Michael Wood is a freelance journalist and proofreader living in Sheffield. As a journalist he has covered many crime stories throughout Sheffield, gaining first-hand knowledge of police procedure. He also reviews books for CrimeSquad, a website dedicated to crime fiction. *The Murder House* is his fifth novel.

@MichaelHWood
/MichaelWoodBooks

Also by Michael Wood

The Murder House

DCI Matilda Darke V

MICHAEL WOOD

OneMoreChapter

One More Chapter
a division of HarperCollins*Publishers*
The News Building
1 London Bridge Street
London SE1 9GF

www.harpercollins.co.uk

This paperback edition 2020
1

First published in Great Britain in ebook format by HarperCollins*Publishers* 2020

A catalogue record for this book
is available from the British Library

ISBN: 9780008374839

Set in Birka by Palimpsest Book Production Limited, Falkirk, Stirlingshire

Printed and bound in Great Britain by CPI Group (UK) Ltd,
Croydon CR0 4YY

To Scout Master Kevin Embleton. Aka Kevin the Beagle.

Chapter One

Jeremy Mercer couldn't sleep. The room was spinning. He couldn't remember the last time he had drunk so much. Still, it wasn't a regular occurrence. A blow-out once in a while didn't do any harm. Maybe he should have slowed down though. Looking back, he seemed to have had a glass of champagne in his hand since early evening until he staggered out of the marquee, into the house, and, somehow, managed to crawl upstairs.

He felt sick. He closed his eyes but that seemed to make matters worse. He quickly opened them again and gave a little laugh. He was back in the bedroom he had grown up in, his mother and father asleep in the attic room upstairs.

Jeremy had been sensible in front of his seven-year-old daughter, Rachel, but once she had gone to bed at eight o'clock, he'd let his hair down and allowed his father to continue pouring glass after glass of champagne down his throat.

Today, or rather, yesterday, was a special occasion. His little sister, Leah, had got married. As the fug of alcohol distorted his memory, one image of the happy day stuck out more than others. Just before the ceremony, he had gone into his parents' bedroom where Leah was getting ready and they'd had a chat.

'Wow, you look stunning,' he said. 'You look so grown up.'

'Thank you. I can't stop smiling,' she said. The floor-length gown was an off-white colour. It was a simple design, but the material was sheer and elegant. It may have sounded like a cliché, but she really did look like a princess. 'How's Oliver doing?'

'He's fine. His shoes are hurting his ankles.'

The smile dropped. 'I told him to put wet newspaper in them a few days before the wedding. Well, I don't care if they cause blisters and he's in agony for weeks, he's leading me on that dancefloor.'

Jeremy sat down on the bed. 'Can you believe this?'

'What?'

'It doesn't seem like five minutes ago you and I were in the back garden pushing each other off the swing. Now look at us; you're getting married and I've got a seven-year-old daughter, a mortgage and debts up to my eyeballs.'

'It's fun being a grown-up, isn't it?' she said with a twinkle in her eye.

Jeremy felt a tug of emotion. 'I hope you and Oliver will be very happy together,' he said, a catch in his throat.

'Don't make me cry, Jeremy. I don't want to ruin my make-up.'

'Sorry. I was just thinking of . . .'

'I know. Today can't be easy for you.'

'It's not. But, today isn't about me. It's about you.'

'I'm not looking forward to everyone looking at me in church.'

'Have you taken your medication?'

'You've asked me that three times already,' she said.

'Sorry. I just want your day to be perfect.'

'And me off my medication would ruin it?'

'Shit. Sorry. I didn't mean—'

Leah giggled. 'It's all right, Jeremy, I know what you meant. Don't worry. I'm fine. I feel fine.' She turned to the mirror and looked at her reflection. 'Well, time I made a move.'

Jeremy stood up, held his sister by the shoulders and looked deep into her eyes. 'I love you, Leah.' He kissed her on the cheek.

'I love you too, Jeremy. I couldn't ask for a better brother.'

'One day, I might give you your Barbie doll heads back.'

'Then you really will be the best brother ever.'

There was a knock on the bedroom door. It was time to go.

Jeremy pushed back the duvet and staggered out of bed. He needed a drink of water. Or maybe he needed to vomit, he didn't know which.

Wearing only a T-shirt, boxer shorts, and, for some reason, one sock, he fumbled along the landing. He was tempted to look in on Rachel but didn't want to wake her. He was sure she was fine. She had Pongo to keep her company.

Gripping the bannister firmly, he looked down the stairs. This must be what mountain climbers see when they're at the top of Everest; a long and treacherous way down. Each step seemed to reverberate throughout his entire body. Even his hair hurt. He decided, right now, he was never drinking ever again. Well, maybe a glass at New Year. And at Christmas. And on special occasions, but not to excess. Apart from that, he was never drinking ever again. Obviously, he'd have a pint on his birthday, too.

He somehow made it to the bottom of the stairs. He felt a cold draught coming from somewhere and wondered if a window had been left open.

'Jesus! You scared the life out of me. I thought everyone had gone home.' Jeremy smiled. The figure in front of him was blurred. He tried to focus his vision, but he couldn't make out who was standing in the doorway of the kitchen, or even if there was someone there at all.

The figure moved towards him. Jeremy felt a sharp pain in the side of his body. He placed a hand there, looked at it, and saw red. He staggered backwards and fell into the hall table and onto the floor. He looked around, but the figure had gone.

What the hell had just happened?

His T-shirt was turning red. His left hand was red. This didn't make any sense. It took a while for his brain to make the connection. Then, the pain kicked in. He'd been stabbed.

He heard the sound of heavy footfalls on the stairs and the muffled yap of Pongo.

'Rachel,' Jeremy uttered.

He scrambled along the hall to the stairs and tried to stand up, but he couldn't. He reached the bottom of the stairs, put a red-stained hand on the first step, and dragged himself up. It was no use. The life was seeping out of him and he had no energy to pull himself up a whole flight of stairs.

'Who are you?' That was his father's voice. 'What do you—?'

'Dad,' Jeremy whimpered.

His father was cut off from finishing his sentence, and all Jeremy could hear was the sound of gurgling and grunting followed by a heavy thud. Then, more heavy thuds as the figure ran up the next set of stairs to the attic bedroom. A loud piercing scream from two floors up was obviously from his mother.

'Daddy?' A pitiful cry from his daughter in the room next to his.

'Fuck,' Jeremy said to himself. He tried to stand up but the mixture of alcohol and heavy blood loss made him weak. 'Rachel, sweetheart, it's OK. Stay where you are. Don't come out of your bedroom.' His voice was slow and sounded like it was coming from someone else.

There was another yap from Pongo.

'Daddy. I'm scared. What's happening?'

'It's all right. You're going to be fine. Just stay where you are. I want you to be a big girl for daddy. Can you do that?'

'I don't know.'

'Rachel. The chair next to your bed, I want you to put it under the handle of your door so nobody can come in.' His voice was full of urgency. Slumped at the bottom of the stairs, one hand holding onto his side to stem the blood flow, the other trying to pull himself up the stairs. It was futile.

'Daddy,' Rachel cried.

'Rachel, you need to do this. Please.' He tried to keep the fear out of his voice for his daughter's sake, but it was no good. He was petrified at what was happening. He waited for her to say something, but she didn't. 'Let me know when you've done it.'

He listened intently but he couldn't hear any sounds apart from the grandfather clock in the living room.

'Rachel?'

There was no reply.

'Rachel?' He shouted louder.

'I've done it, Daddy,' Rachel wept.

'Good girl. Now, get back in bed and Pongo will look after you.'

'Will you come and look after me, Daddy?'

'I won't be long sweetheart. I'm just . . .'

The figure stood at the top of the stairs looking down at Jeremy. His vision was still slightly blurred but there was no mistaking the amount of blood he was covered in. Jeremy tried to focus, tried to make a mental picture of his image, but it was no use. He had a balaclava covering his face.

'What have you done?' Jeremy asked.

The figure disappeared from view.

'Not my daughter,' he whimpered. 'No. Not Rachel. Please. Kill me but leave her alone. Please. She's only seven.'

The sound of yapping grew louder as the bedroom door was forced open, then a yelp and a whine as Pongo had obviously come to harm.

'Daddy!' Rachel screamed.

'You bastard,' Jeremy tried to shout. He was struggling to breathe, and tears were streaming down his face. 'I'm going to kill you,' he screamed. 'Fucking kill you!'

With what little energy he had left in his body, Jeremy tried to pull himself up the stairs. It was no use. He had lost so much blood, he was weakening by the minute. He looked around him. The cream-coloured carpet was saturated with his blood.

The figure reappeared at the top of the stairs and slowly began to descend. There was a large knife in his right hand.

'If you've done anything to my daughter. If you've hurt her, I promise your life won't be worth living.'

He looked up and saw the glint from the bloodstained knife. He didn't feel it enter his neck, but he could taste blood and his breathing became erratic. He looked down and saw his T-shirt turn red as the blood from a ruptured vein pumped out of his rapidly dying body. He tried to speak but he couldn't. He choked as the knife was slowly pulled out of his neck and let out a small groan of pain as it was plunged into him once again.

As he lay at the bottom of the stairs, he looked up and saw the one-year-old Dalmatian puppy staring down at him. Jeremy smiled. Pongo was Rachel's best friend. She loved him from the second he brought him home. She often tried to count the spots on his chubby little body, but Pongo was a wriggler, so she never managed to count them all. It wasn't only black spots Pongo now had; some were red. Blood.

The last thing Jeremy thought of before he died was how do you get blood out of dog fur. He laughed at the implausibility of his thought as he slumped on the stairs and closed his eyes.

Chapter Two

Monday, 15 January 2018

09.30

Sally Meagan stood in the middle of the living room and looked around her. She couldn't remember the last time she had used this room, sat on the sofa, snuggled up to her husband and watched television with her feet up. The family room. That was a joke. They were no longer a family. How could they be when their only child was still missing?

The life had been drained out of Sally when Carl was taken on the 25th of March 2015. She no longer lived, she could merely exist, until the fate of her son was known. After that . . . who knew?

The house was empty. As usual, Philip was at one of their restaurants. He'd left before she'd even woken up. He seemed to be leaving the house earlier and getting home later each day. He only used the house to shower, change his clothes and sleep. She hardly saw him anymore. A few weeks before Christmas, when the restaurants were at their busiest, she followed him to one and stood outside, watching him, seeing how he was at work. It was like looking at a total stranger. He was laughing and joking, schmoozing with the customers, smiling, engaging in pointless small talk, dealing with any issues that cropped up, getting on with life as if everything was peaches and cream. Sally couldn't do that. She tried, but every time she found herself smiling, having fun, or living a seemingly normal life, she remembered Carl was missing, and she hated herself even more for trying to live while goodness knows what was happening to her child.

How could Philip continue with life as if nothing had happened? On that spring day almost three years ago, someone had broken into their home, killed her mother, who was babysitting, and stolen their seven-year-old son. It was a parents' worse nightmare, and while Sally was still suffering, her husband had returned to normal life.

Maybe it was different for a father. A mother has a stronger bond with her child, as she's carried him inside her for nine months. Was that it? Was that the reason? Maybe Philip was looking at the bigger picture; without the restaurants, they wouldn't be able to pay the bills and the mortgage, and they'd have to sell their home. Sally couldn't allow that to happen. This was Carl's home.

She went into the kitchen, took out a bottle of vodka from the freezer, and poured herself a large glass. She slugged it back in one and poured another. She didn't care it wasn't even ten o'clock in the morning yet. She looked down at the golden Labrador who was permanently at her heels.

'Don't judge me, Woody,' she said.

Woody had been bought for Carl's sixth birthday. He'd been asking for a puppy for years, and they'd finally relented. They loved each other on sight and were inseparable. Woody even slept in Carl's bedroom. He accompanied them on the walk to school and pulled Sally on the way to pick him up. When he disappeared, Woody felt the effect of the loss. He stopped barking, he lost his bounce, and spent every night on Carl's bed, pining, sighing, aching for his best friend to return.

Now Sally was home all the time, Woody had latched himself on to her. He didn't want to lose another member of the household. He followed Sally everywhere. While she was working on the computer in the study to find her son, he sat on the floor by her feet. When she left the room to go to the toilet, he followed, and sat outside the bathroom door until she was finished. At first, it annoyed her, but as time went on, it was comforting. She spoke to Woody all the time, told him her feelings, and fears. She'd sit on the floor with him, his head on her lap, and she cried buckets as she poured her heart out to him. He seemed to understand. She told him things she couldn't tell anyone, not Philip, not Matilda, and he never judged her. Even now, when she drank to dull the pain, he still looked at her with those big brown eyes and he seemed to sympathize with her.

'Come on, Woody, let's check the emails. Fingers and paws crossed, eh?'

The study at the back of the ground floor was the nerve centre for Sally's campaign in finding her son. She connected with people all over the world who were missing children to offer a shoulder to cry on. She had a website where people could message her with possible sightings, though they were getting fewer and further between. The room was full of files, missing persons posters, copies of the book she had written. Sally spent more time in this room than anywhere else in the house.

She sat down and powered up the computer. Woody assumed the position at her feet, circling a few times before he found the right spot for him.

On the desk were several framed photographs of Carl. She often looked at them, remembered the exact moment when the picture was taken, what they were doing, what she said, what Carl said, and shed a little tear. Why was this happening to them?

Her first job was to check the emails. There were none. This was the ninth day in a row without a new email. Several people had contacted her from Sweden in the past few months with a possible sighting. She wondered if it would be worth going out there, maybe visiting a few schools. Philip and Matilda didn't think it was such a good idea, and she didn't fancy going to a strange country on her own.

Last year, a former detective with South Yorkshire Police had done some digging of his own. He had an ulterior motive, of course. He wanted to solve the case DCI Darke couldn't. What he'd uncovered made no sense to her, but Matilda was working hard to salvage order out of the chaos of paperwork. If only she didn't have her day-to-day police work getting in the way of finding Carl. It was a selfish thought, Sally knew that, but . . .

Her mobile rang, making her jump. She didn't look at the display. She knew it would probably be Philip asking her if she'd made the changes to the menu she had been promising to do for the past week.

'Hello,' she answered. Her voice was tired and lacked emotion.

'Mummy?'

'Carl?' Sally shot up out of her seat, frightening Woody. 'Carl? Is that you?'

'Mummy?'

'Oh my God.' Tears fell from her eyes and she didn't wipe them away. Her entire body shook with fear, adrenaline. She gripped the phone tighter. 'Carl, sweetheart, it's me. It's your mummy. Where are you?'

Silence.

'Carl? Carl?'

'I'm scared, Mummy.'

'It's all right, Carl. There's no need to be scared. I'm here. I'm going to find you. Can you tell me where you are? Look around you. What do you see?' Her words were tripping over each other as she panicked to find her son.

The line went dead.

'Carl? Carl? Are you still there? Answer me.'

She looked at the phone, but the call had been disconnected. In the call log, she saw a number she didn't recognize. It was a mobile number. With a shaking hand, she picked up a pencil and quickly scribbled it down on a scrap of paper. She then looked up her husband's number and called him.

'Philip, it's me,' she said. She spoke quickly. Her voice was high-pitched. There was an urgency behind it. 'You need to come home right now. I've just had a call from Carl. He's alive, Philip.'

She looked down at Woody who was sitting bolt upright. His ears were pricked, and his tail was wagging.

'Carl's alive.'

Chapter Three

Monday, 15 January 2018

09.45

Rose Bishop diverted from her journey in to work to head for the Mercer house in Fulwood. She had drunk so much at the wedding reception yesterday that she hadn't realized she had gone home wearing only one shoe. She had tried to call Serena this morning to make sure the shoe wasn't casually thrown away with all the leftover food and empty bottles, but she wasn't answering her mobile or the landline.

She pulled up at the top of the drive and trotted down it. She knocked on the door, rang the bell and stepped back, looking up at the house. The curtains were drawn in every room. Serena had been just as drunk as she was, but Clive wasn't a big drinker. Surely they should have been up and getting ready to go to work by now. She knocked again, louder, and leaned into the door to listen for the sound of footsteps. It was deathly silent.

She went around the back of the house and entered the marquee. Rose vaguely remembered complimenting Serena on how gorgeous and elegant everything looked when she first saw it after the church service, but, looking at it now, you would be forgiven for thinking a group of eight year olds had held a birthday party here. It was a mess. She made her way through the tent, and, surprisingly, she found her shoe on a table near the wedding cake. She picked it up and headed for the house. It would be rude to leave without saying hello.

Rose was shocked to find the back door wide open. Clive and Serena were so security conscious. They wouldn't have gone to bed and left the house exposed like this. Maybe Clive was already up and had gone out for a newspaper or something.

'Hello? Clive, Serena, are you up?' Rose called out from the kitchen. She looked at the remains of the food on the island. She picked up a smoked salmon canape and popped it into her mouth. It was as delicious as she remembered. She had eaten dozens of them. She made a mental note to ask Serena for the recipe.

'Jeremy? Rachel? Anyone awake?' Rose asked as she made her way along the ground floor.

She poked her head into the living room but it was empty. This had been off-limits to party guests yesterday and it was, as it always was, spotlessly clean and tidy.

Rose stopped in her tracks at the bottom of the stairs. It took her brain a few long seconds to realize what it was seeing. Jeremy Mercer was slumped against the wall. His eyes were closed and there was so much blood surrounding him.

'Jeremy,' she whispered. It didn't seem real. This was a practical joke, surely. She leaned down, and, with shaking fingers, felt for a pulse on his wrist. He was freezing cold and there was no beat coming from the vein. 'Oh my God.'

She looked up the stairs and saw the trail of blood on the cream-coloured carpet. She stumbled back and almost tripped over the remains of the hall table. On the floor, the cordless phone was out of its cradle. She reached out for it and saw her hands were covered in blood. She silently screamed, picked up the phone and dialled 999.

'999. What's your emergency?'

Rose was about to speak when she heard the sound of barking coming from upstairs.

'Oh my God. Rachel.'

'I'm sorry?' the operator asked.

'You need to come quickly. Someone's been killed, and I think there may be more bodies.'

She tried not to look at Jeremy as she stepped over his lifeless corpse. The carpet on the stairs was full of bloodstains in the shape of paw prints.

'Where are you calling from?'

'Rachel?' Rose screamed, ignoring the 999 operator.

Rose reached the top of the stairs, stepped onto the landing and saw more horror before her. She screamed and continued to scream until her voice was hoarse. The operator was asking questions, but she didn't hear them. She fell back against the wall and slid down it. She clutched the phone firmly against her chest and couldn't take her eyes off the nightmare inches away from her.

Chapter Four

'According to Rory, it's the worst crime scene he's ever seen.'
'Bloody hell.'

DS Sian Mills was driving; DCI Matilda Darke was in the front passenger seat. They had been informed of a triple murder in an affluent part of Sheffield. Uniformed officers were on the scene and forensics were en route.

'Do we know who the victims are?'

'We think so. Ranjeet is looking them up for me back at the station.'

Sian's mobile beeped an incoming text message. It was in a cradle attached to the dashboard. She opened it. 'It's from Rory. He says, "I hope you haven't had your breakfast yet".'

'Jesus,' Matilda muttered as she looked out of the window.

It was another cold morning. Winter had started early in Sheffield with the first snowfall way back in mid-November, and despite there being no white Christmas (again), snow had returned in the new year. The days were cold and the nights were colder. As Sheffield passed by in a blur, Matilda looked at the bare trees. The branches were white with a thick layer of frost. Grass looked beautiful as each white blade sparkled in the glint of the cold sun. Pavements were tricky to walk on and pedestrians took their time over the patches of black ice. Despite the heating being on in the car, Matilda shivered just watching people as they braved the elements.

'Are you all settled in to your new house, now?' Sian asked, filling the silence with a safe topic of conversation so neither of them had to think about the horror that awaited them.

'More or less,' Matilda said with a smile. 'Just one more room to sort out.'

'I bet you're glad. There's nothing like your own home, is there?'

'No,' Matilda replied. She returned to looking out of the window. She had only officially moved in a week ago. It was a bit early to be calling it her home. When she thought of home, she thought of the house her husband built; the one they both agonized over the plans of: how big the kitchen should be, where the downstairs toilet should go, the colour of the tiles in the bathroom. James had put his blood, sweat, and tears into that house. That was her home – their home. This new house was . . . at the moment she didn't know what it was; somewhere to lay her head.

They pulled up as close as they could to the police cordon. From here, they couldn't see the house but the faces on the uniformed officers who were milling around were grim. It was not a good sign.

Matilda looked around at the nosy neighbours as they stood on the side of the road gossiping among themselves. 'You know those cases that you always go back to, that you can't shake off? I get the feeling this is going to be one of them.'

'Haven't we had enough of those, lately?' Sian quipped, pulling her coat tight against the cold.

Pathologist, Adele Kean, parked behind them. Her assistant, Lucy Dauman hesitantly got out of the front passenger seat, flicking back her blonde hair, a habit she was well known for.

'Rory told me to imagine the worst crime scene I can, then times it by a hundred,' Adele said, her face pale with worry. 'Please tell me he was exaggerating.'

'I haven't been in yet,' Matilda said. 'I've been told it's bad.'

'Oh my God,' Lucy muttered.

'Lucy, get a couple of suits out of the back and we'll probably need to double up. We'll need extra gloves and overshoes too.'

Lucy remained where she was. She was relatively new to this job and only in her mid-twenties. She was fine assisting in post mortems, but crime scenes always seemed to upset her. Adele, however, was a seasoned professional, yet even she looked green. This was going to be a nightmare for Lucy. She slowly walked to the boot of the car to get what they needed.

All four women made their way down the driveway to the beautiful stone-built double-fronted house with its sash windows, side breast chimney, and a cast iron shoe scraper by the door. Neither of them spoke. A uniformed police officer was standing on the doorstep. He knew who they all were and began writing their names down on his clipboard. His hand was shaking.

'I'm sorry, I can't recall your name,' he said to Lucy in a quivering voice. She told him and spelled her surname. He gave her a smile of thanks, but it wasn't genuine. He looked too frightened to smile.

An ambulance was parked close to the house, its back doors open, but nobody was inside.

The front door was opened from the inside and Rory greeted them. He was wearing a white forensic suit which was covered in bloodstains. To the untrained eye, Rory looked like the murderer and had been caught in the act. Usually, DC Fleming was the life and soul of the team, always ready with a joke or a sarcastic comment to lighten even the most difficult of moods.

However, he was looking down at the floor, his expression ashen.

'Rory?' Matilda asked.

'Ma'am, nobody needs to see this if they don't have to,' he said quietly.

'Oh God,' Lucy said.

'Where am I heading for, Rory?' Adele asked.

'Forensics are on the top floor in the attic bedroom. There's a body on the stairs, be careful. And . . . prepare yourself for what you see on the first-floor landing.'

'Thanks. Let's suit up then, Lucy.' Adele tried to sound professional, but there was a definite tinge of fear in her voice.

Matilda angled her head to look past Rory into the kitchen. A uniformed officer was comforting a fellow officer who was bent over, in tears.

'Who's that?'

'PC Tranter, ma'am. She's not handling it very well. I told her to have a break.'

Matilda and Adele exchanged glances. Both looked worried.

'There'll be nothing we can do until forensics say it's OK for us to go in. Rory, is there anywhere we can go for you to talk us through it?'

'The living room is free,' he said.

The lounge was a huge space, expensively decorated in neutral colours, though the feature wall with a real fireplace was painted in a warm deep blue. The carpet smelled new, the curtains were rich and expensive. The whole room oozed class and taste.

Rory headed for the sofa and slumped down in the middle. 'I have never seen anything like this before in my life. It's like a horror film up there.'

'Are you all right?' Sian asked, sitting next to him.

'No,' he said. 'I will be. I just need a minute.'

Matilda sat on the edge of an armchair. She looked at a gorgeous grandfather clock in the corner of the room and listened to the heavy ticking. It would look great in her new hallway. There was a photograph on the mantelpiece of a couple raising a glass of champagne to the camera. They looked happy.

'Rory, what have we got here?'

He swallowed hard then looked up at his boss. 'There's a young guy on the stairs, about my age, I'd say. He's been stabbed a fair few times.' He blew out his cheeks and took a deep breath. 'On the first-floor landing there's an old-ish bloke who's practically been decapitated.' He swallowed hard. 'I'm sorry. It's just . . . there's so much blood. I've never seen so much blood. Every time I close my eyes, I'm just seeing red.' He ran his fingers through his short dark hair and took a deep breath. 'On the top floor there's a woman. You can't make out her face at all.' He took another breath which shook with fear. 'In the small bedroom at the top of the stairs there was a young girl. She was tied to a chair.' His voice quivered with emotion. 'She was drenched in blood.'

'Is she dead?'

'No. She hasn't got a mark on her. I think the blood must belong to the other victims. God only knows what she must have seen. There was a dog with her too; a Dalmatian, only a puppy. He was covered in blood as well.'

'Where are they now?' Matilda asked.

'The girl is at the hospital. I think she's in shock. She didn't say anything. A PC is with her. The dog is in the back of the forensics van.'

'OK. The dog is a crime scene. He'll need checking out. Maybe the killer touched him. Or maybe the dog bit him.'

Rory nodded. 'I carried her to the ambulance,' he said, a tear rolling down his face. 'You should have seen how she was looking at me. She couldn't take her eyes off me. I didn't know what to say to her.'

'Rory, do you want to go outside, get some air?'

'I think I will, thanks,' he said, standing up. 'Scott's upstairs in the bedroom the girl was found in. He'll be able to give you more information.' He left the room while he was still talking.

'I don't think I want to go up there,' Sian said.

'If only we had that option.'

* * *

Dressed in white forensic suits, Matilda and Sian stood at the bottom of the stairs and looked at the young face of Jeremy Mercer.

'Poor bloke,' Sian said.

Matilda looked up the stairs, at the bloody footprints and paw prints on the carpet, the sprays and smeared stains on the wall. 'Come on.'

She led the way, taking the stairs slowly. She didn't touch the bannister, despite wearing gloves, in case she smudged any fingerprints. Sian was close behind. Matilda could hear her breathing heavily. The metallic smell of blood was heavy in the air. She could already taste it. Something caught her eye. She turned right and looked through the spindles at the landing.

'Shit,' she muttered under her breath, quickly looking away.

'How bad is it?' Sian asked from behind. Her voice was quivering with nerves. Her eyes remained fixed on the back of Matilda's head.

Matilda composed herself, still with her eyes closed. She took a deep breath and eventually opened them. 'Don't look until you're on the landing.'

She held out a hand and Sian took it, gripping it hard. Matilda pulled her up. As she turned around, she gasped and slapped a hand over her mouth. On the floor in front of them was a grey-haired man. His face was deathly white from having bled out. The carpet was saturated. The walls were dripping in blood. The man's head was barely attached to his body. This was a scene of pure carnage. As much as they wanted to, neither was able to take their eyes off the destruction at their feet.

The door to a room on the left was slightly ajar. Inside, muffled voices were heard, and a brilliant yellow light was coming out from the gap.

Matilda walked over to it and pushed the door open. Sian followed close behind. DC Scott Andrews saw them enter and went over. His white forensic suit was stained with dried blood.

'Ma'am,' Scott said quietly, nodding at his boss.

'Scott, I thought the girl was unharmed?' Matilda frowned at the scene laid out before her.

'That's right.'

'So where did all this blood come from?' Matilda looked down at the white carpet. A trail of blood ran from the door to the bed. The pink duvet was smeared with blood.

'Well, there was a puppy. He was on the floor next to the girl when the first officer on the scene arrived. It was as if he was looking after her. If you look, there are paw prints all over the carpet. I'm guessing the dog kept going out onto the landing and coming back in, not wanting to leave her.'

'Poor thing,' Matilda said.

'The dog or the girl?' Scott asked.

'Both.'

Sian, gloved hand slapped to her mouth, looked down at the floor. She couldn't take her eyes from the horror. 'Are you sure she wasn't hurt in any way?'

'Not physically.'

'She wasn't . . . you know . . . interfered with?'

'We don't know that yet. I'm sure they'll check her out at the hospital.'

'How was she tied to the chair?' Matilda asked. The chair was a small pine children's chair. It was painted cream and the name 'Rachel' was written in pink copperplate on the back with a picture of a Dalmatian drawn on the seat.

'She was tied around the waist, which held her arms in too. Her legs were tied together. She was also gagged but she'd managed to work that loose somehow.'

'Why tie her up and not hurt her yet go on to kill like he did?' Matilda asked, more to herself than her colleagues.

'I don't know. Have you seen the other victims?' Scott asked.

'We've seen two,' Matilda replied.

'Prepare yourselves. This is horrific.'

Matilda turned to Scott. He was looking at the ground, but she could see him struggling to keep hold of his emotions. 'Are you all right?' Matilda placed a comforting hand on the young DC's arm. She could feel the tension.

'No, I'm not. You don't expect anything like this, ever.'

'I've sent Rory outside for a break. Do you want to go?'

'No. I'm fine.'

'Right. Well, I need a team to go door to door. I want to know who these people are and if anyone saw anything. Sian, can you sort that?'

'Sure.'

'Obviously, don't go into any details on what's happened here. Not yet.'

'There's a marquee in the back garden,' Scott said. 'According to the woman who found them, there was a wedding reception here from yesterday evening onwards.'

'We're going to need a list of all the guests. Sian, give Christian a ring. Get him to bring a team out. I want everyone questioned.'

Sian left the room, dialling as she went.

'Where's the woman who found them, now?'

'She's been taken to hospital. She was hysterical when we got here. Oh, there's a wet patch on the carpet on the landing. It's where she wet herself.'

'OK. I'll let forensics know.'

'What do you want me to do?' Scott asked.

'Go to the hospital and keep me informed of the girl's condition. Take a uniform with you to keep guard.'

'Do you think the killer will come back?'

'I've no idea, but it's a possibility.'

Matilda made her way carefully around the butchered man at the bottom of the stairs leading up to the attic. She felt her mobile phone vibrate in her pocket but ignored it. She couldn't take her eyes from the man. Despite the horror of his final minutes, he looked at peace. Who would do something so violent, so shocking to another person?

The stairs leading up to the second floor were drenched in blood; smeared footprints and the odd paw print. Matilda looked down at her feet. The protective overshoes were covered in blood. When she got to the landing, she pulled another pair out of her pocket and replaced the saturated ones.

The attic was a hive of activity as Adele worked with the crime scene investigators. Arc lights had been erected and lit up the scene in an intruding bright white. Matilda entered the room and saw Lucy to one side, tears streaming down her face.

'I'm sorry. I'll be all right in a minute,' she said.

Matilda felt sorry for her. She tried to remember when she was new to the job and the first crime scenes she had attended. In her whole twenty plus years on the force, she had never seen anything as horrific as this. If she had entered the scene as a twenty-something, she would have fainted and probably handed in her notice.

'Why don't you go outside for some air?'

'I can't. I'm needed here,' she said between sobs.

'I'm sure they can spare you for five minutes.'

'I don't think I can go down. I don't want to see that man. Did you see his head? Oh God.'

Matilda didn't know what else to say. She placed a reassuring hand on her shoulder then moved away towards the bloodshed.

Adele, crouched over the bed, stood up when she caught Matilda approaching out of the corner of her eye. Her blue forensic suit was stained red. She looked like the killer in a slasher film.

'Late-fifties, early-sixties, at a guess,' she said. 'I've no idea how many times she's been stabbed. Once we get her to the mortuary and cleaned up I'll give you a better idea. Most of the wounds are to her face, chest and stomach. Look around you, the length of the sprays, this was savage.'

Matilda looked up at the ceiling and took in the sight of red lines, flicked up as the knife was pulled out of the body.

'Lucy, I need your help here to turn her over,' Adele called out.

'I'll leave you to it,' Matilda said.

Matilda backed away and watched as Adele and Lucy gently

turned the woman over. She tried to get a look at her face, see if she recognized her from somewhere, but there were no definable features. This woman had been destroyed.

Lucy turned away and made a gagging noise as if she was about to be sick. Matilda looked back at the body.

'Is that what I think it is?' she asked.

'Her intestines? Yes.' Adele nodded.

'What the hell has he done? Removed her organs?'

'I won't know until I conduct a full PM. It's not unusual, though, for someone to stab so frenzied that they dislodge the intestines.' Adele sounded so calm, so professional. How was that possible?

'You've seen something like this before?' Matilda asked.

'Only in text books.'

More photographs were taken by the forensic team. Matilda couldn't take her eyes from the butchered woman. She was reminded of one of Jack the Ripper's victims. The carnage, the sense of anger and hatred the killer must have had to perform an act of pure evil. Matilda uttered a goodbye to Adele, but she was wrapped up in her work so didn't hear. She turned to the staircase, and headed back down, frowning at the position of the bloody footprints. A flash of something entered her head, then disappeared just as quickly.

As she reached the landing, she stepped over the man again, looking him directly in the eyes. There was nothing there. She was staring death in the face and it was looking right back at her.

'Matilda.' She heard her name being called from the hallway downstairs. Glad of the distraction, she turned away.

Walking downstairs, she saw how her white forensic suit and gloves were smeared with blood, even though she hadn't touched anything. It was everywhere. Her plastic overshoes were slippery on the wood flooring of the hallway. She closed her eyes as she carefully stepped around the body at the bottom of the stairs.

'I've got an ID on our victims,' Sian said, heading into the living room.

'Go on.'

'Clive and Serena Mercer live here alone. They have two children: Jeremy and Leah. Now, according to neighbours, Leah got married yesterday and she and her new hubby left for their honeymoon early evening. Jeremy came home from Liverpool for the wedding with his daughter, Rachel, and stayed the night.'

'So he's our other victim?'

'It looks like it.'

'And the little girl is his daughter.'

'It would appear so.'

'Where's her mother?'

'Apparently, she died a few years ago.'

'We need a contact number for Leah. I don't want her hearing about this on the news. Do we know where she's gone for her honeymoon?'

'Paris,' Sian replied, looking down at her pad.

'OK. Have a look around, try and find something that tells us whereabouts she's gone and we'll arrange for the local police to go around and tell her. Where is everyone?' Matilda asked, looking around and seeing no police officers.

'I've just seen Scott drive off. Rory is in the back garden. He looked dreadful. I haven't seen anyone else.'

'Give Christian another ring. We need more people here. I need to go and see Valerie. This is going to go international once the press gets to know about it.'

Matilda left the house and peeled off the forensic suit. She passed a police car with its back door open. Behind a grill was a puppy Dalmatian caked in blood. Laying down, his head between his front paws, he looked up at Matilda with large sad eyes as she approached.

'Hello sweetheart.' She put a few fingers through the grill and scratched the top of his head. His tail wagged, but he didn't stand up. 'You're missing Rachel?' His ears pricked at the sound of a familiar name. 'Poor thing. What did you see in that house?' She tore herself away from the dog and headed to her car.

At the top of the drive she turned back to look at the house. It was a beautiful family home. Yesterday, there was a wedding. Everyone would have been so happy to watch two young people begin their new life together. They will have laughed, danced, and drank well into the night. Within hours it was a scene of horror.

It reminded Matilda how fragile life was. She knew that only too well. She took her phone out of her pocket, ignored the missed calls from Sally Meagan and looked at the photo she had as her wallpaper. It was her husband, James, smiling back at her. She loved that smile. She missed him so much. She walked away with tears stinging her eyes.

Chapter Five

The knock on the door made ACC Valerie Masterson jump. She was perusing a brochure on motor homes, which she quickly hid under a file on her oversized desk, before calling for her visitor to come in.

Matilda entered the room. She had driven to the station from Fulwood and gone straight into the toilets to scrub at her hands and face. Yet, even though she had been wearing gloves at the crime scene, she felt as though her hands were covered in blood and no amount of washing would make her clean.

'Matilda, come and sit down. I've just heard. How bad is it?' she asked. She went over to her coffee machine and started making Matilda a cup.

Matilda shook her head. 'It's like some kind of sick horror film.'

'How is everyone?' she asked, handing Matilda the coffee.

'Not good. I think we're going to have to offer counselling. Rory is taking this hard.'

'That's not like him.'

'I know. I'll ask Scott to keep an eye on him. Since he was attacked he's been more sensitive.'

'Do we know who they are yet?'

'I think so. Clive and Serena Mercer.'

'The Mercers?' Valerie asked. Her eyes wide.

'You know them?'

'No. There was something in the local paper about them last week. Hang on.' Valerie opened her laptop and began searching the Internet. 'Yes, here we are. He's an anaesthetist and she's a neurologist. They're always in the news for helping to raise money for various charities. Serena's been doing a lot of protesting about saving the Sheffield trees. If memory serves, she was arrested late last year,' she said with a hint of a smile. 'Anyway, it was their daughter's wedding, and the vicar who married them all those years ago came out of retirement to marry their daughter. They had the same church and everything. You're saying they've been killed?'

Valerie turned the laptop around and showed Matilda the article on the site of the local newspaper. The main photograph was of Clive and Serena standing next to their daughter and soon-to-be son-in-law, who were hugging. All four were grinning to the camera.

'So has their son. His daughter has been taken to hospital. We don't think she's physically injured though.'

'Oh my goodness.'

Matilda closed the laptop. She could feel the smiling eyes boring into her. 'The press is going to be all over this when it gets out.'

'Well, leave that to me,' Valerie said. 'I want you and your team to put all your efforts into this. Drop whatever you're working on and get this solved as soon as you can.' Valerie returned to her side of the desk. 'I don't mean to sound heartless here, Matilda, but this has come at the best time for us. You're now running a Homicide and Major Enquiry Team and this is your first test. Solve this, and solve it fast, and it will show those upstairs they did the right thing putting you in charge. We could get more money out of them for more officers. Then we can tackle some of these cold cases.'

'I'm short of detectives as it is. I haven't had a replacement for Faith yet and now Kesinka's on light duties.'

'I'll get some drafted in but it will only be for this case. You can't have them on a permanent basis.'

'I need at least one permanent to cover Faith.'

'I'm working on it.'

Matilda drained her coffee cup and stood up to leave. She hadn't failed to notice the brochure for motor homes sticking out of her in-tray. Valerie wasn't fully focused on getting more detectives for the HMET at all. She was due to retire in less than two years and the plan was for her and her husband to travel around Europe while they were still able to. Valerie's mind was on one thing – buying the right camper van.

When Matilda Darke was first promoted to detective chief inspector, she was put in charge of the Murder Investigation Team. Budget cuts soon intervened and, five years later, the MIT was closed down and Matilda was put in charge of CID. When the press got hold of the information that South Yorkshire Police had more than twenty-five unsolved murders on their books, the pen pushers on the top floor decided to launch a Homicide and Major Enquiry Team which would deal with all serious crime and, in their spare time, tackle some of these cold cases. It was basically the Murder Investigation Team with a new name. Matilda was, once again, put in charge, and she was able to hand pick her team. She purposely chose the same team she had when running the MIT. They were even in the same open-plan office the MIT worked from.

The new unit had been up and running for less than a month.

However, a lack of resources had meant the cold cases hadn't even been touched yet. The murder of DC Faith Easter last year had been a blow to everyone on the close-knit team, and now DC Kesinka Rani, who was heavily pregnant, was on restricted duties, following a health scare in which she collapsed at a crime scene, until it was time for her to start her maternity leave. So, Matilda had only a DI, two DSs and two DCs. It was not enough.

As Matilda headed for her office she was stopped in the corridor by DI Christian Brady. He was usually composed, neat and professional, but this morning, his shirt was sticking out of his trousers and his tie was loose around his open-neck shirt.

'You look harassed,' Matilda said.

'You'd think being a DI would give you some power, wouldn't you? I've spent almost an hour having an argument with a sergeant to send a team of uniforms out to Fulwood. He was behaving like they were his own personal PCs.'

Matilda smirked. 'Have they gone?'

'Yes. They're on their way now. Aaron's already on site. He's going to tell them what to do.'

'Excellent.'

'There are several DCs on the fast-track in CID. Can't we steal them?'

'Only if you want to give the ACC a heart attack. We need her say-so before we do anything.'

'We're going to end up with a couple of trainees, aren't we?'

'Not if I can help it.'

They walked down the corridor at speed, taking long strides to get to the HMET suite.

'Rory called a few minutes back. He said forensics are going to be there all day, possibly tomorrow too. There's a lot to process.'

'I know. I've never seen anything like this before in my life.

It's shocking,' she said, shaking her head. 'Fingers crossed house-to-house will give us something. Whoever did this is going to have been drenched in blood. You don't take a change of clothing with you to commit a crime, so someone must have seen something.'

'Famous last words,' he said as he held the door open for her.

'You're getting as cynical as I am.'

'I know. Horrible, isn't it?' He smiled.

Matilda made her way along the suite towards her office. She couldn't help it, but she threw a glance at the desk Faith used to sit at. Her heart sank. It wasn't getting any easier. Faith wasn't the first detective under her charge she had lost in the line of duty. They all tore away at her conscience, caused a piece of her to die inside.

'Boss,' Kesinka struggled to stand up. She seemed to be getting bigger by the day. 'I've just had Sian on the phone. You're not going to believe what she's found at the murder house.'

Chapter Six

Matilda and Christian drove to the crime scene in silence. Christian was driving while Matilda sat staring out of the window with a heavy frown on her face. She had been so sure the neighbours would have spotted a bloodstained man fleeing the scene. Now, her theory had been thrown out of the window.

A larger crowd had grown at the entrance to the cul-de-sac. Police tape was keeping them at bay, but uniformed officers were still battling with the neighbours who chanced their arm and stood in the middle of the road. Christian beeped, making a few onlookers jump.

'Ghouls,' he said quietly.

'At least there are no reporters here, yet.'

'I doubt they'll be much longer. One of these lot will have called them, hoping to snag a few quid.'

They drove up to the drive and Christian parked haphazardly on the pavement. Sian was waiting for them.

'Have you heard from Scott?'

'Not yet.'

'I just wondered how the young girl was,' she said as she led the way down the gravel drive to the large house.

'How are forensics getting on?'

'There are plenty of fingerprints but as there was a wedding reception here yesterday it's hardly a surprise.'

'True. Give Scott a call, see if the woman who found them is ready to talk to us. She might know who the guests were. Then we can start eliminating people.'

'Will do.'

Matilda paused at the bottom of the stairs. Jeremy Mercer was still slumped in the corner. It seemed disrespectful for him to have been left alone here with nobody sitting with him, but depending on what you believed, the person previously known as Jeremy Mercer was no longer here. He was dead. What remained was a shell, an empty body.

'By the way,' Sian continued, 'we've found about a dozen digital cameras in the marquee. It seems there was one on every table and guests were invited to take snaps.'

'I wonder if our killer will be on any of those photos. Maybe it was a fellow guest. Sian, get them sent back to the station. I want every photo downloaded and every person identified.'

'That's going to be a full-time job in itself,' Christian said. 'We don't have anyone available for that.'

'Then draft someone in from uniform,' Matilda raised her voice. There always seemed to be some obstacle to every little task. 'Sian, what did you want to show us?'

Sian led them into the kitchen where several evidence bags had been placed on the central island. They were sealed but through the little window, Matilda could see bloodstained clothing.

'Where were they found?'

'In the main bathroom. There's a hooded sweater, jeans and a T-shirt.'

'How do we know they belong to the killer?' Christian asked.

'We don't, but, there are no stab holes,' Sian said.

'So, what are we saying, the killer comes in, murders three people and has brought a change of clothes with him?' Matilda asked.

'It looks that way.'

'Are there any clothes missing from any of the bedrooms?'

'I don't know. We still can't get in to have a look yet. I doubt robbery was a motive though. Have you seen some of the expensive stuff they've got down here?'

Matilda picked up the bag with the hooded sweater inside. It felt heavy. 'Get this back to the lab. I want every centimetre of these clothes analysed. If they belong to the killer there'll be something on here, a stray hair or sweat or something. Maybe even his own blood. The attacks were that frenzied I'll be surprised if he didn't cut himself.'

'If he came here with the intent to kill, why not just stab them once each? Why be so violent if he's going to have to change his clothes? He's left us vital evidence, here,' Sian said.

'Unless . . .' Matilda began, thinking aloud.

'What?' Christian asked.

'Either, he's really dumb and he's basically handing himself to us on a plate, or, he's incredibly smart and those clothes will give us absolutely nothing.'

'And if they give us nothing?'

She thought for a while. 'Then they're a plant, and the killer will strike again.'

On the M1 motorway between junctions 28 and 29 was the Chesterfield Motorway Service Station. The bay for lorries was mostly empty. One was just pulling away, and the driver of another was exiting the coffee shop, carefully carrying his provisions that would tide him over until he was able to stop again.

At the side of the bay was a patch of grass with a few wooden tables so people could have somewhere to sit if they wanted to eat outside before continuing with their journey. As it was a freezing cold day in January and there was a fine drizzle in the air, most of the tables were empty. However, sitting at one of them, furthest away from the glow of the services, was a man, hunched over his rapidly cooling coffee. He was wearing a hooded sweater that was too large for him. The hood was pulled up and covering his face. When he heard the sound of a wagon pulling up behind him, he risked a glance.

A heavy-set man jumped down from behind the wheel and bent down to tie his shoelace. He was on his mobile.

'I should be with you in about three hours, depending on traffic. I've been told there's roadworks just outside Milton Keynes but I should be in Luton before five. Is that any good to you?' He stood up and headed for the Costa kiosk.

The man waited until the driver was heading back to his truck before he approached him.

'Excuse me, mate. You couldn't give us a lift to Luton, could you?'

The driver eyed him with a frown. Usually when someone wanted a lift they had a rucksack or bag with them. 'Who are you running from?'

'No one. I got mugged yesterday. They took my bag. It had my train tickets in and everything. I had to take this out of one of those charity bins or I would have frozen to death last night,' he said, pulling at his oversized hoodie.

'Okay. Jump in.'

The man breathed a sigh of relief. He was surprised by how quickly he was able to lie, and how convincing he sounded, but he'd always been told he could talk his way into and out of any situation. He ran around to the passenger side of the truck and pulled open the door. He was smiling as climbed in. In three hours he'd be in Luton. From there he'd try and get to Dover and see if he could get someone to drive him through the Channel Tunnel. This time tomorrow he'll be lost in Europe.

Chapter Seven

It was almost half past six by the time Matilda and her team were assembled for the evening briefing. It was a very sombre affair. The atmosphere was heavy. The whole room was quiet. Sian, who had a snack drawer full of chocolate bars and biscuits, pulled the whole drawer out of her desk and began handing out Mars bars, Snickers and Crunchies to anyone who needed a sugar rush, something to get them through the rest of the day.

'Right. We've all had a bad day. I don't think any of us has attended a crime scene like this one before. Now, I've been speaking to ACC Masterson and if anyone feels they need to talk to someone, anyone, in confidence, help will be made available to you. However, if you want to chat to me, my door is always open,' Matilda spoke slowly and with determination. She had an earnest expression on her face. Who do I talk to about this, though?

'Obviously, today has been a bit of a non-day. We've not been able to get into the house properly to have a good scout around. Hopefully, that will change tomorrow. Now, our first, lucid witness so far is Rose Bishop, who found the bodies. Sian?'

Sian had just put a handful of Maltesers in her mouth. She quickly chewed and took a gulp of tea to wash them down with. 'Yes. Poor woman. She only went round this morning because she left a shoe behind yesterday.'

'Did she say how many guests were at the wedding reception?'

'She thinks about one hundred and fifty, maybe more. She didn't know a lot of them, but she's going to work on a list of the ones she did know. I've said I'll pop round tomorrow morning to see how she's getting on.'

'That's great, Sian. So, we've got Clive Mercer, his wife Serena, and their son Jeremy killed, and his daughter, Rachel, left alive for some reason. Scott, how's she doing?'

Scott looked up from where he had been doodling on his pad. He hadn't touched the coffee Rory had brought him or the Twix Sian had placed in front of him. He looked drained. 'She's in shock. She's not responsive to anyone. It's like she's in some form of trance. However, she hasn't been injured in any way and there is no sign of sexual interference.'

'One saving grace,' Sian muttered.

'Unfortunately, we don't know what she's seen,' Scott continued. 'There's probably a reason why she's not talking. There's a uniformed officer sitting guard outside her room all night. If there's any change he'll ring and let me know.'

'What do we know about the Mercer family?' Matilda asked. She looked at Scott out of the corner of her eye. It had only been a few months since he had been attacked by Steve Harrison. His physical injuries had healed quickly but who knew what was going on inside his head. Scott had always been the quiet one of the group. She didn't want him suffering in silence.

DS Aaron Connolly approached the white board. He'd begun to stick photographs up. 'Clive Mercer, aged sixty, was an anaesthetist and Serena, fifty-seven, a neurologist. Both worked at the Northern General. Jeremy, aged twenty-eight, was a junior doctor in Liverpool. We're looking into their backgrounds, any known enemies, money problems, et cetera, but, so far, all the neighbours are saying they're a lovely family. Clive and Serena raise money for local charities and the hospital. They're regular churchgoers and both children are following in their parents' footsteps. The perfect family.'

'The ACC mentioned something about Serena being arrested last year while protesting about the trees being cut down,' Matilda said.

'Yes. Officially, Serena Mercer does have a record. In November while protesting in Ecclesall, she got a bit carried away and physically assaulted a bloke from the council.'

'How?' Sian asked. There was a glint in her eye.

'She gave him a backhander across the face. According to the report, he went down like a sack of spuds. The whole thing was caught on camera and has over a million views on YouTube.'

'Good for her. Bloody council,' Sian said.

'OK. I very much doubt this is some disgruntled council worker getting his own back after being embarrassed online, but, stranger things have happened. Pay the bloke a visit, Aaron, find out his alibi for last night.'

'Will do.'

'Have we managed to track down Leah yet?' Matilda asked.

'We've got a mobile number,' Rory said.

'Rose says she knows the name of the hotel they're staying in in Paris but can't remember it. She's still a bit fuddled. She's going to have think,' Sian said.

Matilda took a deep breath. 'What about forensics?'

'Still at the scene. According to Sebastian Flowers, it will be at least another day before they're through,' Sian said.

'Point of entry?'

'Rose said the door from the marquee leading into the kitchen was open. The killer could have got over the fence at the back of the garden,' Aaron said.

'Anything missing?'

'Nothing we can find so far. Maybe when Leah gets back from Paris she'll be able to give us more information on that,' Sian replied.

'What about the clothing found at the scene?'

'Nothing yet. It's going to take time.'

'Did any of the neighbours see anything suspicious?' Matilda's questions came faster. It was early days in the investigation. Unfortunately, the first hours were the most important. It was frustrating the crime scene was so intense they were unable to get into the house and have a good look around and try to understand the victims more.

'The majority of the neighbours were at the reception. Apparently, the drink was flowing quite freely and most of them didn't surface until they noticed flashing blue lights out of their windows,' Rory said.

'Which tells us times of death was sometime after the reception on Sunday night or the early hours of Monday morning. We need to find out what time the last person left.'

'Rose said it was just after midnight when she left,' Sian said. 'There were still a few others milling around.'

'And she was up and ready to go to work by ten o'clock?' Rory asked.

'She said alcohol's never affected her badly. It doesn't matter how much she drinks she's always fine the next morning.'

'Lucky cow,' Rory said to a ripple of laughter from around the room.

'CCTV?'

'Some of the properties have cameras up. We're working on it,' Aaron said.

'The digital cameras?'

Matilda had managed to snag a uniformed officer and recruit

him as a trainee DC for the length of this case. Finn Cotton was in his early-twenties but looked to be in his late teens. He had the young fresh face of a children's television presenter. He had strawberry blond hair and wore designer frameless glasses. The ravages of working through the night on a difficult murder hunt, surviving on a few hours' sleep, missing meals and the stress of a dedicated homicide unit had not been felt by this man. Yet.

He looked up and cleared his throat. 'I've uploaded all the photos and put them on an iPad. There's over three hundred of them.' His voice was soft with nerves at being the newbie in the group. 'I've been able to tag names to those I know, but that's only the victims and the main players like the bride and groom. I'll need to go through them with one of the guests who'll be able to identify them.'

'I'll have a word with Rose,' Sian began. 'As soon as she feels able enough, we'll bring her in.'

'Thanks,' he said.

'Good work, Finn,' Matilda said.

Finn smiled. His eyes lit up. He seemed pleased he was doing something right and hadn't screwed up on his first day.

Matilda looked at the ashen faces of her team. 'OK, I think we should call it a night. I want you all to go home, try and have a good night's sleep and we'll look at this afresh tomorrow. Again, if any of you need to talk, please do so. Do not let this eat away at you. Off you go.'

Matilda watched while the team slowly packed up and headed for the door. There were some sights you could never unsee, and the bloodbath they had all witnessed today would stay with them all for the rest of their lives. They would all see this through to the end, of that Matilda had no doubt; but how many would ask for a transfer, or resign when it was over? Aaron and Sian would stay, Christian too, but Scott and Rory were young. Would they think a career in the police force wasn't for them? They had both been viciously attack in the past year or so. How would the hunt for a depraved madman change them? Valerie wanted this case solved at any cost. That was not going to happen. Matilda's primary concern was for her colleagues. If they needed to finish early for their sanity, then so be it.

Matilda waited until everyone had left before going into her small office. She closed the door behind her and went over to her desk. She sat down and released a long, heavy sigh. Today had been a challenge, but they had all made it to the end pretty much unscathed. Who knew what tomorrow would bring?

Matilda looked at her reflection in the laptop screen. She looked tired, was getting dark circles underneath her eyes, and her hair was dull and lifeless. She slammed the laptop closed. She felt in urgent need of a shower, or a long soak in the bath followed by a bottle of wine or two and a plate of something unhealthy. She lifted her hands up and looked at them. They were clean but, in her mind, they were covered in blood. She could almost feel it dripping through her fingers.

As usual, Matilda was the last to leave the office. She passed the white board and looked up at the smiling faces of the Mercer family. It was deplorable what people did to each other. Throughout her career she had met murderers who had stabbed, shot, hanged, run over their victims, but what she had seen today was depraved. Her phone rang. She looked and saw it was Sally Meagan calling her again. It was the fourth time today she had phoned, and each time Matilda had ignored it. She waited until the phone stopped ringing before putting it back in her pocket. She couldn't put off speaking to her for much longer.

In a private room in Sheffield Children's Hospital, Rachel Mercer lay in bed. Her eyes were wide open, and she stared at the ceiling. Outside, a uniformed police officer was standing guard. She could hear the distant sound of life continuing as normal. Nurses came in on a regular basis to see how she was. It was always a different nurse. They spoke to her, checked her breathing, her blood pressure, her heart rate, but she didn't reply. She couldn't.

'Daddy, I'm scared.'

'It's all right, Rachel. Everything is going to be all right. Just keep your door closed. Pongo will look after you.'

'Who are you?' she heard her granddaddy ask. He sounded shocked. He sounded close.

Pongo yapped.

'Quiet, Pongo,' Rachel hissed.

She crept to the door and pushed down the handle. Slowly, she pulled it open just a crack. Not wide enough for Pongo to escape, but wide enough so she could see out onto the landing, see what was going on.

There was a man. She couldn't see his face as it was dark. Her granddaddy was on his knees. The man was holding him by his hair and he was stabbing him repeatedly in his neck. Blood was spraying everywhere. Her granddaddy was choking, gasping as each stab with the knife caused more blood to flow down his pyjamas, soak into the carpet, spray onto the walls. Rachel felt a warm splash of something on her face. She screamed. Her granddaddy looked her in the eye as he was thrown to the floor.

'Rachel! Close your door!' her dad shouted from somewhere.

Rachel couldn't move.

Chapter Eight

It was pitch-dark by the time Matilda arrived in Bradway on the outskirts of the steel city. She parked her new Range Rover at the top of the drive and looked at it with a smile while she stood on the doorstep waiting for her knock to be answered.

The door opened and bathed Matilda in a warm glow coming from inside.

'Matilda, this is an unexpected . . . erm . . .'

'Surprise?' She finished with a smile.

'That depends on what favour you want.'

'You're a suspicious woman, Pat Campbell. What makes you think I want a favour?'

'Oh, so you've come round for coffee and cake? You're more than welcome. Come in. I'll get out my photos for our holiday in Italy,' Pat said, her reply oozing with sarcasm. The former detective inspector stood to one side to allow Matilda to enter.

'You're going to cut yourself with that sharp tongue of yours one of these days,' Matilda said as she stepped into the warm hallway.

'You're holding a file behind your back. I may be retired but my detecting skills are still razor sharp.'

Matilda blushed as she brought the heavy file around to the front of her body.

Pat rolled her eyes and showed Matilda into the living room.

It was minimalist and spacious, neat and tidy, yet homely. Anton was sitting in a recliner by the fire, feet up, reading the evening local paper. Wearing a grey cardigan, comfortable trousers and carpet slippers, he looked every inch the retired gentleman.

'We've got a visitor, Anton, put the rag away.'

'Matilda, lovely to see you,' Anton said.

'You too. You're looking well.'

'He's looking old,' Pat said with scorn. 'Bowling, cardigans. He's only thinking of booking us on one of those Saga cruises. I've told him, he can go on his own. Mind you, if the boat sinks, at least everyone will float with their plastic hips and their plastic knees.'

'Ignore her. She looked in the mirror this morning and realized that expensive skin cream she's been lathering all over her face for the past thirty-odd years doesn't work. Would you like a drink, love?'

'I'd better not, I'm driving.'

'As you're up, you can get me a gin and tonic,' Pat said, taking his place in the recliner.

Anton made to leave the room, rolling his eyes at Matilda as he left.

'Have a seat. Tell me what's on your mind.'

Matilda sat down opposite Pat. 'Is everything all right between you two?'

Pat sighed. 'Yes. Everything's fine. He's just getting into the pipe and slippers routine a bit early for my liking. I'm getting old, I know that. I'm not dead, though. A Saga cruise. Can you think of anything worse? I want to go walking in the Rockies or skiing in Aspen. He wants to go to Norfolk because it's nice and flat. I learned the flamenco in Italy. He twisted his ankle in the first couple of minutes and wore his comfortable shoes for the rest of the trip. Ignore me, I'm just having a moan.'

Matilda leaned forward. 'How would you like a job?'

She half-closed her eyes. 'Depends what it is.'

'I want you to find Carl Meagan.'

'What?' Pat's eyes widened. She sat up. A plethora of emotions ran across her face: excitement, fear, horror, wonder. 'You've got new evidence?'

'I'm not sure. A few weeks after Ben Hales killed himself, Sally Meagan got a letter from his solicitor. Since he'd been kicked out of the force, he'd been working as a sort of unofficial private investigator, trying to find Carl, another way to stick the knife into my back. Anyway, when Ben's wife was clearing out his house, she found a load of paperwork. The solicitor gave it to Sally and Sally contacted me.'

'I bet that was a frosty first meeting,' Pat said with a hint of a chuckle.

'It wasn't the most comfortable of meets, no. We're not best friends or anything, but we've sort of reached an understanding. We've been going through Ben's information. I don't know how he did it but he'd been speaking to child traffickers in prison and missing persons groups abroad. He may have been a dick, but I can't fault his work.'

'Have you found him, then?'

'A couple of weeks ago, we were going through some photos Ben had come across. They were of kids in a school playground, wide-angled shots, but the schools weren't in this country. They were in Sweden.'

'Sweden?'

Matilda nodded. 'Sally suddenly got it into her head that Carl was taken abroad. He's blond with blue eyes, he fits the Swedish look. She wants to go out there. Me and Philip have been trying to put her off. It's a ridiculous idea, but she's dead set.'

'I suppose she's clinging to any form of hope she can get.'

'True. I'm not a parent, I can't imagine how she's feeling.'

'That's why you've come to me?'

Matilda took a deep breath. 'I attended a crime scene this morning that is possibly the worst crime I've ever come across. I can't go into details, obviously, but imagine the worst thing a person can do to another person, then times it by ten. It's that bad. I'm not going to have time to listen to Sally crying at me down the phone.'

'So you want her to cry down the phone at me?'

'I want you to work with her. Just while I'm on this case, then I can take over. She's rung me about half a dozen times today. I haven't called her back. I can't be dealing with it right now.'

'I don't know, Mat. Didn't she go a bit weird at one point, especially after she'd written that book?'

'That was only because she felt she was in limbo. She's got a purpose now. She's doing something positive to find her son,' Matilda said, almost pleading with Pat.

'But he was kidnapped and held for ransom. Why would she think he'd been sold abroad? From the original investigation, it sounds like it was a couple of chancers trying to get some money from a rich couple. You wouldn't go from that to child trafficking.'

'You would if it was the only way you could make some money and you had a kid on your hands you needed to get rid of. What do you say, Pat? Please?'

'Will you let me sleep on it?'

'Sure, no problem,' Matilda said, slightly dejected. She thought Pat would have jumped at the chance of a project to test her brain power.

'Pat, where's the Gaviscon?' Anton called out from the kitchen. 'Those kippers I had for lunch are repeating on me.'

'I'll do it,' Pat said quickly to Matilda.

Chapter Nine

DS Sian Mills was a married woman with four children. As much as she tried to leave work behind when she left the station, it was difficult not to take the emotions home with her, especially on difficult cases such as what had happened with the Mercer family. She was preparing a quick and easy meal for the family – spaghetti and meatballs. It was only when she took the mince out of the fridge, slapped it onto the chopping board and went to take a handful to roll into balls when it hit her. She couldn't face touching the raw, pink meat. She started crying.

'What is it?' Stuart asked, coming into the kitchen with a basket full of dirty clothes for the laundry.

'I can't do this.'

'Do what?'

'This. I can't touch the mince. I keep looking at it and seeing . . .'

Stuart put the basket on the floor and took his wife in his arms. He was much taller than Sian; in fact, he towered over her. He was a large-built man and would not have looked out of place on the rugby pitch at Twickenham. He held her close, her head on his broad chest.

'I'm sorry,' she cried, her words muffled.

'Don't be. We've been through this before, we'll go through it again. I'm here for you, you know that.'

'I've never seen anything like this before, Stuart.'

'Come on.' He led her to the kitchen table, pulled out a chair for both of them and sat Sian down. 'Do you want to talk about it?'

Sian and Stuart had been married for twenty-four years. Although Sian was not supposed to discuss delicate work matters with anyone outside of the station, she often unburdened herself on Stuart. That's what kept their marriage so strong. They supported each other and didn't keep secrets. She refused to be a cliché detective who hid things from her husband, bottled things up and turned to drink to ease her pain. She lowered her voice so the kids in the living room couldn't hear and told her husband what she had spent the day doing. When she finished, he grabbed her in his massive arms and pulled her towards him once again.

Being a detective, especially working on a Homicide and Major Enquiry Team, you saw the worst side of human beings, the depraved behaviour, the evil they inflicted on others. Eventually, it began to seep into your subconscious, and suddenly, you were seeing potential killers everywhere. Having someone stable in your life, just one person, to talk to, to lean on, made all the difference. Sian could tell Stuart anything and knew it wouldn't go any further. She trusted him with her life. She felt safe in his arms.

'Don't tell the kids any of this; they don't need to know,' Sian said when she'd finished crying.

'Are you going to be all right? You can ask Matilda to reassign you. She'll understand.'

'I know she will, but, no, I can't do that. This is my job,' she said, trying to sound positive and determined. She looked over at the chopping board, at the pink flesh of mince waiting to be cooked. 'Tell the kids we're having pizza tonight,' she smiled.

'Will you slow down? You're killing me.'

Chris Kean stopped running and leaned against an oak tree in Graves Park. Further ahead, Scott Andrews was speeding up the incline. He stopped, turned and headed back down.

'What's wrong with you?' Chris asked, breathing rapidly. 'You're like the Duracell bunny on acid.'

'Sorry. Bad day,' Scott said, stretching his limbs to keep them warm while Chris caught his breath.

'Must have been. I've heard about taking your frustrations out through exercise, but this is ridiculous.' He tried to laugh, but couldn't.

'I'm not frustrated, I'm just . . .' Scott couldn't finish. 'Besides, you want a good time for the marathon, don't you?'

'Yes. I don't want to kill myself though.' Chris lowered himself down carefully and sat on the rough tarmac.

It was dark and the wind had picked up, an ice-cold stiff breeze was blowing. The temperatures hadn't risen much above zero degrees all day. Now night had fallen, the temperature had plummeted. The clear sky, the billions of twinkling stars, the hard frost on the ground, it all looked stunning, but not when you were running in it, not when your face was bright red and your nose wouldn't stop running.

Scott went over to him and joined him on the ground. He let out a heavy sigh.

'Mum told me about the crime scene,' Chris eventually said, referring to his pathologist mother, Adele Kean. 'She said it was one of the worst she'd ever seen.'

'It was.'

'You stayed with the girl, didn't you? The survivor?'

'Yes.'

'How is she?'

'I was going to say she's lucky to be alive, but is she? She's going to live with the memory of what happened for the rest of her life, and with the fact that her father and grandparents were butchered. Would you want to live with that?'

'She's got an aunt. She won't be alone.'

Scott wiped his eye before the tear fell. 'Fuck.' He turned away.

'It's OK to cry, Scott.'

'It's times like this that you wish you had someone to go home to.'

'You've got Rory.'

Scott laughed. 'He's my flat mate. I meant, someone to . . . you know . . . hold you. I hate being single, sometimes.'

Chris put his arm around Scott and placed his head on his shoulder. 'I know, mate. It's been a while for me too. I know it's no substitute, but you've got me if you need to talk.'

'Thanks, Chris,' he replied, not comforted.

'And we've got running.'

Scott laughed.

'And as a last resort, there's always alcohol.'

'And turn into Matilda Darke? No thank you.'

Scott and Chris ended their training session early. Neither were in the mood after that. Chris suggested going for a drink but was secretly pleased when Scott turned him down. He had a busy day tomorrow and a lot of marking to get done tonight. His job as an English teacher was originally temporary to cover someone on maternity leave. Fortunately for him, she decided not to return to work, so he was given the job full time. As they left Graves Park, Scott asked Chris not to tell his mother how he was dealing with this case. He didn't want it getting back to Matilda. Chris promised.

Scott and Rory shared a two-bedroom apartment on the third floor of Riverside Exchange, on the outskirts of the centre of Sheffield. The view from the lounge overlooked the dirty water of the River Don and the sprawling city, which, at present, was a building site. Sheffield seemed to be going through a new burst of regeneration with ugly concrete eyesores being demolished and replaced with modern office blocks, cinemas and coffee outlets. Soon, the extension on Meadowhall that nobody wanted would begin. More roads would be built, more traffic would come into the city, more noise. It wasn't shops and hotels Sheffield needed it was affordable housing. Scott and Rory were in their mid-twenties and the only way they could afford to leave their parents' homes was to share. How long would they be doing that for? It didn't look like either of them would be settling down soon. Another few years and they would have to decide who was going to be Jack Lemmon and who was going to be Walter Matthau.

Still wearing his Lycra running gear, Scott dragged his heavy feet along the corridor to his apartment. The bag with his work suit screwed up inside was dragging along the floor behind him. He'd pushed himself too hard tonight in Graves Park, but he needed to do something to forget what he had seen that morning in Fulwood. Not that it would make much difference: he would be seeing it again tomorrow.

He opened the front door, slammed it closed behind him and stopped still in the hallway. He could hear the sound of sex coming from Rory's bedroom. Scott rolled his eyes. Since breaking up with his long-term girlfriend and having the freedom of his own place, Rory had been living life to the full. There was a new woman every weekend, it seemed. Although, this latest one seemed to be sticking around longer than the others.

Scott walked past Rory's bedroom and the sound of grunting and the headboard hitting the wall grew louder, as did the woman's groans. Scott couldn't remember her name. He gave up learning names around the fourth one. He knew them as the blonde one, the dark one, the thin one, the one with glasses, the American one . . .

As Scott stripped off in the kitchen and put his running gear into the washing machine, the sounds became louder, the banging on the wall harder.

'Jesus, Rory, for fuck's sake, stop, you're hurting me.'

By the time Rory came out of the bedroom, Scott was in the living room in his dressing gown, eating a bowl of cereal.

'What's wrong?' Scott asked.

'Nothing. Why?'

'Didn't sound like it.'

'I think I got a bit carried away,' he said, sheepishly.

'Everything all right?'

The Scottish one came into the lounge, putting her earrings in. 'I'm going now. Do me a favour, Rory, lose my number. Nice to see you again, Scott.'

Scott smiled. They both remained silent until the door slammed closed.

'Don't judge me,' Rory said, taking in Scott's hard stare.

'I'm not judging.'

'I was feeling a bit . . . I don't know . . . I just wanted to let off some steam, that's all.'

'You should have come for a run with me and Chris.'

'I hate running.'

'You're going to need to apologize to her.'

'You heard her. She just told me to lose her number.'

'She didn't mean it. Apologize. Tell her you had a rough day.'

He shook his head. 'It's not like it was going anywhere. We were just having fun.'

'You said the other night you really liked this one.'

Rory stood up and went to get a bottle of lager from the fridge. 'Did it work for you?' he asked, ignoring Scott's comment.

'What?'

'Going for a run. Did it help you to get the crime scene out of your mind?'

'Yes, it did.'

'You're a bad liar, Scott.'

'I'm going to bed,' he said, placing his half-eaten bowl of cereal on the coffee table.

'It's not even ten o'clock yet.'

'I'm tired.'

Scott had a quick shower then went into his room, locking the bedroom door behind him. He picked up his phone from the bedside table and began scrolling through the photos. He smiled. There was one of Matilda and Adele crossing the finishing line of the Sheffield Half Marathon last year. They both looked like they were ready to drop dead. There was one of Chris crossing the line in the same race. Then Chris sat at the side of the road panting, sweat running down his face. Chris in the pub afterwards drinking a much-needed pint. Chris, once again in his running gear. Chris running. Chris running. Chris. Chris. Chris.

Chapter Ten

The man had been dropped off in Luton. He'd fallen asleep just after Nottingham and hadn't woken up until Milton Keynes. Now, it was dark. He was still in Luton and he wasn't tired. He needed to get to London. He knew that if he could get to the capital, it would be easier to get to Dover, and then through the Channel Tunnel and into France. Once he was on mainland Europe he could go anywhere. He thought briefly about his sister. Would she be sad if she never heard from him again? Probably not. He had caused her nothing but trouble their whole life. He remembered their last conversation, the argument they'd had. He called her a frigid, stuck-up bitch. She called him a loser and a waste of space. They were probably both right. Chalk and cheese, they'd never got on, even as children.

Well, he wouldn't bother her anymore. She wouldn't have to think about him again. Once he was in France, he knew he'd be safe. He could go anywhere from there.

He stole a biro from a petrol station, found a piece of cardboard in a bin and wrote LONDON in large capitals on it. He would have to wait until morning to be seen by drivers. He found shelter between two industrial bins and tried to get comfortable on the cold tarmac. At one o'clock he was still awake. The smell of rotting food didn't help. He wasn't tired. He was freezing cold and he was trying to work out where that rat had run off to as he quickly tucked his jeans into his socks.

Matilda Darke missed her silver Ford Focus. It was comfortable, familiar, and she felt safe in it. Unfortunately, it was no longer practical, and, as she turned from the smooth tarmac on Ringinglow Road down the bone-shaking track, she realized she had made the right decision in upgrading to a Range Rover. She could hardly feel the pot holes, the broken road, the jagged edges as she headed for her new home. A mile down the track, a narrow turn to the left and a sharp incline and there it was – the farm-house she had bought because she felt sorry for it.

After former Detective Inspector Ben Hales had committed suicide in her house – the house her dead husband built – she no longer felt like it was home. That had been Ben's plan; to ruin the last thing left in her life she truly loved. The bastard. It was in that house where she had felt a connection to her husband, as if he was still alive. He had designed the house, he had put his heart and soul into the place. Whatever room she went in she remembered James enthusing about it. Once it was built, once the decorators had left, the furniture had been moved in and it was just the two of them, alone, James had grabbed Matilda, lifted her up onto the granite worktops in the kitchen and made love to her right there. It was the best sex they had ever had. It wasn't long before they had christened every room, including the double garage which wasn't the most romantic place to make love in, and the toilet under the stairs was just silly and resulted in James pulling a muscle in his back. However, in the long lonely nights since James's death, she remembered these moments of happier times and she smiled. She'd go into the downstairs toilet and she'd laugh as she remembered how James had struggled to get up off the floor and hit his head on the sink. She went out into the hallway, looked at the chair in the corner and . . . no, all she saw in the hallway now was Ben's lifeless body hanging from the bannister above. The house had been ruined for her. She'd had to move.

While driving out of Sheffield she'd found a dirt track she had never seen before. Being Sheffield born and bred, Matilda thought she knew the city like the back of her hand, obviously not. Curious to where it might lead, she felt every bump in the road, and hit her head on the roof of her car twice as she plunged into cavernous pot holes. This was a bad idea. Her car wasn't used to such roads, but something told her to continue. She almost became stuck at the sharp turn and the wheels spun on the incline, but she made it to the top eventually. She was glad she did.

A dilapidated farmhouse with four unstable chimneys, tiles missing from the roof, uncared for brick work, tired window frames with dirty panes, an overgrown garden, untended driveway and a front door that probably only required a swift kick to open. Matilda was in love. She got out of the car and walked up the driveway, her eyes fixed on the unloved house. There was a 'for sale' sign that had fallen down at some point, lying in the tall grass. Surely this was fate giving her a sign.

The house needed work doing to it before Matilda could even think about moving in. As her home sold quickly, she moved in with Adele while her new home, the aptly named Hope Farm, was made habitable. Fortunately, James had known many people in the building industry, and she contacted one of his trusted friends, Daniel Harbison. He'd been more than happy to help out, and when he had seen the enormity of the project, he rubbed his hands with glee. The windows were replaced, as was the roof. The chimneys were made safe, the whole house was rewired, the kitchen and bathrooms were ripped out and new, modern ones installed. Matilda and Adele spent many evenings going over colour charts and carpet samples and soon the house was ready for her to move in. There was just one room that needed finishing. On the ground floor, behind the living room, tucked away in a corner was a split-level room that led to the conservatory. This would make a perfect library, and as this was the room she would spend most of her time in, she wanted to make all the decisions herself.

Now, she stood in the doorway to the library and looked around at the floor-to-ceiling shelves which Daniel had designed and installed. The wood had been treated and needed a few days to settle before Matilda could unpack the many boxes of books she had piled up in one of the spare bedrooms. This was to be her sanctuary. When work got on top of her, when life became too difficult, she would come in here, close the door behind her, relax in the Eames chair and lose herself in a novel.

Matilda went into the living room and curled up on the large Chesterfield sofa. The walls were painted a deep red, the log fire was burning, and the entire house was warm, homely and welcoming.

On the reclaimed railway sleeper above the wood burner, was a framed photograph of her and James on their wedding day. The marriage only lasted five years before James was cruelly taken from her, another cancer statistic. She used to spend hours with the photo in her hands, crying hysterically, screaming for him to be returned to her. Now, she looked into his ice-blue eyes and smiled.

'You'd hate this house, wouldn't you?' she asked him with a laugh in her voice. Of course he would. James was an architect. As much as he admired period buildings, his job was creating new ones. That's what he loved. Hope Farm was built in 1891, the same year Conan Doyle moved his Sherlock Holmes stories to *The Strand Magazine*. Everything about it screamed Victorian.

Matilda was finally home. She was settled. She was almost happy.

Following a couple of hours of reading the new Eva Dolan novel in the lounge, she felt her eyes grow heavy and decided to go up to bed. She closed the door on the wood burner so no burning embers would fall out and set the house on fire while she was sleeping, picked up her book and made her way upstairs.

The house was deathly silent, apart from the usual noises houses made as they cooled down. She stood at the top of the stairs and looked over the bannister at the floor below. Through the stained glass in the front door, she could see thick branches swaying. They cast long shadows on the tiled floor in the hallway. They looked like gnarled fingers, crawling under the door, scraping across the floor. She shuddered at the thought. She'd have to buy a heavy curtain or something to hang in front of the door, block out the light.

Something woke her. She opened her eyes to find she was still sitting up in bed. The lamp on the bedside table was still on, and the hardback novel was open on her lap. She looked at the clock; it was just past one o'clock. She placed a bookmark between the pages, closed the book and placed it next to another framed photo of James on the table. She turned out the light and was about to turn over to hunker down under the duvet when she heard a noise from downstairs. Her eyes widened. She remained still and listened intently. She heard the noise again. It was a creaking sound followed by a tap. Was it the floorboards or the stairs? Was somebody coming up? Matilda sat bolt upright and turned the lamp back on. A few seconds later, she heard the same noise again.

'Shit,' she said to herself.

Matilda flung back the duvet and climbed out of bed. Next to the bedside table, one of James's old cricket bats was leaning against the wall. She'd never had cause to use it in the past, but always felt safer knowing a weapon was to hand if she should ever need to defend herself.

She put on her dressing gown, tying it at the waist and went over to the bedroom door. The brass knob was cold. She twisted it carefully to the right so as not to make a sound, pulled the door towards her and stepped out onto the unfamiliar landing.

'Hello,' she called out. Her shaking voice echoed around the empty house. 'Is anyone there?'

Creak. Tap.

Her mouth dried. She tried to swallow but couldn't. She gripped the bat hard and went to the bannister to look over the edge and into the hallway. There was nobody there.

She was halfway down the stairs when she heard the creak and the tap again. It was coming from outside the front door.

Creak. Tap.

A branch outside the house creaked each time the wind blew and the tip of it tapped against the door.

Matilda released her breath and sighed. She almost laughed. First thing in the morning, she was cutting that branch off. Standing on the stairs, cricket bat aloft, she suddenly realized how ridiculous she was being. Is this how life was going to be from now on? Every time she heard a noise, would she think someone had broken in or the ghost of Ben Hales had followed her here to torture her all over again?

In the old house, even living on her own, she had never felt this frightened, this paranoid before. Was the fact she was living in the middle of nowhere worrying her? The isolation, the rolling countryside views from almost every window, the lack of neighbours – that was what had sold her the house in the first place. It was perfect. It was everything she had been looking for. She had thought.

Maybe I do want people around me.

Instead of returning to bed, Matilda headed for the living room. She pushed open the door and felt the warmth, despite the fire having died a couple of hours since. She turned on the light and almost screamed.

The walls. The walls she had agonized over the colour of for weeks, the deep red which made the room warm and homely, in the haze of the room, looked like blood dripping down. She immediately thought of the Mercer house, the lifeless, mutilated bodies of Clive, Serena and Jeremy. She looked at her hands, still wrapped around the cricked bat, and for a split second she thought they were covered in blood. She dropped the bat and staggered out of the living room.

She would have to redecorate.

Chapter Eleven

Matilda woke to the sound of her mobile ringing. She turned on the light, and, while her eyes adjusted, she fumbled on the bedside table for it. She answered without looking at the display.

'Hello,' she croaked. She sat up and looked around her. She couldn't remember coming back to bed, but she'd obviously dragged herself back up somehow. She threw back the duvet and looked down at her body. There was no blood.

What the hell was I dreaming about last night?

'Morning, Mat. Haven't woken you, have I?' Adele asked. Her voice didn't have the usual bounce and lightness to it.

'No. I was just getting up,' she lied. The clock told her it wasn't even six o'clock yet. 'You're up early. Couldn't sleep?'

'No. I kept having bad dreams,' Adele said. 'How did you sleep?'

'Fine,' she lied.

'I wanted to let you know that we'll be removing the bodies from the Mercer house at some point this morning.'

'That's great.'

'I'll let you know when the post mortems are.'

'Thanks. How's Lucy?'

'She was very quiet when I gave her a lift home yesterday. I'll have a word with her this morning. Chris went for a run with

Scott last night. He said he was behaving, erm, strangely,' she said, choosing her words carefully.

'Strangely? In what way?'

'Well, when he asked him about it, he started crying.'

'Oh,' Matilda was surprised. Scott was well known for keeping his cards incredibly close to his chest. Sian had her husband to confide in. Aaron and Christian both had wives they could talk to. Rory used Sian as an informal therapist, but Scott was stoic. Matilda often wondered whether he had an outlet for his emotions, apart from running. She wouldn't have guessed Chris.

'Scott told Chris not to say anything and Chris told me not to say anything.'

'So you're telling me,' Matilda said with a smile.

'Well, we have to look out for the people we work with, don't we?'

'And we all know you love a gossip.'

'True. You won't tell Scott, will you?'

'No. I noticed he was quiet in the evening briefing anyway. I'm going to keep my eye on him. Fancy meeting for lunch?'

'If I get time for one, yes.'

Matilda ended the call and decided to get up. She had a quick shower while the coffee was brewing then found a cereal bar in one of her many empty cupboards; that would keep her going for a couple of hours. She really needed to do some shopping. She left the house, snapping off the brittle branch that had caused her such panic last night, and headed for her car. Her mind kept going back to Scott. He had been quiet and more thoughtful looking before the Mercer killings. It couldn't just be the carnage he'd witnessed that was causing such angst. What else was going on in his life to warrant such a change in his personality?

* * *

He woke up in agony. A night spent slumped between two industrial bins at the back of a petrol station was not anyone's idea of a comfortable evening. He ached in places he didn't realize he could ache and he was chilled to the core. Slowly, he unfolded himself from the position he had been curled up in and managed to stand up amid the sounds of clicking bones. He stretched, yawned, scratched and breathed in a lungful of rancid exhaust fumes and petrol. There was a hint of pleasure; freshly ground coffee coming from the kiosk. He emptied his pockets and counted the money he pulled out – £47.63. That was all he had in the world. Less than fifty pounds between him and poverty. It needed to last.

He went into the petrol station and headed straight for the toilets at the back. He washed his face with the pink handwash above the sink. He took off his sweater and washed under his arms. He was beginning to smell and didn't want to draw attention to himself. He looked in the mirror at his tired face, his blond stubble and unkempt hair. He could go another couple of days without shaving, but soon he would look like a vagrant, and he'd never get a lift to mainland Europe without drawing suspicion. He'd think of something once he was at Dover. There was plenty of time, he was sure of it.

He bought himself a large black Americano, as strong as he could stomach it, and a bacon sandwich. If the forty pounds he had remaining was going to last, he would need to shop more creatively. No more chain coffee shops. He went back to the bins and picked up his 'London' sign before heading for the motorway.

It was still early in the morning, but it was filling up nicely with commuters. Cars with just one person in them flew past without giving him a second glance, as did coaches and mini buses. His best chance of a lift would come from a lorry. He walked along the hard shoulder, sign in one hand, coffee in the other, cursing every single vehicle that failed to stop.

'Bastard!' he shouted at an oil tanker that had applied its brakes, slowed down, only to quickly speed up again and beep its horn.

People were twats. That was something he'd discovered a long time ago. Nobody cared about anything but themselves. He'd tried his best, but he'd been screwed over too many times. Is there no wonder he turned to crime? It started with a bit of shoplifting; he'd been good at it too. It soon escalated. His mother told him he was on a slippery slope. It wouldn't be long before he found himself in a situation he wouldn't be able to get out of. He should have listened. She was right. If the police found him now, he was fucked. He should never have taken a glove off. The bloody latex made him itch. He'd left a print behind. He knew it.

Chapter Twelve

Sian didn't attend the morning briefing. She sent a text to Matilda saying she couldn't sleep and had called Rose Bishop to see if she could visit her early. Fortunately, Rose also had trouble sleeping and looked forward to having some company.

When Sian arrived, the briefing was almost finished. The main task of the day was getting into the Mercer house and finding out who the family really was. For someone to kill and destroy a whole family like that was personal. According to the neighbours, they were the perfect family. Matilda and her team, from experience, knew there was no such thing. There had to be something lurking in their past that someone would kill for.

Matilda was in her small office with DI Christian Brady when Sian knocked on the glass door.

'Anything?' Matilda asked.

'I managed to get the name of the hotel Leah and her new husband are staying at in Paris out of her. I've contacted the Foreign and Commonwealth Office in London. They're going to contact the British Embassy in Paris and send the local police round.'

'That's great work, Sian. Did she tell you anything else?'

'No. She's a mess. Her hands were shaking, she keeps crying, and I swear she'd already had a drink when I got there. I mentioned the photos and she's going to try and come in later today to go through them with Finn.'

'Is she married?'

'Yes. Her husband had gone to work.'

'How considerate of him,' Christian said with sarcasm.

'She took a few photos herself on her phone. She started showing them to me but began crying. I told her to email them over.'

'I bet a number of other guests took their own photos too,' Christian said. 'It might be worth setting up an email address for people to send them to. We could get Finn to see what matches up.'

'Good thinking, Christian. Call tech and get them to set it up. Also, I'm assuming they had an official photographer too, especially to take photos outside the church. We'll need copies of those.' Matilda looked up through the glass and saw the young TDC Finn Cotton at Faith's old desk, staring intently at his computer screen. 'We'll use Finn for all the photos so nothing is missed. Sian, can you liaise with him?'

'Not a problem.' She was about to leave the office when Matilda called her back in.

'Close the door, Sian,' Matilda said. She lowered her voice. 'While you're both here, I need to ask a favour. Now, we all know how bad the scene was yesterday, but you two are my toughest officers.'

'I don't know about that,' Sian interrupted. 'I was crying on Stuart's shoulder for most of the night.'

'I just went to bed early. Jennifer knows not to ask about work. I talk to her when I'm ready.'

'I'm worried about Scott and Rory,' Matilda said. 'They were both quiet yesterday and this morning. I don't want them bottling anything up. They're also not the type to freely talk about how they're feeling, especially Scott. Now, I think we should limit the amount of people going to the crime scene. Aaron went to the house but didn't go inside, neither did Ranjeet. So we'll keep them here. The less people caught up in this the better.'

'I agree,' Christian said. 'Well, I'll keep an eye on Scott and Sian can keep an eye on Rory.'

'And I'll keep an eye on the both of you,' Matilda smiled.

'But's who's watching the watcher?' Christian asked, a menacing tone added to his voice.

Matilda's mobile rang. It was ACC Masterson. She held it up and showed them both. 'That's who's watching me.'

Chapter Thirteen

Matilda met with Crime Scene Manager Sebastian Flowers outside the Mercers' house. He looked as if he had been there all night. Usually clean-shaven and neat hair, his black mane was uncombed, and his stubble was patchy. Strangely, the unkempt look suited him.

'My wife's two days overdue. I keep seeing red patches every time I close my eyes and I haven't had a decent meal since breakfast yesterday morning.'

'Oh. Good morning to you too, Sebastian,' Matilda said as she approached him.

'The bodies have gone and forensics finished up about an hour ago. You're still going to need overshoes and a face mask,' he said before disappearing into the house.

'Really?'

'Unless you want to ruin your shoes.'

She glanced down at her cheap, sturdy slip-ons. 'They're hardly Jimmy Choos, but fair enough.'

In the hallway, Matilda looked at the framed photographs on the wall as she struggled into the paper suit. There was a different atmosphere to the house now the bodies had been removed. There was still a chilling darkness about the place, a sense that something horrific had happened here, but the immediate tension had lifted and been replaced with a great sadness.

The framed photographs on the walls showed the family at different stages in their lives. There was one of a handsome young man wearing his graduation outfit of cap and gown. His smile was beaming, and he was flanked either side by proud parents. They were now all dead. Butchered. Usually, Matilda reserved judgement as to the type of person who could commit this level of crime, but now, here, she didn't care what excuse he used, was he mentally ill, high on drugs, to her, he was an evil, cold-blooded killer, and she would relish catching him.

'I do have other crime scenes to attend,' Sebastian called to her from the bottom of the stairs.

'Sorry. I was looking at the photos.'

'OK,' he began, reading from his iPad, 'this is where Jeremy Mercer was found. As you can see he lost a lot of blood, so the killer hit his target. Jeremy wasn't stabbed as many times as his parents, but Adele can fill you in on that. Why is he on the stairs? Well, best guess is that he got up in the middle of the night and surprised the killer. There's no sign of a head wound, so he wasn't pushed or fell down the stairs. As you can see from the stains on the stairs there are some good shoe prints. Hopefully, we'll be able to identify what kind of shoes. You can see the distinctive Nike tick logo in one on the landing.'

'What about fingerprints?' Matilda asked as Sebastian made his way carefully up the stairs.

'This was a high traffic area. Don't forget, there was a wedding here on Sunday. People will have been up and down the stairs on a regular basis. The bannister is covered with prints. None of them identifiable.'

'Point of entry?'

Sebastian stopped once again mid-way up the stairs. He gave an audible sigh. 'The marquee at the back of the house. The patio doors were open. The front door was locked and bolted from the inside. Nothing broken on any of the windows. No sign of forced entry. It's all in my report which is in your inbox. Onwards and upwards,' he said in a flat monotone as he returned to going up to the first floor.

Matilda remained where she was, looking at the amount of blood soaked into the carpet, and sprayed onto the walls. She wondered what had killed him: the loss of blood as his heart stopped pumping – a slow and agonizing death – or the stab wounds. She took a deep breath and headed up the stairs. She knew the sight that would greet her: the pool of blood where Clive Mercer had been murdered. As Sebastian was in the doorway of the room Rachel was found in, she went straight in there, leaving the horrors of what lay on the landing until she needed to see it.

Reading from his iPad again, Sebastian ran through what had been found in this room. 'As you know Rachel Mercer was found tied to the chair. She was tied with a dressing gown belt which matches the one hanging on the back of the door, so the killer didn't come equipped to tying anyone up. It's been sent for analysis. There are three sets of identifiable latent fingerprints on the bedside table, fortunately it's a nice smooth silk finish so we've been able to get some prints.'

The bed had been stripped of the bedding, including the mattress, so all that remained was the oak frame. There was no blood on the walls, but the carpet was stained with flecks of blood and small bloody paw prints.

Although Matilda was listening to the crime scene manager, her eyes were darting around the room. She wondered how long

Rachel had been held prisoner here: what had she been forced to endure? Had she known all along that her family had been killed? If the murders had taken place in the early hours of Sunday morning and Rose hadn't found them until just before ten o'clock, that was possibly six to eight hours of being tied to a chair, terrified, cold and hungry. What would that do to her mental health?

'Did you hear what I said?'

'Yes, you've got good prints from the bedside table.'

'No. I was telling you about the stains in the carpet.'

'Oh. Sorry. Go on.'

Sebastian rolled his eyes. 'As you can see, forensics have cut a patch out of the carpet. Depending on what they get from them they may need to come back for more. This is going to need to remain an active crime scene for a while.'

'Not a problem.'

'The little girl—' he looked down at his iPad. 'Rachel. She wasn't physically harmed in any way. So, identifying the various blood groups will give you information as to who was killed in relation to when Rachel was tied up. No tampering with the window. The main light was on when she was found. Now, this is interesting,' he said, going to the bedroom door.

Sebastian closed the door and Matilda suddenly felt her blood run cold. She inhaled a deep breath and held it for several seconds longer than usual. There was the distinct aroma of metallic blood with a hint of dog in the air. She put herself in Rachel's shoes; trapped in the bedroom, tied to the chair, covered in the blood of her dying relatives. She shivered at the thought.

'On the back of the door is a very clear print of an ear.'

'An ear?'

'Yes. Only small, so we're assuming it's Rachel's.'

'Why would her ear print be on the back of the door?'

He shrugged. 'Best guess is she heard something out on the landing and pressed her ear against the door to have a listen. We've all done that at some point in our lives, to be nosy.'

'So she could have heard – I don't know – raised voices or something,' Matilda surmised. 'Maybe she heard the killer arguing with her dad. Perhaps.'

Sebastian raised his eyebrows. 'I don't relish you interviewing her. Poor thing,' he said in his usual monotone.

He opened the door. Matilda was relieved. She was beginning to feel trapped.

'Now, on to the landing.'

Matilda swallowed hard. All she could see when she thought about the landing was the head hanging off the body.

'Nothing of interest here forensically, so we'll move on upstairs.'

'Really?' Matilda asked. She was pleased not to have to linger but was surprised by the lack of forensics.

'Everything around here has been fingerprinted, the doors, the walls, the bannister, and we've found nothing. Obviously, not nothing, the bannister was full of prints, but all of them smudged. Don't forget, this is the landing – a main thoroughfare of the house. People will have come up to use the toilet, get changed. We haven't found a decent print at all.'

'It was a frenzied attack,' Matilda said, looking up at the ceiling at the sprays of blood. 'There must have been something, hairs, anything under his fingernails.'

'Nope. Shall we?' he said, eager to get to the next bedroom.

Matilda frowned. When a crime scene was as frenzied as this one, when it was obvious the victim had put up a fight, something was usually left behind of the assailant – a hair, a fingerprint, a fibre from his clothing, a bead of sweat. She would have a word with Adele, see if she could find anything from under their fingernails.

'Are you sure? What about something in the fibres of the carpet?'

'Matilda, every scene of crime officer who was here has had more than five years' experience on the job. If they'd have found something they would have documented it and I would have known about it.'

'I'm not doubting the SOCOs. I'm just saying, a man was stabbed so many times he was almost decapitated, yet the killer left nothing of himself behind.'

'I can only tell you what we find,' he said, hugging the iPad close to his chest and walking slowly up the attic stairs.

Matilda remained on the landing. The image of Clive Mercer's stricken body was etched on her brain. He was white from having bled out. The number of stab wounds to his neck were many. The attack was frenzied. How could the killer not have left something, anything of him behind? This crime scene did not make any sense.

The stairs leading up to the attic were also smudged with bloody footprints where the killer had run up and down. The wall behind the bed was an explosion of blood. The sprays were high and long. It was difficult to understand how one person could perform such a lengthy, brutal attack, unless they had superhuman strength. Unless there was more than one person involved.

'We managed to get an excellent bloody footprint from the left side of the bed.' Sebastian pointed to where a square of carpet had been cut out. 'Now, judging by the shoes in front of the wardrobe, Clive Mercer was a size eight. The bloody print was from a size ten.'

'Only one print?'

'Yes. Best guess is he put his foot up on the bed, for whatever reason, stood in the pool of blood, and placed it back on the carpet. It also matches the print from the landing with the Nike tick.'

'Is that the only decent print in this room?'

'Yes.'

'Shouldn't there be more prints? What about when he left the room? Unless he levitated.'

'There probably were, but look around you, the carpet is saturated.'

Matilda looked at the floor. Her overshoes were stained red. She pondered the sight before her. She looked at the route the killer would have taken from the left side of the bed to the door after killing. The single footprint didn't make sense.

'What happened here?' Matilda asked looking at a large smudge of grey powder by the dressing table.

'Lindsay knocked over her fingerprint kit. Lucky the carpet's stained with blood or she'd have a hefty cleaning bill on her hands,' he said with a smile. 'Anyway,' he said, clearing his throat, 'you'll like this next bit.'

'Really?'

'Oh yes. We have a hair.'

'Just one?'

'Sometimes it only takes one. It was under the woman's little finger on her right hand. It's only small but the root is attached.'

'Fingerprints and a hair, I'll take that.'

'You can't commit a crime this frenzied and leave nothing of yourself behind,' he said, unknowingly echoing her earlier thoughts.

But he didn't on the first-floor landing, she thought.

'Have forensics finished now?'

'No. They've finished up here but there's the marquee in the back garden. I doubt we'll get anything from there as there will have been hundreds of guests here for the reception. However, it has to be done.'

'True,' Matilda said. 'Well, thank you for this, Sebastian. You and your team have done an amazing job.'

'That's what we're here for. Obviously, the fun starts now, back at the lab. As soon as we've got anything, I'll let you know. I'll email you across the crime scene photos once I've been through them all. As you can guess, there's a lot to go through.'

'Thanks, Sebastian.'

'Well, I'll leave you to it. I'm off to see if my wife has gone into labour yet.'

'Give her my best.'

'Will do,' he said, waving as he left the room.

Matilda stood in the middle of the bedroom and looked around her. She went over to the dormer window and looked outside. It was a beautiful area of Sheffield. She pushed open the window and leaned out. It was a cold morning and she shivered as a stiff breeze entered the room. Looking down, she saw white-suited forensic officers going in and out of the marquee. Everything had to be bagged and tagged. It was probably useless and no relevance to the case, but, maybe the killer had taken a sneaky drink from a champagne bottle, or bit into a lump of cheese and left behind a pattern of some distinct dental work.

Wishful thinking.

She turned back and looked at the bloodbath before her. Serena Mercer had been obliterated. She frowned as she thought. Jeremy Mercer was stabbed only a few times, and, according to

Sebastian, it appeared he surprised the intruder, which meant he was killed first. If that was the case, why did he receive only a couple of incapacitating stab wounds while his parents were subjected to a fierce attack? He was a young man. He was tall. He wouldn't have been as easy to overcome as a couple in their sixties. What did that mean? Was it just the couple who were the focus of the murder? Did the killer think they were alone which is why Rachel was unharmed?

'Ma'am?'

Matilda jumped at the sound of being called. She turned to see Scott standing in the doorway.

'Sorry. I didn't mean to startle you.'

'No. It's fine. What's wrong?'

'Nothing. We've found a few laptops and tablets we're taking back to the station. I've found a file in the boxroom being used as a study. It's got a load of bank statements. I thought you might want to have a look.' There was definitely something wrong with Scott. He was subdued, and he had a permanent worry frown on his forehead, giving him the impression he was about to burst into tears at any moment. Maybe he was.

'Sure,' she replied. 'So, is everything all right?' she asked as they carefully made their way down the stairs.

'Yes. Fine.'

'Are you sure?'

'Yes. Fine,' he repeated, more firmly.

He stormed into the boxroom at the end of the corridor and opened the top drawer of a filing cabinet.

Matilda immediately went to the bookshelves. Since she had acquired the book collection from Jonathan Harkness, a killer she hadn't wanted to be guilty, she had been addicted to reading, and collecting books in general. Whenever she went into someone's house, she headed straight for the book-case to see what they had in their collection. The Mercers had no crime fiction. They were mostly biographies of historical figures and international monarchs. Although some of the covers were striking, the content held very little interest to Matilda, so she joined Scott at the filing cabinet.

'They were very meticulous people,' Scott said. 'A file for everything. Gas, electricity, phone, water, council tax, pension plans.'

'Anything juicy in the bank statements?'

Scott handed his boss a box file from the top of the cabinet. 'All in monthly order.'

Matilda placed the box on the desk, now free of the desktop computer, and opened it. 'Bloody hell look how much they made every month. I'm in the wrong job. What did they do, again?'

'She was a neurosurgeon and he was an anaesthetist. Or it could have been the other way round.'

'There doesn't seem to be much of interest here,' Matilda said, scanning the statements. 'They have quite a few direct debit payments to charity. They really are the perfect family.'

'Were,' Scott corrected.

'Take them back to the station and see if you can find anything. Don't spend too long on it, though.'

'Will do.' He took the file from her and headed for the door.

'Why would someone want to kill an entire family, and in such a horrific way?' Matilda mused.

Scott stopped in the doorway. He turned back to his boss but gave her a shrug for a reply.

'I mean, all killers believe they're killing for a reason. So, if you have a gripe with someone, fair enough, you come in and you kill them, but this? This is overkill. And if someone has that level of anger towards them, then surely their friends or neighbours would know about it. Yet, according to everyone around here they're Mr and Mrs Perfect. What aren't we seeing?' she asked, folding her arms.

'A secret life. Maybe they're in the witness protection programme and they've been found out.'

It sounded far-fetched but, in this instance, it had a sense of realism about it.

'I get the feeling this is going to be a very complex investigation.'

Scott didn't say anything. He stayed where he was and looked at Matilda, as if waiting for her to continue. When she didn't, he turned and left the room. Matilda followed.

'Scott, come into the living room for a moment,' Matilda said once they were at the bottom of the stairs. She took off her overshoes and went in.

'What is it?' he asked, standing in the doorway, still holding the file.

'Put the file down and take a seat.' She patted the seat next to her on the large sofa, but he went over to the armchair. 'Scott, what's wrong?'

'Nothing. I'm fine.'

'You're not. You've been quiet for weeks. Are you having personal problems?'

'No.'

'Everything all right at home? Rory isn't pissing you off or anything?'

'No. We get on well.'

'How's the training for the marathon?'

'Fine.'

'You can talk to me, you know, Scott.'

'I know I can, but I've nothing to say,' he said. Not once had he made eye contact with Matilda.

'OK,' she gave in. 'I don't believe you, but OK. Look, if you want to talk to me, about anything, please, come and see me.'

'I will.'

'Either in the office or you can come to my house. You know where I live. I may give you a paintbrush, but you're welcome.'

'Thanks,' he said with a fake smile. He stood up and left the room, taking the file of bank statements with him.

Matilda's phone rang. It was Sian. 'I've heard back from the FCO,' she immediately said. 'Leah and Oliver are going to get the next available plane back to England. They should be in Sheffield by this evening. They've been told to come straight to the station.'

'How did they take it?'

'Well, language barrier aside, Leah didn't seem to believe what she was being told.'

'I can understand that. We'll meet her at the station and take her to the hospital when we've had a word with her. She'll want to be with her niece.'

'Adele called as well; she wants you to pop in and see her at the mortuary.'

'Will do.'

'Oh, and one more thing,'

'Go on,'

'Rory's handed in his resignation.'

Chapter Fourteen

Matilda sat behind the wheel of her car. She had a perplexed look on her face. She didn't have a clue where this case was heading. The neighbours painted Mr and Mrs Mercer as Mr and Mrs Perfect. Nobody saw anything suspicious as they were all suffering the effects of the wedding reception. Now, her team was falling apart. She couldn't have that. She needed them.

She lowered the window and allowed the sub-zero degree air to roll in. It instantly helped her relax as she took in a deep breath. She would need a clear mind to think straight if she was going to keep a strong hold of the case and her team. No distractions were allowed. She looked at her mobile and saw three more missed calls from Sally Meagan. This was one distraction she didn't need.

Matilda called Sally. It was ten minutes before she was able to get a word in. It was obvious she'd been drinking, despite it not being lunchtime yet. She tried to tell Matilda about the phone call from Carl, but her words came out of her mouth so quickly they were falling over themselves into one long garbled mess. In the end, Matilda interrupted. She apologized for not contacting her, told her, briefly, about her current workload and talked-up the excellent skills of retired Detective Inspector Pat Campbell who was coming out of retirement to help her. Once placated, Matilda ended the call. She felt exhausted.

She started the engine and drove away looking in the rear-view mirror as she went. The house belonging to the Mercers was a beautiful stone-built building, tastefully decorated, in manicured grounds. She wondered if it would have to be knocked down. The house would now be synonymous with a multiple murder. It was such a waste of a stunning building.

Matilda's to-do list was growing all the time. On her way to the mortuary on Watery Street on the outskirts of Sheffield city centre, she planned in her head everything she needed to do. There were the post mortems to attend, Rory to talk to, forensics to liaise with, Valerie to brief, Leah returning from Paris, Rachel's condition in hospital to keep an eye on. She may only be seven years old, but she was a material witness, and she would need careful handling.

Matilda drove along, not paying attention to the road signs or the speed limit. How she made it to Watery Street without causing a crash was anyone's guess.

She pressed the buzzer and waited to enter.

'Matilda, come on in.' The door was opened by radiologist Claire Alexander who performed the digital autopsies. She was dressed in oversized scrubs. Her face was red, and her hair was stuck to her forehead from sweating. Despite the grim nature of her job, Claire always had a smile on her face and welcomed Matilda with open arms.

'You're going to love me when I tell you what I've found,' Claire began, heading straight for the Digital Autopsy suite.

'Oh,' Matilda was slightly taken off guard. She was hoping for a cup of tea first, maybe five minutes to compose herself.

'We've scanned all three victims this morning. I think Adele is ready to get started on the invasive post mortems. Are you on your own?' Claire asked, stopping in the middle of the corridor and turning around.

'For now. I've got Ranjeet coming down.'

'Right. Come on through.'

Claire opened the door into the small ante-room next to the main suite. As usual, the heat was stifling due to the bank of computers and scanning equipment. The atmosphere was heavy, not purely because of the heat, but the knowledge of what went on in this room. It seemed to be embedded in the walls. The usually clear desk had birthday cards dotted about, a reminder than even though this was a place of death, life does go on.

'Whose birthday is it?'

'It was mine on Monday. I should probably take these down now.'

'Many happy returns.'

'Thank you. Don't even think about asking how old I am; I'm trying to put it out of my mind.'

'Did you do anything special?'

'I had a meal out with a couple of friends and I'm off to London this weekend to see a play,' she said, a beaming smile lighting up her face.

Matilda smiled back. It seemed strange to talk about the usual practices of everyday life in a mortuary. She often wondered how people like Claire and Adele were able to do their job without it encroaching on their private lives. Matilda often took her work home with her. She spent many sleepless nights going over conversations, interviews, and statements to see if she had missed anything. Watching Claire deftly hammer away on the keyboard, bringing up images of dead bodies on the large computer screens, she doubted Claire would still be awake at 2 a.m. torturing herself about a bullet entry wound.

'I'm going to talk you through Serena Mercer's killing first. Now, we believe this to be the last of the killings. I'll come to the reason why in a moment. However, this is an image of Serena's face and chest.'

A black-and-white X-ray filled the screen. Matilda had no idea what she was looking at. She didn't know one artery from another. Fortunately, she didn't have to.

'As you know, the attack was frenzied. Now, it's difficult to establish the trajectory of the stab wounds as there was a lot of haemorrhaging which is obscuring the soft tissue. However, air tracks through the soft tissue and we can follow the path of the air to the initial stab wound.' She looked over at Matilda who had a blank expression on her face. 'Do you follow?'

'I think so.'

Claire turned to another computer screen where a more detailed image of Serena Mercer appeared. In glorious technicolour, Matilda could see every muscle and vein in the dead woman's face, neck and chest.

'From the outside, we can see that she was stabbed twenty-eight times. Eight in the face, six in the neck, five in the chest, and nine times in the stomach.'

'Can you tell which one killed her?'

'The ones to the neck did the most damage. They cut through the major nerves and arteries. Both the internal and external jugular veins were severed,' she said, pointing to them on the screen.

'I'd have thought you'd have said the ones that ripped out her intestines.'

'She was most likely dead by then. Also, I think your killer was getting tired by that point too. You can see where the knife dragged along the stomach, almost tearing it open rather than stabbing. Either he was getting tired or his knife was getting blunt.'

'So why do you think she was killed last?'

'Ah, this is the clever part. Take a look here.' She zoomed in close and pointed to the clavicle bone in the chest. 'Do you see that white line?'

'Yes,' Matilda said, leaning in to look at the pure white, but incredibly small, line. 'What is it?'

'That is the tip of the knife.'

'Really?'

'Yes,' she replied with a smile. 'The knife hit the clavicle, the shoulder blade, and snapped the tip right off. Obviously, I don't know how many knives your killer had but all three victims have similar size stab wounds. I'm guessing two different sized knives, but he could have had more than one with the same sized blade.'

'Oh.'

Claire closed down the images of Serena and brought up the ones of her twenty-eight-year-old son.

'Judging from where Jeremy Mercer was found, on the stairs, we can surmise he was the first victim. He also has the least amount of stab wounds – three. A fairly deep one to the trunk of the body but managed to miss the stomach. Another stab to the neck and one to the chest.'

Claire zoomed in on Jeremy's stomach. 'See this line, this is from a much larger knife compared to these two,' she said, pointing to the stab wounds on his chest and neck. 'Now, the tip from the large knife is what is embedded in Serena Mercer's clavicle. The tip from the smaller knife is here,' she pointed to a bright sliver of light in Jeremy Mercer's chest. 'It's broken as the blade hit the sternum manubrium and it's stuck here in the pectoral muscle.'

'So, if he killed him first, damaged his knife, why haven't we found it? Surely he would have thrown it to one side or something as his spree continued.'

'In an attack this frenzied, knowing your killer had at least two knives, you'd imagine him to have one in each hand and be stabbing remorselessly. When one knife breaks you'd throw it away and keeping stabbing with the one you had left,' Claire surmised.

'That's what I was thinking, too. He's hardly going to stop, put the knife away, then continue.'

'Unless he did throw it away then went back to collect it once he'd finished.'

'Hmm,' Matilda thought. 'If he's killed in the way he has done, with such ferocity, then gone back around the house to check he hasn't left anything behind, that shows a man of such cold-blooded calculation. To walk around a house, having tied up one of his victims and leaving her alive, he is basically one disturbed and sick individual.'

Claire shuddered. 'I am so glad I'm in here and not doing your job.'

'Right now, I think I'd rather be doing your job too. This is one killer's head I do not want to attempt to get into.'

Claire blew out her cheeks and unbuttoned her top button. It was getting stifling in the small room. 'Do you want me to show you Clive Mercer or would you like to take a break?'

'Let's carry on,' Matilda said. Her voice lowered and her eyes were wide. She was genuinely frightened by this killer.

'Clive Mercer's injuries were all to the neck. Thirty-seven stab wounds in total. His head was just hanging on with two tendons.'

'Bloody hell,' Matilda uttered.

'He cut through the lot; the carotid artery, the auricular nerve, the supraclavicular nerve, the anterior jugular vein. He's even managed to get through to the thyroid gland. This is taking frenzied to a whole other level.'

Matilda looked at the colourful image of Clive Mercer's neck. The man was an anaesthetist. He was intelligent. He was on the board of two local charities. He was a regular churchgoer, and this was how his life ended.

'Jesus Christ,' she said under her breath. 'Would the killer have been covered in blood?'

'Absolutely. He would have been drenched in it. Unless . . .'

'Unless what?'

'Unless he was wearing a forensic oversuit.'

'Well, you can buy anything on Amazon these days,' Matilda half-smiled.

'Now, I've saved the best until last. Are you ready for this?' There was a glint in Claire's eye which Matilda found almost sinister.

'Go on.'

'Clive Mercer was dying.'

'I'm sorry?'

More tapping on the keyboard and up came a close-up of Clive's head. She zoomed in on a dark patch. 'That is a rather aggressive-looking tumour on Clive's frontal lobe.'

Matilda swallowed hard. She should have noticed the shading of a tumour as soon as she saw it. She'd seen enough of James's in the early stages of his illness.

'Is it cancerous?'

'Adele will take samples and we'll find out the severity.'

'Would he have known about it?'

'I would have thought so. It will be in his medical notes.'

'I haven't seen them yet. Poor bloke.'

'I know. A double blow to his family.'

'What's left of them.'

The door opened and Adele Kean entered. She wasn't scrubbed up yet for the post mortems and was wearing black trousers with a beige sweater.

'We're all set next door when you want to come and join us.'

'I feel sick,' Matilda said.

'Have you eaten this morning?' Adele asked.

'I can't remember.'

'How about we all go for an early lunch?' Claire said.

'That's a good idea. Mat?'

'I don't know. I've got a lot on at the moment,' Matilda said, running her sweating hands through her hair.

'You need to eat.'

'Maybe just a sandwich.'

Adele and Claire were the first to leave the room while Matilda stood looking into the main scanning suite.

'Did Matilda tell you she's seeing someone?' Adele asked Claire.

'No. Who?'

'The bloke who's renovating her new house.'

'I'm not seeing anyone,' Matilda shouted as she followed them into the corridor. 'He took me for a meal last week, that's all.' She rolled her eyes at Claire.

'I don't blame you,' Claire said. 'The only way I'll get involved with a bloke again is if I've seen his bank balance and a cardiogram first.'

'You're a ghoul, Claire,' Adele said with a smile.

Matilda found herself smiling. Sometimes you needed to take a break from the horror of the day job, even if it was a quick lunch with two women who spent their days surrounded by dead bodies.

Chapter Fifteen

Pat Campbell had spent all of last night and most of this morning reading the information Matilda had given her about Ben Hales's private investigation into the disappearance of Carl Meagan. As she had sat up in bed flicking through the file, her husband snoring loudly beside her, a realization dawned on her – sometimes, a fresh pair of eyes is all it takes to find that one missing piece of the jigsaw. Matilda was too close to the Meagan case. Ben was too full of rage to solve it. Maybe Pat could. She'd gone to sleep with a smile on her lips.

She was up bright and early and was back to reading the file when Anton dragged himself down the stairs. He didn't want her getting sucked into police work again. She was retired, they both were. This was their time to go on breaks to the country-side, long walks along the coast, trips abroad to countries they'd only read about in brochures. However, Pat looked content when she was poring over a case in a way she rarely did otherwise.

'Have you solved it yet?' he asked with a smile.

'Yes. I'm pretty sure Lord Lucan took him, and they fled riding Shergar,' she said, looking up from the file spread out on the sofa. 'To be perfectly honest with you, most of what Ben has got here is all random.'

'What do you mean?'

'Well, it's like he's thought of all the possible motives for kidnapping someone – trafficking, ransom, tiger kidnapping, stealing a child to order, and has just researched it. There's nothing specific here to Carl.'

'What's tiger kidnapping?' he asked, sitting down on the recliner and putting his feet up.

'Tiger kidnapping is where you kidnap someone for someone else to do something. Like, say I was kidnapped to get you to commit a crime on their behalf for my safe release.'

'Oh,' he replied with a frown. 'Then why is it called tiger kidnapping?'

'It's like a tiger on the prowl. Look, we're moving away from the point here. What I'm saying is, all this information can be found online. There's nothing constructive, and nothing that could tell us what happened to Carl.'

'But surely Matilda will have noticed that?'

'She would have done . . . eventually.'

'What does that mean?'

'It means that she wants to find Carl so much she'll have looked for any ray of light in here.'

'And I'm guessing there is no ray of light?'

'None at all.'

He nodded towards the thick folder. 'You mean in all that file, there's not one thing that can help find him?'

Pat shook her head.

'What are you going to do?'

'What I promised I'd do; go and talk to Sally Meagan.'

'Rather you than me. I read that book; she sounds doolally to me.'

'Thanks.'

* * *

Anton dropped Pat off outside the imposing Meagan house in Dore. The grounds were secure with an eight-foot-high wall surrounding it. Electronic gates at the bottom of the drive, and a sophisticated-looking entry system would keep out journalists and glory hunters. Pat shivered, and she didn't know why. She wasn't especially cold, but the house was giving off a dark and disturbing vibe. She wondered how Sally could continue living here. Yes, it was Carl's home, but her mother had been murdered in this house. She pressed the button and waited. There was a camera above the speaker. She wondered if Sally was studying her right now, wondering whether to let her in or ignore her, hoping she'd go away. Pat didn't think she looked like a reporter.

'Yes?' A voice asked through the speaker.

'I'm here to see Sally Meagan. She's expecting me. I'm Pat Campbell.'

'Oh. Yes, sorry. Hello. I'm Sally. Come on in.'

The gate opened slowly, and Pat began the ascent up the gravel driveway to the front door. No sooner had she crossed the threshold onto private property than the gate started to close again. It slammed shut with a heavy clank of iron on iron. The echo caused Pat to turn around. It was like being locked into prison grounds. The small stones crunched under foot, and Pat had the feeling she was being watched from somewhere. She looked up at the house but couldn't see any cameras pointing at her.

Pat stood at the door. She thought Sally would have opened it, waiting for her, but it remained closed. She rang the doorbell and waited. It was a beautiful building; nineteenth century. Large sash windows throughout, a double front door, ivy crawling up the brickwork. It was stunning. A real family home. All that was missing was the family.

The door opened just wide enough for Sally to poke her head around. She gave a weak smile then opened it further for Pat to enter. She closed it firmly behind her.

'It's nice of you to come,' Sally said.

'My pleasure,' Pat said, studying the frail-looking woman.

Sally Meagan was thirty-seven years old but looked much older. The stress and torment of losing her only child and not knowing what had happened to him had taken its toll. Her skin was dry, and, despite lathering her face in make-up, it couldn't hide the bumps of acne she was so desperately trying to conceal. The lines under her eyes were dark and thick. She had the permanent expression of a woman on the verge of bursting into tears. Pat wondered if she had any more tears left to cry.

Pat had never met Sally Meagan. She had seen pictures of her in newspapers and the odd appearance on daytime television, but seeing her up close for the first time, Pat saw how fragile and on the brink of collapse the woman seemed to be.

Pat had two children of her own, both grown up, and she had grandchildren. She couldn't imagine how she would continue with life if anything happened to any of them. Was it worse having a child killed or not knowing their fate? That was a question nobody should ever have to try and answer.

'Can I get you a drink?' Sally asked. Her voice was quiet, hardly above a whisper.

'I'll have a coffee, please, it's nippy out.' Although, wrapped up in layers, Pat was warm.

'Come on through to the kitchen.'

Sally led the way along the corridor and opened the door to the large kitchen. A golden Labrador came bounding across the tiled floor to greet Pat.

'You don't mind dogs, do you?' Sally asked quickly.

'No. I love them,' she said, bending down to stroke the young dog.

'This is Woody. Let him lick you and you'll have a friend for life.'

Pat scratched behind his ears. This seemed to be all Woody needed to accept a stranger into the house. He dropped on the floor, rolled onto his back and assumed the position for Pat to scratch his belly.

'I dread to think what would happen if we were burgled,' Sally said. 'He has a mean bark on him, but he'd just lick the burglars to death.'

Pat got on her knees and began fussing the dog who seemed to appreciate the attention. Sally went about making the coffee.

'We got him for Carl for his sixth birthday. He always wanted a dog. They were inseparable. Sometimes, I can't find him. I shout him and he doesn't come. I go up to Carl's bedroom and there Woody is, curled up on Carl's bed. He misses him so much.'

Pat looked up from her position on the floor. She saw the sadness and faraway look in Sally's eyes. She gave her a weak smile. There was nothing else she could do.

Once the coffee was made, Sally took Pat into the living room. Woody stuck close to his new friend and sat by her feet once she sat on the oversized sofa.

'Will you apologize to Matilda for me, please?'

'Apologize? What for?' Pat looked up. Over Sally's shoulder, on the mantelpiece, was a photograph of the smiling Carl Meagan. He looked straight at Pat. He looked about five or six years old, full of life, happy and content. A brief flicker of horror swept through Pat's mind – what horrors had this boy witnessed when he was taken? She looked down into her coffee cup and took a sip of the strong liquid. She tried to avoid eye contact with the photograph, but it wasn't easy.

'I heard about what happened at Fulwood on the radio. Matilda's got her hands full by the sound of it. She's not going to want me hounding her with my problems. It's just . . .'

'Sally, Matilda is anxious to do all she can to find Carl. If she could, she'd be tearing the country apart day and night looking for him. That's why she's got me involved. I'm retired. I can devote more time.'

'I hope you don't mind, but I looked you up on the Internet.'

Pat smirked. 'I doubt there's much of me on there. Most of my successes came before the Internet. God, that makes me feel old.'

'There's a lot about you, actually. Most of it about the McFadden case.'

'Ah.'

'Is it true he sends you Christmas cards every year?' Sally asked leaning forward, eager for any juicy details.

'He used to,' Pat said, looking away. It had been a long time since she'd heard the name McFadden. The case almost killed her and was the reason for her taking early retirement, not that she told people that. 'So, Matilda tells me you're thinking of going out to Sweden,' she said, keen to change the topic of conversation back towards Sally.

'There have been a few sightings out there. I've been sent blurred photographs of children who may or may not be Carl. I don't know what to do. Do you think I should go?'

'To be perfectly honest with you, Sally, no, I don't. If you have something concrete, then fair enough, but don't go on a whim. You'll convince yourself you'll find him, and when you don't, it will hurt you all the more.'

'I don't think I can hurt anymore.' She tried to smile but her bottom lip betrayed her and wobbled.

'I've looked at the photographs.' Pat placed her coffee cup carefully on the table and picked up the file she'd brought with her. She opened it and took out the photos of a young blond-haired blue-eyed boy playing in a school yard. 'I don't think this is Carl at all. There is a strong resemblance, I grant you, but I wouldn't have even considered this as possibility.'

'Matilda said she wasn't sure. She thought it could be Carl. I think I wanted it to be him.'

Pat smiled. 'That's the thing. You and Matilda are too close to this. You need a fresh pair of eyes, someone objective. That's where I come in. The bone structure of this little boy is all wrong compared with Carl. Yes, it's been three years, so he will have changed, grown, but there are some things that don't change. The thing is, the information you received from Ben is very generic. Personally, I'd throw it all in the bin.'

Sally let out the breath she'd been holding. A tear fell down her face. 'But that would mean starting from square one. There must be something there.'

Pat shook her head. 'I'm sorry. All of this information can be found on the Internet. There is no solid evidence to show that Carl was sold to traffickers or to a couple who couldn't have kids. Towards the end of his life, Ben was a very sick man. He was fuelled by getting revenge on Matilda for his own failings. He would have loved to have found Carl and shown Matilda up. That's what he was doing. Unfortunately, he had nothing.'

'So, I've wasted all these months . . . ' Sally began to cry. Woody put his head up and tilted it to one side as he looked at her.

'No, you haven't. You've been productive. Also, Ben did go to visit child traffickers in prison. They didn't tell him anything but, reading between the lines of the interviews, there was nothing to tell because they didn't know anything. We can rule that out.'

'Did Matilda tell you about the phone call?'

'Yes, she did.'

'I was going out of my mind yesterday,' she said, running her fingers through her knotted hair. 'I was hysterical by the time Phil came home. I wanted to dial 999. He said we should leave it to Matilda. What do you think?'

'I don't know.' Pat frowned. 'What did Philip say?'

'He hugged me. He hasn't done that for a long time. He said to call you, well, Matilda, and see about tracing the number.'

'We can do that. Sally, do you really think it was Carl calling you?'

'Of course. Who else could it have been?'

'I'm guessing you've had many people over the years claiming to know where he is, maybe try to extract money from you.'

Sally nodded as she wiped her nose. 'I've had a couple of people saying they were clairvoyants who could possibly find Carl. For a fee, of course.'

'I hope you told them where to go.'

'I certainly did,' she said with a hint of a smile.

She leaned over to the coffee table and tore a page from a pad, handing it to Pat with shaking fingers.

'This is the number the call came from. I didn't imagine it. I mean, that number is proof. And it was Carl's voice. I know it was.'

'Have you called it back?'

'No. I wanted to. Philip said not to.'

'Sally, I don't want to raise your hopes. We need to remain realistic, here. Look, I'll give you my number. If you get any more calls, let me know straight away.'

'Thanks. Pat,' Sally wiped her eyes and leaned forward, 'can I ask you a question?'

'Of course.'

Sally took a quivering breath. 'Do you think Carl is still alive?'

'Yes, I do,' she answered quickly.

Sally smiled. 'Do you think he's still in this country?'

'Yes, I do,' she repeated.

'Thank you.' She smiled through the tears. 'Will you excuse me a moment?' Sally quickly got up from the sofa and left the room, wiping her eyes as she went.

Woody looked up at Pat and mewled.

'Sometimes a lie is better than the truth,' she said quietly to the dog.

Pat dug her mobile out of her bag and sent Matilda a text:

Sally is in a bad way. I need you to look up a number for me. I've had to lie to her to keep her from cracking up. Call me soon.

Chapter Sixteen

DC Kesinka Rani had decided to keep her own name once she'd married DC Ranjeet Deshwal. As she sat outside the hospital room where Rachel Mercer was sleeping, she twirled her wedding ring and smiled. So much had changed in the past year. She had lost her closest friend, DC Faith Easter, something she was still having trouble coming to terms with, she had married her boyfriend after a whirlwind romance, and she was now six months pregnant.

Ranjeet's proposal had come from nowhere. They were sitting in her rented flat when a power cut plunged the whole street into darkness. It might have been the candle light, it could have been the four bottles of wine they'd shared, it might have been Kesinka still feeling the loss of her friend, but Ranjeet felt the romance of the occasion sweep over him and he went down on one knee and popped the question. Kesinka didn't give herself time to think and said yes straight away. She truly did love him.

As house prices in Sheffield weren't the most reasonable in the country, they decided on a basic honeymoon and to put a large chunk of money towards a deposit. So, instead of two weeks on a sun-kissed beach in Florida, they settled on a long weekend in the Lake District. Unfortunately, it rained for all four days. They left their rented cottage very little and spent most of their time in bed, hence the pregnancy.

When Kesinka first found out she was pregnant, she was mortified. She always knew she wanted to be a mother, but the plan was for kids to come along when she was further into her career, a sergeant at least. Here she was, a DC in HMET, a prestigious unit and she was about to go on maternity leave and take a year out. She was more anxious about her return to work than she was about giving birth.

'Hello.'

Kesinka jumped out of her reverie and looked up to see her husband standing over her. A sandwich in one hand and a bottle of water in the other.

'What are you doing here?' she asked.

'I thought you'd be hungry.'

'Thanks.' She smiled, taking the sandwich from him. 'I'm starving, actually.'

He sat next to her and kissed her on the cheek. 'You looked deep in thought. What's on your mind?'

'Nothing. Just thinking about poor Rachel in there,' she lied. 'How's it going?'

'Slowly. It's going to take ages to process the scene. In the meantime, all we've got to go on is what the neighbours are saying. Leah and Oliver are due back from Paris later this afternoon.'

'I can't begin to image what she's going through. The wedding would have been the best day of her life and it turned into a nightmare so quickly.'

'No chance of her getting pregnant on her honeymoon,' Ranjeet said, patting his wife's stomach.

'You look very smug when you say that, like it's some kind of testament to your masculinity that you hit the back of the net on our honeymoon.'

'I hit the back of the net when you agreed to marry me.'

'Smooth talker.'

Ranjeet leaned in for a kiss but his phone rang. He answered. He only said three words then hung up. 'That was DCI Darke. I'm needed for the post mortems.'

Kesinka shivered. 'Rather you than me. I've attended four and fainted at every one.'

'I suppose I'd better go then,' he said. His eyes had widened, and a sheen of sweat had appeared on his forehead. 'I'll probably be late home.'

'Liver and onions OK for tea?' Kesinka smiled.

'It's funny how quickly you can go off people,' he said before turning away and heading off down the corridor. At the doors, he turned back, waved at Kesinka and flashed that perfect smile she had fallen in love with.

Kesinka continued to eat her sandwich when the sound of screaming came from behind. She jumped up, threw the sandwich on the chair and burst into Rachel's room.

The seven-year-old was sitting up in bed. Her face was red and tears were streaming down her face. She was looking at her hands, turning them over, studying them, as if there was something there that shouldn't be. She screamed louder and called out for her daddy.

* * *

He wasn't having much luck trying to get to London. He stood at the side of the road for an hour waiting for someone to stop before he decided to set off on foot. He supposed if he'd been a woman he wouldn't have had any trouble trying to get a lift; some horny trucker on a long-distance trip would have pulled over the second he'd put his thumb out.

It was cold. The blast from passing high-sided vehicles at 70 miles per hour added to the chill. There was a fine rain and he was already soaking wet and frozen to the core. He could end up with flu or pneumonia at this rate. He was gasping for a fag, too. Even a scabby tab end would do right now.

Walking at the side of the motorway, he was taking his life into his own hands. He could easily have slipped on the wet embankment and fallen into the carriageway. Maybe it would be better if he did. Nobody would miss him if he was dead. He watched as a truck passed by at high speed. If he'd stepped in front of it, he would have been dead by now. That's how easy it was. The thought shook him. He didn't have the guts to step out into speeding traffic. He suddenly realized how tough Ruby had been after all these years.

Was this really his life? Twenty-seven years old and on the run. Very little money left, nowhere to go. Suddenly, all the advice given to him by his teachers and his sister telling him to knuckle down or he'd end up in prison was coming back to haunt him. Big deal. The country was going to hell anyway. So, you went to college and university, then what? Yes, you leave with good grades and knowledge, but you can't get a job because there aren't any. So those years in uni have been a waste of time because you don't need a degree to be a barista in Costa. You're on shit wages so you can't pay off your student debt and you can't get on the property ladder because you need a year's salary for a deposit. Was there any wonder why he'd turned to crime? If educated people can't get on in life, what hope did he have?

He tossed his soggy cardboard sign into a ditch and continued walking, head down, shoulders hunched, thumb out, hoping someone would take pity on him. Eventually, someone did. An articulated lorry pulled up on the hard shoulder in front of him. He picked up speed, pulled open the door and climbed inside.

'Where you going?' the driver asked.

'London.'

'Get in.'

'Cheers, mate. I don't think I could have walked any further.'

He slammed the door closed and the wagon set off. He pulled down the visor and opened the flap for the mirror. He looked a state. His blond hair was wet and plastered to his head. He was unshaven for three days and was beginning to get a designer stubble. He quite liked it. He'd never had a beard before.

'You haven't got a fag have you, mate?'

The driver nodded to the glove box. 'Only roll-ups. Help yourself.'

He found the pouch of tobacco and a pack of papers. He rolled himself a fat cigarette with cold, shaking fingers.

'Do one for me, will you?' the driver asked.

They'd been travelling for an hour when the driver indicated and left the motorway, pulling into a deserted rest stop.

'How come we're stopping here?'

'No choice. Law says you have to take regular stops, and I've not had a kip since Northumberland.'

They pulled up into the far corner, away from the main carriageway. The driver applied the brakes and turned off the engine. Silence descended. A distant hum from the faraway traffic was all that could be heard.

'So, how long are we staying?'

The driver turned slowly to look at him. He ran a hand through his greased-back hair. There was a disturbing glint in his beady eyes as he licked his lips. 'As long as it takes. Get in the back,' he said, unbuttoning his trousers.

Suddenly, he wished he was still standing by the motorway getting wet.

Chapter Seventeen

'Look, before you say anything, it's got nothing to do with this case. It's something I've been thinking about for a while.'

As soon as Matilda arrived back at the station, she entered the HMET suite and asked Rory Fleming to join her in her office. He closed the door behind him and spoke before Matilda had the chance. She sat down behind her desk and looked up at the young man before her. Rory had changed over the past year or so. While investigating the Starling House murders he had been attacked by a teenage killer. Earlier last year, he watched his best friend and flatmate, Scott Andrews, suffer at the hands of a killer. Add into the mix the murder of DC Faith Easter and it was no surprise Rory had reached the decision to leave the force.

'Rory, I don't want to lose you from my team,' Matilda pleaded. 'You're one of the best DCs I have.'

'Only one of the best?' he asked with his trademark smile.

'This isn't a rouse to have your ego stroked, is it?'

'No. Look,' he pulled out a chair and sat down, 'when Faith got killed, it made me evaluate a few things. Maybe this case has just tipped things a little, but, I don't want to be one of those coppers who's in their forties and have no personal life and are screwed up by everything they've witnessed over the years.'

'Like me.'

'Shit, no, I'm sorry. I didn't mean . . . I didn't . . .' Rory stuttered.

'Rory, it's fine.' She smiled. 'I love being a detective. It's all I've ever wanted to do.'

'Me too,' he interrupted. 'The reality is different from when you're eight years old and playing cops and robbers, though.'

'I won't lie to you and say this case is going to be a piece of cake, because it isn't. And, I think we're all going to be affected by it for years to come. However, I've been a detective for more than twenty years and this is the worst I've seen. These cases don't come along very often, thank goodness. This is not the norm.'

'I know it isn't. It's just . . . I don't know . . . I want more out of life than to come to work in the morning, not knowing what time I'm going to get home, then passing out from exhaustion. What kind of a life is that?'

'For a man of your age, it's no life at all,' Matilda relented. 'I really don't want to lose you, Rory,' she repeated. 'You're a major asset to this team. I wouldn't have picked you for it otherwise.'

'I know, and I'm really very grateful to you for the opportunity.'

'I tell you what, don't hand your notice in now; wait until we've solved this case. Then we'll have a chat, you and me. What do you say?'

'What if the case never gets solved?'

'Then you never leave.' She grinned.

'You're harsh.'

'I have to be if I want to get what I want.'

Rory was silent while he mulled over what Matilda said. She looked past him and out into the main suite. She saw Scott sat at his desk. He too had the same lost expressions as Rory.

'I'll stay until we've solved the Mercer case,' Rory said reluctantly.

Matilda relaxed. 'Good. I'm glad. Rory, if you ever want to talk to me, about anything, you know I'll always listen.'

'I know. Thanks.'

'It won't go any further either. I'm very good at keeping secrets. You won't believe some of the stuff Sian's got up to over the years,' she said with a sly smile.

'Oh I believe that.'

'Speak of the devil,' she said as she saw Sian approach the door.

'Am I OK to interrupt?' she asked, knocking lightly and pushing the door open.

'It looks like you just did.'

'I've had Kesinka on the phone. She said Rachel woke up screaming for her dad. Nothing would calm her down, so they've had to sedate her.'

'Shit. I wish her auntie would hurry up and get here. She's going to need her right now.'

'Do you think we should contact social services? They'll be able to arrange temporary care for her.'

'Let's wait to see what happens when Leah gets back.'

'OK. All the neighbours have been interviewed, not that we've got much to go on, and since the ACC gave a statement we've had the papers calling asking for more information.'

'They can wait.'

'Medical report on Clive Mercer has come through. He knew about the brain tumour, but, he was being treated in Leeds, not Sheffield.'

'Why?'

'No idea. I'm guessing he didn't want his colleagues to know about his condition.'

'Talk to his consultant. Find out everything you can about the tumour, how Clive was taking it, that kind of thing. Also, should he still have been working? And, did his bosses know about it?'

She nodded. 'Speaking of Clive Mercer, I've been doing some digging into the Mercers' background. Clive was reported to the GMC on three occasions due to malpractice.'

'Excellent. Keep digging, Sian.'

'Will do.' She left, closing the door firmly behind her.

'See, you'd miss all this if you left,' Matilda said to Rory.

'I think I'd prefer to keep my sanity.'

'Sanity? What's the point in being sane when the rest of the world is completely crazy? Come on,' she said, standing up. 'I want you to come with me to the Mercers' house. I'm going to show you why you're a born detective.'

It didn't take long for the conversation to die out. Rory told Matilda how jealous he was of her car. He played with the seat controls and flicked through the menu on the touchscreen on the dashboard like an excited child. Eventually, he sat back and looked out of the window. Matilda's mobile rang. It was in between the front seats so she ignored it. When the ringing stopped, Rory looked down at the phone.

'You've missed two calls from someone called Daniel H.'

'Oh,' was her reply.

'Someone's keen to get hold of you.'

'Yes. He's the bloke who's doing up my house.'

'Shouldn't you call him back? There might be a problem.'

'It'll be fine. Rory, how's Scott?' Matilda asked, wanting to get the conversation away from her private life.

'He's fine. Why?'

'He seems quieter.'

'Is that possible?' He sniggered.

'Quieter than usual then.'

'I hadn't noticed.' He shrugged.

Matilda turned down the driveway and the Mercers' house came into view. It was almost as if a heavy mist had descended. They stopped talking, and both of them could feel the intensity of the situation.

'It's a shame, isn't it?' Rory said as Matilda turned off the engine. 'A beautiful home like that. What do you think will happen to it?'

'I don't know. That's for Leah to decide, I suppose.'

They remained seated. They knew what was in store for them behind the front door. Even though the bodies had been removed, all evidence had been bagged and taken to forensics, they were left with the detritus of a crime scene, the aftermath of a vicious knife attack.

A police cordon was still in place and a bored-looking PC sat in a marked car parked next to the front door. He didn't bother to get out. Matilda showed him her warrant card through the window. He nodded.

As they made their way upstairs, Matilda booted up the iPad she'd taken from her bag.

'Go into the bedroom in the attic, Rory,' she said.

They were both wearing overshoes to protect their footwear from any bloodstains. As much as they tried their best not to walk over the area where Clive Mercer had died on the landing, it was difficult to get around it. In places, the carpet still squelched.

Rory walked up the stairs but kept looking over the bannister at where Clive had been slaughtered. At the top of the stairs he stood in the doorway of the attic and went no further.

'It's just a room, Rory. What's happened is over,' Matilda said. She was trying to comfort him but force him into action at the same time.

'I know,' he said quietly.

'Take a good look, Rory. Look at the blood sprays on the walls and ceiling. Tell me what you see.' Matilda studied her iPad. She had the report from the crime scene investigators.

Rory took a deep breath and entered the room fully. He slowly looked around him, taking in the scene of carnage. 'There's so much blood. The sprays. They're so high.'

'What does that tell us?'

'It was frenzied. He pulled the knife out, lifting it high so he could stab with great ferocity, which caused the sprays, before stabbing again.'

'Keep looking.'

He walked around the front of the bed, eyes darting in all directions. 'There's a footprint by the bed.'

'OK. What do you notice about it?'

'It's a good print.'

'Yes.'

'But there's only one.' He frowned. 'There should be others.'

'Why?'

'Like I said, it's a good print. It's soaked in blood; there should be other prints as the killer left the room.'

'Good.' Matilda smiled. He was picking up on what she had noticed. 'What does that tell us?'

'The killer either took his shoe off, or he covered the shoe with something, like what we're wearing, overshoes, and was careful where he stood upon leaving.'

'But would he have time for that? He's killed three people. There's a dog yapping down there, and a seven-year-old girl. We can guess he went into Rachel's room last because of all the blood on him. Wouldn't he just want to leave and go to them?'

Rory frowned as he thought. He looked from the footprint to the door and back again. 'Maybe the killer came back. After he killed everyone, he returned, used a shoe to make a footprint to throw us off.'

Matilda smiled. 'Well done, Rory.'

He returned her smile. 'But why would the killer do that?'

'I don't know. Either there's something under that footprint that the killer couldn't take with him and he needed to cover up, or it's to make us believe that it is the killer's shoe when it isn't.'

'You mean say this is a size ten print and the killer is only a size seven or something.'

'Something like that. Look around the rest of the room, Rory. Look at the furniture,' Matilda said, looking down at her iPad once again.

'On the chest of drawers, there's evidence of arterial spurts.'

'Good. What does that tell us?'

'She was facing that direction when he stabbed her. She was low down, probably lying down on the bed. The knife hit an artery and it sprayed all that blood out.'

'So there's less cast-off stains because . . .?'

'Because the blood had run out of her here. This is probably one of the first stabs,' he said, going over to the chest of drawers and leaning down.

'If Serena is incapacitated so early on in the attack, how do we account for the hair under her fingernail?'

'Maybe she fought back.'

'Maybe. Anything else?'

'Maybe it's not the killer's hair. It could already have been there under her nail when he came in. It could be her own hair or her husband's.'

'Anything else?'

Rory suddenly looked up at Matilda, a wide-eyed look on his face. 'Another plant?'

Matilda smiled.

'So, what are you saying, this whole crime scene is a lie?'

'I think this is staged. It felt wrong as soon as I first came through the door.'

'But, why?'

'That is the million-pound question. I don't know. However, this is not just some random killing. This family was targeted for a reason, and the killer went to great lengths to cover their tracks.'

'But what about those clothes we found? Do you think they're planted too?'

'I wouldn't be surprised.'

Matilda turned and left the room, leaving Rory standing in the middle of a bloodbath. She was in the hallway on the ground floor of the house by the time he caught up with her.

'But everyone says they're a lovely family. She's a neurologist or something and he's an anaesthetist. They can't be involved in anything that results in this kind of violence, surely.'

'That's what we need to find out. So, still thinking about resigning?' she asked with a grin on her face.

It was a while before he answered. 'Not just yet.'

Chapter Eighteen

The HMET suite was a hive of activity as the evening briefing was about to begin. The murder board was full of crime scene photographs and pictures of the family taken in happier times extracted from the laptops and iPads officers were still going through. However, there were plenty of gaps left to be filled. Leah Mercer should be able to help join the dots when she turned up.

Matilda called the room to order. Phones were hung up and laptops closed.

'This case is moving very slowly,' she began. 'Now, I'm aware we have a large crime scene which is taking time to process, and, as most of the neighbours were pissed or asleep when the murders took place, we are lacking in eyewitnesses. However, we need to put in some ground work. The vultures are swarming and are looking for something to put on their front pages. I hate to be held to ransom by the press but if we don't give them something, they'll make it up, or go down the sensational route. I don't want that to happen.

'I want Rachel interviewing as soon as possible. Now, I think she might feel less frightened when Leah gets back and she knows she's got some family left. Any news on when that will be?'

'I called her about half an hour ago,' Scott said. 'She'll be here within the hour.'

'Good. Is she coming straight here?'

'Yes. I've told her not to go to the house or the hospital.'

'Thank you, Scott.' Matilda had won the battle with Rory but needed to keep an eye on him for the rest of the war here. However, there was something eating away at Scott and she was worried about him.

'Aaron, the bloke from the council who Serena smacked.'

'He's been in Doncaster nick since last summer. Armed robbery.'

'That's one avenue we can rule out. Ranjeet, anything on the post mortems?'

'Yes. Dr Kean was able to extract the tips of the blades from Serena Mercer and Jeremy Mercer,' he said, looking down at his note pad. 'Now, there are a couple of knives missing from the kitchen, but we've bought a block of knives like they had and matched the tips to the missing knives.'

'So the killer didn't come prepared?' Sian asked, looking in her snack drawer for something to eat.

'It would appear not.'

'But he obviously came with a change of clothing,' Scott said.

'That doesn't make sense,' Sian continued, tearing into a Ripple. 'Nothing was stolen, nothing obvious, anyway, so if he didn't come prepared to kill, what did he come for?'

'Rory, would you like to fill everyone in on what we've discovered?' Matilda asked.

Rory smiled and stood up. He smoothed down his tie and cleared his throat. 'We went back to the Mercers' house this afternoon to go through the report from the CSM. There are several points in the crime scene that don't make sense.' He told them about the single bloody footprint in Serena's bedroom, and the hair under her fingernail. 'Also, if the killer didn't come prepared, I'm guessing he wasn't wearing a mask or anything, yet he tied Rachel Mercer up. She must have seen his face, so why leave her alive?'

'Do you think the crime scene was staged?' Sian asked, wiping away the crumbs of chocolate from her desk.

'We do.'

'But why?'

'The answer to that,' Matilda picked up, 'lies in the Mercers' past. Now, we know Clive was brought before a GMC hearing on three separate occasions. Any news on that yet, Sian?'

'Yes. I spoke to someone from the GMC earlier. He's going to email me the case files through.'

'OK,' Matilda said. She noticed how harassed and shattered Sian looked. 'Try and make it a priority. Has anyone pulled Clive Mercer's medical records yet?'

'I have,' Aaron said. He was texting on his phone and quickly put it down. 'He had an aggressive tumour in his frontal lobe. It was diagnosed around eighteen months ago. I spoke to his consultant, Ravi Mukherjee, at Leeds General Infirmary. He said Clive took the news pretty well when he was first told. He said he'd spoken about it to his family, who were all supportive, and he'd cut down his working hours to the bare minimum. However, when I spoke to a couple of his colleagues at the Northern General, they had no idea of his diagnosis and said he'd been working his usual hours, sometimes more.'

'I can't say I'm surprised about that,' Matilda said. 'I bet he didn't even tell his family. Thanks for that, Aaron. We'll bring it up with Leah.'

'Doesn't a tumour on your frontal lobe affect your behaviour?'

Rory asked. He'd moved from his desk to Sian's, where he was rummaging through her snack drawer. He picked up a Bounty and went back to his desk.

'Yes, it does,' Matilda said quietly. Whenever cancer or a tumour was mentioned, she immediately thought of James. His tumour wasn't in the frontal lobe. His was imbedded deep within the brain making surgery practically impossible. His moods hadn't been affected. James remained the same sweet, caring, intelligent, funny man he'd always been, right up until the end. They'd gone through their dark days during treatment, but he always maintained a level of optimism Matilda found inspiring.

She looked up and noticed everyone staring at her. How long had she been drifting away in her own memories? Shit.

'OK. We need to interview the people he worked with. Had they noticed a change in his personality, his work ethic recently? Also, see if this ties in with the reports from the GMC.'

'I'll do the hospital. You do the GMC,' Aaron said to Sian. She nodded.

'What about the others in the family?' Matilda asked.

'I've been through their bank statements and credit card bills, there is nothing dodgy going on with their finances,' Scott said. 'They both make a very healthy living. They have private pensions, savings accounts that made me weep, but they're not in debt, and the only loans they have are the mortgage, which is almost paid off, and their cars.'

'We still need to keep digging. If someone had a vendetta against the family, the reason may not be in plain sight. Do the Mercers own any other properties? Do they have bank accounts in other names or going to other addresses? Were Serena or Clive having an affair? Do they have a secret family or other children we don't know about? We need to tear this family apart in order to find out what killed them. Also, who would gain from the Clive and Serena's death? Let's try and get a copy of their wills. Christian, tomorrow I want you, Scott and Ranjeet working on this.'

'No problem,' Christian said, hurriedly writing down notes with one hand while trying to open a Mars bar with the other.

'Photographs. Finn?'

The fresh-faced trainee detective was looking less fresh-faced than this morning. He'd unbuttoned his top couple of buttons on his shirt. His hair was a mess from running his fingers through it, probably through frustration, and he looked tired. It didn't take him long to fit into the team. The desk once occupied by Faith Easter was a mess of photographs from the wedding reception.

'Rose Bishop came in just after lunch to look through the photographs. She was a bit . . . well . . . she wasn't in a great state . . .'

'Pissed?' Rory asked.

'Just a bit. Anyway, she went through the pictures and identified the majority of the guests at the reception. We've contacted most of them who have given us alibis for where they were around the time of the murders. The majority also had photos of their own they'd taken and have emailed them across to me. I'm still going through them as there are hundreds, as I'm sure you can guess. Now, out of the photos from the digital cameras, there are twelve people who Rose Bishop didn't know the names of. I'm guessing either Leah or Oliver might know.'

'Print them off for me, Finn, and we'll get them to have a look.'

'I've got them right here,' he said, holding up an envelope. 'Also, I've been on to the official photographer. He said he hadn't even uploaded them to his computer yet. He's had two other weddings and a christening to do. I told him it was urgent, so he's coming in tomorrow with his laptop. I should be able to identify the main players pretty quickly after all the photos I've been looking at today.'

'Excellent work, Finn, thank you,' Matilda said with a genuine smile of gratitude.

'I tell you something, I'm not in a great hurry to attend a wedding any time soon. I feel like I've lived through this one a dozen times already,' he said. A ripple of laughter echoed around the room.

Matilda's gaze lingered on the trainee detective a little too long. She blamed herself for Faith Easter's death. Looking back, she should have realized the danger she was in and acted sooner. Hindsight is a wonderful thing. Trainee DC Finn Cotton was the next generation. Life went on. He seemed to be fitting into the team with ease, and he was more than capable.

'Any news from forensics about the fingerprints and hair?' Matilda asked.

'Yes,' Aaron chimed up, flicking through his notebook for the relevant page. 'They're processing them now, we should get the results tomorrow. Although, if we think the scene is staged, are we going to trust the results?'

'That depends what they are. We'll cross that bridge when we come to it. Has anyone been looking into the new member of the Mercer family, Leah's husband, Oliver?'

The room fell silent as officers exchanged guilty glances.

'I'm guessing that means no.'

'He'll probably accompany his wife when they come here. I'll keep an eye on him, ask him a few questions,' Sian said.

'Thank you, Sian. Right then, I think we should call it a day.

Hopefully, Leah and Oliver will be able to give us more information so tomorrow we can make some headway. In the meantime, go home and have an early night. It may be your last one for a while.'

Noise levels in the suite rose again as detectives began to pack away and file out of the room. Matilda went into her office and sat at her desk. She angled herself so if anyone looked it would seem she was reading something on her laptop. In fact, she was looking over the top of the laptop and keeping an eye on Scott. Usually at the end of the day, he and Rory would leave together. They shared a flat so there was no reason why they'd bring two cars to work. Sometimes they went to the gym after work, or maybe for a few pints, depending on how stressful the day was. Scott slapped his laptop closed, yanked his jacket from the back of his chair and left the office alone. By the time Rory was ready to leave, he looked shocked to find his flatmate had gone without him.

Sian was the only one left. She and Matilda were going to interview Leah and Oliver when they eventually turned up. Once everyone had left, Sian picked up the phone to make a private call to her husband. As Matilda left her office, she turned to one side and lowered her voice.

Matilda walked over to Scott's desk and had a good look. Scott was always neat and tidy, in his appearance and in his work. So far, his appearance hadn't changed. He still came to work in a clean suit and shirt every day, smart tie and a neat haircut. His desk, however, was a mess of paperwork, files, crumpled chocolate wrappers and dirty cups. This was not the Scott Andrews Matilda liked and admired.

'I've just had a call from downstairs. Leah and Oliver have arrived,' Sian said, making Matilda jump. 'What's wrong?'

'Have you managed to have a word with Scott yet?'

'Yes. Well, sort of. I spoke to him very briefly at lunchtime.'

'And?'

'He said he was fine. I asked him if the case was affecting him and he said no, it's just another case.'

'Do you believe him?'

'Yes. He's right. We can't treat cases any differently.'

'So you don't think there's anything wrong with him?'

'You do, I take it.'

'Look at his desk.'

'Ah,' she said, looking down. 'Maybe he's got something on his mind. Girl trouble, perhaps.'

'Is he seeing someone?'

'He hasn't mentioned anyone. Do you want to me to have a word with Rory?'

'No. I'll do it.'

'OK. I'm just going for a quick wee before we interview Leah.'

Sian left the room ahead of Matilda. While alone, the DCI took the opportunity to rummage around on Scott's desk. There was nothing apart from work here so she opened the drawers. She felt slightly guilty as she picked her way through notebooks and files, but if she found something that gave her a hint of what was troubling Scott, she'd be able to carefully broach the subject with him.

In the bottom drawer, face down, was a photograph. On the back, written in Scott's neat hand, it said 'Blackpool. January 2008'. She turned the photo over and looked at the happy, smiling face of a young Scott Andrews. She smiled back as she looked into his warm eyes. She'd never seen him smile so wide before. This was genuine happiness. He was standing on the pier, the Tower in the background. He had his arm around someone who was kissing Scott's cheek. Matilda mused. Could this represent what was troubling Scott? If not, Matilda had found Scott's second secret.

Chapter Nineteen

The desk sergeant knew the importance of Matilda's visitors so put Leah and Oliver into one of the family rooms. It was much nicer than the interview rooms with their smell of desperation and guilt, stained tables and chairs screwed to the floor. There were a couple of cheap sofas in here, a small kitchenette, and a TV in the corner along with a selection of toys and children's books. This room was mostly used for child witnesses, to put them at their ease. This was where Rachel Mercer would end up when she was in a fit enough state to talk through the nightmare she was forced to endure.

Matilda entered the room with Sian following. She introduced them both, and Leah immediately started crying.

Leah was a tall, slim, attractive young woman of only twenty-five, although her crying and screwed-up face made her look ugly and old. Her long dark hair was greasy, and her clothes looked thrown on. She had obviously dressed in haste, not caring how she looked to the world. Sitting next to her was new husband, Oliver. He was two years older. He had the same dark coloured hair, but his was closely cropped. He was broad shouldered and had a patchy stubble. He had a heavy brow which gave him a menacing look. Maybe he was worried for his wife. This would not have been the start to married life either of them was expecting. They both sat rigid on the edge of their seats looking nervous, scared, frightened.

'Can I get you anything to drink? Mrs Mercer?' Sian asked.

'It's Ridgeway now. She's Mrs Ridgeway,' Oliver interjected, his voice strong and level.

'Of course, sorry.'

'I'd really like a cup of tea, if that's possible?' Leah said through her tears.

Sian smiled. 'Mr Ridgeway?'

'Same. Thank you. I'm sorry for snapping.'

'That's fine. Don't apologize.'

Sian went over to the other side of the room to make the drinks. Matilda sat opposite the sofa in a matching armchair.

'I'm sorry to meet you under these circumstances, Leah. I do need to ask you some questions about your family.'

Leah leaned forward and whipped up a tissue from the box on the coffee table. She sniffled hard and wiped her eyes.

'That's fine. It's weird but, on the way home, I kept thinking there'd been a mistake, that you'd got it wrong, but as soon as you came in, I knew. I just knew.' She started to cry again. Her accent was pure Sheffield, but her voice was light and weak.

Matilda noticed the distance between Leah and Oliver. As newlyweds their love should be at its strongest. Even at a tragic time like this, they should be touching, holding hands. Oliver should have his arm around her, supporting the love of his life. But they were sitting apart like strangers next to each other on a train.

'I want you to know that I am truly sorry about what has happened to your family, but my team and I will be working around the clock to find out who has done this, and why,' Matilda said. A little white lie never hurt anyone.

'I don't understand,' she sniffed hard. 'Everyone loved my mum and dad. They were good people. They went to church. My dad organized events for charity for crying out loud. Why?'

'We don't know that yet. We're hoping you can give us as much information as you can about your family so we can find out.'

Sian brought the drinks over on a tray and placed them on a table. Oliver leaned forward and took his tea. He added milk and one sugar. Leah didn't move.

'When can I see Rachel?' Leah asked.

'We'll take you to her as soon as we've finished here.'

'Is she OK?'

'We don't know. Physically, she's fine. She keeps screaming. We don't know what she saw.'

'Oh my God. She loved her dad so much. They were inseparable.'

'Leah, we've been told Rachel's mum died. Is that correct?'

She sniffled and wiped her dripping nose. 'Yes. She died when Rachel was three. There was a pile-up on the motorway, several died. She was one of them. If you look back into our family, you'll see we're bad luck.'

'That's not true,' Oliver said, hesitantly placing a hand on Leah's lap. He quickly removed it.

'Oh it is. Aunties and uncles dying in their thirties from cancer. My Uncle Phil, my dad's brother, he was caught up in a terrorist attack. My Aunt Monica, she wasn't my real aunt, we just called her that, she was mugged. She hit her head on the kerb and never regained consciousness. We're bad luck.' Leah gave in to her emotions once again, leaned forward and let out a torrent of tears.

Oliver tried to ease her pain. He sat closer to her and put his arm uncomfortably around her shoulders. 'Can we do this another time?'

'I know it's difficult, Oliver, but we need to know if there was anyone in Leah's life who could have had a grudge against your family.'

Leah shrugged out of Oliver's hold. Her hands were fists, her knuckles white and her leg left was shaking involuntarily. The tears were streaming down her face and she was biting her bottom lip hard. Matilda studied her and recognized the signs of anxiety.

'There isn't. You heard what she said. Serena and Clive did a lot for the community. They were the perfect family.'

Matilda and Sian exchanged knowing glances.

'We've already found out about Clive being investigated by the GMC on three occasions. Could that have had anything to do with it?'

'I was waiting for that to be brought up,' Leah sobbed. 'He was cleared of any wrongdoing on all occasions. I told you, we're bad luck.'

'What about Jeremy?'

The tears increased. 'Jeremy,' Leah pined. 'I couldn't have asked for a better brother.'

'Could this have something to do with him?' Matilda asked. 'Did he have any money worries, for example?'

'He's a junior doctor, of course he's got money worries,' Oliver said.

'Were you close to Jeremy, Leah?' Matilda asked.

She nodded.

'Is there anything in his background that we need to know about? Do you know of anyone who would want to harm him in any way?'

'No. He lived for two things; his work and Rachel. That was his life. Oh God,' she descended into a wreck of emotions once more. 'Fuck. Shit. Fuck,' she silently screamed through gritted teeth.

'Is everything all right?' Sian asked Leah, looking confused.

'Yes. I'm fine. I mean, I'm not fine. I'm . . .'

Matilda looked to Sian and briefly shook her head, telling her not to push it.

'Mr Ridgeway, what about you?' Matilda asked.

'What about me?' he replied with scorn.

'You've just joined the Mercer family. Is there any way this could be connected to you?'

'Connected to me? What are you talking about?' His face reddened and a vein throbbed in his neck.

'Oliver, please, calm down,' Sian said in her best soothing tone.

'I'm sorry,' Matilda continued. 'Some of these questions aren't going to be easy, but we have to ask them in order to find out the truth.'

Oliver took a deep breath. 'You're right. I'm sorry. You're just doing your job. As far as I know, there's nobody who would want to harm me in this way.'

'What do you do for a living, Oliver?' Sian asked.

'I'm also a junior doctor. I work at the Northern General.'

'Is there anything either of you can tell us that you think might help us in finding who did this to your family?' Matilda asked, a slight edge to her voice. While she sympathized with the newlyweds, she needed information about the Mercers to move this case forward, and quickly.

Leah shook her head.

'Not that I can think of,' Oliver replied.

Matilda sat forward. 'Leah, during the post mortem of your father, we discovered he had a tumour on his brain. Were you or anyone else in your family aware of this?'

She looked up, eyes red and blotchy, tears streaming down her face. 'A tumour?'

'Yes.'

'You mean he was dying?'

'I'm afraid so.'

'He didn't . . . I mean, he never . . . no. No.' She fell into Oliver's arms.

'Is it possible he didn't know about it?' Oliver asked.

'He was seeing a consultant at Leeds General Infirmary. He told him he'd cut down his working hours and his family were very supportive.'

'We didn't know,' Leah said quietly into Oliver's chest. 'We didn't know.'

'I'm very sorry,' Matilda said.

Leah sat up, sniffled and wiped her nose. 'Why didn't he tell us? We're a close family. We didn't keep secrets. He could have told us.'

'Leah, you know what your dad was like,' Oliver said. 'He lived for his work. He would have been made to give it up. He would have hated that.'

She nodded. 'You're right. He still should have told us, though.' She turned to Matilda. 'Do you see what I mean; we're bad luck. The whole family is jinxed.'

They sat in silence for a long minute. Leah tried to control her emotions but the tears refused to stop. Oliver sat with his arm around his wife. His right hand gripped her right shoulder a little too firmly for Matilda's liking. Whenever she made eye contact with him, he quickly looked away.

'Can I see Rachel? She's going to need me. I'm all she's got left now,' Leah said, sitting up and wiping her eyes.

'Of course. We can continue this discussion tomorrow,' Matilda said, standing up. 'Do you need a place to stay tonight? We can put you up in a hotel.'

'No. Thank you. We can stay at my parents' house,' Oliver said.

'Right. Well, we'll get a car ready and take you to the hospital.'

The journey to the Children's Hospital wasn't long, but it was fraught with tension and a heavy atmosphere. In the back seat, Leah tried to stop her sobbing but was failing. On the opposite side, Oliver looked out of the window, his face blank, devoid of emotion.

As they walked along the corridor, Oliver held his wife's hand. It disappeared inside Oliver's huge fist, his knuckles were almost white.

'Leah, you need to stop crying. You need to be strong for Rachel,' he said quietly.

'I know. I'm trying.'

Sian had sent a text to Kesinka to let her know they were here and to get the armed guard out of the way. Leah was in a state already. A tactical support officer armed to the teeth wouldn't do her any good. A doctor was waiting with Kesinka outside the door when they approached.

'How is she?' Leah asked.

'Physically, she's fine. She has no injuries apart from slight bruising around her waist from where she was tied up. Please, don't stay too long. She gets distressed easily,' the doctor said in her well-used soothing tone.

Leah took a deep breath. She wiped her eyes and blew her

nose and put the tatty tissue in the pocket of her skinny jeans. With a shaking hand, she pushed down the handle and opened the door.

'Rachel, sweetheart, it's me, Auntie Leah.'

Rachel was on her side, her back to the door. She stirred, sat up, looked over to the doorway and let out a scream that only a wounded animal should make.

Chapter Twenty

Typical. He had been waiting all day for someone to stop and give him a lift to London and the one person who did had only one thing on his mind. The trucker had practically dragged him into the cab at the back. Luckily, he was fat and slow. A quick punch to the throat winded him just long enough for him to make his escape. As he jumped down from the cab, he noticed the trucker's wallet on a shelf under the dash. He swiped it as he left. It was the least he owed him.

Once far enough away so the trucker couldn't find him, he hunkered down behind an abandoned garage. There was a cold wind coming from somewhere that chilled his bones. In the background, the distant hum of the motorway told him life was close. He opened the wallet. There were a few credit and debit cards he immediately dismissed. There was no way he'd be able to use them. The driving licence was in the name of Peter Denny. He was fifty-one. There was a photograph of him with a woman of a similar age who he assumed was his wife. Two young girls surrounded him. Were they his children? The dirty bastard. They probably had no idea what kind of double life their husband and father was leading while he was away from the family home. How many people had he successfully raped up and down the country on his travels?

There was £140 in ten and twenty pound notes in the wallet. His eyes lit up. He should be able to get a room for the night in a cheap hotel and pay for a one-way ticket to London in the morning. He grabbed the notes, tossed the wallet to one side and headed for the bright lights of the motorway.

It was another half an hour of walking before he came to a Premier Inn. He signed in under the name of Peter Denny, paid cash, and went up to his room. It was bright, airy and clean. The first thing he did was take off his clothes and have a long, hot shower. He hated the feeling of being dirty. He scrubbed at his hair and under his fingernails. He didn't want to get out. The hot needles of water raining down on him was shear bliss.

He looked at himself in the mirror. His hair was clean and shiny. There was nothing he could do about the beard, but he was starting to like it. It made him look older, which was no bad thing at the moment. He put on the white dressing gown and flopped down onto the big comfortable bed. Heaven. As exhaustion took over and sleep enveloped him, he crawled under the covers. His eyes were almost closed when the realization of who he really was dawned. He was a wanted man. How far would he get before all ports had his photograph and were looking out for him?

Sally Meagan was in the office of her home, replying to the emails she had received throughout the day. Most were from women around the world who had children who were missing, offering their advice and support. A couple were replies from pleas for help she had sent out. One stood out more than the others. This email only had a few lines of text, but there was a photo attached. She opened it and was looking at a long-range shot of a group of children playing in a park. One of them was circled. Her heart sank as she looked at the smiling young boy with blond hair. She wanted it to be Carl, but she knew straight away that it wasn't. There was something not right about his smile, and his build was all wrong. However, the email had come from someone in Sweden. This couldn't be a coincidence. Surely. What was the link between Carl and Sweden?

The phone rang, making Sally jump and Woody sit up, giving a whimper. She looked at the phone. Philip was at one of their restaurants. She immediately thought of those new menus she hadn't done, but it wasn't Philip calling. She didn't recognize the number. Her heart rate increased. Please let it be Carl.

'Hello?' she answered. There was the sound of heavy breathing coming from the other end. 'Hello?' Sally asked again, pressing the phone harder against her ear to try and hear something, anything.

'Mummy?'

It was faint, but there was no denying what the caller said. Sally started crying. Her whole body was shaking.

'Carl?' she called out. Woody jumped up from the floor and sat bolt upright next to Sally, his head tilted to one side. 'Carl? Sweetheart is that you?'

'Mummy?'

'I'm here, Carl. Mummy's here for you. Tell me where you are, Carl.'

'Mummy.' It sounded like he was crying.

Sally sniffled back her emotions. She needed to be strong for her son. 'Carl, listen to me. I need you to tell me where you are so I can come and get you. Look around you. What do you see?'

The call ended.

'Carl? Carl?' Sally screamed into the phone. She looked at the display, but it was blank. She threw it onto the desk and fell off the chair onto the floor. Woody, sensing her distress, sat beside her and rested his head on her lap. She held onto him. 'Carl's alive, Woody, I know he is. I'll bring him home for you. I promise,' she said through her tears.

Chapter Twenty-One

There was a loud knock on Matilda's front door.

'Shit,' she said under her breath.

By the time she had arrived home, the last thing she wanted to do was entertain guests. She felt physically and mentally drained after the day she'd had. On the way home all she could think about was the brief interview with Oliver and Leah. Was Leah upset enough about the murder of her family? Why did Oliver give off such negativity? Could any of their reactions be used as an accurate description of their feelings? This was a highly unusual situation they had found themselves in. One minute they were basking in the glow of their wedding, the happiest day of their lives, the next they were plunged into a living nightmare.

At this stage, Matilda had no idea who the killer could be. It was a cruel fact that the majority of murder victims know their killer, but would Oliver or Leah inflict such pain and torment on their family? Would they leave Rachel alive to carry the horror of what she saw around with her for the rest of her life? Whoever the murderer was, they were cold-blooded, they were pure evil, and that kind of person struck again.

By the time Matilda had showered off the detritus of the day, she made herself cheese on toast and planned to have an early night and start the latest Elly Griffiths novel with a large bag of Maltesers. That's when someone knocked on the door and ruined her plans. She really wanted to be on her own. She stood in the doorway to the lounge and looked at the oak front door. There was another knock and the sound of the doorbell ringing echoed through the house.

'Shit,' she said quietly again.

It was obvious she was home as the garage needed to be made safe and secure before she could park her car in. Until then, it was parked on the drive near the front door. She hoped it wasn't Daniel Harbison. She genuinely liked him, but she thought he wanted more out of their relationship than architect/client.

Her mobile started to ring. She dug it out of her pocket and saw it was Pat Campbell calling her. Breathing a sigh of relief, she turned into the living room and closed the door behind her so whoever was at the door wouldn't be able to hear her talking.

'Hello,' she answered, speaking quietly into the phone.

'Are you in the shower or something?'

'What? No. Why?'

'Because I've been knocking on your door for the past hour and I'm bursting for a pee.'

Matilda shot out of the living room, ran to the door and pulled it open. 'Pat, I am so sorry.'

'Toilet?'

'Through there.' Matilda pointed.

Pat ran to the small bathroom at the bottom of the stairs and closed the door behind her.

'Slight exaggeration, Pat. You've hardly been standing there for an hour,' Matilda called out.

'When you're my age and have a full bladder, a few minutes feels like an eternity. You're lucky I didn't ruin your rose bed.'

Matilda smiled to herself. 'Would you like a tea or coffee or something?'

'I'll have a coffee and put something Irish in it as well, please. I'm chilled to the bone.'

Matilda was in the kitchen making coffees when Pat poked her head around the doorway.

'Bloody hell, Mat, you've got a gorgeous house here.'

'Thanks.'

'You're all settled now then?'

'More or less.'

Pat stood in the kitchen and looked around her, mouth agape. 'I'd kill for a kitchen like this. Last year, I mentioned to Anton about moving. I said I wanted a bigger kitchen and an en suite. He said "what's the point in moving, we'll just get comfy and we'll have to move again to the cemetery". Honestly, Mat, what did I marry? He's just turned seventy and he's already got one foot in the grave.'

Matilda smiled as she handed Pat her drink. 'Here we go; one Irish coffee. Shall we go through to the living room?'

Matilda led the way and Pat headed straight for the roaring fire where she turned her back on it to warm herself up.

'Another gorgeous room. Aren't you worried it's a bit . . . you know . . . big?'

'It's actually smaller than the last house.'

'Not by much, I'm guessing. Still, you could always take in a lodger.'

'You think of leaving Anton?'

She looked up over her coffee cup and winked at Matilda. 'You're tucked up out of the way here, too, aren't you?'

'It's how I like it.' Matilda smiled.

'It sounds like you're running away from someone.'

'Only ghosts.'

'All my ghosts live in here,' Pat said, tapping her temple.

'Do you have a lot of ghosts?'

'Too many to mention.'

'I know that feeling.' Matilda looked down. An expression of sadness swept across her face.

'Are you all right?' Pat asked, sitting on the opposite sofa. 'I heard on the radio this afternoon about the triple murder. Is it really the Mercers?'

Matilda looked up. 'You know them?'

'I don't. Anton does. Well, he knew Clive Mercer.'

'Oh. What was he like?' Matilda asked.

'Well, you know Anton, he doesn't like to speak ill of anyone, but he struggled to find something good to say about Clive Mercer.'

'Oh.'

'He was a bit of a control freak, by all accounts. Loved himself. You know the type, swaggering about the hospital like he owned the place.'

'So how did Anton know him?'

'I'm not sure. I don't think he knew him as in knew him, but knew about him, if you know what I mean.'

Matilda looked confused. 'I think so. Did Anton say anything else?'

'I'm guessing you know about Clive facing the GMC on a couple of occasions?'

'Yes. We're looking into that.'

'Well, according to Anton, they made him worse.'

'In what way?'

'He didn't like being told what to do. As far as he was concerned, he knew his job like the back of his hand, and nobody could do it better than he could.'

'Wow.'

'Told you he was a control freak.'

'It sounds like my list of suspects is going to get bigger the more people I talk to.'

'Do you have any suspects yet?'

Matilda immediately thought of Oliver and Leah Ridgeway. 'Not at the moment, no. I think this is going to be solved with forensics. You should have seen the crime scene, Pat, it really was a bloodbath. The killer must have left something of himself behind. It's just going to take a lot of hard work finding it.'

'You'll get there,' she said, a positivity in her voice.

'I hope so. Did Anton say anything about Serena Mercer?'

'He only met her a couple of times. He liked her, but he thought she was holding herself a bit too much.'

'What do you mean?' Matilda frowned.

Pat moved away from the fire and sat on the opposite sofa. 'You know when you're at a party and you really don't want to be there; you're all tense and rigid. Well, that's what Serena was like on the occasions he met her.'

'Like she wasn't comfortable in her surroundings?'

'Kind of. And you know the rumour about Clive and Jeremy, don't you?'

'No.'

'Really? I thought one of the nosy neighbours would have told you.' Pat leaned forward. 'There's a rumour, but it's never been denied, that Jeremy wasn't Clive's son.'

'Are you serious?'

'Anton said Serena had an affair not long after they were married and fell pregnant. He forgave her and brought up the child as his own.'

'Why would he do that?'

Pat shrugged. 'I'm not sure. I don't think I could forgive someone cheating on me.' She chuckled. 'Mind you, who'd be mad enough to throw themselves at Anton?'

'You did.'

'When he was a strapping twenty-year-old with a full head of hair and a flat stomach, yes, but now? No. I think I'm safe. Would you have forgiven James if he'd had an affair?'

Matilda looked over to the wedding photo on top of the mantle. 'No. Absolutely not.'

'There you go then. So, why did Clive forgive Serena?'

'Is Leah his child?'

'I assume so.'

'Bloody hell, Pat, fancy a job on my team?'

'With you as my boss? Not bloody likely,' she laughed. 'Anyway, the reason why I've driven out to the middle of nowhere this evening is because I wanted to talk to you about Sally Meagan. This call that she claims to have had from Carl.'

'Claims? You don't believe her?'

Pat sighed. 'I really don't know.'

'Go on.'

'The thing is, there have been no real sightings of Carl for months, the case is going nowhere, and Sally is living on her nerves. She's getting really desperate.'

'So you think she's made up this call? Why?'

'Sympathy, maybe. Or maybe she's wanting to attract attention to keep the case in the public eye. Or maybe she doesn't know she's doing it.'

'What do you mean?'

'I think she might be losing her grip on reality.'

'Oh my God,' Matilda said. 'Was Philip there when you went round? What did he say?'

'He wasn't there.'

'No. I haven't seen him for months. Every time I've gone round he's always been at one of their restaurants.'

'So Sally is left on her own for her mind to mutate and come up with all kinds of scenarios.'

'It would appear so. What do you think we should do?'

'First of all, we need proof.' Pat dug around in her bag and pulled out a scrap of paper. 'This is the number Sally said the call came from. Can you check it out?'

'Of course. I'm guessing it'll no longer be in use, though.'

'I'm guessing that, too.'

'But that doesn't necessarily mean it's Sally making the call.'

'No, but you might be able to triangulate whereabouts the call was made.'

'You're wasted as a civilian,' Matilda smiled.

'I know. But South Yorkshire Police couldn't afford me now,' she laughed. 'I'm going to have a word with Philip, see what he thinks about all this. Also, I'd like to wait to see if Sally gets any more calls, and if there's anyone around to witness it.'

'I really hope she isn't cracking up,' Matilda said.

'So do I, but she's been doing nothing for the past few years but look for Carl. It's slowly killing her.'

'Shit.' Matilda put her cup down on the coffee table with a bang. She stood up and walked over to the fireplace. She looked into the flames. The heat stung her eyes and she blinked away the tears that formed.

Matilda blamed herself for Carl going missing. It was her fault the ransom drop went awry and every time the Meagans were mentioned she remembered that dark time in her life when her husband, James, succumbed to the cancer that was killing him. He died on the day of the ransom drop and Matilda was not focused on anything. The days that followed were now a blur. She remembered nothing of that time. The only reminder was the deep-seated guilt that still rattled around inside her.

'Matilda, you're not to blame for any of this,' Pat said. 'I know what you're thinking, but you can't beat yourself up for the way Sally is living her life.'

'She isn't though, is she?' Matilda turned around from the fire. Her face was red. 'She isn't living. I just keep thinking that she's going to die a lonely old woman, not knowing what happened to her son.'

'But you can't go through life tormenting yourself like this. We all make mistakes, errors of judgement. You can't solve every case.'

Matilda looked into the deep eyes of former Detective Inspector Pat Campbell. For the first time, she saw a long career of successes, but there was something there, something on Pat's mind that added a touch of despair to her gaze.

'Which case keeps you awake at night?' Matilda asked.

Pat took a deep breath. 'Do you remember the Pauline Clover murder? Monday, the tenth of April 1989. I'll never forget that date. She was twenty-eight-years-old. She'd been married for three years and had an eighteen-month-old daughter, Charlotte. Everything in her life was going so well for her. Then, this particular Monday night, she doesn't return home from work. She was found in Graves Park the next morning. She was literally hacked to pieces.'

'I remember,' Matilda said.

'We put it down to a random act of violence. We had no suspects, no motive, no witnesses. Pauline Clover keeps me awake at night. I often see her lying there in the middle of the woods. But even after all this time, I don't blame myself. It was just one of those things that we didn't catch her killer.'

'But I should have caught Carl's kidnappers. If my mind wasn't . . .'

'No. You can't say that. You don't know what would have happened even if your mind was one hundred per cent on the case. You can't spend the rest of your life feeling guilty.'

'Don't you feel guilty about Pauline Clover?'

'No. I feel incredibly sad for not finding her killer, but I didn't kill her. I've nothing to feel guilty about. I did everything in my power.'

'I didn't.'

'Yes, you did. Now, leave Sally to me.' She looked at her watch. 'I'd better be off. If I stay out any longer, Anton will think I've left him and start leaving the toilet seat up,' she joked.

'You'll keep me informed?'

'Of course I will. Promise me you'll try and get over this self-hatred thing you've got going on.'

'I am trying. That's another reason why I've moved. I want to restore some life into myself.'

'Good for you.' Pat gave Matilda a kiss on the cheek and saw herself out.

Matilda remained in front of the fireplace. The living room was temporarily lit up as the headlights from Pat's car shone through the windows. She turned to look at her reflection in the mirror. She studied herself, tilting her head one way then another.

'I don't hate myself,' she told herself. 'I'm just not happy.'

And why's that? She heard James's voice in her head asking.

'Because you're not here.'

You need to let go.

'I can't,' she said, looking into his photograph on the reclaimed railway sleeper.

*You have to. It's going to be a long time until we're together
again. In the meantime, be happy. Have fun. I'm waiting for you.*

'I've forgotten how to have fun.'

You had fun in Monaco with Adele.

Matilda smiled at the memory. It seemed like a lifetime ago
since Monaco. 'But I had to come back here.'

*Then move. Leave Sheffield. If it's difficult here, go somewhere
else. I'll be with you wherever you go, but the bad parts can stay
here.*

Matilda blinked and felt a few tears fall down her cheeks. He
was right. When she thought of Sheffield she thought of Carl
Meagan, Ben Hales, her husband dying. When she was in Monaco
with Adele, they had a great time. She'd laughed, danced, swam
in the sea. She thought of James, obviously, but they were good
thoughts. It was only in Sheffield where her mind went over to
the dark side. Maybe, instead of moving to a new house, she
should have moved cities.

Chapter Twenty-Two

Matilda felt positive as she walked the corridors of South Yorkshire Police HQ to the HMET suite. The team would be interviewing Oliver and Leah Ridgeway again today, which should cover more ground, and, fingers crossed, maybe the forensic team would have some results from the tests and DNA from the hair found under Serena Mercer's little finger. By the end of today, they may be closer to a suspect, or at least have a person of interest to pursue.

Upon entering HMET, Matilda was greeted by a buzzing team. Rory and Sian were chatting loudly by the drinks station, Aaron and Ranjeet were listening to something on Ranjeet's phone. Matilda guessed it wasn't work related as they were both trying, but failing, to stifle laughter. Kesinka was fanning herself with a folder and looking very uncomfortable as she sat at her desk. At his desk, Scott was sitting with his head down, a heavy expression on his face. He looked forlorn. He wasn't reading anything or doing any work, his gaze was somewhere else.

Nobody had seen Matilda enter the room. She went over to Scott and put her hand on his shoulder, making him jump.

'Is everything all right, Scott?' she asked.

'Yes,' he said quietly. He tried to smile, but nothing happened.

'Are you sure?'

'Yes. I'm fine. Just . . . thinking.'

'OK,' she replied reluctantly.

'DI Brady called,' Scott said, quickly changing the subject. 'He said to start the briefing without him as he's with forensics.'

'Thank you.'

Matilda made herself a strong coffee and took a Twix from Sian's snack drawer before beginning the morning briefing. They went through everything they knew about the Mercers so far, which wasn't much. However, Oliver and Leah were due into the station at any moment, so, hopefully, by the end of the day, they would know more about the Mercers than they did their own families.

'I've been doing an online search of the Mercers,' TDC Finn Cotton said. 'Most of what I can find out about Serena Mercer is her arrest for protesting about the tree felling last year. There's a few mentions of the charities she was involved in but that's about it. There's nothing derogatory and she became a bit of a hero after her arrest.'

'What charities did Serena work with?'

'Local homeless charities, mostly. I found an interview she did with *The Star* in 2016. She was passionate about those who drop out of society, rehabilitating them, finding them a home and a job.'

'What about Clive?' Matilda asked.

'There's plenty about the marathons Clive Mercer ran. And he and a team of medics spent a week up a mountain with Bear Grylls.'

'I wouldn't mind spending a week with Bear Grylls,' Sian said, licking her lips.

'I can't see you up a mountain, Sian,' Rory said.

'Who said anything about a mountain? I was thinking about a hotel room.' She smiled.

Matilda tried to hide her smile and told Finn to continue.

'There are two years between Leah and Oliver, so they finished university at different times. However, when Leah finished, she took a year out and decided to go travelling. Oliver took a year out from his studies and went with her. They joined an aid organization and helped out during the Ebola virus outbreak in Sierra Leone in 2014.'

'Bloody hell, they really are the perfect family,' Rory said.

'No such thing,' Sian said. 'Trust me, I've got four kids. Each one of them has some form of rebellion in them.'

'Well, someone didn't think them too perfect or they wouldn't have been killed,' Ranjeet said.

'And we're no closer to finding who that someone is,' Rory added. 'Every bit of research just reaffirms how bloody goody-goody they were.'

'Someone obviously found a reason to kill them.'

'Maybe that was the reason,' Rory said with a slight smile on his lips.

'What about the neighbours?' Matilda asked ignoring Rory's comments. It was good to see the old fun-loving, joke-making Rory back, but there was a time and a place for that sort of thing. 'Surely there has to be dispute over how high the trees were growing in their back gardens, fence boundaries or where they put their bloody bins.'

'I was looking through the statements this morning,' Aaron said. 'Most of the neighbours we spoke to all said how lovely the Mercers were, how shocked they were by what happened. However, I think we should go back and talk to them again. The news will have settled by now. Maybe we'll get something else from them.'

'Good thinking, Aaron. Take Ranjeet with you and dig a little deeper. We need to know if they overheard any arguments coming from their home, who visited them, did any of them say anything about unwanted attention, work problems, money worries, that kind of thing. I've also been told of a rumour that Clive wasn't Jeremy's real father. Can we get that confirmed and if it's true, who was his dad?'

'Where did you hear that?' Sian asked.

'A little bird told me.' Matilda turned to the murder boards and looked at the smiling faces of the victims in happier times. 'I refuse to believe this was a random murder. Nobody kills in this way on a whim.' She turned to Aaron. 'While you're chatting to the neighbours, try and find out who Serena's best friend was.'

'Will do,' Aaron said, quickly scribbling in his notebook.

'Who is talking to the colleagues?'

'We've been through the house,' Sian began. 'And we've found out exactly where Clive, Serena and Jeremy worked. I'm going to send a team around to the hospitals today and have a chat with their co-workers. Jeremy worked in Liverpool at the Royal Liverpool University Hospital, and I happen to know a sergeant working in Liverpool . . .'

'Why do you seem to know people all over the place?' Rory interrupted.

'I'm very popular and friendly.' She smiled.

'You bribe them with your snack drawer, don't you?'

'I don't care what she does, providing it gets us some answers,' Matilda said. 'Sian, I'll leave you to contact Liverpool and get them to find out about Jeremy Mercer. Who knew he was going to be in Sheffield for the wedding? Who did he live with in Liverpool? What do his colleagues say about him? Again, any money worries, relationship problems, that kind of thing.

I want to know who the intended target was, why they all had to die, and why Rachel Mercer was left alive? Any word on her, by the way?'

Kesinka waved to get Matilda's attention. She had her mouth full of crisps and quickly swallowed. 'Sorry, can't seem to stop eating at the moment. I phoned the hospital this morning. Rachel woke up a few times in the night screaming. There's a family liaison officer in the room with her. Apparently it took them ages to calm her down last night after she'd screamed at Leah and Oliver coming into the room.'

'Why did she do that?' Matilda asked, more to herself than anyone else.

'According to the FLO, Leah didn't want to leave. She was in floods. Oliver practically had to drag her out of the hospital room,' Kesinka continued.

'I bet that didn't help Rachel much. Is she physically well enough to leave hospital?'

'I believe so, yes.'

'Then I want her brought here and interviewed. Kesinka, you can do that.'

'Won't we need an appropriate adult present?'

'We'll see if Leah is up to it. The way she was yesterday, she'll do more harm than good. If not, call social services.' Matilda clapped her hands together. 'We all have tasks to do. By the end of the day, I want us to know the Mercer family inside out. I want a person of interest named and I want an arrest imminent. Understood?'

'And I want Mila Kunis in my bed by ten o'clock,' Rory said, nudging Scott who didn't react.

'Ma'am, Leah and Oliver are here,' Kesinka said, putting the phone down.

'Thanks. Right then, Rory, you're with me, Scott, you're with Sian. Let's see what the newlyweds have to say.'

As they filed out of the room, Matilda pulled Sian to one side. 'Ask Oliver what he really thought of his in-laws. He might open up more with his wife out of the way. Really get under his skin.'

'It'll be a pleasure.' She smiled.

'When you've finished, take Scott out for lunch and have a quiet word with him. I don't care what he says, something's bugging him, and it's starting to bug me.'

'Can I claim the lunch back on expenses?'

'As long as it's only a three quid meal deal from Boots.'

'I was hoping for three courses in Strada.'

'I'm not that concerned.'

Matilda's mobile started ringing. The display told her DI Christian Brady was calling. 'Christian, you were missed at the briefing,' she said, a hint of humour in her voice.

'It was worth it. We've got a match from the hair found under Serena Mercer's fingernail.'

'Excellent. Who?'

'Keith Lumb. He's got form, and, get this: he's on the run.'

Chapter Twenty-Three

Christian's revelation would have to wait. Matilda told him to get as much information on the suspect as possible and meet her back in the HMET suite in an hour or so. Leah and Oliver needed to be interviewed separately and now was the perfect time.

'I'm sorry. I can't seem to stop crying,' Leah said, dabbing at her eyes.

They were sitting in interview room one. Leah on one side, Matilda and Rory on the other. On the desk between them were three mugs of tea and a packet of biscuits. Neither had been touched. Leah's expensive-looking handbag was on the seat next to her. She kept reaching inside it for a packet of tissues when the one she was using was saturated with tears. She looked as if she had aged ten years overnight. Her face was red with constant crying. Her shoulder-length hair was lifeless and lank. Her clothes were creased, probably pulled straight out of her suitcase. She should have been in Paris right now, lounging in bed with her new husband, in a haze of sexual glow, not sitting in a police interview room with an underlying smell of stale sweat and cold coffee.

'I can't believe any of this is happening. It doesn't feel real. I keep picturing us leaving. Everyone was smiling and waving.

Mum was crying. She gave me a hug, told me to enjoy myself. Dad wasn't much of a hugger but he gave me a kiss on the cheek. I could tell he had tears in his eyes. Jeremy hugged me too. I threw the bouquet. Rachel caught it. She looked so . . .' her words were lost to tears.

Rory and Matilda exchanged glances.

'Leah,' Matilda said after clearing her throat, 'how many people were at your parents' house?'

'I've made a list,' she said, wiping her nose and rummaging through her bag. She pulled out two sheets of A4 paper. 'One hundred and fifty were invited to the church service, and about a hundred came back to the house.'

'That's a lot of people in the house.'

'We had a marquee. I've highlighted the ones who came to the reception.' She smoothed down the pages and pushed them across to Matilda.

'Thank you. That's a great help.'

'I've put their phone numbers down too. There may have been a few others who turned up to the house; I wasn't really paying much attention. I've hardly slept. I knew you'd probably want a list of people who came. It gave me something to do.'

'I appreciate it, thank you. We've managed to identify many of the guests from the digital cameras on the tables. There are a few people we still haven't been able to put a name to. Would you be able to go through them with one of our detectives?'

'I think so, yes,' she said, wiping her sore nose.

'Thank you. Now, how long were you at the house until you left?' Matilda asked.

'We got back at about four o'clock. Me and Oliver left about seven.'

'Was the party breaking up by then?'

'No. It was going to go on until late.' She reached for her cup of tea and had a sip. It must have tasted horrible as she pulled a face. 'Everyone was having such a wonderful time. Even I didn't want to leave.' She tried to smile but couldn't.

'Leah, I know this is difficult, but can you think of anyone who would want to kill your family?'

Leah screwed up her face at the mention of the word 'kill' and began crying again. 'I was thinking of nothing else all night and the answer is no. You can ask anyone who knows my mum and dad; they were well liked.'

'What about your brother?'

'Jeremy was the best brother I could have asked for. He was intelligent, a loving father to Rachel. He'd do anything for anyone.'

'Leah, I don't mean to sound disrespectful, but your family sounds whiter than white. Surely they couldn't get on with everyone.'

'That's just it, they did. Mum and dad were very busy people. They worked a lot, but always had time for family and friends. The people they did know they held in great regard.'

'Did your parents have any worries?'

'Like what?'

'I don't know. Money worries?'

'No.'

'Any rows?'

'No. Mum and dad got on so well. They were together for a long time. They loved each other. Why are you looking at each other like that?' She almost shouted. 'Don't you believe me?'

'Leah, people don't get killed for no reason. Nothing was stolen from the house, that we're aware of, so robbery was not the motive. That makes us believe they were targeted. The killer believed they had a genuine reason for doing what he or she did. That's what we need to find out.'

'I can't help you,' she said, sitting up straight and wiping her nose.

'Whatever you tell us will be private. You won't be harming your parents by revealing any family secrets.'

'We didn't have any family secrets,' she said, annoyed by the constant haranguing from Matilda.

'Leah, we've heard rumours that your father may not be Jeremy's father.'

'What?' she asked, her eyes widened. 'Who said that? It's a lie. I can't believe this,' she sniffled. 'My family have been murdered and people are spreading such vicious lies. My mum would never have cheated on my dad. They loved each other far too much.'

'OK. I'm sorry, I had to ask.'

'Mrs Ridgeway,' Rory began, 'would you like to tell us about the three occasions your father faced a hearing at the GMC?'

'Jesus!' She threw her tissue on the table. 'Why are you bringing this up? It was ages ago. That's all you lot do though, isn't it, rake up everything from the past, no matter how mean-ingless, just so you can add your own sordid twist on it.'

'Leah, please, calm down. That's not what we're trying to do,' Matilda said. 'We need to understand your family in order to find out who killed them.'

'Well, you're barking up the wrong tree.' She roughly ran her fingers through her hair several times, pulling on it hard. 'My family was perfect. I know you may not think that exists but in our case, it did. They did everything right. They went to work, they did their job, they paid their taxes. I'm not going to sit here while you try and pick at their good name.'

Leah stood up. She grabbed her bag but dropped it, its contents spilling out all over the floor. 'Fuck!' she screamed, falling to her knees and bursting into tears.

Matilda went around the table to hold Leah in her arms while Rory went about picking up the items and putting them back in the bag; tissues, make-up, diary, boxes of medication, mobile phone.

'I'm sorry,' Leah cried into Matilda's shoulder. 'I shouldn't have snapped. I just can't believe any of this has happened. I loved my mum and dad so much. They were the best parents. What am I going to do now?'

What about Rachel?

Matilda looked at Rory. She looked uncomfortable as she was never any good at other people's emotions, she could barely understand her own. 'Perhaps we should take a break here.'

* * *

In interview room two, Oliver Ridgeway was sitting with his arms firmly crossed. He looked pale under the strip lighting and the rings under his eyes showed signs of a bad night's sleep. Sian wondered if his lack of sleep was due to comforting his wife, not necessarily because he was sad at what had happened himself.

Scott came in with a tray of mugs of tea and a couple of bars of chocolate stolen from Sian's snack drawer. He stood in the doorway for a second longer than he should before walking fully into the room. He placed the tray in the middle of the table, gave Oliver a lingering glare, then took his seat.

Sian began the interview. 'Mr Ridgeway, did you get on with your in-laws?'

'Of course I did,' his tone was accusatory.

'There's no "of course" about it,' Sian said. 'Not everyone gets on with their in-laws. I know I don't.'

'Well I did.'

'That's refreshing to hear.' She smiled. 'How did you and Leah meet?'

'Through a mutual friend. I play tennis and Leah was looking for a partner. I stepped in and we played mixed doubles. It built up from there,' he said with a genuine smile on his face.

Sian copied his smile. 'How long was it before you were a couple?'

'A few months.'

'And did you propose?'

'I did.'

'What did her parents think of you getting married?'

'They were pleased. I think they were happy I was a doctor, too.'

'Status meant a lot to Clive and Serena?' Sian asked.

'No. I don't mean it like that.'

'When you heard about your wife's family being killed, what did you think?' Sian asked quickly.

'What kind of a question's that?' he asked, looking to Scott then back at Sian. 'I was shocked, obviously.'

'You didn't expect anything like this to happen?'

'No.'

'Do you know of anyone who would want to kill your wife's family?'

'No.'

'Tell me about what happened on Sunday.'

He stammered at the sudden change of subject. 'It was my wedding day. We were all busy. Everyone was running around trying to make sure everything went smoothly.'

'And did it?'

'Until someone decided to kill my wife's family, yes,' he said with incredulity.

'Did you notice anything unusual in the behaviour of Clive and Serena, or even Jeremy on the day of your wedding?'

'No. Well, Clive was a bit quiet. I think he was worrying about his speech. Serena was trying to do half a dozen things at once, as usual. Jeremy was just Jeremy.'

'Did you get on with Jeremy?'

'We didn't see each other much.'

'You're both the same age, roughly, you do the same job. I'd have thought you'd have a lot in common, enough to spend time with each other.'

'We went for a few drinks when we met up. He was in Liverpool and a single parent working long hours and raising a daughter on his own. He didn't get much free time.'

'How is your wife coping with all this?' Scott asked for the first time.

'How do you think she's coping? She's in bits.'

'Mr Ridgeway,' Sian began, 'there's no need to be on the defensive. We're trying to find out about your wife's family in order to discover who killed them.'

'I'm not on the defensive.'

'You're acting like this is all a great inconvenience to you.'

'To be honest, it is. I should be on my honeymoon right now. Not exactly the great start to married life.'

'Mr Ridgeway, tell me about your relationship with Clive Mercer.'

He shrugged. 'I didn't have one.'

'Really? You were marrying his daughter.'

'He was a very busy man.'

'Is that it?' Scott asked when Oliver didn't continue.

'I don't know what you want me to say.'

'What did you think of him?' Scott leaned back in his chair and folded his arms firmly against his chest.

'I liked him. He was a kind man. Generous.'

'In what way generous?' Sian asked.

'He paid for the wedding.'

'That's just tradition, though. How about Serena? What did you think of her?'

'I liked her.'

'Was she kind and generous too?'

'What are you saying?'

'I'm saying that for them being your in-laws, your new extended family, you sound like you didn't know much about them,' Sian said.

'Look, I'm a junior doctor. I don't know how many hours a detective works each week, but we work all the hours God sends. In my spare time, I've been preparing for this wedding as well as studying, and trying to find a house I can afford. Any time left in the day, I tend to try and grab a few hours' sleep. I didn't see my in-laws much. I didn't see Jeremy much. I rarely see my own parents and brothers.'

'So you wouldn't know if Clive, Serena, or Jeremy had any enemies? Anyone who would want to kill them?'

'No. I wouldn't.'

'What about you?' Scott asked.

'What about me?'

'Did you want to kill them?'

Both Sian and Oliver looked at Scott with wide eyes. The silence in the room was palpable. The temperature seemed to drop by several degrees.

'No I did not.'

'Are you sure?'

'Of course I'm sure. Besides, I was in Paris at the time.'

'Wanting someone dead isn't the same as actually killing them. You could have put someone up to it.'

'DC Andrews,' Sian said.

'Oh, yes, I put a notice up on the hospital board. Anyone fancy making a few quid? Give me a call, I've got a couple of relatives I want killing. Just who do you think you are asking me those questions?'

'Mr Ridgeway, DC Andrews is merely . . .'

'Now that Jeremy is dead, your wife stands to inherit a great deal of money. But it's not always about money, is it? Sometimes people kill to stop someone finding out about something,' Scott said. His voice was calm and he looked straight ahead at Oliver.

'How dare you?' Oliver fumed, standing up. 'You don't know me. You don't know anything about me. I love my wife. I would never do anything to hurt her. And I did not kill her family,' he said, looking Scott straight in the eye.

'I think we're letting things get out of hand here,' Sian said. 'Perhaps we should take a break.'

Sian ushered Scott out of the room and, holding him by the elbow, marched him down the corridor into an empty office. Scott towered over Sian, so the sight of him being led by a woman almost a foot shorter than him looked comical.

'What the hell was all that about?' Sian said, throwing Scott into a room and slamming the door closed behind him.

'He's lying.'

'What? How do you know?'

'I . . .' He stopped himself.

'What?'

Scott was sitting on the edge of a table. He was playing with his fingers, looking down.

'Scott, what is it?' Sian asked.

He looked up. There were tears in his eyes. 'I'm sorry. I don't know what I'm saying.' His voice was breaking slightly.

'You know something, don't you? Something about Oliver?'

He nodded.

'What is it?'

'I can't say.'

'Why not?'

'Because I can't. I'm not . . . I . . .'

Sian went over to the young DC and placed both hands on his shoulders. She lowered herself so she could look up and see his face. Tears were rolling down his cheeks.

'Scott, whatever is going on, you can tell me. It won't go any further, you know that.'

'But what I need to say will go further now.'

Sian frowned. 'This is personal, isn't it?'

He nodded.

'Bloody hell, Scott. What have you got yourself into?'

Chapter Twenty-Four

DS Aaron Connolly stopped in his tracks as he made his way through reception to the car park. He hadn't expected to see Leah Ridgeway sitting in the corner. Her nose was red from where she'd been rubbing at it. Her eyes were puffy and wide. She was looking into the distance. She was shivering with cold.

'Mrs Ridgeway?' Aaron asked, placing a gentle arm on her shoulder.

She jumped and looked up at him. 'Sorry, I was miles away. Are you a detective?'

'I am, yes. Is there anything I can help you with?'

'I meant to ask DCI Darke, but I completely forgot. I was wondering, would it be possible to see my family?'

'Ah,' Aaron said sitting down next to Leah. He thought for a while, trying to find the correct words to use. 'The thing is, your parents were stabbed many times. It might be better to remember them the last time you saw them, at your wedding, rather than how they are now.'

'I want to say goodbye,' she said, choking back the tears.

'I can understand that,' he said. 'It's just, they suffered serious stab wounds, which might be upsetting to you.'

'What about Jeremy?'

'I think you might be able to see your brother. Would you like me to find out for you?'

'Would you?' She smiled.

He tried to leave in order to make a phone call, but Leah grabbed his arm tight.

Matilda was tucked into the corner of the canteen wolfing down a large bowl of cereal. Christian stood in the doorway and scanned the room looking for her. He went over to her, pulled out a chair and sat down. He looked tired. His dark blond hair wasn't in its usual neat and tidy state.

'Trying to hide?' he asked.

'That was the plan.'

'Sorry. I thought you'd want to know about Keith Lumb.'

'Fire away,' she said, shovelling in a large spoonful of corn-flakes. 'Ignore me, I just realized I didn't have breakfast.'

'OK. Well, Keith has a record as long as your arm. He's only twenty-seven but he's been in trouble since he was thirteen.'

'What for?'

'Theft, burglary, muggings, driving without a licence, driving without insurance, claiming unemployment benefit while working cash-in-hand, more theft and more burglary,' he said reading down a list on his iPad.

'But that's just petty crime compared to what happened at the Mercer house,' Matilda said with a mouthful.

'Maybe he wasn't acting alone.'

'Maybe,' Matilda thought. 'It doesn't make sense. You don't just go from burglary and working while signing on to a frenzied triple murder.'

'Maybe there's another reason why his hair ended up at the scene.'

'Such as?'

Christian frowned as he thought. 'I don't know. Perhaps he was a guest at the wedding.'

'Didn't you say he was on the run?'

'Yes.'

'So, he wouldn't have attended a wedding if he was on the run. Why was he running anyway?'

'He was arrested in Barnsley last week for a spate of burglaries in the area. He was charged and processed. A uniformed officer goes to his cell to take him for questioning and notices the door is open and he's not there.'

'How the hell was he able to escape from a police station?'

'I've no idea.'

'I think you and I should pay a visit to Barnsley.'

'Such a treat. I'll pop home and get my passport,' he said with sarcasm, and a twinkle in his eye.

Matilda smiled. 'We get all the good jobs, don't we?'

'How did it go with the Ridgeways?'

'I haven't had a chance to speak to Sian yet about Oliver but Leah's in bits.'

'Only natural.'

'She's very selfish though. She kept saying how all this is affecting her. She didn't once say how Rachel was going to cope.'

'I wouldn't read too much into that. At the moment, her mind will be all over the place. Once it's fully sunk in she'll think about the practicalities.'

'Maybe,' Matilda mused.

'Is it true Rory's thinking of leaving?'

'He did mention it. Attending the crime scene affected a lot of us. I think I've tried to assuage him.'

'I hope so. Rory's a good copper. He's got the potential to go far,' Christian said.

'I know. I like him. Anyway, we'll sort him out once we've got this case solved. I'll track Sian down, have a word. In the meantime, get a pool car and organize a couple of plane tickets to take us to exotic Barnsley.' She smiled.

'Will do.'

As he left the canteen Matilda could hear Christian singing 'Oh this year we're off to sunny Barnsley, Y Viva South Yorkshire.'

She laughed. It was the closeness of her colleagues, the camaraderie, the laughter and how comfortable she felt around her team that she loved the most about this job. Yes, the crimes were often brutal and shocking, but if you had the right people around you, everything else was manageable. She needed to instil that sentiment into Rory. Then she realized she was considering leaving Sheffield herself only last night. She sniggered. She knew she wasn't going anywhere.

Keith Lumb didn't want to wake up. He was having a wonderful dream where he was living in Spain. By day he worked as a waiter in a restaurant. By night he walked the streets in shorts and a T-shirt, moving from bar to bar. He'd changed his name to something Spanish and affected a local accent to wow the English tourists. He'd romance a different woman every night; buy her a meal, drinks, take her back to his apartment overlooking the Mediterranean and make love to her on the balcony.

He woke with a start and remembered exactly where he was – a generic hotel room somewhere in the south of England with the unromantic sound of a busy motorway coming through the window. He was a long way from realizing his dream. At this rate, he wondered if he'd ever get out of Britain. Everything seemed to be conspiring against him. He looked at his watch and was surprised to see it was after eleven o'clock. He must have been shattered last night.

Keith decided against having breakfast. He had another lingering shower. He didn't know when he was next going to have one. He dressed in the sweaty clothes he'd been wearing for the past three days and left the hotel.

Across the courtyard was a small Costa. He bought a black Americano, and two slices of toast which looked as if they'd never seen the inside of a grill. However, they would fill a hole for now. As he ate, he looked out of the window at life carrying on as normal. He didn't even know where he was. He remembered the rapist truck driver picking him up just outside of Luton. They drove for about an hour before he turned into a darkened layby. When Keith had made his escape, he walked for a good half an hour until he came across the Premier Inn. Where the bloody hell was he? What if he'd walked in the opposite direction? He could be heading back north instead of to the south coast.

He left Costa, taking his coffee with him. He passed a petrol station and stopped as his eye caught the stand of newspapers. They were all carrying the same story as their front-page lead:

MASSACRE AT THE WEDDING

WEDDING DAY HORROR

MURDER AT THE WEDDING

That didn't sound like something that happened in England. He pulled out a copy of *The Sun* and read the beginning of the story on the front page:

Three members of the same family have been killed
in Sheffield in what police describe as a brutal
massacre. The Mercer family were celebrating the
wedding of their daughter when the killer struck on
Sunday night, killing the bride's mother, father and
brother. Her niece was left alive but has been mentally
tortured by what she witnessed. The seven-year-old is
currently under armed guard in the city's Children's
Hospital.

The Mercer family were well known in the affluent
area of Fulwood where they lived, and neighbours were
stunned when they heard of the carnage.

Cont. Page 4&5.

Keith's hands were shaking as he gripped the paper tightly.
He was about to turn to page four to continue reading when
there was a bang on the glass. He looked up.

'We're not a library. You want to read it, you pay for it first,'
came the angry call from inside the petrol station.

Keith placed the paper back in the slot and walked away. He
couldn't believe what he was reading. He knew Fulwood. He
was there only last week. He knew the Mercer family too.

'Fuck,' he said under his breath. 'Fuck, fuck, fuck.'

Chapter Twenty-Five

The viewing room of the mortuary was dank and depressive. Low lighting and dull-coloured furniture gave it an oppressive atmosphere. Aaron had been in this room many times with grieving relatives throughout his career; even if it was decorated in modern colours with a plush carpet and gaudy furnishings, he often thought the room would still have an air of sadness. It leeched out of the walls. Hundreds of people had cried in this room; Leah Ridgeway was simply another inhabitant. There would be more like her. Death was the only constant to life.

The door opened and Lucy Dauman stuck her head through the small gap she allowed. She gave Aaron the nod then quickly left. He knew the drill. There was a switch at the side of the window; you pressed it and the curtain opened to reveal the dead.

'Are you ready?' Aaron asked.

Leah was perched on the edge of the uncomfortable sofa. 'I don't know.' She looked up at him with wet eyes.

'You don't have to do this if you don't want to.'

She took a deep breath. 'No. I do. I'm ready.'

She stood up and joined the sergeant by the window. With the dark curtain closed, Leah could see her frightened expression staring back at her. Aaron pressed the switch and the curtain slowly and smoothly opened.

On the opposite side of the glass, Jeremy Mercer lay on a trolley. A white sheet covered him; only his head was exposed. His hair had been combed, his face washed. He looked peaceful, as if he was sleeping.

Leah reached for Aaron's hand and held it firmly. 'Do you have any brothers or sisters?' she asked, not taking her eyes from Jeremy.

'I have an older brother.'

'Are you close?'

'He lives in Germany. We talk when we can.'

'We were very close. We spoke often. And I popped to Liverpool most weekends to take Rachel out. What do I say to her?'

Aaron released the breath he'd been holding. 'I don't know. Children are very resilient, though. She'll get through this. You both will.'

'He was a good father,' she said, placing a hand on the glass. 'It's so incredibly cruel.'

Leah turned away and fell into Aaron. He placed his arms around her and let her sob. After a while, he pressed the switch and the curtain closed on Jeremy Mercer.

'You're very quiet,' Christian said to Matilda from the driver's seat of the pool car.

'Yes. Just thinking,' Matilda replied. She had her elbow on the door and was resting her head in her hand. She looked out of the dirty window at the grimy view as they headed up the A61 to Barnsley.

When Christian had left her in the station canteen, she went back to eating her soggy cornflakes and thought about the members of her team. Yes, they had a life. Yes, they worked well together, but, apart from Sian, how much did she know them, really know them? It took her a full five minutes to remember Christian's wife's name, and no matter how much she wracked her brain, she couldn't recall what Aaron had called his new child.

'This case is a real head scratcher, isn't it? I was talking to Aaron earlier. He said the neighbours all thought the Mercers were the bees knees. Who would want to kill Britain's most perfect family?'

'Sorry? What?' Matilda asked, realizing Christian had been talking.

'Are you OK?'

'Yes. Fine. Christian, how are you?'

'How am I?' He looked over at Matilda, slightly perplexed. 'I'm OK.'

'Family OK?'

'Yes. Fine.'

'What about the children?'

'They're doing OK. What's this about?' he asked with a nervous smile.

'I always thought I knew my team. We don't seem to chat much anymore, do we? We don't go out for drinks after work.'

'We do.'

'Do we?'

'Well, I've been out a few times with Aaron and Ranjeet. Sometimes Sian pops along.'

'Oh.' Matilda was slightly taken aback.

'We used to ask you, but you always said no so we stopped asking.'

'I see.' Matilda looked hurt. 'What do you talk about when you're having these evenings out?'

'It's hardly an evening out; just a few drinks after work.' He smiled.

'OK. So what do you talk about?'

'Nothing much. Work is off the agenda. We just chat about life in general.'

'Huh,' was all Matilda could reply. So, my team get on perfectly well with each other, but not with me.

'Is this about Rory thinking of resigning?'

'Er . . . yes . . . I suppose it is.'

Matilda had always had a problem in trusting others, in allowing them to get close. When she was younger, she decided she wanted to be a detective and that was that. She wasn't interested in a relationship, getting married and having children, all she thought of was being the best detective she could be. When she met James, all that was thrown out of the window. There was a new purpose in her life. James showed her what else life had to offer: happiness, laughter, fun, a relationship. She could still be a brilliant detective, but she would have someone by her side too. She allowed James to be that someone. For the first time in her life, everything slotted into place nicely. She was happy.

Since his death, the walls went back up and she refused to allow anyone else in. Adele was fine. She'd known Adele for years, but anyone else, no thank you. That was the reason she didn't go for drinks with her team after work. She was afraid of having a few too many and opening herself up, allowing others to see her vulnerable side. Maybe it was because of her icy nature that Scott was reluctant to talk to her, to share what was bothering him.

'We're here,' Christian said.

'Oh.' Matilda looked around and saw they'd pulled up in the

car park of a dilapidated building on the outskirts of Barnsley. She looked up through the windscreen. 'This is the police station?'

'Yes.'

She looked again at the grey three-storey building with rusting window frames. 'No wonder Keith Lumb was able to escape.'

'Who's in charge here?'

'Nigel Eckhart. He's a DI.'

'I don't know him.'

'I've worked with him a few times,' Matilda said. 'He's a decent bloke. Hard-working. He's had a few personal issues though recently.'

'How come?' he asked, looking out of the window at the building.

'Something happened with his daughter, I think,' she said, frowning. 'I can't remember what, exactly, but I know she ended up committing suicide.'

'Really? How old was she?'

'I don't know. Come on, let's see how Keith managed to escape from Alcatraz.' She smiled, unbuckling her seat belt.

Kesinka Rani waddled down the corridor of Sheffield Children's Hospital. The armed guard was no longer outside Rachel Mercer's room as ACC Masterson said the cost couldn't be justified. If the killer did come back, finger's crossed one of the nursing staff knew a few karate moves.

She pushed open the door to find Rachel sitting up in bed eating a bowl of Coco Pops. She was wearing a pair of pink Hello Kitty pyjamas and her brown hair was tied in bunches. As soon as she saw Kesinka, she gave her a smile. It was heart-warming to see she was starting to rally round and was no longer sleeping all the time and hiding away under the blankets. Next to her was a family liaison officer.

'How is she?' Kesinka asked.

'She's fine. The doctors are wanting to release her. Physically, there's nothing wrong with her. The only problem is, there's nowhere for her to go.' The FLO said, keeping her voice low.

'There's the auntie, but I don't think she's in a stable condition at the moment. We'll have to contact social services.'

'Won't she need to be interviewed?'

'Yes. I'll get something set up back at the station. I'll give DCI Darke a call. She might be able to persuade Leah to take her.'

They both looked back at Rachel who was devouring the cereal as if it was the first meal she'd had in weeks.

'Poor thing,' Kesinka said, rubbing her stomach. 'I dread to think what she saw in that house.'

The door burst open and hit the back of the wall with a bang. All three of them jumped. Rachel immediately started crying. Standing in the doorway was Leah Ridgeway.

'Rachel, get dressed, you're coming home with me,' she said. Her hair was pulled back into a severe ponytail. Her eyes were wide and starry.

'I'm afraid that's not possible at the moment,' Kesinka said, standing in front of Leah, blocking her view.

'I'm her next of kin. The doctors said she's fine to leave, so I'm taking her home.'

'She needs to be interviewed.'

'She's seven years old,' she shouted.

'And she's the only witness to what happened. Don't worry, we know how to deal with child witnesses.'

'No. I'm not having you plant ideas in her head. She's suffered enough. She's coming home with me.'

'This is not helping,' the FLO said, shielding Rachel.

'She's my niece. She's all I've got left. I'm taking her.' There was a catch in her throat and she bit down hard on her bottom lip. 'Fuck.'

Rachel started crying.

Leah moved over to a chair, picked up the clothes and threw them at Rachel, telling her to get dressed.

'Mrs Ridgeway, I think you and I should step outside,' Kesinka said. She placed her hands on Leah's shoulders.

'Don't tell me what to do,' she said, shrugging out of the DC's hold.

'Daddy,' Rachel cried from her bed, hugging the pillow.

The FLO went over to the bed and sat next to her, holding her tight to her chest.

'Mrs Ridgeway, please,' Kesinka said. 'Rachel is very distressed. You're not helping. I think we should all calm down and discuss this.'

'There's nothing to discuss. She's my family. I'm her guardian now. And I'm taking her home with me. Rachel, get dressed.'

Kesinka stepped forward and grabbed Leah by the elbow. She pulled her towards the door.

'Don't fucking touch me,' Leah screamed, flinging her arms up at Kesinka, pushing her away.

DC Rani lost her footing, fell into a table and onto the floor with a heavy thud. Everyone stopped and looked around as Kesinka lay on the floor, not moving.

Chapter Twenty-Six

Matilda and Christian were shown into DI Nigel Eckhart's office on the top floor of the draughty building. They were offered tea. Matilda was about to refuse until Christian jumped in and accepted. The man drank close to a dozen cups of tea per day.

'I was sorry to hear about Hattie,' Matilda said, referring to his daughter.

Nigel was a tall thin man with a shiny bald head and a long bony nose. His brown eyes were close together, and his thin lips were permanently pursed. He wore a shirt and tie with the small knot too tight under his neck. It looked painful. The shirt was frayed at the cuffs. He gave the impression of a man who lived on his nerves, forever on edge. He looked at a photograph on his desk with sadness in his eyes.

'Thanks. So, what brings you to Barnsley?' he asked, quickly changing the subject. 'Let me guess, it's about Keith Lumb, isn't it?'

'Yes it is,' Matilda replied. 'Do you want to tell me what happened?'

'Well, I wasn't here on the day he was arrested,' Nigel quickly said, fingering the knot of his tie. 'I was at a seminar in Birmingham. From what I can gather, he was placed in a cell and the door wasn't locked properly. He saw his chance and he took it.' He shrugged as if it was just one of those things.

'Why wasn't the door locked properly? Who was the duty sergeant?' Christian asked.

Nigel let out an exasperated sigh. He swept a few files away and pulled forward the keyboard to his computer. Using a shaky index finger, he hammered a few keys, before looking up at the screen. 'That would be Sergeant Bella Slack.'

'Did you question her about it?'

'Yes. She put him in cell five. Unfortunately, we have had problems with the lock on that door.'

'So the lock was faulty?' Matilda asked.

'Yes.'

'Had it been reported?'

Nigel didn't reply. He looked from the computer screen to Matilda, to Christian, to the screen, then back to Matilda again.

'I'm guessing that's a yes,' Matilda said. 'So, the lock was reported but not repaired?'

'That's right.'

'What was Keith Lumb arrested for?' Christian asked.

'He was caught on CCTV running away from the scene of a burglary in Dodworth. He's known to us, so uniform went to pick him up. He was questioned and admitted a further five burglaries around the city.'

'In what way is Keith Lumb known to you?'

'I'm guessing you've seen his record. He's done it all: theft, mugging, burglary, driving without due care and attention, driving without insurance and without a licence, drunk and disorderly, loitering with intent.'

'Murder?' Matilda asked.

'Murder? God no! Well, not yet. I'm sure he'll get there eventually.'

'I'm guessing you've heard the news about a family being murdered in Sheffield.'

'The Mercer family? Yes. I saw it in the paper this morning. Hang on, you don't think Keith did it, do you?'

'His DNA was found at the scene.'

'The report said it was a massacre.'

'That's right.'

'Good Lord.'

'Did Keith ever have an accomplice?' Christian asked.

'No. He always worked on his own.'

'What about family? Any next of kin?'

'Let me have a look.' Nigel returned to typing with one finger on the keyboard. A knock came on the door and a tired-looking woman in an oversized cardigan came in carrying a tray with three mugs of tea.

'Lovely. Thank you,' Christian said, leaning forward and taking the tea. 'Does anyone here have a snack drawer?'

'A what?' she asked.

'Leave it, Christian,' Matilda said.

'Leslie, could you ask DC Weaving to come up here?' Nigel asked. She smiled and left the office. 'DC Weaving is the one who interviewed Keith Lumb on the day he was arrested. He should be able to answer your questions in more detail. Now, next of kin,' he said, looking back at the computer screen. 'Yes, here we are. He's got a sister, Elizabeth Lumb, who lives in your neck of the woods: Trap Lane in Sheffield.'

'Trap Lane?' Matilda asked.

'Yes. You know it?'

'Yes. It's not far from where the Mercers were killed in Fulwood.' Matilda and Christian exchanged glances. 'When did Keith actually escape from custody?'

Nigel sighed again as he returned to the computer he so obviously despised. 'Friday, the twelfth of January according to this.'

'Two days before the murders.'

'Are you actively looking for him?' Christian asked, slightly annoyed with Nigel's laxity.

'Of course we are. We have a team watching his flat. We visited all his known haunts, talked to friends, neighbours, colleagues.'

'He was working?'

'Yes. He worked as a labourer, casually.'

'What about his sister?' Matilda asked. Her voice had taken on a sharper tone. 'Did you speak to her?'

'Yes. She was interviewed twice. She said she hadn't seen her brother for weeks.'

'And you believed her?'

'We had no reason not to. Look, DCI Darke, it is unfortunate that Keith Lumb was able to escape from our station. However, we're not exactly bursting at the seams with spare cash here. Look around you, the building is falling apart. Yes, I knew about the lock on the cell door. But do you have any idea how much a cell door costs to replace? We had to pay out over a million pounds last financial year in compensation to members of the public who sued for wrongful arrest, or because they said they were unfairly treated. A copper only has to look at someone the wrong way and they're straight on the phone to a tin-pot solicitor claiming harassment. And God forbid a male officer tries to arrest a female suspect these days.'

It was the most Nigel had spoken since Matilda and Christian had arrived. His face reddened as he launched into his diatribe. He had obviously fallen out of love for the job years ago and the changing nature of society was weighing him down.

'I'm sorry,' he apologized, squeezing the bridge of his nose. He took a deep breath. 'An internal inquiry has been launched into how and why Keith escaped. I will accept full responsibility for whatever the outcome is.'

'Nigel,' Matilda lowered her voice. 'I'm not blaming you. I know how difficult it is when you've got the boss on your back moaning about overtime and the cost of the department yet wanting results at the same time. We're doing an impossible job.'

'Tell me about it. I've had officers, good officers, resign because their hands are tied when it comes to dealing with some of the scum we're struggling with. The drug dealers and the rapists out there, the real criminals, are laughing at us. Do you know how many detectives I've got who are on long-term sick, or seeing a therapist? All of this,' he picked up a stack of paperwork and dropped it straight down onto his desk again, 'is not worth the hassle.'

The three remained silent as they absorbed Nigel's woes. A clock ticked loudly in the background. Outside, in the CID suite, a hushed silence descended.

'Nigel,' Matilda began, 'do you know Keith Lumb?'

'I don't know him. I've met him a few times. I know of his track record.'

'Do you think he is capable of murdering three people in such a frenzied way?'

'When you've been in the job longer than I have, nothing surprises you anymore. If you've got forensic evidence saying Keith Lumb killed three people, then that's good enough for me. Catch him and throw the key away.'

Matilda offered a weak smile.

* * *

'Your DI Eckhart is quite a guy,' Christian said to DC John Weaving as they all sat in the canteen nursing another cup of tea.

'You could say that.' John smiled. 'He's a stroke waiting to happen.'

John looked like a young, fuller version of Nigel Eckhart. He was also bald and wearing a shirt and tie, but he was taller and fitter. His eyes were deep-set and had thick dark circles beneath them. He constantly played with his wedding ring. His accent wasn't local, but his voice was deep and quiet.

'What's he like to work with?' Matilda asked.

'He's firm but fair. He doesn't let us get away with much,' he said with a smile which revealed dimples in his cheeks.

'John, tell us about when you arrested Keith Lumb.'

'We went around to his flat in Tankersley. I knocked on the door. He answered wearing only a pair of boxers. I arrested him, told him to get dressed. He saw there was a few of us there so he didn't even try to resist. He got dressed. I led him to the car, sat in the back with him and brought him in.'

'Why did you go and arrest him and not uniformed officers?' Matilda asked.

'Because I've been dealing with these burglaries for months. It was my collar.'

'So what happened during the interview?'

'Well, he was denying it at first. He said he had alibis and then I whip out the CCTV images we've got of him. You could tell it was him. Then the fingerprints came back. He'd taken a glove off at the last house he did and left a print behind on a door frame. He couldn't deny it any longer.'

'Then what?'

'I charged him, put him in a cell. It was getting late so he was going to spend the night here and off to magistrates' court the following morning.'

'Who put him in the cell?'

'That would have been Bella Slack,' he said with his eyes closed as he thought.

'Did you know one of the cell doors was broken?'

'Tell me something that isn't broken around here.'

'What happened when you'd found out he'd escaped?' Christian asked, breaking off a finger of KitKat and dunking it into his tea.

'I didn't find out until the following morning. I went with a team to his flat, but he hadn't been back, and his car was still there. Although we impounded that as it wasn't taxed.'

'Who went to interview his sister?'

'I spoke to her twice. She said she hasn't seen him for weeks.'

'Did you phone her or visit her?' Matilda asked.

'I phoned her.'

'Don't you think you should have visited her?'

'If it had been my decision, then yes, I would have done. But we're that short staffed and rushed off our feet that if it can be done over the phone then so be it.'

'Is anybody actually looking for Keith Lumb now?'

'No.'

'Why not?'

'Ask DI Eckhart. It's all about budget and numbers with him. He told me, and I'm quoting him word for word here: "he's hardly Jack the bloody Ripper. We'll catch him when he breaks into another house".'

'Do you know Keith Lumb?'

'We all know Keith Lumb. He's regularly brought in for

questioning. Twenty-seven years old and he's done sod all with his life apart from ruin a lot of other people's.'

'Is he capable of massacring three people?'

'I've no idea,' he said, scratching his bald head. 'Who knows what people are capable of when they've taken a few colourful pills.'

'He's an addict?' Christian asked.

'Suspected. Have you finished? Only my shift finishes in half an hour and I'd like to leave on time for a change.'

'We might need to speak to you again.'

'You know where to find me.' He drained his cup and left the canteen with his head down, dragging his feet.

'Such a happy bunch of people here,' Matilda said sarcastically. 'And have you noticed all the blokes are bald?'

'Maybe you should think of putting in for a transfer then.' She smiled.

'What are you talking about?' he said, patting down his short-cropped hair. 'I'm not thinning, am I?'

'Come on. Let's go and check out this cell door.'

'Seriously, am I going bald?' Christian asked, running after Matilda out of the door.

Bella Slack was in her fifties. She had dyed jet-black hair which was pulled back into a loose ponytail, wore far too much make-up and whatever perfume she wore, it smelled like she'd bathed in it. Apart from her appearance, she was a warm and welcoming woman with a large smile and bright personality. She took Matilda and Christian to the cell block.

'Bella,' someone called from the end of the corridor, 'I can't get the touch screen to work.'

'Hang on.' She made her excuses to Matilda and Christian

and left them alone. She was back within seconds. 'Sorry about that. We're back to using ink pads for fingerprinting. The touch screen hasn't worked properly since it was installed.'

'How was Keith Lumb processed?'

'The same way. Like I said, it's temperamental. Anyway, it's this one here on the end. I knew one of them was broken but, well, you know what it's like when you're busy, things go out of your mind.' She opened the cell door and slammed it closed. 'Listen, it shuts fine,' she turned the key. 'It even clicks into place. That's probably why I didn't give it a second thought. But, watch this.' She gave the bottom of the door a hard kick and it groaned open. 'See.'

'And we all know prisoners love kicking the door,' Christian said, standing well back to avoid the smell of her fragrance.

'Exactly.' She smiled.

'Were you on duty when he escaped?'

'No. What we're guessing is that he waited until no one was in here. Now, we don't have a night shift as such anymore. If there's a prisoner needs charging then we call upstairs to one of the night staff and they come down to process them.'

'Dare I ask if there's CCTV footage?' Matilda asked.

'There is, but only of the cells and the outside where they're brought in. There's nothing of this area here.'

'Why not?'

'We don't have the capacity to run so many cameras, so we have to choose carefully where we want them to go. You can't even plug your phone in to charge without overloading the system,' she giggled. 'Hang on a minute.' She pushed past them when the door opened and a uniformed officer entered the custody suite. 'Rita, come and sign Dawn's card. There's only you left. And you owe me a fiver for those flowers for Ross.'

'How is this place still open?' Christian said as an aside to Matilda.

'I've no idea. I know budgets have been slashed right, left and centre recently. We're having to share dog handlers with West Yorkshire, forensics aren't going out to burglaries where nothing's been stolen to cut down on cost, it's ridiculous.'

'Yes, but cost cutting leads to bigger things. Look at this, Keith Lumb is arrested, put into a dodgy cell then escapes. A week later he commits three murders. Three lives lost because of the price of a cell door.'

'Sorry about that.' Bella came back into the cell corridor. 'Rita was off on holiday last week. I needed to catch her. If there's a whip-round to be had for someone you can guarantee it's always me who has to organize it. Trying to get money out of coppers can be a full-time job in itself.' She smiled.

'Bella, you'll have met Keith a few times, wouldn't you?' Matilda asked.

'You could say that. He was more like a colleague than a criminal.' She laughed.

'Would you say he was the type of person to commit a triple murder?'

'Is this the Mercer family you're talking about?'

'Yes.'

'No. Absolutely not.'

Matilda was taken aback by such a firm answer. 'Why so sure?'

'Around this time last year Keith was arrested for drunk driving. We had to do a blood test on him. The second the doctor put the needle in, Keith looked down at his arm and passed out. He hated the sight of blood.'

'So he couldn't break into a house and butcher three people to death?'

She fingered her collar. 'Well, who knows what people are capable of when the balance of their mind is disturbed. Also, there was a rumour Keith had dabbled in drugs from time to time. Get started on them and that's it; all rational behaviour goes out the window, doesn't it?'

Matilda smiled. Keith Lumb was looking as guilty as a man holding a smoking gun. For some reason, she was having serious doubts about him as a suspect but had no idea why.

'I've got a headache,' Christian said as they stepped into the fresh air of the car park.

'Yes. This case is giving me one too.'

'No. I meant Bella's bloody perfume. I can smell it on me. God knows what Jennifer's going to think when I get home.'

'Answer me this question, Christian,' Matilda began, ignoring her DI, 'we've got a petty criminal with a phobia of blood who is on the run because he's scared of going to jail for committing a few burglaries. He pops over to Sheffield, and slaughters three people in a vicious bloodbath. What's wrong with that picture?'

'It doesn't make sense.'

'Precisely.'

'So, what does that mean?'

'It means that either Keith Lumb had overcome his phobia and decided to become a mass murderer, or, someone is framing him.'

There was a slight knock on DI Eckhart's door. It opened and DS Jonson entered without being granted permission. Nigel was by the window, looking out over the grey South Yorkshire town.

'I've heard a DCI from Sheffield has been sniffing around,' Ross said from the doorway.

Ross was tall and broadly built. His large brown eyes gave him a sad expression. His tie was loose around his collar, he hadn't shaved for several days and the dark circles beneath his eyes were evidence of a lack of sleep.

Nigel nodded without turning around.

'I kept out of the way. Just in case,' Ross said, closing the door behind him.

'They're just leaving now. DCI Matilda Darke. You've heard of her, I'm guessing.'

'Who hasn't?'

'She's good. She's also like a dog with a fucking bone. She won't let this drop.' Nigel turned from the window and went behind his desk.

'Did she ask about Keith Lumb?' Ross asked. He stood at the back of the room and looked down at his feet.

'Yes. They've found evidence of him at the scene. He's the number one suspect.'

'Do they know where he is?'

'Not yet. Do you?' he asked.

'No. His mobile's turned off. He could be anywhere.'

Nigel opened his top drawer and pulled out a single sheet of A4 paper. 'I received this yesterday. We're being closed down.'

'What?'

'The building needs far too much doing to it to bring it up to standard that they've decided it would be cheaper to close us down.'

'When?'

'They haven't said.'

'What will happen to the staff?'

'Moved around or redundancies. The thing is, if we can bring Keith Lumb in and arrest him before DCI Darke does, that'll give us some leverage when it comes to fighting to keep this place open, or at least moved to another building.'

'What do you want me to do?' Ross asked, looking DI Eckhart in the eye for the first time.

'Find Keith Lumb. I don't care what you have to do, but I want him caught.'

'I'm trying. I don't know . . .'

'Look,' Nigel leaned forward on the desk, 'I'm not pissing about here, Ross. We need him under lock and key. Start with that weird sister of his. Do whatever you have to do.'

Nigel didn't break eye contact. He didn't blink. This wasn't an operational command. This was a threat.

Chapter Twenty-Seven

Keith Lumb dropped a pound coin into the slot in the public phone box and dialled a number from memory. He impatiently listened to the ringing. Around him in the shopping centre, life was going on as normal as people went about their business. He watched an elderly couple in Costa chatting and laughing as they sipped their lattes. A mother and young child holding hands as they went into Waterstones to browse the children's books. A young couple arm in arm outside a jeweller's shop, probably choosing an engagement ring. Life looked so simple. Why was his so complicated? Or had he just made his life so complicated?

'Hello?' The call was eventually answered.

'Elizabeth, thank God.'

'Keith? Is that you?' his sister asked.

'Yes, it's me. I've just seen in the papers about what's happened to the Mercers. Have you heard?'

'Yes. It's all everyone's talking about.'

'Do the police know who's done it yet?'

'I don't know. I don't think so. Where are you?'

'I'd rather not say.'

'Why not?'

'The least you know, the better.'

'Keith, what's going on? What have you done now?'

'I haven't done anything. Why? What have people been saying?'

'Nothing. Keith, you're not making any sense.'

'Elizabeth, I think something bad's going to happen.'

'I don't like this. You're scaring me. Look, come home.'

'I can't.'

'Why not?'

'I just . . . I can't. Look, I want you to know that I'm not a bad person.'

'I know you're not.'

'Has anyone called you or asked about me?'

'No.'

'Good. Look, I'm really sorry for everything I said to you the other day.'

'There's no need to apologize. You were right.'

'No. I wasn't. I never understood how things were between you and Ruby. I should have been there for you more. I wish there was something I could do to make up for it.'

'Keith, you're scaring me. You're not going to do anything stupid, are you?'

He sighed. 'Elizabeth, I have no idea what I'm going to do.'

Elizabeth Lumb was ten years older than her brother. She lived alone in a three-bedroom semi-detached house on a quiet road not ten minutes' walk away from where the Mercers lived in Fulwood. She stood in the neat and tidy hallway of her home with the phone to her ear. She had a confused look on her pale face.

'That was Keith. He sounded very strange,' she said loudly, aiming her voice upstairs. She walked slowly into the living room. 'I think something's happened. I think he might have done something. He mentioned the Mercers. I don't know what I'm going to tell mum when I go over this afternoon.'

She sat down on the armchair and looked ahead at the blank television screen and saw her reflection staring back at her. 'What would you do, Ruby?' she asked herself.

Chapter Twenty-Eight

Christian had felt his mobile phone vibrate in his pocket several times while he and Matilda were in the police station. It was only when they were heading back to the car when he had the chance to take it out and have a look.

'Oh my God,' he said, stopping in his tracks.

'What is it?'

'Kesinka's been assaulted by Leah Ridgeway.'

'What?' Matilda asked.

'According to Sian, Ranjeet is with her now in the Hallamshire. Leah's at the station.'

'Bloody hell! You leave the building for five minutes and all hell breaks loose. Drop me at the hospital then go and interview Leah, find out what she's playing at.' Matilda jumped into the front passenger seat and slammed the door behind her. 'There's something about that family that doesn't make sense. I don't like that Leah and Oliver either.'

'Why not?'

'I don't know yet,' she replied. 'Look, just put your foot down and let's get back to Sheffield. Once we've sorted this mess out we'll go and have a word with Keith's sister.'

Christian slammed his foot down on the accelerator and

skidded the wheels as he took a sharp right-hand turn out of the car park.

'I thought today was going to be such a good day, too,' Matilda said. *I should have kept my big fat mouth shut.*

Matilda was greeted with a huge smile from Kesinka and a look of relief from Ranjeet who was sat by her bed.

'Kesinka, are you all right?'

'I'm fine,' she said. 'It was a bang on the head, nothing more.'

'She's got high blood pressure, too,' Ranjeet said.

'That's got nothing to do with the fall.'

'What happened?' Matilda asked. Before Kesinka could reply, Matilda asked the woman in the next bed if she could steal a chair for a few minutes. She sat down and listened as Ranjeet held his wife's hand firmly. Matilda looked at the array of monitors she was hooked up to. She didn't know what any of them were for, but assumed she was out of danger as she wouldn't be sitting up in bed talking.

'So it wasn't an assault as such?' Matilda asked.

'It was,' Ranjeet leapt in. 'She swung her arm back. She lashed out. She should be charged.'

'Don't be ridiculous, Ranjeet. There were extenuating circumstances. She's just found out her whole family has been murdered. She was on edge, that's all. I don't want to press charges,' she said to Matilda.

'That's not what you were saying half an hour ago,' Ranjeet said.

'Leave it,' Kesinka said through gritted teeth.

'What were you saying half an hour ago?' Matilda asked with a frown.

'She was saying that Leah was possessed. Her eyes were wide and staring. It was like she was determined to take Rachel out of the hospital and nothing was going to stop her.'

'Is this true?'

Kesinka nodded.

'She also said she thought she was on drugs,' Ranjeet continued.

'I did not say that.' She looked at Matilda who looked back with a raised eyebrow. 'I said she had the look of someone who'd taken something. You know, when they get that wide-eyed stare?'

Matilda nodded. 'There's something not right with that family. Oliver and Leah aren't telling us the whole story and I don't like being lied to.'

'Do you want me to . . .?'

'You're not doing anything,' Ranjeet interrupted his wife. 'You're not allowing her back to work, surely? This is the second time something's happened. I will not risk losing you or the baby.'

'What have the doctors said?'

'I've got to stay in here until my blood pressure drops, but apart from that, I'm fine.'

'She's not fine at all.'

'Ranjeet, I think you're probably contributing to my high blood pressure. Will you calm down? And let go of my hand, you're cutting off all the circulation in my fingers,' she said, snatching her hand out of his grasp.

'Sorry.'

'When is your maternity leave due to start?'

'Not for another couple of months yet. Please don't make me go on leave early.'

'I'll have a word with the ACC. You may be restricted to office duties.'

'I don't mind. Anything as long as I don't have to sit at home with my mother calling round every five minutes.'

Matilda smiled. She told Ranjeet to take the rest of the day off, returned the chair to the heavily pregnant and red-faced woman in the next bed and left the ward. Matilda had never wanted children, and often felt uncomfortable around pregnant women.

There was one brief moment, not long after James died, where she wished they'd had children. No baby could have been a substitute, but it would have been nice to have looked into a child's eyes and seen a reflection of her husband. As she walked down the corridor, she wondered what a child of an architect and a detective would have grown up like?

Matilda was almost at the main entrance of Hallamshire Hospital when she heard her name being called. She turned around to see Rory trotting towards her.

'Sorry, I would have shouted boss, but I'm guessing quite a few people answer to that around here.'

Matilda smiled. The old Rory seemed to be back. 'What are you doing here?'

'There was a consultant who knew Serena Mercer. I thought it better to chat to him in person rather than over the phone.'

Matilda immediately thought of the detectives in Barnsley. She wondered how long it would be before Valerie clamped down on the cost of petrol and wear and tear on the pool cars.

'And?'

'Fancy treating me to a coffee?' He smiled.

They went to the canteen, where Matilda bought them both a coffee and a chocolate chip muffin. She rarely claimed money back on expenses for little things like coffees. Matilda was in the fortunate position of having a comfortable bank balance.

James had left her very well off, and he had a good insurance policy which paid out upon his death. The house she sold went for more than she expected, and she didn't spend much as she was always either working or at home reading a book. She understood times were difficult for people like Rory and Scott who were trying to get a foot on the property ladder. Matilda remembered saving up two thousand pounds for a deposit on her first flat. She would be laughed out of the estate agency now if she offered such a little amount.

Rory bit off a large chunk of muffin and washed it down with a slug of tea. 'Lovely.'

'How do you stay so slim with all the crap you eat?' Matilda asked.

'I go to the gym five times a week.'

For such a small word, 'gym' frightened the life out of Matilda. She couldn't think of anything worse than being in a room full of sweating poseurs.

'So, this consultant,' she prompted.

'Mr Edward HillierPendleton, to give him his full name,' Rory said.

'Very posh.'

'Well, he tried to act posh. He had the pinstripe suit and everything, but I saw *The Sun* in his top drawer,' he laughed. 'Anyway, he's worked with Serena Mercer on and off for about twelve years. He said she was a lovely woman, brilliant at her job, couldn't fault her professionally, but he went to a party once where Serena was there with Clive and it changed his whole view of her.' Rory paused while he had another bite of muffin.

'Go on,' Matilda was on the edge of her seat. She hadn't even touched her muffin, or the orange tea.

'When she went to these functions on her own, she was always laughing and joking, joining in, had a few drinks, but as Clive was there, she was very withdrawn. She constantly kept looking at him as if for his approval before she said or did anything.'

'That's not so unusual; a lot of people behave differently when their other half is around. My dad can hardly get a word in edgeways when my mother's with him.'

'He said that after that night, he picked up on things he'd never noticed before. If she was asked anywhere she'd say she'd have to ask Clive. Or it was always Clive's booked us to go here, Clive says we should go there. Everything was always about Clive. And,' Rory leaned forward and lowered his voice, 'he's not sure, but he got the impression that Clive used to hit Serena.'

'Why did he think that?'

'He had no proof, but it was all in her behaviour.'

'So what are we saying; Clive was a bully and Serena was abused?'

'It looks that way.'

'But that doesn't help us. If it was just Clive who was killed, then maybe, but why was Serena killed?'

'I don't know.'

'The crime was frenzied, savage. I can just about get my head around Jeremy and Rachel being in the way but someone hated Clive and Serena. If abuse was the motive, why kill Serena and Jeremy? No. The killer hated the whole family.'

Matilda sat back in her seat and looked around the canteen. The more people they spoke to about this case, the more confusing it became. The neighbours thought they were perfect, but now it appeared Clive may have abused his wife. There was a hair found at the scene but it belonged to a man whose most heinous crime was burglary. Leah's mental state seemed to be all over the place, and goodness knows what Oliver was hiding.

'Are you eating your muffin?' Rory asked.

'What? No, take it.'

'Thanks. I missed lunch.'

'Lunch?' She looked at her watch. It was almost four o'clock.

Matilda caught a lift back to the station with Rory. He drove with one hand on the wheel and the other stuffing his face with chocolate chip muffin. Matilda gazed out of the window. It was starting to rain, only a fine drizzle, but enough for people to put umbrellas up. It was dark outside, but it was still early, still plenty of the working day left. However, Matilda was looking forward to getting home, lighting the fire in the living room and curling up on the sofa with a good book.

Her mobile burst into life, shaking her from her reverie. Typical. She could never have a few minutes alone with a positive thought.

'DCI Darke,' she answered without looking at the display.

'Matilda, Kate Stephenson. How are you?'

Matilda bit her tongue to stop herself from swearing. She was never any good at talking to the press, especially when it was the editor and not just a lowly journalist.

'I'm fine thanks, Kate. Yourself?'

'I'm well. Circulation is up slightly. You'll be pleased to know Danny Hanson was named Young Reporter of the Year.'

'Really? Well, that's great. Tell him congratulations from me,' she said, though it pained her to do so.

'You can tell him yourself. You're on speaker phone and he's sitting right beside me.'

Matilda bit her tongue too hard and tasted blood. 'Hello Danny. Congratulations. You must be thrilled.'

'I am, thank you,' came the cheerful reply from the young

journalist. 'It was my work on the Steve Harrison case that got me the award. I mentioned you in my acceptance speech.'

Why is there never anything around to kick the shit out of when you need it?

'Glad I could be of service,' she seethed. 'So, Kate, did you ring for a reason?'

'Yes I did. I had a call this afternoon from an anonymous source about the killing of the Mercer family. Is it true that members of South Yorkshire Police had the killer in custody and allowed him to escape leading him to commit his crimes?'

Matilda closed her eyes. She had a feeling Kate was going to ask that. Who the bloody hell had given her that information?

'I'm afraid I can't comment on that, Kate.'

'Really? The source is reliable so we will be running the story. I wanted to offer you a right to reply.'

'In that case I'd ask you to contact ACC Masterson's office for an official statement. Goodbye.' She disconnected the call before Kate could say anything else.

'I'm guessing that was the press,' Rory said.

'It certainly was.'

'Not good news?'

'The press doesn't deliver good news. They don't know the meaning of the term.'

She turned to gaze out of the side window. The Sheffield scenery went by in a blur. Dusk was beginning to set. Another day was almost over and the case was still no closer to being solved.

Despite the forensic evidence telling her Keith Lumb was the killer, her instinct told her otherwise. She believed the truth lay closer to home.

Chapter Twenty-Nine

Sian had noticed TDC Finn Cotton was getting fatigued sitting at his desk staring at his laptop all day, so changed the appointment with the professional photographer. Instead of him coming into the station, they would go and visit him. When she told this to Finn, his face lit up. It would be his first journey out of the office since he started in HMET.

'How are you settling in?' she asked in the car as they drove through the busy streets of Sheffield towards Mansfield Road.

'Great, thanks. I'm loving the work. This case is very interesting,' he said with a smile. 'Nice to get out of the office, though. I was getting a bit stiff sat at my desk all day.'

'Not all cases are as interesting as this one. So, whereabouts do you live, Finn?'

'Heeley.'

'Still with your family?'

'No, with my wife.'

'Wife?' She was stunned. Finn didn't look old enough to shave let alone get married. 'How old are you?'

'Twenty-two.'

'Twenty-two and you're married?' She took her eyes off the road and had to brake harshly for a red light. 'How long have you been married?'

'About eighteen months.'

'How old's your wife?'

'Twenty-eight.'

'Oh.'

At twenty-two, the last thing on Sian's mind had been marriage. She was too busy studying by day, partying by night and ignoring every word of warning her parents gave her.

She indicated left and turned into the industrial estate. She found the small unit the photographer worked from and parked in the visitor's parking space. She would love to have continued chatting to Finn, get all the gossip on him and his wife. Maybe on the journey back.

Professional photographer, Peter Parker, didn't match the image Sian had made of him from their conversation on the phone. His deep voice gave the impression he was in his forties, of a large build, and, for some reason, Sian expected a bushy beard. What greeted them upon arrival was a young man in his early-twenties with dark hair and piercing eyes; Elijah Wood but without the Frodo ears.

His small, untidy office was full of Spider-Man memorabilia (obviously). He made them both a coffee from an expensive-looking machine and loaded up his bank of large computer screens. As she looked around, Sian wondered how a man of such young years could afford a set up like this.

Peter seemed to have read her mind. He placed his left leg on the desk and pulled up his trousers showing a titanium leg. 'Roller coaster crashed at a theme park in Germany. I got a good solicitor and a hefty compensation pay out,' he said with a smile on his face. 'My footballing days are over but I'm doing a job I love, and I've got a great life attending weddings and parties.'

Sian found his positive attitude, his confidence, to be infectious. What an admirable young man.

'Is Peter Parker your real name?' Finn asked.

He chuckled. 'Yes it is. I hated it when I was at school. I lost count of the amount of times I was asked if my spidey-sense was tingling. However, now I use it to my advantage. The kids at parties love it.'

Finn looked around the office, wide-eyed. Obviously, a Marvel fan.

'First of all, I've got to say, I'm loving being involved in police work,' Peter said. 'I know it sounds ghoulish, but who doesn't fantasize about detectives needing your help in a big murder case?'

'You have some strange fantasies, Mr Parker,' Sian said, sipping her coffee.

'Call me Peter.'

'Do you get many bookings based on your name?' Finn asked, looking at a wall of photographs.

'I get a lot of kids' parties. I'm sure some of them think I am actually Spider-Man. Still, if it helps business.'

'What can you tell me about the Mercer wedding on Sunday?' Sian asked, getting on topic.

Peter's smile dropped in respect for the dead. 'One of the better, classier weddings I've attended. It's difficult to believe how it's all turned out. Frightening. Life's fragile. I know that more than most. We have to get what we can out of it while we're here. Anyway, it was a brilliant day, bloody cold, but the sun was out so I got some amazing pictures.'

He turned to the bank of computers and brought up a slideshow of the Mercer wedding photographs. 'Now, these are all in a raw state. I don't want you thinking I'm shite at my job,' he said. 'I haven't had a chance to play around with exposition and editing yet, you understand.'

As he spoke, the photographs changed at two-second intervals. Leah looked completely different from the emotional wreck in the interview rooms. The dress was elegant and figure-hugging. Oliver was very handsome in his three-piece suit. Serena beamed with pride in a lilac dress and matching hat. Clive and Jeremy wore grey suits and the same coloured tie. Then there was little Rachel as a bridesmaid. In every picture her smile spread across her face. It was the happiest day of her life and she looked like a princess. Peter was right, life was incredibly fragile.

'Did anyone stand out as being especially awkward, or like they didn't fit in?' Sian asked, not taking her eyes off the display.

'No. Everyone seemed to enjoy themselves. Look at this one of the bride with the bridesmaids. The little girl was loving it. Is she OK?'

'She's fine.'

'Did you go back to the house?'

'Yes. I was booked to take pictures of them cutting the cake, having their first dance.'

'Can we have a look at those ones?'

'Sure.'

In the next series of photos, the atmosphere was less formal, as the reception began. Coats and hats were removed, ties loosened, and bouquets of flowers abandoned. The drink was flowing, and food was being consumed. Leah smiled into the centre of the camera as she and Oliver held the knife to cut the cake. As they danced, Oliver held his wife by the waist. She looked up to him, their eyes locked, smiles almost painfully sweet.

'How long did you stay at the reception?' Sian asked.

'Not long. Once the formalities were over with, I shot off a few casual pictures, had a glass of champagne then left.'

'Did anything out of the ordinary happen?'

'Not that I can remember. Oh, hang on a minute, yes. I was in the kitchen putting my camera away and Mrs Mercer – Serena – was talking to this other woman. I hadn't seen her at the church or during the reception, but she was apologizing to Serena. She said she was sorry and hoped she hadn't hurt their friendship.'

Sian frowned. 'What did Serena say?'

'Nothing. She wasn't really paying that much attention to her. When I was pulling out of the driveway, I saw this woman running down the road, crying her eyes out.'

'Does she appear anywhere on your photographs?'

'I doubt it. Like I said, it was the first time I'd seen her. She would have stood out too; she was wearing something very old-fashioned. She didn't fit in with the rest of the guests.' He studied Sian and Finn's strained expressions. 'Have I given you a massive clue?' He smiled.

'You may just have, Mr Parker. Thanks for your time.'

'No worries. Here, take a couple of cards, hand them out at the station. I do all formal parties and gatherings. Or, if you ever need some artistic crime scene shots, I do excellent black-and-white noir effects.'

Sian took the cards and smiled. She had a mental image of him running around a crime scene asking for the body to be posed in different positions. 'I'll keep you in mind, Spidey.'

Chapter Thirty

Scott had been complaining of a headache, so Sian sent him home. Ranjeet was still at the hospital with his wife, so by the time the evening briefing was due to start there was only Matilda, Sian, Aaron and Christian remaining. Matilda told Rory and Finn to go home too, leaving only the senior officers hanging around. The briefing was to be an intimate affair so they convened in Matilda's office.

Sian entered with her snack drawer and placed it on Matilda's desk, telling everyone to help themselves. Meanwhile, Aaron and Christian went about making everyone a much-needed coffee.

'Who the hell put cereal bars in here?' Christian complained as he rooted around in the drawer for something chocolatey.

'I did,' Matilda said.

'Oh. I'm sure they're lovely,' he said with a fake smile.

'They've got chocolate chips in.'

'But it's a cereal bar. The name alone tells you it's going to be good for you. I like something to dunk in my coffee.'

'Bloody hell, it's like being in charge of a creche sometimes with you lot. Here,' she said, handing him a Snickers from the bottom of the drawer.

His face lit up. 'Lovely.'

'Are you sure the nuts won't count as a health food? I don't want you wasting away.'

'This will do perfectly, thank you.'

Aaron entered, kicking the door closed behind him, carrying a tray of coffees and placing it on the desk. 'They're all the same as we're out of sugar.'

'Typical,' Christian moaned.

'I'll bring some in tomorrow,' Sian said.

'Sian, look at the back of my head,' Christian said, turning around. 'Do you think I'm going bald?'

'No. Why?'

'I just wondered. I feel like I'm thinning on top.'

'Oh dear. You're not entering a mid-life crisis are you? Please don't come to work in a convertible.'

'Or dye your hair,' Aaron chipped in. 'Go grey naturally.'

'Grey? Am I going grey?' Christian panicked and tried to look at his reflection in the back of a teaspoon.

'OK everyone, let's settle down. We can talk about Christian's descent into old age another time,' Matilda said with a smile. 'On the way over here, I had a call from Kate Stephenson at *The Star*. She told me that a reliable source has told her all about Keith Lumb escaping from a police station and going on to commit three murders.'

'Jesus,' Sian uttered. 'Who's blabbed?'

'Nobody's mentioned a call from the press, today,' Aaron said.

'I don't think it's anyone from here, don't worry,' Matilda placated. 'I've had a word with the ACC. The only press contact has been through official channels. No, I think it might be someone from Barnsley.'

'Really?' Christian asked. 'Why?'

'I don't know.' She frowned. 'There's something about that

place that didn't seem genuine. Remember the duty sergeant, Bella Slack? She couldn't do enough for us.'

'And the "if there's a whip-round to be done, it's always down to me to do it". She did seem a bit too good to be true, didn't she?'

'Exactly.'

'I wouldn't have her down as the type to feed the press information, though.'

'Maybe not her, but someone else in the station.'

'What do you want to do?'

'I don't know yet. I'm going to have another word with Valerie. See what the situation is with Barnsley. We'll go from there. Sian, throw us that bag of Minstrels, will you?' Matilda asked. 'Aaron, did you interview Leah?'

'I did. She was full of remorse, kept saying she was sorry and she didn't know what had come over her. I drove her home, but she wasn't too keen on going inside.'

'Why not?' Sian asked.

'I don't know.' He frowned. 'I saw her mother-in-law looking at us through the living room window; she had a face like a slapped arse. I don't think they expected Oliver and Leah to be living with them. It's only a small cottage by the looks of it.'

'Selfish cow,' Sian said. 'How's Kesinka doing?' she asked Matilda.

'She's OK. She's had a scan and the baby is fine. I think she was in shock more than anything. Now, when she comes back to work, she is under strict instructions not to leave this office. She's desk-bound until her maternity leave begins. Understood?' There were nods of ascent from around the room. 'Right then, as day three of the investigation comes to an end, does anyone have any idea who killed the Mercer family?' She looked around at the blank faces. 'Your silence frightens me. OK, the people we need to speak to are, understandably, upset, fragile. However, we need to be more active in our approach.'

'How do you mean?' Aaron asked.

'For a start, I want Rachel interviewed first thing in the morning. Is she still in hospital?'

'She is, but they want to discharge her. There's nothing physically wrong with her and they need the bed. The problem is, what do we do with her?' Sian asked. 'Leah is adamant she wants to take her home.'

'Leah doesn't have a home at the moment. I think we're going have to get social services involved. I don't think Leah is in any fit state to look after a seven-year-old.'

'She does seem very up and down with her emotions,' Aaron commented. 'Understandable, I suppose, given the circumstances.'

'You want her put into care?' Sian frowned.

'No. Just temporary, emergency care. Once this has all died down, hopefully, Leah will be in a more stable position to care for her niece. I want Rachel's interview a priority for tomorrow. We'll get someone from social services to act as a responsible adult and the whole thing handled carefully. I want either Rory or Scott to interview her.'

'Don't you think it should be a woman?' Christian asked, looking at Sian.

Matilda thought, briefly. 'No. I want a DC interviewing her. I think we need to start giving Rory and Scott more responsibility.'

'Rory's not going to resign, is he?' Aaron asked.

'I've managed to get him to hold off on resigning until this case is resolved. Now, if we can give him more to do, allow him to stretch himself, I think it might sway him into staying.' Matilda flicked through her notebook. 'Also, Rory spoke to a consultant at the hospital who knew Serena Mercer quite well. He was under the impression she was being abused.'

'Serena? Who by?'

'Her husband.'

'Bloody hell!'

'I know. Now, it's not something we can ask Leah; besides, I doubt she'd even know. So, we need to go to whoever was closest to Serena. Tomorrow, I want Leah interviewed again, but not here. I don't think she handles the formality of a police station too well. We need to take into account the fact she's had a massive shock. Sian, will you go to her, have a discreet chat. Find out who Serena's best friends were, who she confided in? Then we'll ask them about her being abused by her husband.'

'No problem. Serena was an only child, so there was no sister for her to tell her secrets to, or anything.'

'How about Clive? Did he have any brothers or sisters?'

'He had two brothers,' Aaron said. 'One died at the age of five more than fifty years ago. The other died in 2016. He was caught up in the terrorist attack in Nice on Bastille Day. Remember, when the truck was driven into a crowd of people?'

'Maybe Leah's right, her family are bad luck,' Sian said.

'OK. What about the wedding guests? Have they all been contacted?'

'We've got in touch with more than half the guests so far. They're going to come in to provide fingerprints for elimination purposes over the next few days. It's going to take some sorting out, though,' Aaron said.

'I know, but it needs doing. Aaron, you're in charge of this, but get uniform to handle the drudgery.'

'Thank God for that.' He smiled, reaching out to Sian's snack drawer and helping himself to a Viscount. 'Finn's gone through most of the photos but there's a few he needs either Leah or Oliver to look at.'

'I think probably Oliver would be the best choice for that. He's in a more rational state at present. Have we found out anything about Jeremy Mercer?'

'I've called my contact in Liverpool,' Sian said. 'I'd forgotten what a talker she was. I couldn't get off the phone to her. Anyway, she's sending someone round to his home and the hospital to interview his neighbours and colleagues. She's going to get back to me sometime tomorrow. Now, if my phone rings, I'd be grateful if someone could answer it and take a message. If I speak to her, I'll lose the whole day.' She smiled.

'I'm sorry, Sian, I seem to always be turning to you to see if certain things have been done, but did you get in touch with the GMC?' Matilda asked.

'Yes I did. They've emailed me over everything they've got but my email's down, so I haven't been able to access them yet. I've put the basics up on the board.'

'As soon as it's back up, pass them on to Scott or Rory to go through. That's another avenue to go down.'

'We've got more avenues than Sheffield at the moment,' Christian said, looking down at his notebook.

'I know. I said this was going to be a complex case; it turns out I was correct.'

'You don't know this week's lottery numbers as well, do you?' Christian asked.

'If I knew, do you think I'd tell you?' Matilda smiled. 'Besides, you'd only waste it on hair transplants.'

There was a ripple of laughter from Sian and Aaron. Christian didn't join in, though he did place a hand to the crown of his head.

'Any more from forensics?' Matilda asked.

'The fingerprints that were found in the bedroom Rachel was sleeping in,' Aaron began. 'They belong to Keith Lumb.'

'So that's the hair and the fingerprints then? We need to find where he is if we're saying he's our prime suspect. I'll go and have a word with his sister tomorrow,' Matilda said. *I'm going to be doing a lot tomorrow. Fingers crossed it's about forty hours long.*

'But is he a prime suspect?' Christian asked with a frown. 'Barnsley painted him out to be a petty thief, not a triple killer.'

'I know but we have to go where the evidence takes us. Right now, it's all pointing to Keith.'

'Do you think we should put out an alert? He could try to skip the country,' Sian said.

'I've thought of that, but we'll wait until we see what the sister says. He may have been in contact with her. She could be hiding him for all we know. Aaron, did forensics say anything about those bloodstained clothes they found in the Mercers' house?'

'Yes, hang on.' He placed his coffee cup on the floor and flicked through his notes. 'I've got it here somewhere. Here we go: there were a few hairs on the inside of the hooded sweater. Some had roots, so they're going to test them against the hair that was found under Serena's fingernail. They're really stretched at the moment as they're testing everything found in the marquee too. Do you want me to ask them to make it a priority?'

'Absolutely not. Do you have any idea how much they charge for a rush job?' Matilda glanced out of the window and saw it was dark. 'I think we should leave it there for now. We've covered a lot of ground today, but we've still so much to do. Go home, have a sleep. Maybe when we wake up fresh tomorrow we might have thought of something else.'

'That's the problem with a case like this,' Christian said, standing up, 'it occupies your dreams as well as your waking thoughts.'

Everyone filed out of the room, leaving Matilda alone at her desk. She watched through her open door as they turned off their computers, put on coats and left the suite, chatting as they headed for the lifts. Alone, Matilda opened her laptop and checked her emails. One stood out among the spam and news-letters – the crime scene photos from Sebastian Flowers. She opened the email, read the short message, then clicked on the attachments. There were hundreds of them.

Matilda leaned in close and looked at the scenes of carnage. Jeremy Mercer was found slumped at the bottom of the stairs, lying in a pool of his own blood. On the first-floor landing, Clive Mercer had all but bled out as dozens of stab wounds to the neck almost decapitated him. Sprays of blood hit the ceiling and the far wall. The carpet was saturated. In the glorious technicolour photographs, Clive was deathly pale as his wide-eyed blank expression looked out at her from the richness of the blood that surrounded him. In the attic bedroom, Serena Mercer was hanging half out of her bloodstained bed. The arterial spurts soaked the white cotton sheets, the sprays from the knife were high. A close-up of Serena showed her intestines hanging out of her body, spilling onto the bloody mattress like something from a sick horror movie. Matilda winced at this photo. She could understand why Lucy Dauman found the scene so difficult to process. Some crimes defied explanation. This was savage. Whoever could inflict such pain, horror, torment on another human was beyond evil. She couldn't look at any more. She closed the file. These photographs should only be looked at when absolutely necessary.

Matilda sat back in her chair and frowned as she wondered what kind of a killer she and her team were looking for. She realized she had no idea what Keith Lumb looked like. She logged onto the PNC and entered his details. Up popped a mug shot of their prime suspect. Whatever she had been expecting, it was fair to say, she wasn't expecting this: Keith was five foot seven inches tall, thin, with staring pale blue eyes and full lips. He looked younger than his twenty-seven years. He had the faraway gaze of a lost little boy. This was not the face of a triple killer. Yet the forensics did not lie.

Matilda's mobile rang, making her jump. In the silence of her office, the shrill ring resounded off the walls. She looked at the display and saw it was Pat Campbell calling her. She answered, not taking her eyes from the sad expression of Keith Lumb on her laptop.

'Pat, good evening. What can I do for you?'

'Sally Meagan's had another call from Carl.'

'Oh. Same number.'

'No. A different one. Did you manage to check the first number?'

'I did. It was from a burner phone. No trace.'

'No surprise there. If I give you the other number can you look it up?'

'Sure.'

Matilda changed to a different screen on her laptop and entered the mobile number Pat gave her. 'How is she?'

'A wreck.'

'Was she alone when she received the call?'

'Yes, she was. Apparently, Philip's hardly at home. I'm going to see him tomorrow at one of their restaurants.'

'I wouldn't be surprised if they didn't split up before long,' Matilda said.

'I was thinking the same. If they do, it'll kill her.'

'I'm afraid the second call was from another burner phone too,' Matilda said, looking at the screen.

'Shit. Someone's playing with her, aren't they?'

'I think that's more than likely.'

'Why would someone be so cruel?'

'Do you really need to ask that question?'

'I suppose not. There are some sick bastards out there,' Pat said through gritted teeth. 'When we find them, I hope you throw the book at them.'

'Does Sally really believe it's Carl calling her?'

'Yes, she does. She's adamant it's his voice.'

'I know it sounds daft but maybe it is.'

Pat audibly sighed. 'Sally said she's asked him on both calls where he is, and each time, he's hung up. Now, if it was really Carl, he wouldn't hang up. He'd tell her.'

'Maybe he didn't hang up. Maybe he had the phone snatched from him.'

'He called her mummy. If he's alive, he's ten years old now. How many ten years old call their mother mummy?'

'I don't know any ten year olds.'

'Well my kids didn't call me mummy when they were ten. I won't tell you what they did call me either.'

'So, you think it's some kind of scam.'

'I do. Oh, while I'm on, Mat, I was going through the file you gave me. Now, when you spoke to the kidnappers on the night of the ransom drop, you said they had Yorkshire accents. Can you remember?'

Matilda closed her eyes tight. 'Of course I can remember. I've been over that night thousands of times. It never goes away.'

'And they definitely had Yorkshire accents.'

'They were local, yes. I'd stake my life on it. Why do you ask?'

'Picture the scenario. You're local. You've kidnapped a kid for ransom but it goes wrong. So, what do you do with the kid?'

'Do I have to answer that?' Matilda asked, knowing what Pat wanted to hear.

'You kill him,' she said abruptly. 'Unfortunately, you've now got a dead body to get rid of. What do you do with him?'

'I really wish you wouldn't ask me these questions.'

'You either bury him, or you put him somewhere.'

'Where?'

'I was chatting to the woman next door whose grandson is an urban explorer. She said Sheffield has more abandoned buildings than you'd think. She's going to call her grandson and get me a list.'

'Hang on, you think Carl has been killed and dumped in an abandoned building?'

'I'm saying it's a possibility. One that hasn't been looked into.'

'If there are as many abandoned buildings in Sheffield as you're suggesting, I can't justify sending a search team into every single one.'

'You don't have to,' Pat interrupted. 'Gwen next door said her grandson will look into some for me. He's already been in loads. If he'd come across a body, he'd have contacted the police, so there's probably not that many left. I might ask him to take me on one of his jaunts, it sounds fun.'

'You bloody will not,' Anton called out in the background.

'Ignore him,' she whispered.

'Pat, please, be careful.'

'I will.'

'Promise me you'll keep me informed of everything you're doing.'

'I will,' she groaned. 'I best be off, I'm getting funny looks from someone who doesn't know how to work an oven.'

Matilda laughed. They said goodbye and Matilda hung up. She leaned back in her chair and looked at her laptop and the dead-eyed stare from Keith Lumb looking back at her.

'You've never killed anyone in your life, have you?' she said to him.

Chapter Thirty-One

Matilda was shattered. She wanted to go home, grab a book, and sit in front of a roaring fire. She pictured her living room with the red painted walls that reminded her of blood. She would need to pop along to B&Q at some point and buy some tester pots of paint. There was no way she could live with that now. It was a shame really as it looked good with her furniture. Maybe an earthy green or a deep blue.

On the drive home, Matilda wasn't paying much attention to the roads and the traffic signs. Twice she almost went through a red light. Before too long, she pulled up, turned off the ignition and was about to climb out of the car when she realized she'd driven to Adele's house in Hillsborough.

What the hell is wrong with me?

She knew the answer to that. Despite saying she wanted to be alone and lock herself away from the outside world, what she wanted more than anything else was company. The massive contradiction filling her mind obviously counted for her sleepless nights and her constant headaches.

When Adele opened the front door, Matilda squinted as the warm light from within blinded her.

'You look like you've been ridden hard, and put away wet,' Adele said.

'And on that note, I'll be off home,' Matilda said, turning away from the doorstep.

'I'm sorry. I didn't mean it. Come in.' Adele grabbed her by the arm and led her into the warmth of the house.

The kitchen was bright and there was a smell of something wonderful baking in the oven. Matilda sat down at the breakfast table and had a glass of white wine placed in front of her. Now this is a home.

'How are things?' Adele asked, sitting opposite her.

'You really don't want to know.'

'How come?'

'It's complex.'

'I can imagine. The post mortems alone were a nightmare, especially Clive Mercer's. Did Ranjeet tell you what happened?'

'No.'

'Oh, I didn't think he would, actually,' she said with a twinkle in her eye. 'You know his head was basically only attached with a couple of tendons?'

'Yes.'

'Well, it came off completely when he was on the mortuary table. We opened the body bag, lifted him up and the head came off. It fell onto the floor and landed at Ranjeet's feet. I've never heard anyone scream like that before,' she said, stifling a laugh.

'Oh God. Poor Ranjeet,' Matilda said.

They both burst out laughing.

'I honestly thought he was going to faint,' Adele said, wiping her eyes.

'No wonder he was quiet.'

'Speaking of quiet, have you found out what's wrong with Scott?' Adele asked, going over to the oven to see how the meal was doing.

'Not yet. I think I know but I don't want to say anything until he does.'

'Ooh, gossip. Are you planning on sharing?'

'I'd better not. Has Chris said anything?'

'No.'

'Is he in?'

'No. He and Scott are out running again.'

'They're quite close, aren't they?'

'Chris and Scott? Well, they have a lot in common. I was doing a lasagne until I sniffed the beef, so we're having a veggie one instead. You staying?'

'If you don't mind. It smells lovely. What do they have in common?' Matilda asked.

'Who?' Adele was busying herself with dishing up the meal.

'Chris and Scott.'

'Oh. Well, there's the running. They like the same music and films. They often go to the pictures together.'

'What about Rory?'

'What about him?'

'Does he join them?'

'I don't know. Chris hasn't mentioned him so I guess not. What's wrong?' Adele asked looked up at Matilda's perplexed expression.

'Nothing. Just thinking.'

'You'll give yourself a headache. Shall we eat?'

After the meal, which was exactly what Matilda needed, they went into the living room where they slumped on the sofa with their feet up. The real fire was blazing. Matilda could have fallen asleep, she felt so comfortable.

'Have you heard any more from your hunky architect?' Adele

asked in a dopey voice as she relaxed into the sofa. She was a few glasses of wine ahead of Matilda, so she was feeling the effects of the alcohol.

Matilda rolled her eyes. 'I have. He sent me a photo earlier.'

'What of?' Adele's eyes lit up.

'His wood.'

'The dirty sod. Let's have a look.' She sat bolt upright.

'Not that. Bloody hell, Adele, you're disgusting. I was talking about the wood he's going to be using for the beams in the garages.'

'Oh,' she deflated.

'Do you honestly think he would have sent a picture of that?'

'He might have.'

Matilda started laughing and nudged her friend. 'You're pure filth, do you know that?'

'I've been single for a very long time. I have to get my kicks from somewhere.'

'Are you thinking of going back onto the dating scene?'

'You're joking, surely. The last person I went out with turned out to be a paedophile. I'm probably better off on my own.' She took a slug of wine. 'I do miss sex, though,' she said after a while.

'Who doesn't? James was the best lover I ever had.'

'Robson was . . . well, he was adequate,' she said, talking about her ex-husband and Chris's father. 'He knew where all the buttons were, he just didn't bother to press them.'

'Do you ever hear from Robson?'

'No. Chris does from time to time. He's too busy with his new family. Bastard.'

'Not that you're bitter, or anything.'

'Of course not. I hope he's blissfully happy with Caron. Stupid name. I need more wine,' she said, easing herself up from the sofa and staggering out of the room.

'Not for me. I'd better make a move while I can still drive. Thank you for a delicious meal. As soon as I've got past the stage where I don't want to use anything because it's too new I'll return the favour.'

They hugged on the doorstep and Matilda headed for her car on the driveway. As she drove from Hillsborough to the outskirts of the city, she thought of how sad Adele had looked. Chris was settled into his career, he was socializing more, and it wouldn't be long until he had saved up enough money to move out. Adele really would be on her own, then. Matilda wondered if she had been selfish in choosing a house in the middle of nowhere. She should have moved closer to Adele. They could have grown old and lonely together.

Closing the front door behind her, Matilda stood in the hallway. There wasn't a cloud in the sky and the light from the full moon cast long, sinister shadows through the stained glass onto the tiled floor. Matilda made a mental note to go shopping for a curtain for the door this weekend. It looked creepy.

She went into the kitchen and flicked the kettle on, pulling down the blinds and making the house secure while it boiled. She made her tea in an oversized mug and took it into her library. It wasn't quite eleven o'clock yet. She had time to sort out the books that were still in boxes, waiting to be shelved.

The collection of crime novels, which Matilda continued adding to, was inherited from Jonathan Harkness, a killer she had met upon returning to work after a period of mourning her husband. She had liked Jonathan. She felt great sympathy for him. Unfortunately, he turned out to be a multiple murderer.

When he took his own life, he left instructions with his solicitor to have his vast collection of books given to Matilda. At first she hated the idea, but the more she read, the more she used reading fiction as a form of therapy to distract her brain from tormenting her about Carl Meagan and missing James, the more she understood why Jonathan had sought solace in fiction.

Matilda closed the door on the library, took her cup of cold tea into the kitchen and placed it in the sink to wash at some point and headed upstairs. As she made her way across the landing towards her bedroom she stopped and looked out of the window overlooking the back garden. It was almost as bright as day with the moon so big and full shining down. It lit up the grass, the naked trees, the view looking out into the countryside. It was serene, relaxing. She opened the window.

A blast of cold air hit her and she shivered. She leaned out and took a lungful of the winter cold. It smelled fresh. The sound of branches clacking against each other in the breeze echoed. There was no other sound to be heard; no traffic, no noise from neighbours, no drunks staggering home, nothing but blissful silence.

By the time Matilda had changed and climbed into bed she was freezing cold having stood at the open window for more than half an hour. As much as she wanted to read, she decided to have a night off and hunkered down under the duvet to warm up. She soon drifted off and fell into a deep sleep.

Matilda rarely remembered her dreams. When she woke the first thing she saw was the photograph of James on her bedside table. She smiled and hoped she had been dreaming of him, of them, in happier times. A dream was forming, a smile spread on her lips when her eyes shot open.

She knew exactly why Jeremy had died. She knew why Rachel had been left alive and tied up. The killer was a monster, of that she had no doubt, but this particular monster also had a conscience and, right now, he would be suffering for what he had done. Someone would notice a change in his personality. He would be withdrawn, on edge, terrified every time someone came to the door or the phone rang. He wouldn't be sleeping or eating or going to work. He would be scared of his own shadow. This should make him easier to find. This, however, did not fit with their suspect. For some reason, Matilda knew Keith Lumb was not a triple killer. If she was correct, the entire crime scene and the forensics were a complete lie, which meant the killer was someone very savvy and very dangerous. The only people capable of this were those with knowledge of how a crime scene worked, what the police looked for at a murder scene, and how the case was going to progress.

Matilda's blood ran cold. She knew who the killer was.

Chapter Thirty-Two

Breakfast was a chore for Matilda. She wasn't a fan but knew she'd feel sick by the time she arrived at the station if she didn't have something to eat. She sat at the table in the kitchen, sipping at the strong black coffee and looking at the bowl of cereal in front of her with contempt. She forced a spoonful of cornflakes into her mouth and began chewing.

Matilda had had a disturbed night's sleep. Since the revelation that she possibly knew the killer, she'd been unable to rest. Now morning was here, all she wanted to do was go back to bed and hibernate under the duvet. The doorbell rang making her jump. She was almost nodding off into her cornflakes.

Matilda pulled open the door to find Scott Andrews on her doorstep. He was dressed for work in a smart suit and coat. His shoes were polished. His hair was neatly styled. The look on his face was one of haunting, deep-set worry.

'Scott. Is everything all right?' she asked.

'Not really. Is there any chance of a word?'

'Of course. Come on in.' She stepped back and he entered.

He looked around the hallway at the high ceiling, the Victorian tiled floor and the oak doors. 'Wow. This is really nice,' Scott said. He smiled at his boss, but the smile didn't reach his eyes. They were wide, staring. He looked lost.

'Thanks. Come into the kitchen. I've got a pot of coffee on.'

'I've had a couple already this morning,' he said, following her.

He marvelled at the new kitchen. He ran his hand along the wooden worktops, popped his head around the corner into the utility room, which, he remarked, was larger than his bathroom, and sat at the breakfast table, smoothing down the tablecloth.

She put the bowl of soggy cornflakes in the sink. 'So, what can I do for you?' she asked.

'I think you should take me off the case,' he said, not looking at his boss, but somewhere in the distance.

'I think we definitely need coffee for a conversation like this.'

She chose two mugs from the cupboard, picked up the cafetière and sat directly opposite him at the table so he would have to look up and make eye contact. She poured him a cup, added milk, and pushed it across to him.

'So, why should I take you off the case?'

He picked up the mug and inhaled the caffeine before taking a sip. 'This is good.' He took another sip and gently put the mug down. 'The thing is, I know something. About someone.'

'OK. Someone to do with the case?'

'Yes.'

'Who?'

'Oliver,' he replied, swallowing hard.

'Oliver Ridgeway?'

'Yes.'

'You know him?'

'Yes.'

'Are you related to him?'

'No.'

'Then how do you know him?'

His face reddened. He adjusted himself on his seat. He looked uncomfortable; not only with the conversation but with himself. He swallowed a few more times, which seemed to cause him some pain.

'I'm gay,' he said, looking deep into his coffee cup.

'Right. And?'

He gave a nervous laugh and looked up. 'Oh. You don't seem . . . you know . . . upset or anything.'

'Why should I be upset?'

'Because . . . well, I don't know.'

'To be honest, Scott, I've suspected you were gay for some time. I could tell there was something eating away at you lately, but I've not wanted to push you to open up. Does anyone else know?'

'No.'

'Not even Rory?'

'No.'

'But you live together.'

'I know. It's never been an issue before. I've always wanted to just keep my head down and get on with my career. I've never been bothered about getting married, having children or anything, but . . .'

'You've met someone?'

'Sort of,' he said, blushing.

'You remind me so much of me. When I first started in this job, I wanted to be the best detective I could be. Getting married and having children was something that would get in the way of that, so I took it off the agenda. Then I met James and it was like being hit by a thunderbolt.'

'I know what you mean,' he smiled.

'Look, Scott, your secret is safe with me. I won't tell anyone. However, for your own sanity, your own happiness, it might be best if you tell others, especially Rory.'

'I know. I want to, but, I don't know how people will react,' he said, staring down into his coffee cup.

'To be honest it's got nothing to do with anyone else. What people do in their private life is their own affair. As long as it doesn't interfere with work, it doesn't matter.'

'I'll think about it. I will.'

'I'm always here for you, Scott,' Matilda said, reaching across and placing her hand on top of his. 'Do you know why I chose you for my team? It's because I knew you were good at your job, you have the makings of an excellent detective, but you're also a good man. You care. And I think of you as a friend.'

'Really?'

'Yes. I'm not just here to help you with all things work related. You can trust me, and you can rely on me not to say anything to anyone else.' His features seemed to be softening. She knew it must be difficult for someone as sensitive as Scott to open up, but she was pleased he'd chosen her to confide in. 'So, have you always known you were gay?'

'Yes. Ever since I was a child.'

'Your parents don't know?'

'No.'

Matilda gave the young DC a sympathetic smile. 'I bet this house your mum already does.'

'Probably,' he smirked.

'So, going back to the case, what do you know about Oliver Ridgeway?'

'I'm on a dating app. You know, a gay one?' he said, almost embarrassed. 'I haven't met anyone yet. Most of them just seem to want one thing. Anyway, a few weeks ago, I got chatting to a guy on there. It was Oliver Ridgeway.'

'Are you sure?'

'Definitely.' He took his phone out of his inside pocket. 'We started chatting on this app and got on well, then we swapped numbers. He sent me a few photos. Look,' he handed the phone to Matilda.

'Oh,' was all she said.

'He said he was bisexual. He never mentioned he was getting married. He told me he was single.'

'You didn't meet him?'

'No. He said he was going on holiday. We arranged to meet when he got back. I'm guessing he was talking about his honeymoon.'

'And he didn't recognize you when you interviewed him?'

'No. I only ever sent him one face picture and I was wearing sunglasses. I don't photograph very well so I don't have many,' he said, blushing again.

Matilda smiled. 'Don't be so hard on yourself, Scott. You're a very handsome man. Did Oliver send you any other pictures?'

'Yes. He sent several, including some rude ones, too, which I deleted. I just think maybe I shouldn't be working on this case.'

'On the contrary. Oliver has been hiding something from us. He's leading a double life. We need to confront him about it.'

'But that will mean people finding out about me.'

'Not necessarily. You and I can go and see him and get an explanation from him. Maybe his sexuality doesn't have anything to do with the Mercer family being killed. If so, then it doesn't need to come out.'

'I don't know. I'm not one of those people who like to be defined by their sexuality.'

'And you won't be. Certainly not by me. As far as I'm concerned, you're a detective. Who you sleep with is way down the list of attributes that define who you are. Now, let's strike while the iron's hot.' She drained her coffee cup and stood up, heading out of the kitchen.

On the journey to see Oliver Ridgeway, Matilda had called Christian and told him to lead the morning briefing without her. They knocked on the door of Edward and Sophia Ridgeway and waited for it to be opened.

'Don't look so scared,' Matilda said to Scott.

'Sorry. I get the feeling this is going to be one of those life-changing days.'

'If it is, it will be a change for the better. You'll be able to be yourself.'

'I don't think I know who I am.'

'That will come with time.'

The door opened and a woman in her fifties answered. She was wearing a pink dressing gown and had a white towel wrapped around her head. Judging by her half-made-up face, they had disturbed her getting ready for the day.

'DCI Matilda Darke, South Yorkshire Police. This is DC Andrews,' Matilda said, showing her ID. 'I'd like to speak to Oliver, please.'

'He's not in at the moment. He's at work.'

'Work?' Matilda frowned. 'But he would have been on his honeymoon.'

'Yes, but as he's back home and there's nothing to do he said there was no reason why he shouldn't go to work.'

'But his in-laws have just been murdered,' Scott said.

'Yes. And like Oliver said, the world doesn't stop turning. Bills still need to be paid.'

'How did Leah react to Oliver going back to work?'

'If she ever stops crying, I'll ask her,' Sophia said. Her voice was as harsh as her expression was stern. She looked as if she didn't have a compassionate bone in her body.

'Is Leah in?'

'She's in bed, and I'm going to be late,' she said, making an exaggerated look at her watch. 'If there's nothing else, you'll find Oliver at the Northern General.'

'Have you and your husband given a statement yet?'

'Yes. We were called yesterday. Apparently we need to give our fingerprints.'

'For elimination purposes only. I'm sure you understand.'

'It's a bit out of my way, but I'll pop along one evening after work. Now, if you'll excuse me.' She closed the door before Matilda had chance to say anything else.

'What a lovely woman,' Matilda said to Scott as they headed back for the car.

'Poor Leah. Her family have been murdered and look who she's got for comfort. You can see why she's so desperate to have Rachel with her,' Scott said.

When they found a space in the car park at the Northern General Hospital, Scott took his phone out of his trouser pocket.

'What are you doing?'

'He's online.'

'Who is?'

'Oliver. He's on that dating app now.'

'Show me.' She looked at the phone. 'How can you tell?'

'The green dot on his profile picture means he's online.'

'Is that you?' she asked, pointing at a thumbnail.

'Yes,' he said, taking the phone back.

'It's a good picture. Oh, Scott, I wish you'd get some self-confidence. You're a very good-looking bloke. Let your guard down. Have some fun.'

Take your own advice, Mat.

'I'll try,' he said, putting the phone away in his back pocket.

They eventually found Oliver sitting in the canteen. He was sitting in a corner, looking forlorn. His black coffee and tuna sandwich was untouched. He looked as if he was a million miles away. He probably wished he was.

'Mr Ridgeway?' Matilda asked, making him jump.

'Sorry. I was thinking about . . . something.'

'DCI Darke.'

'Yes. I remember. Sorry. My mind's all over the place.'

'You remember DC Andrews?'

'Sure,' he said, glancing at Scott but not recognizing him.

'Do you mind if we have a seat?'

'No. Do you want to ask more questions?'

'Why have you returned to work so soon?' Matilda asked, pulling out a chair and sitting down.

'There's nothing for me to do at home.'

'Don't you think you should be there for your wife?'

'She keeps saying she wants to be alone. I was just getting in the way.'

'Mr Ridgeway, is there anything you'd like to tell us?'

'Tell you?' He frowned. 'About what?'

'About you.'

He looked from Matilda to Scott then back to Matilda. 'Me? No. I don't think so.'

'Scott,' Matilda turned to the DC.

Scott took a deep breath and licked his lips. He took out his phone and logged on to the dating app. He turned the phone around and showed it to Oliver.

'Shit,' Oliver said. He looked up at Scott. 'Now I recognize you. I thought you looked familiar when you came into the interview room. I didn't think . . .'

'Does Leah know?' Matilda asked.

'Of course she doesn't.'

'Who knows you're on this app?'

'Nobody.'

'You're sure about that?'

'Definitely.'

'Your picture is there for all to see. I'm guessing there are hundreds of men in Sheffield who have seen you online. I doubt it would take much to find out who you are, where you are.'

'So what? What's this got to do with Clive, Serena and Jeremy getting killed?'

'I don't know. Although, if Clive found out his daughter was being lied to, I doubt he's the type of man to keep quiet.'

'Oh,' he said, sitting back and smiling. 'I see. You think I killed Clive because he found out about me?'

'It gives you a motive.'

'No, it doesn't. If Clive found out, do you think he would have allowed the wedding to go ahead?'

'It depends when he found out. Maybe it was too late for him to stop the wedding.'

'Now you're being ridiculous. Look, that app, it's just sex. You should know that,' he said looking at Scott. 'It's meaningless.'

'I don't think Leah would see it that way.'

'Leah doesn't have to know.'

'Really? You don't think your wife, your new wife of less than a week, doesn't need to know what her husband is getting up to behind her back?'

'That's got nothing to do with you,' he said through gritted teeth. 'You're a detective. Your job is to find out who killed her family. This has nothing to do with it.'

'I'll be the judge of that, Mr Ridgeway,' Matilda said. 'We will be talking again.'

'If you threaten me in any way, I'll report you to your superior,' Oliver said, standing up.

'Really? I don't think you're in any position to be issuing threats at the moment, Mr Ridgeway.' Matilda walked away.

'I was going to message you later,' he said to Scott. There was a look of malevolence in his eye. He hadn't liked being caught out and needed to be back in control again. 'We could have had some fun together. Oh well. Your loss, pretty boy.'

Chapter Thirty-Three

The small room was set up to be as comfortable as possible. There was a dark carpet, walls painted a soft, warm colour. Two small sofas and a coffee table. There were tasteless generic prints on the wall, a plastic potted palm in the corner and a box of outdated toys for the younger children to play with. A video camera was set up, pointed towards one of the sofas.

The door opened and Rachel Mercer was shown into the room by the large social worker who had collected her from the Children's Hospital. Everything had been explained to her. So far, she was being incredibly brave.

Rachel was wearing grey tracksuit bottoms and a pink sweater, which Sian had collected for her from the Mercer house. Her dark brown hair was neatly combed and hung lifelessly down her back. Her face was pale, and she looked on the verge of tears. She sat down on the edge of the sofa. She didn't want to be here.

She had already met DC Rory Fleming. He'd shaken her hand and had taken her to the vending machine where he asked her to choose anything she wanted to eat. An extra bar of chocolate had fallen from the machine. This broke the ice. Rory cheered at the free chocolate and said it would taste better because they hadn't paid for it. On choosing a drink, Rachel said her dad didn't allow her to have fizzy pop too often. Rory said, on this occasion, it would be fine.

In the interview room, Rory laid everything out on the table as if they were having a picnic. Behind him was a large window that they couldn't see out of, but Christian and the social worker, Bernice Simpson, could see in.

Rory started the video camera.

'Rachel, tell me about the wedding,' he asked. His voice was light. He wanted to put Rachel at her ease.

She smiled. 'I was a bridesmaid,' she beamed.

'Really? Wow, that's cool. What did you wear?'

'It was an ivory dress with lace on the bodice,' she said with pride.

'I bet you looked lovely.'

'I had my hair done all nice, too. And, Dad said I was allowed to have a bit of make-up on.'

'I bet you looked all grown up. What did you have to do?'

'Well, Auntie Leah had two other bridesmaids but they were older. We each had some flowers, and we walked behind Auntie Leah as she walked up the aisle.'

'Were you nervous?'

'A little bit. But Jane and Angela, they were the other two bridesmaids, they told me what to do.'

'Did you enjoy it?'

'Yes.' She grinned.

'Help yourself to a bar of chocolate.'

She looked down at the selection and picked up a Mars bar and a can of cola. She sat back on the sofa. She seemed to be relaxing.

'Was the wedding fun?'

'It was, but I got bored after a bit. It seemed to go on for ages.'

Rory smiled. 'Church weddings do take a long time. What happened afterwards?'

'Well, we stood outside and had our photo taken. The photographer took so many pictures, but he was funny. He made everyone laugh. He didn't have a real leg. He showed it to me.'

'What was that like?'

'Weird, but kind of cool.'

'Who did you have your picture taken with?'

'Everyone. There were some with me and my dad on our own and some with just us bridesmaids. Auntie Leah said she wanted everyone to be in on the photos.'

'Did you go back to the house then?'

'Yes. We had a big tent up in the back garden.'

'Wow. I bet that was cool.'

'It was. Inside, there were tables around the edges and a massive cake in the corner. There was a dancefloor in the middle. Auntie Leah and Uncle Oliver had the first dance, then everyone joined in.'

'Did you dance?'

'Yes. I had my first dance with Daddy. I stood on his feet,' she beamed. She took a small bite of the chocolate bar but didn't seem to be enjoying it. Rory wondered if it was the thought of her father; their last moments together were so happy. It would have been the biggest day of her life, so far, and it soon turned into a nightmare.

'Did you dance with anyone else?'

'Yes. Grandad, and then Grandma, and Auntie Leah and Uncle Oliver. Then just Uncle Oliver.'

'Do you like your Uncle Oliver?'

'Yes. He's not funny, like Daddy, but he's nice.'

'In what way is he nice?'

'He lets me go out with him and Auntie Leah if they're going anywhere. And, even though we live in Liverpool, they come over to see us a lot.'

'That's nice. What's your Auntie Leah like?'

'She plays with me. She's always buying me clothes for my Barbie. She used to say we were like sisters. I'd like to have had a sister.'

Rory felt sad listening to her talk. She was being incredibly brave, but was it a mask? How long would the nightmares last? What other problems would she have in later life which were born in this massive event? He thought of all the issues teenagers had to deal with; the temptation of sex, drugs, alcohol, the pressure others put on young women to be slim and beautiful. With everything Rachel had been through, those pressures would be magnified.

'Did you stay at the party all night?' Rory asked.

'No. I went to bed early. I was tired.'

'Did you mind?'

'No. Dad took me up to bed. He gave me a plate with a few sandwiches and a slice of cake, and he made me a hot chocolate. I'm not allowed to eat in bed, but it was a special day.'

'And you had Pongo to keep you company, too, didn't you?'

'Yes.' She grinned. 'Where is Pongo?'

'We've got him in our kennels downstairs. He's fine.'

'Can I see him?'

'Soon. I'm guessing *101 Dalmatians* is your favourite film?'

'Yes.' She smiled. 'I love it. I seen it millions of time. I prefer the cartoon version but the puppies in the real version are so cute. Have you seen it?'

'Yes. They're good films. So, did you eat your snack?'

'No. I ate my cake but I gave my sandwiches to Pongo,' she whispered, as if telling Rory a massive secret.

He smiled. 'Did you go straight to sleep afterwards?'

'Not straight away. I played with Pongo for a little bit. Also, the party was really loud downstairs.'

'So, you fell asleep, and you were woken up. Can you remember what it was you heard that woke you up?'

Rachel giggled. 'Daddy said a rude word.'

'Did he?'

'Yes. He was walking along the landing. I think he hit his foot or something because he said a word that sounds like duck that I'm not allowed to say.'

Rory laughed. 'Oh. Naughty daddy.'

'I heard him go downstairs. I tried to go back to sleep but I could hear voices.'

'Whose voices?' Rory asked, leaning forward.

'Daddy's was one of them. I didn't know the other.' She frowned.

'Did you hear what they were saying?'

She thought for a while. 'No. Well, I heard Daddy ask who the other man was, but I didn't hear what he said.'

'But it was definitely a man?'

'I think so. Men talk quieter than women, don't they?'

Rory smiled. 'Sometimes, yes. What happened then?'

'Well, I heard someone coming upstairs. I thought it was Daddy, but then I heard Grandad coming down from the attic. He said that duck word too. I knew he couldn't have been talking to Daddy. Then I . . .' Rachel's bottom lip started to wobble and her eyes filled with tears.

'It's all right, Rachel, take your time,' Rory said. He picked up a box of tissues from the table and handed them to her.

'Grandad screamed,' she said, wiping her eyes. 'It wasn't a loud scream, but it was like a . . . I don't know.'

'Do you think you could make the sound?'

She thought, then nodded. She made a choking sound.

'OK. Could you hear anything else?'

'Yes. There was grunting.'

'Grunting?'

'Yes. And then a loud bang. Then I heard Daddy shouting again, and I heard someone running up the stairs to the attic. Then Daddy shouted for me.'

'He shouted for you? What did he say?'

'He told me to close my door and put a chair under the handle.'

'Did you?'

She shook her head. 'I couldn't. I was so scared. I just stayed in bed with Pongo. I told Daddy I had done, but I didn't. I lied to him,' she cried. Tears rolled down her cheeks and she gasped for breath.

Rory remained where he was on the sofa. He handed her another tissue and took the can of cola from her and put it on the table. He waited until her tears had subsided.

'You didn't lie to him, Rachel, you were frightened. That's OK. Your daddy would have understood that.'

To Rory, it felt like the room was getting hotter. He could feel himself sweating. He didn't know if it was their close proximity, the tension of the interview, or the heat from the radiator but he felt a dampness under his arms and his shirt was sticking to his back. He'd softened his image for Rachel; taken off his tie, undone a top button, and removed his jacket, but he still felt hot under the collar.

'Rachel, what happened next?'

'I was in bed. I was crying,' she sniffled. 'I was holding on to Pongo. The door was kicked open and Pongo started barking. He jumped off the bed and ran towards him and the man kicked Pongo.' She couldn't talk anymore as the tears fell in a torrent.

'Rachel, Pongo is fine. He's not hurt in anyway. We've had a vet look at him and he's walking normally. He's bounding about with his tail wagging.'

'Really?' she asked, a hint of a smile through the tears.

'Yes. As soon as we're finished here, I'll take you to see him.'

'Thank you.'

'Rachel, can you tell me what the man looked like?'

She shook her head. 'I couldn't see his face.'

'Why not?'

'It was dark and he had like a beanie hat on but it was pulled down over his face.'

'OK. Was he tall or short? Fat or thin?'

She took a deep breath to compose herself. 'He was tall.'

'OK. Tall like me?'

'Taller.'

'Right. And was he fat or thin?'

She frowned as she thought. 'I don't know. Sort of . . . medium.'

Rory had an idea. 'Do you watch *The Simpsons*?'

'Yes.' She smiled.

'It's funny, isn't it?'

'Yes. Daddy says I'm like Lisa because I'm always reading.'

'That's good. Reading is important. You should speak to my boss. She loves reading. Anyway, this man, he wasn't fat like Homer?'

'No.'

'Was he big and muscly like Duffman?'

'No. He was normal. Like Principal Skinner.'

'OK. What was he wearing? Was he wearing a suit like Principal Skinner?'

Rachel started crying. The tissue in her hands was soaked. Rory passed her the box. She took one out and placed it next to her on the sofa.

'He was covered in blood. All over.'

'Could you see what he was wearing?'

'It was a onesie,' she sniffled.

'A onesie?' He frowned.

'Yes. Not a Dalmatian one like mine. His was plastic.'

'He was wearing a plastic onesie?'

She nodded.

'Can you remember anything else about him? What kind of shoes was he wearing?'

'I couldn't see his shoes. He had like plastic bags on.'

'Plastic bags over his shoes?'

'Yes.'

'What about his hands?'

She cried again. 'They were red.'

'Did he say anything to you?'

'No. I could hear Daddy shouting but I don't know what he was saying. I was so scared. I didn't move. The man grabbed me and pulled me out of bed.'

'What did he do?'

'He told me to sit in my chair. He pulled the belt off my dressing gown and tied me up with it.'

'Did he tell you to sit in the chair?'

'Yes.'

'So he spoke to you?'

'Yes.'

'What did he sound like? Did he have an accent like mine?'

'Sort of. His voice was deeper, but sort of whispering.'

'Is there anything about him that you can remember? Did he have funny teeth or did his breath smell?'

'Yes,' she said, her eyes widening. 'His breath did smell.'

'What of?'

'It smelled like Daddy's when he gave me a goodnight kiss. Can I see Pongo now? Please.'

'Of course you can. You've been a very good girl, Rachel. You've been really helpful. Now, I'll just go and check we can see Pongo. I'll send Bernice in to look after you for a little bit. Help yourself to some toys.'

He stood up and left the room. As soon as he closed the door behind him, he leaned against the wall and let out an exhausted breath. The door to the observation room next door opened and Christian and Bernice stepped out. Bernice gave him a sympathetic smile before going into the room to be with Rachel.

'Rory, you did brilliantly,' Christian said, placing a hand on his shoulder.

'Really?'

'Absolutely.'

'I'm shattered.'

'It's not easy interviewing kids, is it?'

'Not at all. I'm soaked. Thank God I've got a spare shirt in my locker.'

'You should be proud of that, though, Rory.'

'Thanks. She wants to see her dog. Am I OK to take her?'

'Of course you are.'

'Did you hear what she said about what the killer was wearing?'

'A onesie?'

'A plastic onesie. And he had plastic bags on his shoes. You know what that means, don't you? He was wearing a forensic suit and overshoes. The killer could be someone working within forensics, a scene of crime officer. We could all know who the killer is.'

Chapter Thirty-Four

Matilda looked up to the sound of knocking on her office door. Her eyes widened.

'Ross, come on in.'

DS Ross Jonson from Barnsley stepped into the office and closed the door behind him. 'You looked deep in thought; not interrupting anything, am I?'

'Nothing that won't keep. Have a seat. How are you?'

He shrugged.

'It's not often we see you in Sheffield. Something wrong?' She perched on the edge of her desk.

'I heard you were in Barnsley yesterday, asking questions about Keith Lumb.'

'That's right.'

'I thought I'd better come and have a chat to you about him. I know him. Well, sort of,' he said, looking down at his hands and playing with his fingers.

'In what way sort of?'

'If you look at his record, which I'm sure you have, you'll see petty crimes, a bit of burgling, nothing serious. If you knew him, you'd see a different story.'

'And you know him?'

'I knew his former girlfriend, Tina Law. She was a sweet thing.

She was training to be a beautician. She knew Keith was trouble, but, well, she was young, she was in love, and Keith had his own flat. She was smitten.'

Matilda read the uncomfortable expression on Ross's face. This was a story that didn't have a happy ending.

'What happened?'

'Keith got jealous of anyone he saw Tina talking to. It was as if she couldn't have a good time when he wasn't around or she shouldn't be talking to other men, period. He got quite volatile towards her.'

'Was he violent?'

'You could say that. I was sent to interview her from her hospital bed. One of the nurses had called us when she was admitted to A&E. He'd beaten her black and blue.'

'Why isn't any of this on his charge sheet?'

'Because Tina refused to press charges. She kept saying she was accident prone, kept falling downstairs, or being silly while on a drunken night out.'

'And you didn't believe this?'

'It was obvious she was covering for him. She was frightened. I put her in touch with some refuge groups. I don't know if she ever contacted them.'

Matilda took a deep breath. She was almost afraid to ask the next question. 'Where's Tina now?'

'I've no idea,' he said, looking up. 'The last time I met her was about eight months ago. She was in hospital again, broken arm, fractured jaw, bruised ribs, two black eyes. She said she'd been mugged outside a nightclub in town. When I asked her what had been taken, she'd said her mobile and purse. However, I requested the CCTV footage from the front of the hospital, and it showed her paying for a taxi and taking money from her purse.'

'Keith Lumb again?'

'Who else?'

'Did you ever interview Keith?'

'I had a quiet word with him. I made it out like I was worried about her having so many accidents.'

'What did he say?'

'He said she had a problem with alcohol. She drank too much and fell over. It was bullshit, but what else could I do?'

'Your hands were tied. I don't suppose you know where Tina is now?'

'No. I did a trace on her last known address yesterday when I found out you were asking about Keith Lumb. She hasn't lived there for months and nobody knows where she's gone. If she's run away, then good luck to her, I say.'

'And if she hasn't run away?'

Ross shrugged. 'I dread to think.'

'The killing of the Mercer family,' Matilda said, 'is Keith capable of something like that?'

Ross hesitated as he thought. 'Yes,' he eventually said. 'I've seen him when he's angry. He just flips.'

Matilda was still reeling from Ross's statement when she received a phone call from the desk sergeant. A solicitor had come into the station asking to see the detective in charge of the Mercer murders.

Max Warburton was a short and skinny man with tangled mousey hair and dull blue eyes. He wore a cheap navy suit and scuffed black shoes. He sat in the waiting room holding his briefcase firmly against his chest as if it contained the code for nuclear weapons.

Matilda showed him into an interview room. He refused a

cup of coffee but asked for a glass of water. While she went to fetch him one, he set about opening his briefcase and laying his papers down on the desk.

He drank the glass of water in one drink. His nervousness was evident.

'Sorry, I'm not usually this on edge. I've been fighting with my conscience since yesterday morning.'

A solicitor with a conscience? A new breed.

Matilda didn't say anything. She allowed him to ramble on, hoping he'd say something worthwhile eventually.

'My firm represents the Mercer family. Clive Mercer in particular. Last summer, he came into the office to make out a new will. I didn't deal with him, one of our senior partners did. However, when he retired, I took it over and the message on the front of the envelope states that it shouldn't be opened until the event of Clive Mercer's death,' he said, showing her the brown envelope.

'I see.'

'Inside, was the last will and testament of Clive and Serena Mercer made last summer.'

'It was a joint will?'

'Sort of.'

'What do you mean?'

'If Clive dies before his wife then everything goes to her to support her for the rest of her natural life. However, when she dies, this will comes into effect again and whatever is left of the estate is inherited by the people Clive has stipulated in this will.'

'And as Clive and Serena died at the same time, I'm guessing everything goes to whoever would inherit after Serena's death?' Matilda asked.

'That's correct. It seems as though Clive Mercer thought of every eventuality when it came to his death.'

Matilda remembered the brain tumour he had recently been diagnosed with. He obviously wanted everything sorted before he died.

'So, why have you come to see me? It all seems pretty straight forward.'

'It is. It's just . . . well, who inherits and the reason behind it is slightly odd.'

'Go on.'

Max selected the correct file and cleared his throat. The paper shook slightly in his hands. 'In the event of Serena's death, whatever it left of the estate and after the sale of the house and contents not inherited to family and friends is divided up. There are small legacies to a few trusts and charities Clive supports, but everything else goes to Leah Mercer.'

'Leah? What about Jeremy?'

Max swallowed hard. He looked down at the paperwork again. 'It says here that Jeremy Mercer will not inherit anything as he is not Clive's legitimate son and heir.'

'We had been informed of such a rumour. But surely Serena wouldn't have signed off on that. She was his son and she paid just as much money into the house as he did. They both had very well-paid jobs.'

Max turned the will around to show Matilda both signatures.

'Did he leave anything to Rachel, Jeremy's daughter?'

'No. The will states that in his eyes, Rachel isn't his legitimate granddaughter and does not qualify to inherit any of his estate.'

Matilda bit her bottom lip. She wanted to call Clive Mercer every name under the sun but didn't think it would look good in front of his solicitor.

'Have I done the right thing in coming to you?' Max asked to break the silence.

'Absolutely.' Matilda grinned.

Back in the HMET suite, Matilda stood in front of the murder board and glared into the cold stare of Clive Mercer.

'What a bastard,' Christian said from behind.

'That was my first thought, too.'

'Do you think Leah and Jeremy knew about this?'

'I've no idea. That's something else we'll need to ask her.'

'I can't see Serena agreeing to this,' Christian said, pointing at her photograph. 'She wouldn't allow her son to be cut out of her will.'

'It's her signature.'

'Do you think he forced her into signing?'

'I wouldn't put it past him.'

'I hate men like that.'

'You and me both.' Matilda was about to turn away from the board when she stopped.

'What is it?' Christian asked.

'I wonder if Leah knew Keith Lumb,' she said. 'They're both about the same age.'

'What are you hinting at?'

'Let's say Leah knew the content of her father's will. She knew she was going to inherit everything, but she also knows how controlling and domineering her father is towards her mother. Is it possible she could have arranged for Keith to kill them while she has the perfect alibi of being out of the country on her honeymoon?'

'But why have the mother killed? Why have Jeremy killed? And why leave Rachel alive?'

'Both parents need to die for Leah to inherit. Jeremy, we've already established disturbed the killer. Leah then gets the money and guardianship of Rachel. Instant family.'

'What about Oliver?'

Matilda looked over to the picture of a smiling Oliver. She wondered if Leah had found out about Oliver's secret and simply wanted him out of the way. She could blackmail him into not claiming half of the estate in any divorce, maybe even pay him off. If that was the case, all the tears and the drama was an act and made her one clever, cold, heartless and dangerous woman.

Chapter Thirty-Five

It took Leah Ridgeway a long time to answer the door. By the time she did, Sian was shivering on the doorstep.

'I'm sorry. I thought there was someone else in,' she said in a dopey voice reserved for the permanently tired. 'Come in.'

Sian entered the house belonging to Leah's in-laws and looked around at the brightly lit, tastefully decorated hallway.

'You're on your own?' Sian asked.

Leah nodded. She was wearing a floor-length dressing down, open to reveal heavily creased pyjamas. Her hair was sticking up in all directions. She turned and headed for the kitchen, dragging her heavy legs.

'I'm sorry. I've had a bad night. I don't think I've had more than an hour's sleep. Can I get you a coffee or something?' she asked. She went over to the counter where the kettle was and leaned against it. She was like the walking dead.

'Would you like me to make it?'

'Would you? I'm sorry. I don't think I have the energy.'

She pulled out a chair at the breakfast table and slumped into it.

'Where's Oliver?' Sian asked as she set about making the coffee. Matilda had already called her and told her Oliver had returned to work.

'He's at the hospital. He said there was no point both of us hanging around the house moping,' Leah replied. There was a hint of bitterness in her voice.

'How do you feel about that?'

She gave a slight chuckle. 'I don't know how I feel about anything. I'm just so numb.'

'That's understandable. You shouldn't be on your own though.'

'I may as well be. Oliver doesn't handle emotions very well.'

'What about your mother-in-law?'

'Sophia? She sees crying as a sign of weakness. If it was up to her I would have had my entire family buried by now then continued with my honeymoon.' Her bottom lip began to quiver.

'Did she actually say that?' Sian looked disgusted at the thought.

'No. She may as well have done though. Oliver told me to go to bed early last night as my snivelling was disturbing his parents' mealtime.'

Sian put the mug of coffee in front of Leah along with a matching milk jug and sugar bowl. 'Would you like something to eat?'

'I can't keep anything down.'

'You really need to keep your strength up. For Rachel.'

'I know.' She ran her fingers through her hair but they became stuck in the tangled mess. 'I just can't help feeling . . .' she couldn't finish as the tears came down in a torrent.

Sian allowed her to cry. She had the feeling Leah had been bottling everything up while her in-laws were around. She was obviously encroaching on their perfect life and they didn't like anything that upset their well-oiled routine.

'Have you been to see a doctor? They may be able to give you something.'

Leah sniggered. 'I don't need any more medication.'

'More?'

'Lithium, Lorazepam, and there's something else I can never pronounce.' She looked at Sian who frowned. 'I'm bipolar. Actually, I'm not allowed to say that. My therapist said I have to say I have bipolar, not that I am bipolar as that makes it sounds like I am my illness when I'm not.' She ran her fingers through her hair, but they became stuck in the tangles.

'How long have you been like this?'

She blew out her cheeks as she thought. 'Years. Years and years. I was depressed even as a child. As I grew up it became steadily worse. My moods can change at the drop of a hat. I don't even feel as if I'm in control of my own mind sometimes.'

'Your family was supportive?'

She nodded. As she spoke, tears began to fall. 'Mum and Jeremy especially.'

'What about your dad?'

'He understood, but he was always busy. Shit, I forgot to ask, how's the detective?'

'DC Rani? She's fine. No lasting damage.'

'She's pregnant, isn't she?'

'Yes. Don't worry. The baby is fine.'

'I don't know what came over me. I just suddenly realized that Rachel was all I had left and I wanted to take her away from everything. Will you tell her I'm sorry?'

'Of course. Leah, would you be up for answering a few questions about your family?'

She sniffled and sat up straight. 'If I can.'

'The neighbours all describe your parents as a happy, loving couple, but when we questioned them, we were under the impression they didn't know them all that well.'

'Mum and dad were private people. They got on with the neighbours, chatted in the street, that kind of thing, but they weren't close.'

'Did your mum and dad have any close friends?'

'Oh yes,' Leah's eyes almost lit up. 'Especially Mum. She was very popular.'

'The thing is,' Sian began, shuffling in her seat, 'to be able to find out who killed them, we need to find out who your family were. Who would know your mum and dad best, apart from you, obviously,' she said, giving her a warm, comforting smile.

Leah thought for a while. 'Well, there's Leslie and Ronnie. They were always going out shopping as a threesome.'

Sian took out her notebook and wrote down their names. 'Were they at your wedding?'

'Yes. Leslie Beck was there with her husband, Adrian. I think they went home early. Adrian suffers with anxiety. He didn't like the crowd. I wasn't a big fan either. Ronnie Lister and her husband, Derek, were still there when Oliver and I left. Ronnie loves a party. I'm guessing she was one of the last to leave,' she said with a smile.

'And what about your dad?' Sian asked.

'Dad's friends were mostly work related. He wasn't one for socializing. Well, not without Mum anyway.' Leah looked deep in thought as if trying to conjure up someone, anyone, who she considered to be a friend of her father's. 'You could speak to Emmett Flanagan. He's worked with Dad on and off for years. He was at the wedding. We didn't think he'd come actually as his wife died recently. He stayed for a few hours, which was lovely.' She smiled again at the memory the wedding invoked, but then, she remembered that only a few hours later her entire family had been slaughtered and there was suddenly nothing to smile about.

'Thank you, Leah. That's very helpful.'

'I don't understand any of this. I can't think of a single person who would want to kill my family. It doesn't make sense. If it was a robbery gone wrong, I could perhaps get my head around it, but you say nothing was taken.'

'At this stage, Leah, it's incredibly frustrating, but we will find out who did this and why. All you need to do is concentrate on yourself, and Rachel and Oliver. You need to surround yourself with people who will help.'

Leah shook her head. 'The only people who could help me are dead.'

The front door opened and slammed closed. 'Leah, it's me,' Oliver called out from the hallway.

'Shit,' Leah said under her breath. 'I promised I'd be dressed and ready by now. He'll kill me.'

'Leah?' Sian asked, looking worried.

'Oh,' Oliver said, standing in the doorway to the kitchen when he saw Sian. 'Is everything all right.'

'Just a few follow-up questions,' Sian said. 'I hear you went back to work.'

'Yes. Not a crime, is it?'

'Of course not. I'd have thought you'd be needed here with your wife.'

'Why? What's happened?'

'Mr Ridgeway, your wife is incredibly upset. She needs support.'

He pulled out the chair next to her and sat down. 'Leah, why don't you go upstairs, have a soak in the bath and then I'll take you out for lunch. Cheer you up a bit.' He smiled but to Sian it didn't look sincere. 'Unless, of course, you have any more questions?'

'No. I'm finished here,' Sian said, closing her notebook and putting it in her pocket. 'I'm sure we'll need to speak to you both again at some point.'

'Thank you,' Leah said.

'You're welcome. Take care of yourself. I'll show myself out.'

Sian lingered in the hallway, straining to hear what was being said between husband and wife in the kitchen, but she couldn't make out a single word from Oliver's hushed tones. She left the house and headed for her car. She had a feeling the Ridgeways were people who needed a close eye to be kept on.

ACC Masterson entered Matilda's office and closed the door behind her. It was rare for her to come downstairs. Usually, she made a call and asked people to come to her.

'What's going on with Barnsley?' she asked, her voice low.

'Funny, I was going to ask you that,' Matilda said.

'What's that supposed to mean?'

'The place is falling apart. There's a DI who is on the verge of having a stroke, plain-clothed officers walking around like they have the weight of the world on their shoulders and prisoners able to leave without detection whenever they feel like it.'

Valerie pulled out a chair and sat down. 'I've been told all about this Keith Lumb character. Is he seriously a suspect for the Mercer killings?'

Matilda sighed. 'He's starting to look more and more likely.'

'Any clues on where he might be?'

'No. I'm going to see his sister later today. She doesn't live far from the Mercers. Fingers crossed she knows where he is.'

'And if she doesn't?'

'If she doesn't, I'll put out an appeal for anyone who's seen him to get in touch.'

'If he is the killer, and the press find out we had him in custody and allowed him to escape, they'll hang us out to dry,' Valerie said, scratching her head.

Where is this 'us' coming from?

'You need to do something about Barnsley then. Throw a bit of money at the place.'

'There isn't any money,' Valerie almost snapped. 'I'm already dreading the bill coming in from the forensic services over the number of samples you're sending them from this Mercer case.'

'Jesus!' Matilda said in frustration. 'You can't expect me to solve murders without spending any money,' she said, raising her voice.

'I'm aware of that, DCI Darke, but budgets are being cut right, left and centre.'

Matilda rolled her eyes. 'It's funny how central government can always find money when they want to. Big Ben needs repairing, oh look, here's forty million down the back of the sofa we didn't realize we had,' she said. 'I refuse to cut corners, cut staff, and stop sending detectives on interviews in the name of cost cutting. If we do that, we'll end up like Barnsley,' Matilda said loud enough for everyone out in the HMET suite to hear her.

Valerie took a deep breath. 'I'm not asking you to cut corners. I'm worried about the state of this force.'

'Then you need to give Kate Stephenson at *The Star* a call, because someone already has and she knows we had our chief suspect in custody.'

'Shit. All right, leave Kate and Barnsley to me. I'll sort them out. In the meantime, I want you to find Keith Lumb and get him back in custody.' She headed for the door then stopped, turning back to Matilda. 'And try to cut down on overtime.'

'Fine,' Matilda smirked. 'My staff will be strictly nine till five, Monday to Friday, with an hour for lunch. Let's hope murderers and rapists have a similar working timetable.'

Valerie opened her mouth to say something but changed her mind. She left the office and headed out of the suite, not making eye contact with any of the other officers.

'You handled that well,' Christian said from the doorway.

Matilda rolled her eyes. 'Do you get the feeling this department is going to be made a scapegoat when this all hits the fan?'

'Shall we be terribly British and do what we're supposed to do in a crisis and have a cup of tea?' He smiled.

'Go on then. But only use one bag. Remember, we're on a budget.'

Pongo was waiting in the car park at the back of the police station. One of the handlers was giving him some exercise. As soon as he saw Rachel leave the building he charged straight for her. For such a small dog, he had great power, as he almost dragged the handler with him.

Rachel dropped to her knees and allowed the young Dalmatian to jump all over her and lick her face. She looked genuinely happy to be reunited with her best friend again.

Rory squatted next to her and began stroking the puppy. 'He's a beautiful dog.'

She didn't reply. It was as if Rory wasn't there. She was excited to be with something familiar again.

'He smells funny,' she eventually said.

'We had to wash him.'

'Oh.' Her face dropped when she remembered why they'd had to wash him. 'I opened my bedroom door,' she said, still fussing with the dog.

'Did you? When?'

'When Daddy told me not to. I opened my door to look out.'

'What did you see?'

'Granddaddy was on his knees and the man was holding him by his hair. He was stabbing and stabbing at his neck.'

'That must have been very upsetting,' Rory said. He looked up to the social worker who was standing behind him. She nodded to show she was listening.

'It was. I got some blood on my face. Granddaddy was crying. The man looked at me.'

'Did you know who he was?'

'No.'

'Do you think you'd recognize him if you saw him again?'

'I don't want to see him again,' she cried. She grabbed Pongo who had stopped fussing and help him tight.

'You won't have to, Rachel. I promise you. If we found a photograph of this man and showed it to you, do you think you'd be able to say if it was the man you saw?'

'His face was covered. I could only see his eyes.'

'OK. Rachel, when you saw your Auntie Leah and Uncle Oliver at the hospital, why did you scream?'

'I thought they were dead too,' she sniffled.

Rory sat back on his haunches and watched as Rachel returned to playing with Pongo. It broke his heart to see the torment she was going through. She had been incredibly brave, but soon, the loss of her father would hit home, and the tears and the nightmares would return.

Chapter Thirty-Six

'Elizabeth Lumb?' Matilda asked the pair of eyes peeking out at her from the small gap in the door.

'Yes.'

'DCI Matilda Darke, South Yorkshire Police. Would it be possible to have a few words?'

'Is this about my brother?'

'Yes.'

'Oh. I don't know where he is,' she said, still not opening the door any wider.

'Perhaps if we could come in and have a chat.'

Elizabeth thought for a long while before giving in. Eventually, she ducked out of the small gap and opened the door wide to allow her visitors to enter.

Elizabeth Lumb was a tall woman with slicked back dark hair which she wore in a ponytail. Her face was plain and without make-up. Her dress sense was comfortable yet dowdy; baggy beige linen trousers, thick woollen cardigan with a soft pink sweater beneath. Her shoulders were hunched as if trying to make herself smaller, almost apologizing for being close to six foot.

The hallway was narrow and seemed cluttered due to picture frames of all different sizes taking up every available space on the walls. They all interlocked together perfectly like a game of Tetris but on a much grander scale. In the corner, an oversized coat stand took up a large amount of floor space, yet it had only one coat hanging from it. She showed Matilda and Scott into the living room which was an extension of the hallway. Pictures covered the walls, sideboards were cluttered with ugly ornaments, standard lamps with large shades, busy rugs and old-fashioned beige sofas gave the room an oppressive, sad feel to it.

'Please take a seat.'

Matilda and Scott sat, but they didn't look comfortable. This wasn't a house to be comfortable in.

'Mrs Lumb—'

'Miss,' she interrupted.

'Miss Lumb, when was the last time you saw your brother?' Matilda asked.

'It was a week or so ago, I think.' Her voice was quiet, almost a whisper. Her accent was local, but again, it seemed like something she was apologizing for. She looked as uncomfortable as her surroundings.

'You told police in Barnsley that it was more than two weeks ago,' Matilda said.

'Did I? Oh.' She looked away and bit her thumbnail as she thought. 'No. It was about a week, I think.'

'OK. Did he come to visit you or did you go to see him?'

'He came here.'

'Was there a reason for his visit?'

'Yes. He asked me to lend him some money.'

'Did you?'

'No. I don't have much.'

'Why did he need money?'

'He said he needed to get away.'

'Why?'

'I don't know.'

'Did you ask?'

'No.'

'Weren't you bothered?'

'My brother and I, we're not close,' she said quietly. 'We're very different people.'

'Did you know your brother had been arrested for burglary and had escaped custody?'

Elizabeth looked to the floor and sighed. 'The detective mentioned it when he called. Keith didn't go into details. I guessed there was something wrong. I assumed he was running away from something. Or someone.'

'Do you know about his criminal past?'

'Of course. That's one of the reasons we're not close. It broke Mummy and Daddy's heart the way he was. They had many arguments about him.'

'Are your parents still alive?'

'Mummy is. My daddy died eight years ago. Throat cancer.'

'I'm sorry. Is it possible Keith could have been in touch with your mumm . . . mother?' Matilda asked.

'No. I would have been told.'

'Have you heard from Keith recently? Has he called you at all on the phone?'

'No,' she replied quickly.

'We really need to get in touch with him rather urgently. Do you have any idea where he'd go?'

'No.' Again, she answered quickly.

'Do you know any of his friends or where he hangs out?'

'No. I don't. I'm sorry,' she said, her reply sounded sharp.

Matilda allowed the silence to grow. 'You haven't asked why we're looking for him.'

'Well . . . I'm guessing it's to do with the burglaries.'

'Do you know a Clive and Serena Mercer?'

'Yes. No. I mean, sorry, yes. Well, I don't know them as such. I've met them. Serena, anyway.'

Elizabeth seemed nervous. She struggled to make eye contact with Matilda or Scott. Her gaze flittered around the room as if looking for something that would save her from this interrogation.

Matilda and Scott exchanged glances. 'How did you know Serena?' Scott asked.

'She helps out at a charity I work with.'

'What charity?'

'It's a homeless charity. Did you know that Sheffield is fifth in the UK for homelessness with 1.9 people per thousand without a home? It's shocking. And people don't seem to care anymore. We seem to have lost that sense of community and pride,' she said, her most animated of the whole conversation.

'What did Serena do at the charity?'

'She donated money, helped with fundraising and she got some of the other doctors at the hospital involved to give homeless people check-ups and medical help.'

'A valued member of the team,' Scott said.

'Absolutely.' She smiled.

'Have you heard about what has happened to Serena and her family?'

'Yes. It was on the news last night. Shocking. Absolutely shocking. And on the day of her daughter's wedding, too.' She may have sounded shocked but there were no tears in her eyes, no hint of sadness on her face.

'Did you attend the wedding?' Scott asked.

'No. I wasn't invited. I sent a card. I doubt they knew who I was.' She fiddled with the brooch on the lapel of her cardigan.

'Did you know where the Mercers lived?'

'Oh yes. It's not far from here, actually. About a mile or so.'

Matilda edged forward on the sofa. 'Elizabeth, I need to ask you something very important. Do you think your brother may have had anything to do with Serena's death?'

'Oh no,' she said without needing to think.

'You sound sure. I thought you didn't know him all that well.'

'I don't. But he's not a killer. He's a petty criminal. He breaks into houses. There's no way he could kill someone, absolutely no way. We didn't bring him up to be a killer.'

'What shoe size is your brother?'

'Shoe size?' she asked, completely thrown by the question. 'I've no idea. Oh, wait, I do. He's a size ten'.

'You're sure.'

'Yes. The same as my daddy.'

'OK. Elizabeth, I'd like to show you a couple of photos. They're items of clothing. I'm afraid they have blood on them.'

'Oh. I'm sure not if I want to,' she said, sitting further back in her seat.

'Nobody is wearing the clothes, they're just items on a table, that's all.'

'Why do you want me to see them?'

'I want to see if you recognize them.'

Matilda took three photographs out of her inside pocket and placed them on top of a magazine on the coffee table between the two of them. Gingerly, Elizabeth leaned forward, her arms firmly wrapped around her.

'Take your time,' Matilda instructed.

'I'm not sure,' she said, looking from one to the other and back again.

'Do those clothes belong to your brother?'

'Oh ye . . .' she stopped herself. 'It's difficult to say. They look like just ordinary clothes. There's nothing special about them, is there?'

'You do recognize them, don't you?'

'No. Now I come to look at them, no I don't. I'm sorry,' she said, pushing them away.

'Fair enough,' Matilda said, gathering up the pictures and putting them back in her pocket. 'Would it be possible to speak to your mother?'

'Why? Why do you want to talk to her?' she asked, getting flustered.

'In case Keith has tried to contact her.'

'But he hasn't. I would have been told.'

'Maybe he told her not to tell you.'

'He wouldn't do that. Mummy's in a home. She's not well. She doesn't need this stress.'

'OK.' Matilda put her hands up, trying to calm her down. She dug into her pocket for a card. 'If Keith does call you, would you give me a ring, let me know?'

'Well, yes.' She smiled. 'I don't know why he would, though. I mean, there's no reason for him to.'

'Miss Lumb,' Matilda said, an edge to her voice. 'Your brother has escaped custody. He's on the run. He's wanted for a series of burglaries and we have strong evidence to suggest he was in Clive and Serena's home on the night of their deaths. We need to speak to him.'

'He was in their home?' she asked, fiddling with the collar of her cardigan.

'Yes.'

'Why? Why was he there? He didn't know them. I know them. Serena's my friend, not his.' Her voice grew in volume and anger.

'That's what we need to talk to Keith about. Now, I'm on your side, here, Elizabeth. I don't believe Keith had anything to do with their deaths.' Matilda could feel Scott's eyes burning into her. 'But I do need to speak to him urgently.'

'I see.'

'So you'll call me?'

'Of course. Yes.'

'Right.' Matilda stood up. 'We'll leave you in peace then.'

She moved towards the door with Scott closely following.

Elizabeth showed them out, closed the door behind them and secured it with bolts and a chain. From the hallway she went to the kitchen, opened the door and entered.

'Well,' she said. 'What do you make of all that?'

*   *   *

'Wow,' Scott said, breaking the silence once they were in the car. 'I have no idea what to make of Elizabeth Lumb.'

'Neither do I,' Matilda answered. 'Strange house.'

'Yes. All that furniture is really old-fashioned. I bet it's stuff from her mother's house when she moved into the home.'

'Probably.'

'Do you think her brother has been in touch?'

'Definitely,' Matilda said. 'She seems like the kind of person for whom family is very important. She's protecting her mother from us and she'll protect her little brother from us, too.'

'Who's protecting her?'

'She'll do that herself,' Matilda said, looking out of the window of her car and at the bland house she lived in on Trap Lane. 'It looks so lifeless.'

'Heavy atmosphere. So, where do we go from here?' Scott asked.

'We inform the public of who Keith Lumb is, that we want to speak to him, that he mustn't be approached under any circumstances.'

'If he sees that appeal, he's bound to call his sister. Do you think she'll call us?'

'No. We'll need to put surveillance on her.'

'Masterson won't like that.'

Matilda turned back to Scott. 'The day I start putting budget over people is the day I resign. I'm a detective, not an accountant.' She started the engine.

Chapter Thirty-Seven

DIFFERENT NAME. SAME PROBLEMS

By Danny Hanson

Young Reporter of the Year, 2017

South Yorkshire Police launched their Homicide and Major Enquiry Team late last year to great fanfare and back slapping. It was a turning point in the force which has been dogged by controversy in recent years. However, less than two months since the well-publicized launch and it's safe to say the cracks are already beginning to show.

Headed by DCI Matilda Darke, formerly in charge of the Murder Investigation Team, the new unit aimed to clear up more than twenty-five cold murder cases within the county as well as investigating current crimes.

In the wake of PC Steve Harrison being unmasked as a serial killer last year, hidden from DCI Darke and her team in plain sight, ACC Valerie Masterson said the new unit would 'leave no stone unturned, no avenue unexplored, no question unanswered and no case too big to tackle'.

However, The Star has learned that a man wanted in relation to the brutal massacre of the Mercer family in Fulwood last week was in police custody a few days before and was allowed to escape to commit his crimes.

An unnamed police source said South Yorkshire Police have no idea where this man is now and believe he could have fled the country.

In a statement, ACC Masterson said, 'DCI Darke and everyone in the Homicide and Major Enquiry Team are working tirelessly around the clock to find the person responsible for these crimes. It is unfortunate a man we are keen to interview was briefly in police custody. However, a major internal inquiry has been launched and severe action will be taken once all the facts are known.'

It would appear that beneath the tinsel and glitter of a glamorous new unit, the people of South Yorkshire are no safer now than before, just a few extra million pounds poorer for having to cough up for such a pres-tigious unit.

'Bollocks!' Valerie swore as she slammed her laptop closed. She had spoken to Kate Stephenson, had a thirty-minute conversation in which she had batted back each and every back-handed comment like a Wimbledon champion. She thought Kate had understood the difficulties the force was facing in the days of stringent budget cuts, and she had betrayed her and allowed her star pupil to write such vitriol.

Valerie sat back in her seat and closed her eyes. She should have realized she was talking to a venomous reporter. If they could find any hint of bile in a story, they would run with it.

Her phone rang. She looked at it and immediately knew who would be calling. The tone sounded different, urgent, severe.

'ACC Masterson,' she answered.

'Valerie.' Chief Constable Martin Featherstone didn't need to introduce himself. He didn't have to. His gruff voice, which sounded like he gargled every morning with a mouthful of gravel and his distinct West Country accent, were unmistakable. 'Once again South Yorkshire Police has made the main news headlines, and once again it isn't about impressive clear-up rates.'

'I have just read the story myself.'

'I bet you have. This Danny Hanson seems to have got it in for you. Any particular reason?'

'He's young. He's ambitious. We're easy targets.'

'Of course you are, especially when you're handing him such award-winning stories on a silver platter. Is it true you had someone in custody and allowed him to escape so he could butcher three people?'

'It's not like that.'

'So the story is a lie?' Valerie didn't know what to say so she remained silent. 'I didn't think so,' Martin added.

'Like it is reported in the story, I have begun an inquiry into how Keith Lumb could have escaped. There will be repercussions.'

'Yes there will, Valerie. I trusted you to turn this force around, especially in the wake of the Rotherham abuse scandal, the Hillsborough inquiry and how do you repay me? With allowing a man to escape custody and go on to kill three people.'

Valerie didn't say anything. She couldn't. She knew what was coming next.

'Aren't you due to take early retirement later this year?'

'There's another eighteen months, sir,' she replied quietly.

'Maybe we should have a serious chat when this case is resolved. It might be more prudent if you went on gardening leave.'

'Sir.'

Valerie listened to the dial tone. She did not want her career to end like this. If she wanted to leave with her head held high, a firm handshake and a pat on the back, sweeping changes would need to be made, and she would start with DCI Matilda Darke.

Chapter Thirty-Eight

This was the life Pat Campbell missed. In her heyday she was a much-respected detective inspector with South Yorkshire Police. She was known to be a scary woman who didn't suffer fools. If you were on her team you were there to work until the case was solved. Once she retired, all that was gone, and she was just a regular member of the public. Her days were filled with trips to the supermarket, visits to Meadowhall, coffee dates with friends and neighbours, babysitting duties for her grandchildren. Soon, the novelty wore off, and she missed the dramatic lifestyle a DI commanded.

A few years later, Anton retired too, and he immediately slipped into the comfortable cardigan and slippers routine with ease. He was content to spend his days with a newspaper, doing a crossword, watching daytime television, going for the odd game of bowls, a drive out to the countryside. He was relaxed. Pat didn't see it that way. She saw it as the slippery slope towards the inevitable decline into old age, and she wasn't ready for that yet.

Together, they went on holidays, but they were either too raucous for Anton or too sedate for Pat. When Matilda came knocking and asked for her help, she knew there could be only one answer – a resounding yes.

She found a parking space in Meadowhall's underground car park and headed for the main entrance. Like most people in Sheffield, she wasn't a fan of a shopping centre nicknamed Meadowhell. She visited once or twice each year and that was more than enough. The place gave her a headache just looking at it. It was currently the eighth largest shopping centre in the country. However, an extension of entertainment and leisure facilities was underway and would make it the fourth largest. Pat knew her days of coming here were soon at an end.

Pat found a board with a map of the stores and felt like a tourist as she tried to find the restaurant she needed. Typically, it was at the other side of the centre to where she was at. Still, it would help her achieve her ten thousand steps target. She set off at pace for Nature's Diner.

Nature's Diner was a chain of organic restaurants owned by Philip and Sally Meagan. It used only organic ingredients and every meal was lovingly prepared to order by their award-winning team of international chefs, according to their website. Meals with a conscience came at a price. It wasn't cheap to eat at Nature's Diner. Last year, Pat had dragged Anton along to one of the restaurants in Dronfield. Anton almost cried when the bill arrived.

It was still early, and the restaurant was empty apart from an elderly lady in the corner picking at a walnut salad. It was dimly lit. Each table came with a statement informing diners how the furniture was made from sustained rainforests, and how the Meagans had planted over a hundred thousand trees since they opened their first restaurant over a decade ago.

Pat waited at the bar while a waitress whose name tag said she was called Rainbow went to fetch Philip for her.

Philip Meagan was a tall and slim man. He had made a hole

on his belt where he'd obviously lost weight. His shirt hung from his shoulders like a coat hanger. There was nothing for it to cling to. He was a walking skeleton. As he approached Pat, she noticed how his face was drawn and lifeless. He had the pallor of the defeated. His eyes were sunken, his mouth turned down at the sides and his cheekbones were protruding. She remembered him from the time Carl disappeared and the times he appeared in the newspaper or on television. He used to be a handsome man with a solid build, a thick mound of salt-and-pepper hair. Now, he was a ghost of his former self. His hair was thinning and completely grey.

Pat tried not to make her staring too obvious. 'Nice to see you again, Philip.'

'You too. Can I get you a drink? It's on the house.'

'I'd love a coffee,' she said hesitantly, wondering if he would launch into a long speech about how his coffee was from a once struggling coffee grower in Kenya, who, thanks to Nature's Diner, was now a wealthy man employing a whole team of locals, and their once poor village had been transformed into a mecca for the self-made man.

'Instant OK?' he asked.

'Fine,' Pat replied, slightly taken aback.

'You want to talk about the phone calls, I'm guessing,' he said as he set about making the coffee.

'Yes. What's your take on them?'

He visibly sighed. 'I don't know.'

'Have you received any?'

'No.'

'Just Sally then?'

'It would appear so.'

'And have you been around when she's received them?'

'No.'

'Do you think she's making them up?'

He shrugged as he handed her a small cup. 'I don't want to think it, but I do.'

Pat took a sip of the black liquid. It was like a slap in the face. It was strong, but it was good. 'What can we do?'

'I wish I knew. Look, I miss Carl as much as Sally does, but she really needs to move forward. This brooding and not leaving the house isn't doing her any good. She needs to return to work.'

'Have you told her this?'

'Until I'm blue in the face.'

'What has she said?'

'She said she can't while Carl is missing. I'm out of ideas.' He ran his bony fingers through his hair.

'You need to talk to her, Philip. You need to tell her how you're feeling.'

'I've tried. She won't listen. I try to hold her and she backs off. I offer to take her out and she refuses. I've suggested going on holiday and she looks at me like I'm something she's stepped in.' He sat down behind the coffee machine and slumped on the bar. He was lifeless.

'Is there anything I can do?' Pat offered.

'Try and get her to see sense. Life hasn't stopped for us. She needs to recognize what's around her. I'm still here.'

'Sorry, can I interrupt?' Rainbow said, making them both jump. 'Philip, but that man from the vegetable farm is on the phone and I can't understand what he's talking about.'

'OK. Sorry, Pat, I need to take this.'

'That's OK. You go. I'll talk to you another time.'

Pat watched as Philip headed for the office. His shoulders were slumped and he was dragging his feet. It was sad to see two once happy people suffer in this way. There was no doubt in Pat's mind Carl was dead, but if she could find them his body, they could get through this together.

Sally Meagan stood on the doorstep of the back door and watched as Woody ran around the garden. He caught the tennis ball she threw him and brought it back, dropping it at her feet then looking up at her expectantly. He sat, tongue hanging out, and waited. Sally looked into the distance, her mind a million miles away. The phone rang, which brought her out of her reverie. She turned and went back into the house. Woody followed, soggy tennis ball in his mouth.

She couldn't find the phone, and by the time she did, it had stopped ringing. She looked at the display but didn't recognize the number. It rang again almost straight away.

'I'm scared, Mummy,' the voice said.

Sally fell against the wall in her office and slid down to the floor. 'Carl,' she said, tears already flowing.

'Mummy.'

'Where are you?'

'I don't know.'

'What do you see? Tell me what you see and I'll come and find you,' she said.

'It's dark.'

'Carl. I need you to concentrate.'

The call ended.

Sally screamed. It was a noise full of anger, frustration and lost hope. It scared Woody. He backed out of the room and headed for the safety of his bed.

The phone started to ring again. She looked at it and saw it was Philip calling.

'Philip,' she cried down the phone. 'He's called again, Philip. Carl's scared. He needs me. I'm . . . I . . .'

'Shit,' Philip said. 'Stay where you are. I'll be right home.' The panic was evident in his voice.

Sally, clutching the phone tightly, curled up on the floor as the tears refused to stop. She kept screaming and wailing as the pain ran deep. Ten minutes later, when Philip burst into the house, that's where he found her, a bundle, a mess of emotions, on the floor.

Chapter Thirty-Nine

Matilda and Sian were in her office watching the local news on Matilda's laptop. As soon as Keith's name was mentioned the screen filled with an image South Yorkshire Police had released to all media.

Police have named a person of interest in the investigation into the triple murder in Sheffield on Sunday night. Keith Lumb, twenty-seven, from Tankersley in Barnsley hasn't been seen since last Friday. He is described as blond, of slim build, five feet seven inches tall, and has a youthful complexion. If anyone sees him they are to call 999 immediately and not to approach him as he may be dangerous.'

'That should get the phones ringing,' Matilda said, muting the news and sitting back in her chair.

'You wouldn't have thought the BBC would have allowed her to wear that shirt. You could see her nipples,' Sian said as the newsreader appeared back on the screen.

'Did someone mention nipples?' Rory asked from the doorway. His eyes were wide and smiling.

'What do you want, Rory?' Matilda asked, closing her laptop.

'Are you watching porn?'

'No, we're not,' Sian chastised as she left the office.

'Shame. I know a great site. It's free, too.'

Sian left the office, giving the young DC a playful slap on the shoulder.

'What do you want, Rory,' Matilda repeated, firmer this time.

'Oh. I've had forensics on the phone. They want to release the house. They've done all they can.'

'That's fine. Rory, do me a favour, Sian is going to interview a couple of Serena's friends this afternoon, go along with her.'

'Will do. I've got some news for you. I don't know how you're going to take it.'

Matilda rolled her eyes. 'Go on,' she prompted.

'I showed Rachel a photo of Keith Lumb. She said she wasn't sure as she only saw the killer's eyes, but she doesn't think it's him. She said the killer had more lines around his eyes.'

'Meaning he was older?'

'Yes. Do you still think the crime scene is staged?'

'I do.'

'Even now after everything we've found out about Keith?'

'If I knew that, Rory, I wouldn't be sat here pulling my hair out. Speaking of which, have you seen Christian?'

'Not since this morning.'

'OK. Rory, has Scott said anything to you?' she asked, trying to look nonchalant.

'About what?'

'Anything?'

'No. Oh, well, he mentioned about me not emptying the bin in the kitchen. I'm guessing that's not what you were thinking about.'

'No.' She smiled.

'Have you got something to tell me?' Rory asked Scott when he appeared at the door.

'Like what?' he asked, his eyes widening.

'I don't know. The boss thought you might have something to tell me.'

'No.'

'OK. Fair enough. I'll be off then.'

Rory headed over to Sian and Scott entered Matilda's office, closing the door behind him.

'Before you say anything, Scott, I didn't tell him. I just wanted to know if you already had.'

'I haven't,' he said, sitting down. 'I'm . . . I don't know what to say or whether to even tell him. I feel sick whenever I think about it.' He sat with his shoulders hunched and his arms folded firmly across his chest. 'I hate all this. Why do I have to tell people? It shouldn't be a thing in 2018 where we have to state our sexuality.'

'Scott, you don't have to say anything if you don't want to. But if you keep secrets, if you keep things bottled up, it will cause you all kinds of pain and anxiety. Trust me, I know.'

'I'm just worried how people will react. I don't want people treating me differently or taking the piss. I'm not strong enough or confident enough to handle things like that.'

'I know. However, and whenever you want to do this, is up to you. I will stand by you and support you whatever you decide to do.'

'Thank you,' Scott said, looking up. 'I'd better go and check on those extra phones for when the calls start coming through.' He stood up to leave. He put his hand on the door handle then stopped. 'Is . . .?'

'Yes?' Matilda asked when he stopped.

'No. It's OK.' He smiled and quickly left the room.

* * *

Keith Lumb managed to flag down a truck on a layby on the A23 just outside of London. The driver was a woman with a thick Scottish accent and was a fast talker. It helped pass the time and he was quite sad to leave her in Maidstone.

He treated himself to a bacon roll and a mug of tea before he tried to find someone to take him to Dover. He was so close. He finished eating, wiped his mouth with his sleeve and looked up. When he saw what was on the small television in the corner of the café, he almost brought his bacon roll back up again. His face was staring out at him. The police were onto him.

Keith quickly downed his strong tea and couldn't get out of the café fast enough. He needed to get to a phone. He was beginning to regret having that haircut and a shave. He was back to how he looked when he was first arrested. The beard and unkempt hair had been a perfect disguise.

'Elizabeth, it's me. What's going on?' he whispered loudly into the phone. 'I've just seen the news. I'm all over it.'

'I know. I saw it too. I had the police round here this morning asking about you. A DCI Darke. She left me her card.'

'What did she say?'

'She wants to know where you are. She mentioned the Mercers. She said you were in their house on the night they were killed.'

'What? That's ridiculous. I don't even know where they lived. I only met Serena a few times.'

'Keith, what have you done?'

'I haven't done anything.'

'It sounds like they've got evidence of you being in their house. Now, come on, tell me, what's happening?'

Keith was silent as he tried to think. 'Elizabeth, I swear, honest to God, I have never been in their house and I would never kill anyone. You know that. You know me.'

'I want to believe you.'

'Then believe me. It's the truth. Shit!'

They both fell silent.

'This DCI Darke, she wants me to call her if you call me,' Elizabeth eventually said.

'Are you going to?'

'I don't know. I should do. Look, why don't you ring her yourself. Tell her you've never been in their house.'

'What good will that do? They've got me down as a triple killer. They'll lock me up.'

'Not if you tell them where you really were on Sunday night. You can't be in two places at once. I'll give you DCI Darke's number and you can call her. Do you have a pen?'

Keith dug around in his pockets and found the pen he'd stolen from the petrol station. 'Go on.'

Elizabeth gave him Matilda's mobile number and he wrote it on the back of his hand.

'Promise me you'll call her, Keith. She'll listen to you. I know she will.'

'She's a copper, Elizabeth. They'll say anything.'

'No. She seemed really nice. She reminded me of that detective who spoke to me about Ruby: kind, genuine, a listener. She certainly wasn't like DI Ben Hales when he questioned me about Mum. I'll never forget his name. He put me through hell,' she said with venom.

'Oh God. I don't know what to do,' he said, almost crying. 'This is a mess. I think someone might be setting me up.'

'Who would do that? And why?'

'I don't know.'

'What are you going to do?'

'I don't know that either. I've got to go. My money is about to run out.'

'Keith, wait . . .'

He ended the call. He wanted to scream and shout and kick the crap out of the phone, but he couldn't draw attention to himself.

'Shit,' he said to himself. 'Fuck! Shit!' he said under his breath.

As he walked away from the phone box, head down, hood up, he looked at the back of his hand at the number his sister had given him. Maybe he should try and reason with this DCI Darke. He couldn't cope with the prison sentence from a few burglaries; a life sentence for three murders would kill him.

Chapter Forty

Sian and Rory drove in silence to Firshill Crescent in Shirecliffe where Leslie Beck lived. Hopefully, she would give them some insight into Clive and Serena's married life.

It was early afternoon. The grey sky and ominous clouds made it feel later than it was. Another freezing cold night was forecast. Sian looked out of the front passenger window. People were layered up in thick clothing and sensible shoes. It seemed a long time ago since she'd left the house without a coat. There didn't seem to be an end in sight to this current cold snap. The Beast from the East the media were calling it. There weren't wrong. The icy cold wind was biting.

'You're not leaving the force, are you?' she asked, turning to Rory. The question shattered the silence. Rory visibly tensed and gripped his fingers tightly around the steering wheel. They weren't far from their destination. He waited until he'd pulled up before he replied.

'Can I tell you something in private?'

'Of course you can.'

'You won't tell anyone. Not even the boss.'

'I promise.' She edged closer to him in her seat as if there was a risk of them being overheard.

'I love being a detective,' he said with a smile. 'It's all I've ever wanted to be. But . . .' he swallowed hard, 'I don't want to turn into DCI Darke.'

'Ah.'

'Don't get me wrong, she's an amazing woman. I think she's brilliant at what she does,' he quickly added. 'But, she's sacrificed so much to get where she is. When I look at her sometimes, she looks so unbelievably sad. I don't want to be in my forties and realize my career had defined me and nothing else. Does that make sense?'

'Yes, it does.' She nodded. 'We're in a strange job. It seems like you can either have a family or be a detective, but not both. I've taken so many years out having four children. I'm the same age as Matilda yet I'm a DS and she's a DCI. Could I have been where she is if I hadn't had a family? Possibly. But I'm happy as a DS. I've never wanted to go any higher. It's different for men, Rory. They don't take as long off work when they have a child. They can have a home life and a career.'

The expression on Rory's face was one of frustration and despair. 'But look how many men at the station are divorced. Jim Young is on his fourth marriage and he never sees his kids. Ali Bankroft's wife left him, and it was over a week before he noticed because he was at work all the time. And look what happened to DI Ben Hales? I don't want to turn out like them.'

'Have you met someone? Are you considering settling down?'

'No,' he sighed. 'I'm hardly likely to meet anyone in this job.'

'Rory, you're still only young. You're a born copper. I don't think you should worry about this until you do meet someone. In the meantime, think about what you want from the job, where you want to go.'

'I've found something.'

'Another job?'

'Yes. It's research with a university down in London in the criminology department. My degree is in psychology. When I contacted them they seemed really excited about me joining them as I'm a detective.'

'A researcher for a university? That's not going to be well paid, Rory.'

'And being a detective is? It's not about more money, it's about trying to keep hold of what is left of my sanity. It's about having time to go to the pub, see my mates.'

'Have you applied?'

'I've filled out the form. I haven't sent it yet.'

'I would be incredibly sad to lose you, Rory. Despite you nicking all the good chocolate out of my drawer, you're a decent bloke, and a bloody good detective. Think about that before you make a decision.'

'I will. Thanks, Sian.'

'You're welcome. You can talk to me anytime, you know that. Come on, she's looking at us out of the window.' Sian nodded to the house opposite, where a woman was staring daggers at them from behind a curtain.

* * *

Leslie Beck was in her early sixties, yet she tried her best to hide it. Her hair was dyed dark red, her face was heavily made up and her clothes were at least a decade too young for her. She let the detectives in with a smile and pointed them in the direction of the living room. A cafetière of coffee was already waiting for them along with a plate of carefully arranged biscuits.

Sian and Rory sat on one sofa; Leslie on the one opposite.

'I can't believe what's happened. I just can't believe it. Why would someone want to kill Serena? She was such a kind-hearted, warm woman. She'd do anything for anyone. It's shocking,' she said, shaking her head. 'It comes to something when you're not even safe in your own home, isn't it? Leah must be devastated. Poor girl.'

Sian waited until Leslie had finished. She noticed how she hadn't mentioned anything about Clive. 'Leslie, how long had you known Serena?'

'Oh, years. We worked together at the hospital for a long time. I had to give work up in 2005 after a car crash we had in Potenza, but, you know, Serena was always on hand to help me out. She took me to my physiotherapy sessions, she went shopping for me. Like I said, she'd do anything for anyone.'

'Did you know Clive much?'

Leslie's face dropped for a split second and her lips thinned. 'I didn't know him as well, obviously. He was such a hard worker.' She smiled a large, fake grin.

'Leslie.' Sian leaned forward on the sofa. She dropped her voice slightly. 'Were there any problems in Serena and Clive's marriage?'

'No. They were the perfect couple,' she replied, again with the painted-on grin.

'I think we're both old enough to know that the perfect couple doesn't exist,' Sian said. 'You won't be betraying anyone's confidence if you tell me a secret you've been asked to keep.'

'I don't know what you're talking about. Help yourselves to biscuits. They're homemade,' she said, picking up the plate and aiming it in Rory's direction.

'Mrs Beck,' Rory began, taking a biscuit and dunking it in his coffee, 'we've had a few people tell us they thought Clive might have been a bit of a bully. Did Serena ever mention that to you?'

'No. That's ridiculous. Ludicrous,' she said, not looking at them. 'He was a professional, at the top of his game. I suppose some people may have seen him as . . . I don't know,' she waffled, struggling for the right word, 'aloof, perhaps, but certainly not a bully.'

Sian leaned forward. 'Leslie, your best friend was murdered. She was butchered. We don't know who's done this or why, that's why we're here. We need to know everything about her, to try and understand who could have done this.'

Leslie's bottom lip began to wobble, and her face muscles suddenly gave up. A tear escaped from her right eye. She quickly swept it away, but it didn't go unnoticed. It was a while before she spoke as she wrestled with her conscience.

'What you need to remember about Clive Mercer is that he was a brilliant man with a brilliant mind. He was often misunderstood.'

'Is that you talking or Serena?' Sian asked.

Leslie relaxed and let out a heavy sigh. 'Those were Serena's words. She came to visit me once and something happened, I can't remember what, and she just burst into tears for no reason. I asked what was wrong. She wouldn't tell me at first. She said she was overtired and working too much. I knew there was something more. It took a while, but it all came out. Clive put himself up on a pedestal so high that even he couldn't live up to his own expectations. It irked him that Serena was getting so much recognition for her work in neurology and her charity work. Then, when he was reported to the GMC, well, he really did see red.'

'What happened?' Rory asked.

'An elderly woman died on the operating table. She had a bad reaction to the anaesthetic. If I remember rightly, there was something in her notes about it but he hadn't read them. It was all whitewashed anyway and he escaped with a warning, but mud sticks, and from his point of view, he was tarnished while Serena continued to flourish.'

'He was jealous?' Rory asked.

'Absolutely. The thing is, Serena wanted to project this image of her belonging to the perfect family. She wanted to prove that a woman could have the best of both worlds, a loving family and a career.'

Sian and Rory exchanged glances. They had been discussing this very topic in the car.

'And, she really did have it all,' Leslie continued after stopping for a sip of her coffee. 'It's just, behind closed doors, Clive wasn't the saint she painted him as. He was jealous. He was cruel.'

'Did Clive ever hit Serena?'

It was a while before Leslie answered. She gave a brief nod.

'Did this start after the first GMC hearing?'

'Yes.'

'How many times did he hit her?'

'I don't know.' She shrugged.

'Did she ever consider leaving him?'

'No,' Leslie answered quickly. 'I told her on many occasions to leave him but she wouldn't. It wasn't even an option. You see, Serena didn't have a very happy childhood. She came from a very poor background. Her father was a brute to her mother and he eventually walked out when Serena was eight. Her mother brought her up alone. They were poor, living well below the breadline. She had an idea in her head of what the perfect family was and she made sure she was going to have it.'

'But she wasn't doing herself any favours. She wasn't showing herself any respect,' Sian said.

'I know. I told her that myself. I think Serena had created a character of who she wanted to be rather than who she was. She had a wide circle of friends, but I don't think any of us knew the real Serena. I doubt she did either.' A look of sadness drifted across Leslie's face as she thought about the life of her best friend.

'Did you know about Jeremy not being Clive's son?' Sian asked.

Leslie nodded. 'Only recently. I noticed a bruise on her arm and the topic of her leaving him came up again. She said she couldn't after everything he'd done for her. I asked what she meant by that and I got full chapter and verse. She had a one-night stand, not long after they were married. It was years before Clive found out. He told her he'd stay with her, bring up the child as his own, but he'd never let her forget her betrayal.'

'He was using her affair as a hold over her?'

'Yes. I told her she didn't need to worry about any of that now. The kids were grown up, but she still wouldn't listen to reason. You were right, when you said Clive was a bully. He really was. I think he taunted Serena about her affair at any opportunity he got; anything to bring her down.'

'Tell me about the wedding,' Sian said, sitting back in the sofa and crossing her legs.

Leslie's face lit up once again. 'Oh, it was such a lovely day. Leah looked gorgeous. She's always been pretty but when I saw her walking down the aisle, my heart skipped a beat. And Oliver, well, let's just say, if I was thirty years younger . . .' she laughed.

'What were Clive and Serena like on the day?'

'Serena couldn't stop crying. She kept running to the bathroom to check her make-up. Clive was acting the dutiful father. You see, if I hadn't seen the bruises for myself, I would have thought

Serena had been lying. He was a wonderful public persona. The last true family man. But when you know something about someone, and you see them acting in a different way to what you know, you see through the façade. On the day of the wedding, I saw a damn fine actor in Clive Mercer. It's sad. The man had everything, but at the end of the day, it wasn't enough. He was jealous and bitter of a woman who loved him.'

'What time did you leave the reception?'

'We left early. My husband, Adrian, he suffers very badly with his nerves. He doesn't cope well with large groups. We stayed for a couple of hours, but we were both home and in bed by ten o'clock.'

'Did Adrian know Clive at all?'

'He couldn't stand him,' she chuckled. 'He thought Clive was arrogant.'

'Leslie, do you know of anyone who would want to kill Serena, Clive and Jeremy?' Sian asked, purposely talking slowly to drive home the severity of the crime.

The tears came once again. Leslie leaned forward and whipped a tissue out of the box on the coffee table. 'No. It was Mrs Mottershead, two doors down, who told me something bad had happened at the Mercers. Do you know what I thought? I thought Serena had killed Clive. I thought she'd finally snapped. I wouldn't have blamed her either.'

'But you've no idea if anyone would want to kill them all, as a family?'

'No. Absolutely not. Clive may have been a bastard, but he did good work. His motives may have been selfish for notoriety, but he helped a lot of people.'

* * *

On the other side of Sheffield, in Beighton, DS Aaron Connolly and DC Ranjeet Deshwal were interviewing the only person the HMET team could find who knew Clive Mercer better than anyone else – Emmet Flanagan.

Emmet was a tall, thin man with a deep commanding voice. He could easily have been employed as a double for Christopher Lee. He had arched eyebrows which gave him a frightening, sinister look. His living room was devoid of life. There was no radio on and no sign of a television. Several clocks were dotted around the room, all ticking at different beats.

'I'd offer you a coffee but I'm out of milk,' he began in a tone which said that he wouldn't have offered them a drink even if he had a dairy in his back garden. 'I took early retirement in 2012 when my wife died. I kept in touch with a few people from the hospital, not many. Clive was one of the few. A hard-working man. Dedicated. Professional. A bit of a wanker.'

Both Aaron and Ranjeet looked at Emmet with wide eyes as if they'd misheard him.

'In what way?' Aaron asked.

'I think if he'd had his way he would have changed the name of the hospital to Clive Mercer's Northern General Hospital. Does that answer your question?'

'So he was conceited?'

'That's putting it mildly. I often had to check his name badge to make sure he wasn't calling himself God,' he said with a hint of a chuckle.

'Was he good at his job?'

'Too good.'

'Can you be too good at your job?'

'Absolutely. You become complacent. Clive thought nobody could do his job better than he could. He also thought he knew everything. Given half a chance he would have performed every role in the operating theatre single-handed.'

'It sounds like you didn't like him,' Ranjeet said.

'It does, doesn't it? I can't say I've ever given much thought to whether I like him or not,' he said with a frown.

'What was he like away from the hospital?'

Emmet thought for a while. 'He was friendly. Always ready with a quip. And he played everyone off the table at snooker.'

'Did he talk about his family much?'

'Occasionally.'

'What about Serena?'

Emmet frowned as he tried to conjure up a memory. 'He didn't speak about her much. When he did, he called her "the little woman". To be honest, I don't ever remember him saying very much about her.'

'What did you think of Serena?'

'I thought she was one of the most wonderful women on God's earth. How she put up with him, I've no idea.'

'They weren't matched?'

'Heavens, no.'

'How did Clive react when he was reported to the GMC?'

'On which occasion?'

'All of them.'

'The first time it happened I honestly thought he was going to explode. He was absolutely livid that someone was calling his judgement into question. It seemed like a darkness had descended. It remained hanging over him ever since.'

'And by the third time?'

'I'd retired by then but he came to see me. He knew it had the potential to ruin him. He was angry, but Clive Mercer was one of those people where if he fell into a vat of shit he'd come out smelling of roses. He knew of a way out of it.'

'Did he say what?'

'No. But I wouldn't be surprised if it wasn't something underhand. The man would have lied, cheated, deceived, and even sold his own mother to get out of a tricky situation.'

'Did you go to the wedding?' Ranjeet asked.

'I did. I showed my face at the reception but I didn't stay long.'

'How were Clive and Serena on that day?'

'They were the dutiful parents.'

'Would you know of anyone who would want to kill them?'

'I'm sure there are many people who would have happily done away with Clive, but not his son, and certainly not his wife.'

'I get the feeling Clive Mercer was one of those people where you'd want to slap his face as soon as you looked at him,' Ranjeet said as they made their way back to the car.

'Yes, but is that a reason to kill him?' Aaron asked.

'I don't know. If he'd rubbed someone up the wrong way, really riled them up, maybe.'

'But why kill Serena, and why Jeremy?'

Ranjeet frowned as he tried to think of an answer. 'Because they were there.'

'So then why leave Rachel alive?' Aaron asked, getting behind the wheel.

'I'm not sure.'

'Although,' Aaron began, 'if Clive had used his influence, his cunning, to get out of being prosecuted by the GMC, maybe the families of the patients might have had a reason to kill him.'

'But again that leaves us with the question of why kill Serena and Jeremy yet leave Rachel alive,' Ranjeet said.

Aaron started the car but Ranjeet stopped him.

'Hang on a minute, let's try and work this out. The killer was obviously pissed off at the whole family but didn't have a big enough grudge to kill the little girl. So, who did Clive, Serena and Jeremy have a shared dislike in? Who didn't they like?'

Aaron frowned. 'Oh my God!' he exclaimed. 'The man marrying into the family.'

'Oliver Ridgeway? But he was in Paris with Leah.'

'Wanting someone dead doesn't mean actually going through with it. His honeymoon is the perfect alibi.'

'But what's the motive?'

'That's what we need to find out. We crack Oliver, we find the killer.'

Chapter Forty-One

Following the evening briefing, Matilda closed the door to her tiny office and slumped into her chair. She had a headache. It seemed Clive Mercer had a queue of people who would happily see him breathe his last, but only kind words were said about Serena and Jeremy. Sian's contact in Liverpool had been in touch. He had spoken to Jeremy's colleagues who said he only had two things in his life – his work and his daughter. He had little time for anything else. His neighbours said he was a quiet man who doted on Rachel. Jeremy didn't know many people, but the ones he did were all his friends.

So, the question of motive still remained unanswered. Clive was the centre of the crime, but why not wait until he was alone and knock him over or hit him on the head from behind? Why did Serena and Jeremy have to die too? That was the head scratcher. That was why Matilda was now rummaging through her desk drawers trying to find some paracetamol.

Towards the end of the briefing, Aaron had brought up Oliver Ridgeway. Did he have some secret that Clive, Serena or Jeremy had found out? Was he worth trying to break? Matilda and Scott looked at each other. They both knew Oliver's secret. But who else knew?

She found a blister pack of paracetamol in the bottom drawer but there was only one left. She had no idea how long it had been there. Did paracetamol have a best before date? She shrugged and dry swallowed it.

Her mobile started to ring. She dug it out of her pocket and looked at the display. No Caller ID.

'Hello?' she answered. She sounded tired and listless. That was probably because she was.

'Is that DCI Darke?'

'Yes.'

'My name is Keith Lumb. I believe you're looking for me.'

Matilda's headache was soon forgotten. She sat up and quickly rooted around on her desk for a pad and pen to take down anything that may be important.

'That's right, I am. Where are you calling from, Keith?' She tried to listen to anything in the background, but it was a muffled.

'I'm calling from a phone box.'

'OK. Where are you?'

'I can't tell you.'

'Why not?'

'I just can't. Look, I don't have much time. I know you've been to see my sister. She gave me your number. She said you might be able to help me.'

'Help you? How?'

'I'm not a killer, DCI Darke. I've not led the best life so far. I've stolen; I've broken into people's homes; I've driven without a licence and without insurance. I'll put my hand up to all of that, but I have never murdered anyone. I promise you,' he said with firm determination.

'Why were you at the Mercers' house on Sunday night?'

'I wasn't,' he said, his voice pleading.

'We have evidence to suggest you were.'

'I don't know how because I wasn't even in Sheffield on Sunday night.'

'Then where were you?'

He was about to say something but instead he sighed. 'What's the point? In your eyes I'm guilty. I've seen the news. You've told the whole world I killed three people.'

'No, we haven't. You're a person of interest. You might have seen something.'

'How can I have seen something when I wasn't even there.'

'Keith, why don't you come into the station and we can talk about this properly.'

'No way. Look, you're not fitting me up for this. I did not kill the Mercers. I've never killed anyone. Do you understand that?'

Before Matilda had a chance to reply, Keith had ended the call.

She sat back in her chair and squeezed the bridge of her nose. The headache was pulsing. Keith hadn't left a number but it was easy to track the call. She'd need Valerie to give the go-ahead from the phone company but that wasn't a problem. Even if he was calling from a phone box, they'd have his location. She dialled ACC Masterson and, as she waited for the call to connect, she couldn't help but go over the conversation she'd just had. Keith was adamant he was innocent. It was obvious he didn't have an alibi for Sunday night, so why was he protesting his innocence?

'Because he is innocent,' Matilda said to herself.

Scott was sitting in his car with the heater turned up and the engine off. He'd been sitting in the car park of a supermarket, tucked into the corner with the recycling bins, for what seemed like ages as he agonized over what to do next. Aaron mentioning Oliver possibly having a secret he was hiding from the Mercer family was too close to the truth and Scott was tying himself up in knots. He needed to do something constructive, for the sake of his own sanity rather than anything else. He'd deleted his profile on the dating app and quickly created a new one. Instead of using his own photo he used one of Chris. He hated himself for doing so but it was the only way to flush out Oliver. He had found a picture in his phone of Chris in his running gear. It showed his firm stomach, his strong legs and muscular arms. It would definitely get Oliver's interest.

Scott scrolled through the men who were nearby looking for Oliver's profile. He found it. He was three kilometres away and there was a green dot on his photo. He was online. Scott took a deep breath. His fingers were cold. He was shaking. He sent him a message. It didn't take long for Oliver to reply.

Cute pic.

Thanks.

What are you looking for?

Fun. You?

Same. You accomm?

Not tonight I can't.

You into outdoor?

Sure. Where?

Weston Park?

OK. When?

6

See you there.

Scott felt sick. He had no idea what Oliver was like as a person. He was the kind of man who was leading a double life, hiding his sexuality from his wife. How would he react when he found out he had been duped? Did he have a temper? Maybe Scott should take someone with him for support, but who? There was nobody he could confide in.

He would have to do this alone.

* * *

Less than ten minutes after Matilda had put the request in to the phone company who provided the network for her mobile, than her phone rang her with the result. Keith had indeed called her from a phone box. It had the 01622 dialling code, which was the code for Maidstone in Kent. It would seem that Keith was trying to flee the country. That didn't help Keith's claim that he was innocent.

Matilda phoned Valerie who contacted the chief constable of Kent Police and asked them to launch a manhunt as there was a potential murderer in their area. Keith's details were sent down and all local media were to be informed. Hopefully, it wouldn't be long before he was caught and on his way back up to Sheffield for questioning.

Keith had made a mistake. He knew DCI Darke wouldn't understand. All coppers were the same. They didn't care about the truth; they just wanted a result. Someone had placed him at the scene of the murders; he had no idea who or how but they had. So, as far as South Yorkshire Police was concerned, Keith Lumb was obviously guilty. The chances of him getting out of the country now were slim to impossible. He'd have to remain in Britain, but away from the ports, train stations and airports as they were the obvious places they'd look for him.

It was getting dark and it was getting cold. He didn't relish spending another night curled up in a bus stop or a vandalized phone box trying to keep warm. He couldn't survive on the streets for much longer, but he didn't have anywhere to go. He couldn't go to Elizabeth's, especially now DCI Darke had been round; she'd keep visiting and pushing his sister until he was found.

'Fuck,' he shouted to release some of the pent-up aggression he was feeling. How had he managed to get himself into this impossible situation? He was a petty thief, a burglar. All of a sudden, he's Britain's most wanted man.

He ran into a motorway service station and accosted the first driver he saw getting into his truck.

'Here, mate, you couldn't give us a lift, could you?' He sounded desperate. He looked desperate. He didn't care if the driver was a rapist or a murderer, he'd take his chances.

'Where you are heading?' the man asked in a thick Scottish accent.

'I don't care. Anywhere,' he replied.

'Who are you running from?'

'The girlfriend's husband,' he said, not knowing where that came from.

The trucker laughed. 'I know that feeling,' he said, lifting up his left hand and showing the white mark where his wedding ring used to be. 'Get in.'

'Cheers, mate. Where are you heading?'

'Back up to Glasgow. Far enough for you?'

A smile spread across Keith's face. 'Perfect.'

Elizabeth Lumb was sitting in the armchair opposite the television. On her lap was a wooden tray with a simple meal of a mini quiche, four boiled potatoes and a handful of green beans. She picked at it carefully with her cutlery.

The local news came on and started with the story of South Yorkshire Police hunting for her brother.

'Have you seen this?' she called, aiming her voice out of the living room. 'They've got Keith down as some kind of serial killer. I liked Serena, I really did. She didn't deserve this. I hope Mum isn't watching this. It'll break her heart. Do you think I should go over there tomorrow, fill her in on everything that's happening?'

She waited for a reply, but one didn't come. She never received a reply.

Chapter Forty-Two

Sian was late leaving work. She had been in conversation with a man from the GMC who had the dullest voice she had ever heard. He also insisted on giving her every single detail of all three occasions Clive Mercer had been brought to their attention. By the time she put the phone down, she was the last one in the HMET suite. Even Matilda had left for the day. She called Stuart and told him she'd be late home, tidied her desk, put on her coat and headed for the stairs.

'You're late going home, Sian,' the sergeant on the front desk commented. 'I thought everyone had already left.'

'I'm beginning to get jealous of Kesinka going on maternity leave in a few months.'

'It must be bad,' he laughed. 'How is Kes? I heard she'd had a fall.'

'She's fine. She'll be back at work on Monday. Sam, what's that smell?' She wrinkled her nose and lowered her voice for fear of offending someone within earshot.

'You're going to regret asking that question,' he said with a smile.

'Why?'

'DS Sian Mills? Is that you?' A loud voice came from the other side of the reception area.

'Oh God, no. I don't need this. Not now,' she said through gritted teeth. She turned around and saw two women approaching her. Both were in their mid-forties but were dressed much younger. They wore far too much make-up and whatever fragrance they had sprayed on themselves was strong enough to strip paint. The contrasting smells congealed to make one very pungent aroma.

Bev and Sarah were well known to South Yorkshire Police. They were prostitutes who plied their trade on the outskirts of the city centre. They had been walking the streets for years and looked out for each other, especially the younger, more vulnerable girls. Whenever they saw police they didn't shy away or hurl abuse. They were old hands at this game and knew they were there to protect them.

Bev stepped forward. She was wearing shiny black leggings, high heels that were far too high for her to walk on and a low-cut top that revealed a sagging bosom and a wrinkled chest. She had a black quilted jacket over the top which was hanging off her shoulders. Her skin was the colour of leather. It was difficult to work out if it was the grime of the Sheffield streets having tinted her over the past twenty years or whether she was using a cheap fake tan.

'We've lost another one,' she said. Her heavy local accent was deep; the effects of the copious amounts of cigarettes she had smoked. 'Danielle. She was only with us three weeks, wasn't she, Sarah?'

Sarah, standing slightly behind her, nodded. 'A month tops,' she said. Sarah didn't ooze as much confidence as Bev. She wasn't as brash and showy and often allowed Bev to do the talking for her.

'She says she's nineteen but we reckon she's younger than that, don't we, Sarah? She's got a Geordie accent. She's small, slim and very pretty. Nobody's seen hide nor hair of her for days.'

'Maybe she's gone home.' Sian shrugged, standing back to avoid the smell of cheap perfume.

'And maybe she's lying at the bottom of the River Don. You need to do something about this, Sian. Do you know how many have just disappeared in the last couple of years? Six. People don't just disappear.'

Sian took a deep breath. At this rate she wouldn't be getting home until midnight. 'Come through to an interview room. I'll take some details. Sam, can you fix us a few drinks?'

Scott spotted Oliver straight away standing under the shelter of trees by the tennis courts. It was past six o'clock and pitch-dark. Few people were using the park apart from the odd dog walker and the late finishers who used the park as a cut-through to the main bus route outside the Children's Hospital.

As Scott approached, he looked at Oliver who stood with his hands in his pockets, head high, shoulders back. He oozed confidence. Why had he decided to get married if he was gay? He wasn't being fair to Leah, or himself.

Everything in his logical brain was telling Scott to turn around and go home. This was a bad idea. He swallowed hard, took a deep breath and headed over to the junior doctor. He was still wearing his work suit, and his smart shoes echoed around the empty space.

'Oh look, it's the gay detective,' Oliver said. 'I should have known it was too good to be true. The guy in the photo was far too handsome to be real. So, why are you here? No, let me guess. You repress your feelings while you're at work but once you clock off you realize you're a red-blooded male just like the rest of the world and fancied some fun?'

Scott was not a violent man, but he had a sudden urge to knock that smirk of his face.

'I just wanted to talk.'

'Typical. You're one of those – all talk and no action.'

'Why are you doing this?'

'Doing what?'

'Going behind your wife's back like this. Why get married at all?'

Oliver stepped forward so he was almost nose to nose with Scott. 'That is none of your fucking business,' he spat.

'It could be. I'm looking into the murders of your wife's family. We're trying to find a motive. I think if your father-in-law found out what you were doing behind his daughter's back and confronted you with it, that's all the motive you'd need.' Scott tried to sound confident but his shaking voice betrayed him.

Oliver rolled his eyes. 'That's a shame. You're a very good-looking bloke. As usual, pretty but dumb,' he said with a smile. 'You seem to be forgetting, pretty boy, that I was in Paris when my wife's family were murdered.'

'You're not the type to get your hands dirty. In fact, you're the type to set the whole thing up. Let me see if I'm right, here,' he said, finding the confidence from somewhere. 'You've always wanted to be a doctor but you're not cut out for all the hard work. You've seen Leah's parents with their big house, fancy cars, and you want that. However, you don't want to work for it, you want it now. So you arrange for your in-laws to be killed while you're out of the country. The perfect alibi.'

Oliver mockingly laughed. 'You're wasted in the police force. You should be writing for soap operas. Do you have any idea how ridiculous you sound? Where do you look for a killer? Do you put an advert in the newsagents' window? Is there a special page on Facebook where you can advertise your services?'

Scott stepped forward. 'You killed them. I know you did. And I'm going to prove it.'

'You can't prove a negative. I was in Paris,' he repeated with a smile. 'I was just as shocked as Leah by what happened.'

'And what if Leah found out about what you get up to behind her back? How long do you think your marriage will last then? I imagine she'll apply for divorce before the contents of the will have been revealed. Actually, I think she may even be able to get the marriage annulled. She could be a free woman within a week. And then where will you be?'

Oliver's face dropped. 'Don't threaten me.'

'Believe me, it's not a threat. It's a promise.'

Oliver took a step back. He looked around him. 'What do you want?'

'Sorry?' Scott frowned.

'I'm guessing you're not out. Despite this being the twenty-first century, it's still not easy to be out in the police force, is it? However, we all have urges. Is that what this is about? You'll keep quiet for a shag once a week?'

'What?' Scott backed up in disgust. 'No.'

'Liar. I know what coppers are like. You're all corrupt. You're all after one thing.' He took small steps to Scott who was backing away, not knowing he was being backed into a corner behind the shed where the park keepers store their equipment. 'You arrest a drug dealer and I bet just enough makes it to court as evidence for him to be sent down and you share the rest among yourselves. You've stumbled upon my secret and you've thought of a way to turn it to your advantage.'

'That is not what I'm after at all.'

'So why are you here? Why send me that picture, pretending to be someone else, to lure me here?'

'I want the truth.'

'I've told you the truth,' he said with a grin. 'I was in Paris with my wife. I enjoy being a junior doctor. Yes, it's hard work. Yes, it's long hours. Yes, it's poorly paid, but it's a job I love. So, what else are you here for?' He started to unbuckle his belt.

Scott backed away further and banged into the shed. He looked around and noticed he was trapped. 'Shit,' he said under his breath.

'Not so cocky now, are you, pretty boy?'

Chapter Forty-Three

'Oh my God,' Matilda said. She suddenly burst into laughter. 'What is it?'

'Look at this.'

Matilda had received a picture message on her phone and immediately showed it to Adele who also laughed. The photo was of Pat Campbell, who, as she was going urbexing tonight, had gone out and bought herself a new wardrobe so she would be warm and comfortable for the night-time excursion. Dressed in a black beanie hat, black fleece jacket and waterproof black trousers, she looked like she was about to commit her first burglary.

'Isn't urbexing illegal?' Adele asked.

'Technically, no. You're only a burglar if you're on the premises to steal or damage it in some way. If you enter a property just to look around then you're a civil trespasser which isn't illegal.'

'You're well informed.'

'I looked it up when Pat said that's what she was doing.' Matilda smiled.

After work, Matilda had decided against going home. Instead, she'd phoned Adele and asked if she fancied a takeaway, a few glasses of wine and a bad film. Adele replied yes to all three.

Sitting on the sofa in Adele's warm living room, foil containers discarded, wine bottles opened and a bad Hollywood blockbuster playing out noisily on the TV, they relaxed, leaning against each other as the effects of the alcohol swept over them.

'Where's Chris tonight?' Matilda asked as, on-screen, London seemed to be suffering the brunt of a violent storm.

'He came home to change then said he was going out running with Scott. Did I tell you he's found a flat?'

'No. Where?'

'Norton.'

'That won't be cheap.'

Adele sniffled. 'I'm going to be on my own, Mat. I know I can't expect him to live with me forever, but, I don't think I like the idea of being in here on my own.'

'You get used to it. I did.'

'It's silly. I mean, Chris is out a lot anyway. He's either running or at the gym or on a night out. I hardly see him. But he's here. This is his home. It'll just be me rattling around.'

'You could always move. Buy somewhere smaller.'

'I like it here.'

'Take a lodger.'

'And get murdered while I'm asleep?'

Matilda stifled a laugh. 'Find a bloke.'

Adele poured herself a large glass of wine and took a sip. 'I think I've been on my own too long. I mean, it would be nice to wake up in the morning and have someone next to me. But then I think of the mess they make in the bathroom and I wonder if it's worth the hassle.'

'It's funny; Pat moans about her husband yet here we are, lonely without one.'

'Sod's law.'

The front door opened and slammed closed making them both jump. The living room door was pushed open and Chris, in his running gear, came in with his arm around Scott, still suited and booted from work.

'Matilda, thank God you're here. Scott's been attacked,' Chris said.

'What?'

'I haven't been attacked,' Scott said.

Chris put Scott into the armchair and all three stood over him. Whatever had happened to him had resulted in his being hit in the face. His left eye was rapidly darkening.

'What happened?' Matilda asked.

'Nothing.'

'If you don't tell them, Scott, I will.'

'Shit,' Scott said quietly. He tried to make eye contact with Matilda but couldn't out of embarrassment. 'I went to see Oliver Ridgeway.'

'What? Why?'

'I wanted to get the truth out of him. Put a little pressure on him.'

'And he hit you?'

'No. Well, not . . . it's not that simple,' he said, looking at Adele and Chris.

Matilda frowned. She turned to Adele and asked if she and Chris could leave them alone for a few minutes. They disappeared into the kitchen. Matilda sat down on the edge of the coffee table. 'What happened?'

'I sort of suggested that he'd arranged to kill his in-laws when Clive found out his secret.'

'So he hit you? I'll have him charged with assault.'

'No. Wait. He tried to . . . you know . . . he backed me into a corner and he undid his trousers.'

'What?' Matilda jumped up.

'No. Nothing happened. I went to move and he thumped me, so I elbowed him in the ribs. Then I did a runner.'

'Jesus, Scott. What were you thinking?'

'I don't . . . I just.'

'You could have been seriously injured. Or worse.'

'But don't you see what this means? It shows how quick he is to anger. He's got to have played some part in the murder of his in-laws.'

'But he has an alibi, Scott.'

'He could have paid someone to do it for him. This Keith Lumb bloke. He could have offered him a few grand or something. It's possible.'

'Possible, but unlikely.' Matilda sat on the sofa. 'You did a reckless thing tonight, Scott. You were lucky.'

'I'm sorry.'

'I don't want you doing anything like that again.'

'I won't.'

'I should hope not. You've only just recovered from what happened with Steve Harrison. Do you enjoy being in hospital?'

'Look, I said I'm sorry,' he said, standing up, wincing as he did so.

'Where are you going?'

'Home.'

Matilda stepped in front of him. She lifted his shirt and saw the bruises on his body. 'I thought he just hit you in the face. Adele,' she called out. 'This is assault, Scott.'

'And if I press charges it'll all come out. You promised,' he said through gritted teeth as Adele and Chris came back into the room.

'What's going on?' Adele asked.

'You're medically trained. Have you got anything for this?' Matilda asked, lifting Scott's shirt up once again.

'Jesus, Scott, why didn't you tell me?' Chris chastised.

'Come on,' Adele took charge. 'Upstairs. I've got something that will take care of the bruising.'

Adele led Scott out of the room while Matilda and Chris went over to the sofa.

'Is everything all right with Scott?' Chris eventually asked.

'Why do you ask?'

'Well, since this new case, you know, the nasty crime scene, he's been a bit quiet, a bit off.' He shrugged, struggling to find the right words.

'Has he said anything to you?'

'No. That's just it. Mum mentioned how bad the crime scene was. I just think it's affecting him more than he's letting on.'

'Chris, I know you and Scott spend a lot of time together, but do you talk much, you know, about private things?'

'Not really. I don't think Scott has much to talk about. He works a lot. He goes home and puts up with Rory's antics.'

'He hasn't mentioned anything else?'

'No. Well, he said he's lonely a few times. But then, aren't we all?'

'You're lonely?' Matilda asked, surprised.

'It's not fun being single in twenty-first century Britain. I think it's since he moved in with Rory and he's seen how he lives his life, he wonders why he can't be like that – a different woman every weekend. They're very different people. Rory's loud, confident, and makes chatting up women look simple. Scott's more reserved, shy. It's not easy being like that.'

Adele came back into the living room. 'I've run him a bath. I've got some of those muscle relaxing crystals that dissolve. They stink the place out, but they work.'

'I think I'll go up and have a word,' Chris said.

'What's going on?' Adele asked quietly as her son left the room.

'I wish I knew, Adele. I think I've reached that age where I no longer understand the youth of today.'

'Oh God, that's a depressing realization.'

'Tell me about it.'

'More wine?'

'Definitely.'

By the time Oliver arrived home the house was almost in darkness. He unlocked the front door and stepped in to see his mother at the top of the stairs.

'You're late,' she said.

'Yes. Busy day. Where's Leah?'

'She's in bed. Has been all night.' She rolled her eyes. 'Have you eaten?'

'I'm fine, Mum.'

'OK. Well, goodnight.' She turned the landing light off and headed for her bedroom, plunging Oliver into darkness.

He was sore from the attack by the detective, but he would heal. Though it would take more than a few paracetamol to help what was going on inside his head. He wondered if the gay detective was out at work. He knew they all stood by each other. If Scott's secret did come out, nobody would care, they would stand by him and it would be Oliver whose career would lie in ruins before it even started. Fuck.

He went into the living room and poured himself a large brandy from his father's supply and necked it in one gulp. This wasn't how he expected his life to have turned out, certainly not his married life. The plan had been to move into Leah's parents' home once they returned from their honeymoon for a few months until they found a place. They had enough between them for a deposit on a house and there were several new builds they liked the look off. Clive and Serena Mercer had a house large enough for them all to live in quite happily for a while without being in each other's pockets. If only the same could be said for his own parents' cottage. Even downstairs in the living room he could hear his father's light snoring.

He poured himself another drink and took it over to the sofa where he slumped into it. He took out his mobile phone and logged on to the dating app. There were several blokes currently online within a few kilometres who he liked the look of. Sex with Leah was comfortable, pedestrian, safe. When he was with a man, it was completely different. It was exciting, dangerous, and tinged with a hint of violence. He loved the roughness as he took another man between his legs, looked into his steely eyes and saw the same urgent determination that was racing through his own veins.

He felt himself grow hard and he rubbed his hand over his erection. He was married now. He had a wife upstairs who was there to satisfy his urges. But the sex on the night of their wedding had been incredibly tedious. He had to bite his bottom lip to stop himself from yawning. What was wrong with Leah? Why wouldn't she give herself to him?

His phone vibrated. He looked down at the screen and saw he'd received a message from a cute nineteen-year-old. He messaged back. Within five minutes they knew just enough about each other to realize they were compatible to satisfy each other's needs. The teenager gave him his location and Oliver texted back saying he'd be there in ten minutes. He snatched up his car keys from where he'd thrown them on the coffee table and left the house, slamming the door closed behind him.

* * *

Upstairs, Leah couldn't sleep. She had heard Oliver come home and expected him to come straight to bed. She needed him. She needed someone to hold. Earlier in the evening, she had tried to talk to her mother-in-law, but it was obvious she wasn't interested. They had never really got on. A clash of personalities. She had expected the murder of her family to have changed things, maybe brought down the walls Sophia built around her emotions, but no. She was as cold and as icy as ever.

As soon as Leah heard the front door close, she jumped out of bed and went over to the window, peeling back the curtains to look out. Oliver headed for his car. He looked at his watch as he turned on the internal light and entered something in his satnav, probably a postcode. He was obviously going somewhere specific, but where, and why now at this time of night? Despite being in her pyjamas, Leah picked up her car keys from the bedside table, took a jacket from the wardrobe and ran downstairs.

Leah shivered as she left the house. She had been warm and comfortable in bed. Now, in the freezing cold night, the low temperature bit into her. She ran to the bottom of the drive and saw Oliver's car turn left at the end of the road. She jumped into her Fiat Punto, turned on the ignition and followed at speed.

She eventually caught up with him at the traffic lights, but kept well back so he didn't recognize her. She hated herself for distrusting her husband of less than a week, but why had he been heading back out when he had only just come home? It didn't make sense.

Leah slowed down. She was getting too close. They left Limb Lane and turned onto Ecclesall Road South. They were heading into the city centre, but at this time of night, nothing was open. Leah turned up the heating. She was freezing cold. Her hands were shaking, though it was mostly through nerves at what she might discover than the low temperatures.

At the end of the long road, Oliver slowed, indicated left, and pulled up in a small car park next to Endcliffe Park. The lighting was poor, and Leah couldn't see well, but she was sure there was someone there waiting for him. She pulled over and turned off her lights. The front passenger door to Oliver's car opened, lighting up the interior. She saw her husband smile as whoever had been waiting for him got into the car and closed the door. The light went off, plunging them into darkness.

Leah immediately thought the worst. Oliver was dealing in drugs. Maybe he was selling what he could steal from the hospital. She wondered how he had managed to come up with his half of a deposit so quickly, especially after his parents said they wouldn't help him. This was not the way she wanted to buy a house. She did not want to start married life on a lie, and she certainly didn't want to be married to a drug dealer.

Fuming, she stepped out of her car, slammed the door closed, and headed for Oliver's black Toyota. She took long strides, not taking her eyes off the car once. Her breath formed in the cold night and drifted away. She was breathing heavily. She was angry, full of rage and disappointment. With a shaking hand, she took the handle and opened the door. The young man, whoever he was, was leaning back, his eyes closed, a smile on his face and his trousers open. Her husband was bent over and performing oral sex on him.

Oliver opened his eyes as the cold from outside wafted over him. As soon as he saw his wife, his expression changed to one of abject horror.

'You bastard,' she eventually said. Her voice was calm, despite the fact what was left of her life had just been chewed up and spat out.

She slammed the door so hard she heard a crack in the glass and headed back for her car. She had no idea where she was going to go. She wanted to be away from Oliver, and everything that reminded her of him.

By the time she reached her Punto, she had calmed down, a little. The image of what her husband was doing in the car filled her head and she vomited into the side of the road.

'Leah. Leah,' Oliver shouted her. She looked up and wiped her mouth.

'Don't come anywhere near me.' She held out a hand to stop him. 'I don't want to hear your excuses.'

'Leah, it's not what you think?'

'Really? So I didn't see you with that lad's cock in your mouth?' Oliver recoiled.

'What? Embarrassed? Ashamed? Good. So you should be. You're my husband, Oliver,' Leah spat. 'We're married. If you didn't love me, why marry me?' She felt tears roll down her face which angered her more. Why should she feel so upset?

'I do love you,' he pleaded.

'You're pathetic.'

He stepped forward and put a hand on her arm which she quickly shrugged away.

'Don't touch me,' she screamed. Her voice echoed through the night. 'If you'd told me you were gay, I would have understood. I'm not a bigot. But this? This is disgusting. You disgust me. I don't want anything to do with you.'

She jumped into the car, started the ignition and drove at speed. She looked in the rear-view mirror and saw the man she had loved standing in the middle of the road looking sad and pathetic.

Chapter Forty-Four

It was almost midnight but Sian and Stuart Mills finally had the house to themselves. Stuart came in from the kitchen carrying a cup of tea in each hand and offered one to his wife. She was shattered and wanted to go to bed but didn't have the energy to get up off the sofa.

'You were going to tell me why you were late home,' he said, sitting next to her and putting his arms around her.

All four of Stuart and Sian's children knew what their mother did for a living. They knew the potential dangers she could face on a daily basis, but it was never spoken about in front of them. Whenever they wanted to discuss her work, it was usually last thing at night before they went to sleep, or, like now, when the kids were all in bed and they had some alone time.

Sian tossed the note pad onto the coffee table and relaxed in her husband's arms. 'I had a visitor just as I was leaving the station. Bev. She works as a prostitute. She's like the mother to all the young girls on the streets. She came in about a year ago saying one had gone missing and now she says another one's gone missing too. I'm not sure what to do about it.'

'Maybe they've moved on,' he said, taking a sip of his tea.

'It's possible. I just . . . I don't know. I'll have a word with Matilda. I left Bev to make an official missing person's report.

The thing is, there has been talk over the past year or so of street workers going missing.' She scratched her head. There was a worrying look on her face. 'You know when there's something wrong, but you can't put your finger on it?'

'What are you working on?' he asked, nodding at the note pad.

'I'm trying to make sense of the notes I took from a bloke at the GMC. This Clive Mercer, he faced three hearings over the past six or seven years. An elderly lady, a man in his forties and a child aged three all died in his care.'

'Did he kill them?'

'No. On each occasion he was found to have acted lawfully. Mistakes were made, and lessons would be learned. The usual guff. I'm giving myself a headache trying to find someone who would want to kill him and his family and just can't seem to find anything.'

She snuggled deeper into her husband's arms and rested her head on his chest.

'There's more than you working on that team, Sian. Delegate.'

'I know. I will.'

'Would you like me to carry you up to bed?'

She laughed. 'I'd love that. I think I'm going to spend a few more minutes on my notes. You go up. I won't be long.'

Stuart stood up, kissed her on the forehead and left the room, taking his cup of tea with him. 'Love you.'

'Love you, too,'

Sian picked up her note pad and looked at the three names she'd written – Margo Sanders, Martin Walken and Milly Johnston. They had all died on the operating table while Clive Mercer was monitoring their anaesthetic. In each case he had been forced to justify his actions to the GMC. In each case he had been found to have acted responsibly. However, after the hearings, Clive had grown in confidence, or was that arrogance? He hadn't appreciated having to explain himself in a position he thought he ruled.

Clive's anger had grown. He wasn't used to being questioned. He'd become complacent in his duty and it wasn't appreciated by those he worked with.

It didn't seem to matter how many people Clive had pissed off in his work, it didn't alter the fact that if someone wanted to kill him they could have done so in a different way. There was no reason for anyone to have caused such a brutal and violent attack against Serena and Jeremy and left Rachel alive to witness the slaughter of her family.

Sian threw her notebook on the table and decided to sleep on it. There was something they were yet to uncover in the Mercers' history, something so bad it warranted the butchering of three family members. Something that big would soon come to light. She hoped.

'Can I come in?' Chris asked, knocking on the bathroom door.
'Sure.'

Chris opened the door. His nose wrinkled at the smell of the muscle relaxant his mother had put in the bath. Through the steam of the heat, Scott was just about visible. He had wrapped a towel around his waist. Chris saw, for the first time, the full result of his attack. Scott was pale. His skin was smooth and hairless. The dark purple bruises were stark.

'Oh my God.'
'It looks worse than it feels.'
'Are you sure about that?'
'Yes.'

'Look, I think you should stay over tonight.'

'I'll be fine,' he lied.

'Matilda's staying over so you may as well. Mum loves a full house.'

'Is there enough room?'

'Sure. You can have my bed.'

'And where will you sleep?'

'I'll take the sofa.'

'No. That's not fair. Look, give me a hand to get dressed and I'll give Rory a call. He can come and fetch me.'

Scott struggled to walk out of the bathroom. Chris led him into his bedroom and sat him down, carefully, on his bed. He sat next to him.

'I don't suppose you're going to tell me what really went on tonight.'

'It's to do with this case. Occupational hazard,' he tried to laugh but it hurt.

'You going to press charges?'

'No. Like I said, all in a day's work.'

Scott looked ahead. His face was a map of worry. His frown lines were heavy. His eyes were large and wet as if he was about to burst into tears.

'Scott, what's wrong?' Chris asked quietly.

Scott tried to reply but his emotions betrayed him. A tear fell and his bottom lip wobbled. 'I'm all . . . knotted,' he said. 'I feel . . .'

'What?'

Scott turned to look at Chris. He immediately leaned forward and kissed him on the lips. 'Fuck,' he said. 'I'm sorry. I don't know why I did that. I'm sorry.' He tried to get up off the bed but cried out in pain.

Chris grabbed him to stop him from falling and sat him

down on the bed. He reached out, took hold of his chin and turned his head towards him where he reciprocated his kiss.

'What did you do that for?' Scott asked.

'I've been wanting to do it since the first night I saw you in Endcliffe Park all those months ago.'

Scott let out the breath he'd been holding. 'Really?'

'Oh yes.'

Scott smiled. It was the first genuine positive emotion he'd felt in months, years. 'You can do it again if you like.'

Chris took Scott's head in both hands and kissed him firmly and passionately on the lips. It was a kiss so powerful, so electric, neither of them wanted it to stop.

Chapter Forty-Five

Matilda entered the HMET suite with a takeaway latte in hand. She'd asked the barista for an extra shot of caffeine, but as she'd walked up the stairs and taken a sip, it didn't taste any stronger. She had slept fitfully last night in Adele's spare bedroom which was next to Chris's room. She had strained to hear the muffled conversation between Chris and Scott which went on into the small hours of the morning, but couldn't make out what they were talking about.

The room was already abuzz of activity. Matilda took another sip of the coffee, asked Sian to throw her a Boost from her snack drawer and opened the morning briefing.

'Where's Scott?' Aaron asked.

'No idea,' Rory said. 'He didn't come home last night.'

'He's finally pulled? About bloody time. I was starting to get worried about him.' Aaron smiled.

Matilda cleared her throat. 'Scott suffered an altercation last night. He'll be taking today off,' she said. As she'd left Adele's she'd sent Scott a text telling him not to come in today after being attacked last night.

'An altercation? What does that mean?' Rory asked, looking worried.

'He was involved in an incident.'

'Is he OK?'

'He'll be fine. He just needs today to rest.'

'Where is he?'

'Rory, we'll talk after the briefing,' she said, silencing his questions.

Rory sat back in his seat. He had the confused look of someone trying to recite their thirteen times table. He took his mobile phone out of his jacket pocket and ran off a quick text at speed.

'Right then, developments,' Matilda began. 'I had a phone call yesterday evening from Keith Lumb. I'm guessing he's been in contact with his sister and she passed my number on to him. He is adamant he was nowhere near the Mercer house on Sunday night. The call was traced to Maidstone in Kent, which makes me believe he's trying to flee the country.'

'Why run if he's innocent?' Aaron asked.

'My sentiment exactly. The thing is, he sounded scared. So, is he running because he's committed three murders or is he running because he's been set up by someone?'

'Maybe we should talk to the sister again.'

'Me and Rory spoke to her last time, so I think we should pay her another visit. Now, Kent Police said they were going to step up their patrols in trying to find Keith. His photo has been sent to all airports, bus and train stations and the port at Dover, just in case he tries to cross the Channel. ACC Masterson has put out an appeal to all press for anyone to get in touch if they see him. If any of you have seen this morning's national newspapers, you'll have seen Keith looking up at you from the front page. So far, we've had no genuine leads.'

'The phones are ringing off the hook by all accounts,' Aaron said.

'It's a sad fact that a lot of them will either be pranks or false leads. However, they all need to be followed up. Any information that comes through with sightings in other jurisdictions needs passing on to that police force for them to check out. We will deal with all South Yorkshire sightings. In the meantime, we still need to work on a motive for why the Mercer family were killed.'

'I spoke to someone at the GMC yesterday,' Sian said, putting down her bag of Maltesers. 'My goodness, he was dull. Also, my email is back up and running so I've got the files of the three cases.' She flicked through her note pad. 'We've got Margo Sanders aged eighty; Martin Walken, forty-six; and three-year-old Milly Johnston. All from Sheffield.'

'Oh God. A three-year-old?' Aaron asked. 'What happened to her?'

'She had a brain tumour. There was a fault with her oxygen levels during the surgery to remove the tumour. They couldn't restart her heart.'

'Poor kid.'

'Adele Kean would have worked on the post mortems on each of the patients, I'm guessing, so I'm going to have a word with her and see if there was anything unusual about them. Just on the off-chance,' Sian said.

'Good thinking,' Matilda said. 'Contact each of the next of kin and find their alibis for the night of the murders.'

'I'm a step ahead of you there,' she said with a smirk. 'The benefit of working on a case that won't allow you to rest is that it affects your sleeping patterns, so, I was on the phone from seven o'clock this morning. Margo's next of kin was her husband, Vince. He died about eighteen months after his wife of a stroke. I spoke to his daughter who lives in Dorset and has an alibi for Sunday night. Martin Walken's next of kin is his wife, Louise.

She accepted the GMC ruling and has no ill will against the Mercers. She's emailed me several photos of herself at a concert on Sunday night. As for Milly Johnston, her next of kin were obviously her parents. I've called the house and spoke to a bloke called Zack Fisher. He's house-sitting while the parents are away on holiday in southern Spain.'

'And all that before breakfast?' Matilda asked.

'I'm dedicated, what do you expect?' She said with a smile.

The glass double doors were opened, and a uniformed ACC Masterson entered the suite. She was only a small woman but she commanded a great presence. Everything stopped when she entered a room.

'Ma'am,' Matilda said, surprised by the visit.

Valerie nodded. She remained standing by the door. 'Are we any closer to finding this Keith Lumb?'

'I haven't had a chance to call Kent Police yet, so I don't know if they've had any sightings.'

'Don't bother. I had a call from Manchester Police an hour ago saying a truck driver dropped him off at Piccadilly Station late last night.'

'What? How genuine is the sighting?' Matilda asked, looking confused.

'Very. The driver said it was definitely Keith Lumb. They're emailing through his statement. Apparently, when it came on the news about him being in the Maidstone area he panicked and asked him to drop him off at the station. When the driver let him out, he looked him up on his phone, saw his picture on the BBC News app and called it in.'

'Why has he come back north?'

'He has family here, doesn't he?'

'Yes.'

'Maybe he's come back home.'

'OK. He has a flat in Tankersley. I want that watching and his sister's house needs keeping an eye on too. His mother is in a home. I need to know which one and that needs monitoring too,' she said to Christian, who made a note and said he'd get right on to it.

Sian's phone rang. She answered it before the end of the first ring.

'Matilda, the press is all over this,' Valerie said, dropping her voice. 'This story has gone worldwide – three professional people in a middle-class part of Sheffield butchered on the day of their daughter's wedding. This sounds like the plot of a Hollywood movie.'

'Matilda would be Liam Neeson though,' Rory said with a smile. He looked down when it was met with steely glances.

'I need a development on this by the end of today,' Valerie said, wiping a hand across her brow. She looked tired and drawn. She had obviously been on the receiving end of an awkward conversation with the chief constable. 'I do not like Sheffield being on the front pages for the wrong things. Are we clear on this, Matilda?'

'Very,' she replied icily. She did not like a dressing-down in front of her team. It wasn't good for morale.

'Good.' She glanced around the room before turning away and leaving the suite.

The silence developed as all eyes returned to Matilda.

'Right, Rory, we're going to see Elizabeth Lumb again. She must know where her brother is heading. Sian, you're on motive. Christian, use Aaron and Ranjeet to cover Elizabeth's house, the flat in Barnsley and the care home their mother is in.'

'We don't have enough people for all this.'

'I'm aware of that,' Matilda almost shouted. 'Get uniform on it. Get the Barnsley police to lend some officers. If it wasn't for them letting a prisoner go in the first place we wouldn't be in this fucking mess. Today would be good, Rory,' she said, charging out of the suite.

'Ma'am, that was reception on the phone,' Sian called after her. 'Leah Ridgeway is downstairs. She said she needs to see you. She's in a bit of a state.'

Scott opened his eyes. For a moment he couldn't remember where he was. The wallpaper wasn't familiar, neither were the curtains. He coughed. The pain shot through his entire body and he remembered everything about what happened last night. A smile spread across his lips when he recalled the long conversation with Chris. He turned over and looked at the empty space next to him. Maybe he'd been dreaming.

He picked up his mobile from the bedside table and saw a note underneath it. He rubbed his eyes until his vision was clear enough to read it:

Morning, I tried to wake you but you just turned over and went back to sleep. I enjoyed our chat last night. It was good to hear you feel the same as I do. I'm looking forward to seeing where this goes. I'll text you when I get a free period. Chris, xx

Scott smiled as he read the note. He read it a second time and folded the small piece of paper carefully. He'd be saving this note.

Last night, Scott had opened up and told Chris everything. From his point of a view, it was a gamble that could have ruined their friendship. They were very close, shared similar interests and got on well with each other. When Scott had finished, he looked Chris in the eye. He was surprised to see him smiling. Chris didn't need to say anything. He leaned forward and kissed him firmly on the lips again. It was passionate and spoke a thousand words. When they pulled apart, reluctantly, their entire relationship had changed. They were no longer friends. They were a couple. They spent the night sleeping in each other's arms. For the first time in as long as he could remember, Scott had a deep sleep. He felt warm, wanted and safe.

Looking at his phone, Scott saw several missed calls from Rory and a frantic voicemail from just before midnight asking where the bollocking-hell he was. There was also a text from him sent an hour ago asking what incident had taken place yesterday. Scott's heart sank. Had Matilda told him everything?

Before replying, he read the text from Matilda telling him not to come in today and spend the day recovering. He put the phone back on the cabinet and turned over, pulling the duvet over his head. As much as he wanted to revel in the happiness and warm glow his developing relationship with Chris made him feel, he couldn't fully relax as the reality of his colleagues finding out, being the centre of attention, the constant questions, filled him with dread. Would they treat him any differently once they knew he was gay? Would they accept him? Would they want to work with him?

Leah Ridgeway had been led into an interview room to wait for Matilda. When the DCI opened the door she saw a different woman sitting behind the desk. Gone was the grieving daughter and sister who had lost the majority of her family, replaced by a determined, strong woman. Her face was free of make-up. Her hair was tied back in a severe ponytail. She wore a black coat and a cream-coloured sweater beneath. She sat perfectly still, her hands clasped on her lap in front of her. Her lips were pursed so tightly they were almost white. Her eyes were wide and staring, they couldn't focus as she blinked rapidly and took in everything going on around her.

'Leah, is everything OK?' Matilda asked.

'No,' she said firmly. 'I want you to arrest my husband.'

'What? Why?' Matilda sat down opposite her.

Leah swallowed hard. A tear fell down her face but she didn't wipe it away. 'Last night, he tried to rape me, and, I think he arranged for my family to be murdered.'

Chapter Forty-Six

Everywhere Keith looked he saw his face. He was on the front of all the newspapers. It was the picture he had taken the last time he had been arrested. He looked, dead-eyed, to the centre of the camera. There was no smile, no sneer, no look of regret, just a blank expression of a man hurtling towards his thirties with no future, no hope and no prospects.

In the centre of Manchester, he looked around and saw people going about their business. Nobody cared anymore. Everyone lived in their own little bubble. He was grateful that the majority of people seemed to be charging full pelt with their heads down. Students and young people were more interested in what was going on in cyberspace via their smartphones to worry about a potential triple killer standing next to them in the queue for a coffee. Those of a working age were too caught up in the complexities of life – work, home, bills, childcare, lack of a pension, the instability of the future thanks to Brexit – to concentrate on who was around them. As long as it didn't have a direct impact on their own lives, they weren't interested. The elderly seemed to go around with a look of fear on their faces. They were distrustful of the young with their self-aggrandizing want for the superficial, and who could blame them.

Keith knew he wasn't at risk of being identified by the public.

Obviously, there was always one nosy parker who noticed every-thing and would ring the police if they recognized him, but he thought he'd changed his appearance enough for the untrained eye not to pick up on him. The one thing Keith feared, was the all-seeing eye of CCTV cameras. They were everywhere. He had read somewhere that England had more security cameras than any other country in Europe. He wondered if it was true. Suddenly, he was seeing cameras wherever he looked. He pulled the hood up on his sweater, and, with his head down, made his way quickly north. He had no idea where he was going. He didn't know Manchester well. He felt he had to get away from the city centre, head for the motorway, try and grab another lift. He'd been spooked in the truck yesterday when he was mentioned on the radio. He guessed the driver saw a change in his behav-iour, that's why he'd asked him to drop him off at the next station. He was shocked to find he was only at Manchester. Glasgow would have been ideal.

He found a phone box, dug for a pound coin in his jeans pocket and called his sister. He needed help and he had very few people he could turn to.

'Elizabeth, it's me.'

'Keith. Where the hell are you?'

'I can't tell you.'

'The news said you were in Maidstone. What were you doing there? We don't know anyone in Maidstone.'

'I'm not there now. I was trying to get abroad.'

'Keith, what the hell have you got yourself mixed up in?'

'That's just it, I haven't done anything.'

'Then why are you running away? Did you phone DCI Darke?'

'Yes. I called her last night. I told her I was innocent.'

'Did she believe you?'

'I doubt it. They don't care about guilt and innocence. They just want someone to lock up.'

'No. She's not like that. She'll listen to you. I looked her up on the Internet. Do you remember that place in Sheffield, Starling House? It was a youth prison for all those violent teenagers? There was a lad in there who was innocent, and she got him out. She'll listen to you; I know she will.'

'You're sure?'

'Positive.'

'Will you call her for me? Will you tell her I'm innocent?'

'It would be better coming from you.'

'I've tried.'

'Try harder. Keith, you can't keep running away like this. They'll find out. If they do it will look worse. It would be better if you gave yourself up.'

'Elizabeth, you know me, there's no way I could have killed three people.'

'I know.'

'So tell them that. Please,' he begged.

'Think about it, Keith, they're not going to listen to me. They'll have looked into my background too. They'll know all about me. They won't believe a word I say. You've got to come home.'

Keith was silent for a long moment while he made a decision. 'I want to.'

'Then come home,' Elizabeth pleaded. 'For me. For Mum.'

He took a deep breath and released it in a heavy sigh. 'Look, call DCI Darke. Tell her I'll talk to her, but it's just going to be me and her, and you. Nobody else.'

'OK.'

'Thanks. I'll call you later. I love you, Elizabeth,' he said quickly before ending the call.

Elizabeth Lumb stood in the living room with the phone in her hand. She looked at the blank display. Her heart was racing. If her mother found out what her son was involved in, it could kill her.

'That was Keith,' she called out to the kitchen. 'He wants to come home. I'm going to call that DCI Darke, see if she'll meet him.'

Still clutching the phone to her chest she headed for the kitchen. She opened the door and went to put the kettle on.

'Don't look at me like that. I can't leave him out to dry. Do you want a coffee?' She turned to the table. There was nobody there. 'I'll just make myself one then.'

Chapter Forty-Seven

'What's going on?'

'Rory, not now.'

Matilda was charging down the corridor with the young DC on her heels.

'What's happened to Scott? I've tried calling him and texting him but he's not responding. Has he been hurt? Is he in hospital? Do his family know?'

Matilda stopped dead in her tracks. Rory almost collided with her.

'Rory, I don't have time to answer your questions right now.' She saw the look of hurt on his face. 'Look, Scott is fine. He just needs to take today off. I'm sure he'll tell you everything tomorrow.'

'But it doesn't make sense . . .'

'Rory, I've got a woman in there who says her husband killed her family. I've got a suspected triple killer running around Britain and the world's press breathing down my neck. I'm short staffed. I haven't showered since yesterday morning and I'm wearing yesterday's knickers. I haven't got time for this,' she shouted.

She turned and continued to head towards the HMET suite. Rory picked up the pace and followed.

'I'm sorry,' he said, quickly.

'That's OK.'

'What do you want me to do?'

'Get a car and go and arrest Oliver Ridgeway.' Matilda kicked open the door, which banged against the wall. 'Christian, I need a team to keep an eye on Elizabeth Lumb. I'm not going to be able to get there this morning.'

'I don't have the manpower for another team.'

She looked around at the empty room. 'Shit.' She could feel the prickly heat of a panic attack rising up through her body. It had been a long time since she had been under such stress. Usually everything was manageable. Not this time.

'Christian,' she said, taking a deep breath, 'I don't care how you do it, but I need a team to watch Elizabeth Lumb's house in case her brother comes back. Use Specials, use Community Policing, use the fucking boy scouts, I don't care. As long as there is someone keeping an eye on her house until I can find time to get over there,' she said quietly.

'Leave it with me. I'll sort it.' He backed away.

'Thank you.'

She turned to head to her office; her vision blurred. She tried to take a deep breath but she was too tense for it to have any effect. She bit the inside of her mouth hard to try and relieve the aggression she was feeling, but even with the taste of blood, there was no release.

Her phone started to ring. She fished it out of her pocket and saw it was Elizabeth calling her. *What fresh hell is this?*

'DCI Darke? It's Elizabeth Lumb. I don't know if you remember me, you came to my house—'

'Yes, I remember,' Matilda interrupted.

'I've had a call from my brother. He'd like to talk to you.'

Her eyes widened. 'Where is he?'

'I don't know. But he said he'd like to talk to you and explain everything, but he wants to talk to you on your own. Well, with me there too, but just you from the police.'

'That's fine. I can do that. Where?'

'I don't know. He's going to call me back later.'

'OK.' Matilda ran her fingers through her hair. She dug her nails into her scalp. The pain sent a shiver down her spine. 'When he calls, tell him to name the time and the place and I'll be there.'

'Will do.'

Matilda ended the call. She felt a wave of relief sweep over her. She was making some headway. Finally. She turned to face the room but there was only one other person there.

'It's Tim, isn't it?'

'Finn.'

'Of course. Sorry. Do me a favour, look up a woman named Elizabeth Lumb. She lives on Trap Lane in Sheffield. I want to know everything about her.'

'How do I . . .? I mean, is she a suspect or . . . you know . . .?' He waffled. His fingers were poised over the keyboard of his laptop. They were shaking with nerves.

'Just do what you can.' She rolled her eyes and left the room.

* * *

Matilda found herself heading for the toilets. The last cubicle near the window was always her place of refuge; where she went to lock herself in and have a good cry. It was usually her depression, the empty feeling of loss when she thought of James that made her feel like this, but now, it felt different. Why did she want to cry? She pushed open the door and was about to cross the threshold when she stopped herself. She took a deep breath and inhaled the toxic fumes of toilet cleaner, cheap liquid soap and urine.

You're bigger than this.

She turned on her heels and headed for the stairs. Maybe she needed some fresh air. Maybe she needed just a few minutes to herself. Maybe she needed a clean pair of knickers.

As she ran down the stairs she looked at her phone. There was a text from Pat saying she had thoroughly enjoyed urbexing last night. She'd been in four buildings on the outskirts of the city centre but hadn't found anything. She was going again next week at some point. Matilda smiled to herself as she remembered the selfie Pat had sent her. She dialled Scott.

'Scott, it's Matilda. I'm sorry but I need you to come in. I know I said you could have today off but we're seriously short staffed.'

'Oh.'

'Problem?' she asked in a way where even if there was a problem he would be unable to refuse to come to work.

He hesitated. 'No. It's just . . .'

'Look, Scott, I'm sorry. I know you're going through a lot in your personal life but you're going to have to put it on the back burner.'

'Does anyone know what happened last night?'

Are you referring to your attack or the kissing noises I could hear from the spare room?

'They think you were involved in an incident. That's all. We're arresting Oliver Ridgeway. His wife has made a serious allegation against him.'

'Shit,' he said under his breath. 'OK. Give me an hour.'

Matilda ended the call. No sooner had she put the phone in her pocket than it started ringing again. She answered as she pushed open the double doors and was hit in the face with a blast of cool air. She shuddered. It was just what she needed. She was able to breathe easily again.

'Is this DCI Darke?'

'Speaking.'

'It's TDC Finn Cotton. I'm on your team.'

'I remember.' She smiled.

'I've looked up Elizabeth Lumb for you. She has a record.'

That stopped Matilda dead in her tracks. 'Really? What for?'

'For a start, her mother isn't in a nursing home. Well, she kind of is, but it's not a home that you go to just because you're old.'

'What are you talking about?'

'Her mother has locked-in syndrome. She was involved in an accident in 2001.'

'What happened?'

'She fell off a balcony and landed on concrete.'

'Elizabeth said she was in a nursing home. Why would she lie?'

'Because, according to this, it was Elizabeth who pushed her.'

Chapter Forty-Eight

Elizabeth put the phone back in its cradle in the hallway. She liked it to be fully charged. She put on her coat and stepped into her ankle boots. In the mirror, she checked her appearance, neatened her hair and made sure she didn't have anything in between her teeth.

'I'm going out now,' she called up the stairs. 'I won't be long. Keith said he'll call. If he does and I'm not back, tell him to try again later. Will you be all right on your own?' She waited as if listening to a reply. 'That's good. You just relax. Bye.'

She let herself out, locked the door behind her and placed the door keys carefully in her pocket. As she made her way down the pavement she looked back up at the house and gave a wave to the front bedroom window.

Oliver Ridgeway was sitting in interview room one. His solicitor had been called and was on his way. Watching from the observation room, Matilda was joined by a flustered Scott who looked like he'd run all the way to work.

'We're not going to mention the assault on you at all,' Matilda said. Her voice was low and severe. 'We're not going to talk about anything connected with you. It'll just be the assault on his wife and the murders. Understand?'

'Yes,' he said, swallowing hard.

'Are you all right?'

'No,' he almost snapped.

Matilda opened her mouth to speak when a PC knocked and entered, telling them Oliver's solicitor was here.

In the corridor, Hilary Morrison stood with her back straight and her head held high. She was only a short woman, five foot two in heels, but she made up for it with her reputation. Hilary was a formidable woman who oozed attitude. She was as vicious with her clients as she was with the police. She wasn't here to make friends but to get to the truth of the matter. Above all, she hated being lied to and had been known to walk out during an interview, leaving her client stranded if she felt she was being sold a lie. Matilda had a great deal of admiration for her.

'Hilary, long time no see,' Matilda said, shaking her hand.

'Matilda, always a pleasure. I've been told you've moved house.'

'Yes. I had no idea how much of a project it was going to be, but it's getting there.'

'You're moving on then?'

'Trying.'

'You'll get there.' She smiled a natural smile. 'Can I have a private chat with my client?'

'Of course. We'll be in in a few minutes.'

Hilary entered the interview room and closed the door firmly behind her. Ten minutes later, when Matilda and Scott entered, Hilary had made herself comfortable. Her expensive jacket was draped over the back of her chair and she was sitting next to Oliver with her pen poised over an open folder. She had already made comprehensive notes by the look of it.

Matilda watched as an icy exchange was made between Oliver

and Scott. Scott turned away first but Oliver's steely gaze was fixed firmly on the DC.

Scott started the recording equipment and they each stated who they were in turn. Eventually, he looked up. He was sitting opposite the accused. They were in each other's line of sight.

'Before we proceed,' Hilary began, 'my client denies all knowledge of an assault on his wife. Last night, they had a row and Leah left. She didn't come home all night. As for Leah claiming he is responsible for the murder of her family, he is dumbfounded by these allegations, and, as you know, has a cast-iron alibi for the time of the killings.'

Matilda opened a file in front of her. 'Mr Ridgeway, when you were arrested we seized your mobile phone under section nineteen of the Police and Criminal Evidence Act of 1984. Section twenty of that act allows us to sift it for evidence. We have found the text message you sent to your wife this morning at nine o'clock in which you apologize for absolutely everything. They were your exact words. This is all the evidence we need for your guilt.'

'Taken out of context, that text could mean anything,' Hilary interrupted.

'Mr Ridgeway, do you know what Grindr is?'

The temperature seemed to drop several degrees in the room as, once again, Oliver and Scott made eye contact. Again, it was Scott who looked away first.

'Mr Ridgeway?' Matilda prompted.

'No,' he said quietly.

'Are you sure?'

He took a deep breath. 'Yes. I'm sure.'

'OK. Grindr is a social networking app used by gay men in order to meet other gay men whether that's for a drink, casual sex, or dates. Why is this app on your phone?'

All eyes were on Oliver as he remained stoic.

'Mr Ridgeway, are you bisexual?'

'My client's sexuality is not under scrutiny here. Surely he's here to answer questions about the alleged assault on his wife. An assault he has vehemently denied.'

'True, but we need to find a motive for the assault. I'm guessing if his wife found out about his secret other life, that would be a motive for assault. It could also be a motive for the murder of his in-laws?'

'My client, and his wife, were both in Paris at the time of the murders. You know this already, DCI Darke.'

'Indeed. I didn't say he committed the murders. I said his secret life could be a motive. Mr Ridgeway, would you answer my question?'

'I don't use it very often,' he eventually said. His head was down and he was nervously picking at his fingernails.

Matilda referred to the file again. 'You downloaded the app in October 2010. That's almost eight years ago. You have messages on there going back several years and in your message history you have over one hundred conversations with men which are still active. You even logged on to the app while you were in Paris and messaged seven men. If you're going to lie about your usage of this app, you really need to clear your history more often.'

'May I have a few more minutes' private chat with my client?' Hilary asked as she quickly scribbled on her pad.

'Not yet,' Matilda replied with a hint of a smile. 'Mr Ridgeway, does anyone know about you using this app?'

'No,' he said, looking up at Scott.

'Does anyone among your circle of friends or family know about your sexuality?'

'No.'

'Are you ashamed?'

'DCI Darke, please?'

'How do you think your parents would react to knowing about you being gay? You're their only child yet they don't seem very warm and loving parents.'

'My parents.' Oliver's face twitched and he started to stutter. 'My p-parents are hard-working people. They've done a lot for me over the years.'

'And all they want is for their only child to get married to a lovely woman, settle down and start a family. But that's not what you want, is it?'

'DCI Darke, I think we're deviating from the purpose of this interview,' Hilary intervened.

'Mr Ridgeway, were you frightened of your father-in-law?'

'What? No.'

'Our investigations have uncovered that he was quite a violent man, quick to temper. If he found out you were gay, cheating on his wife, or even if you called off the wedding to his daughter, he wouldn't have allowed you to simply walk away, would he?'

'I don't know.'

'I'm guessing Mr Mercer would have enacted some form of punishment. His daughter would have been distraught, naturally.'

'I wasn't scared of him.'

'Did you arrange for Clive Mercer, Serena Mercer and Jeremy Mercer to be murdered?' Matilda asked firmly.

'No.'

'Did you arrange for Clive Mercer to be murdered but now, after finding out two other people were killed in the attack, you're ashamed at the destruction you've caused?' Matilda almost shouted.

'No,' he said, a tear falling down his face.

Matilda rifled through the file once again and brought out a photograph of Keith Lumb. She placed it in front of Oliver. 'For the benefit of the recording, I'm showing Mr Ridgeway a photograph of Keith Lumb. Do you know this man?'

He glanced at it, frowned, and turned away. 'No.'

'Take a longer look.'

He did and repeated his answer.

'Are you sure?'

'My client has already told you twice he has no idea who this man is.'

'This is Keith Lumb. He's known to police as a petty criminal. He's committed a few burglaries, driven without any insurance, drunk and disorderly, nothing earth shattering. However, his DNA is all over the Mercer household. He's currently on the run. We're trying to trace him in connection with three savage murders. Unfortunately, that doesn't sit well with me. Every police officer we have spoken to about Keith has said he is not the type of person to commit murder. So, if he is the killer, the question is, why?'

'Isn't that a question to put to this Keith Lumb and not my client who has no knowledge of him?' Hilary asked.

'Yes it is. And as soon as we trace Keith, we will be asking him that. We'll also be showing him Oliver's photograph and asking if he knows him. I'm guessing he will. Now, Mr Ridgeway, do you know Keith Lumb? Before you answer that question, please bear in mind you have already lied about the contents of your mobile phone.'

'I don't know who he is,' he said, pushing the photograph away.

Matilda audibly breathed in. 'I'm disappointed. You're in a

position to end the suffering your wife and your niece are going through yet you continue to lie.'

'You have no evidence my client is lying.'

'Let's talk about the assault on your wife last night.'

'I didn't assault my wife.'

'She claims you came to bed angry. She could feel the rage coming from you. You asked her for sex and when she said she was too upset you forced yourself upon her.'

'That's not true.'

'You don't like being told no, do you, Mr Ridgeway?'

'I didn't . . .'

'It's a sad fact that a lot of women seem to marry their fathers. Clive Mercer was a domineering, violent man and Leah seems to have followed in her mother's footsteps and married a man exactly like that.'

'No.'

'We've already uncovered evidence of Clive being violent towards Serena and now we have evidence of you attacking your wife.'

'I didn't attack my wife,' he stated loudly.

'Mr Ridgeway, I am charging you with assaulting your wife. You will go to magistrates' court tomorrow morning and I will be requesting we keep you in custody while investigations into the murders of your in-laws are ongoing.'

'But I didn't kill them,' he called out. 'I wasn't even in the country. I don't know this man. Look, I'm sorry, OK? I've told her I'm sorry. Can I see her? I'll tell her everything about my . . . sexuality. Let me explain to her.'

'I'm sorry, Mr Ridgeway, that would be classed as interfering with a witness.'

'She's my wife,' he shouted.

'A wife you attempted to rape.' The room fell silent at the mention of rape. Even Hilary Morrison couldn't think of anything to say. 'Scott.'

Scott looked at his watch. 'Interview terminated, 11:37.'

Chapter Forty-Nine

Sitting in an interview room wearing a white paper suit, Leah Ridgeway looked every inch the victim. She had undergone a rape examination and given a statement to a specialist female police officer. Now, DC Aaron Connolly was about to enter the interview room and ask her why she was wasting their time.

He watched her from the observation room with DC Angela Tanner next to him.

'According to the doctor, there's no evidence of rape or any sign she's recently had sexual intercourse,' Angela said. She spoke softly, something she did purposely to disguise the lisp she was self-conscious about.

'Why would you lie about being raped?'

'I've absolutely no idea.'

Aaron looked back at Leah who was rocking slightly in her chair. 'Is she on any form of medication?'

'I don't know,' Angela replied, looking down at the report in front of her.

'OK. Let's go and see what she has to say.'

Aaron entered the interview room first with Angela Tanner following. They hadn't even sat down before Leah jumped out of her seat.

'Have you arrested him? Did he admit it? I bet he didn't. The smarmy bastard. I don't know why I agreed to marry him in the first place.'

'Mrs Ridgeway—' Aaron began.

'Don't call me that,' Leah spat. 'I'll be reverting to my maiden name. I'm Leah Mercer. Call me Ms Mercer.' She looked at the detective sergeant from the top of her eyes. She had a frightening, menacing look about her.

'Ms Mercer, please, take a seat.'

Reluctantly, she sat.

'Is there any chance I can have my clothes back, please?'

'A change of clothes will be provided,' Angela said.

'Ms Mercer,' Aaron began, 'before we begin taking a formal statement, is there anything you would like to say?'

'No.'

'It isn't too late to change your mind about your allegations.'

'I don't need to change my mind,' she replied firmly.

'Ms Mercer, according to the doctor who examined you, you haven't had sexual intercourse recently at all. There is no sign of bruising or assault.'

Leah breathed in hard. She opened and closed her mouth several times as if wanting to say something but not knowing what.

Angela leaned forward and placed her hand on top of Leah's. 'Leah, your husband didn't rape you, did he?'

Leah's bottom lip wobbled. 'He may as well have done. The way he made me feel. I feel violated. Dirty.'

'Leah, what happened?' Angela asked.

'Do you know, I've known him for four years,' she said, looking into the middle distance. 'I fancied him the moment I saw him. I thought he fancied me, too. He said he did. It turns out it's all been a lie. Looking back, I suppose the signs were there. I guess

I just didn't want to see them.' She was visibly shaking. She ran her fingers firmly through her knotted hair, pulling hard at it. 'He's been meeting men, behind my back, sleeping with them, virtual strangers. It's disgusting. He could have caught anything. He could have infected with me all kinds of things. Wouldn't you feel like you'd been raped?' she asked, looking directly at Angela.

'When did you find all this out?' she asked.

'Last night. I followed him. Do you know where I found him? In a car park sucking off some teenager. I don't have a problem with him being gay. We're all free to do as we please. But why did he get married to me?' She started crying. 'Why tell me he loved me? Why go through the whole charade of a wedding? Why make—' She stopped, roughly wiped her face and ran her fingers through her hair again.

'What was your sex life like?' Aaron asked.

'Trust a man to ask that question. What's it got to do with you?' Leah snapped.

'I'm trying to build a picture of your relationship.'

'I . . . I'm not a big fan of . . . you know . . . sex,' she said quietly. 'When I was at school, all the girls were talking about losing their virginity, saying how great it was. I was the last one in my class to have sex. It never really bothered me.' Angela handed her a box of tissues. She pulled one out and wiped her nose. 'I had this boyfriend, Damien Curry. He was always asking me when we were going to do it. Eventually, I gave in. I hated it. It was horrible. It was uncomfortable. I remember looking at Damien afterwards and he lay there with a grin on his face like it was the most magical thing ever. I just wanted him to go home so I could have a shower and cry.

'I thought it was me, at first. You know, the first time is never the best, is it? Me and Damien did it again, but I still didn't like it. He did, though.' Leah was gently rocking back and forth in her seat, her fingers fiddling with the zip on her paper forensic suit. 'We broke up. Well, teenage romances don't last longer than a few weeks, do they? At college, I went out with a few more lads but I didn't like it with them either. I always tried to avoid it, if possible, but, well, we all know what men are like when it comes to sex; it's all they think about, day and night.'

Angela smiled and nodded in agreement. Aaron looked uncomfortable as he adjusted himself in his seat.

'What about your sex life with Oliver?' Angela asked.

'I genuinely fell in love with Oliver the second I saw him,' she said with a hint of a smile on her face. 'I'd never felt like that before with anyone. I decided to be honest with him. I told him I wasn't a fan of sex, that I didn't really like it. He said it was fine. We cuddled, kissed, and spent nights holding each other. It was lovely. It was what I wanted. I couldn't believe I'd found someone who was happy with the way I am. Now I know why.'

The room fell silent. Throughout her telling, Leah seemed to have calmed down slightly. Her breathing was back to normal and she didn't have the steely, deranged look in her eye.

'I'm sorry,' she eventually said, turning to Aaron. 'I shouldn't have come here saying what I did. Oliver didn't try to rape me and I don't think he arranged for my family to be murdered. I was just so angry when I caught him. Will I be charged with wasting police time? I don't mind. You can send me to prison if you like.'

'I don't think it will come to that,' Angela said.

'This is a fucking mess,' Matilda said waiting impatiently for the kettle to boil in the HMET suite.

Aaron had filled her in on the interview with Leah. 'I know.

She was just in such a state finding her husband last night, she didn't know what she was saying. I asked her where she'd stayed overnight and she couldn't remember. I wouldn't be surprised if she hadn't just parked up somewhere and nodded off.'

'OK,' Matilda said, spooning three heaped teaspoons of coffee into her mug. 'With everything going on in her life at the moment, I suppose we should expect someone with mental health problems to act out a bit. Don't charge her with anything and release Oliver without charges too.'

'Will do.' Aaron smiled.

'Hang on,' Matilda called him back. 'I still don't like Oliver. Just because she's retracting her statement doesn't mean he's innocent. He may have the perfect alibi but that doesn't mean he's not involved somehow. I still want him tailed.'

Aaron walked away, and Matilda added a fourth spoonful of coffee to her mug. If Oliver was innocent of the murders, she would have to work on Scott to convince him to press charges for his assault. There was no way she was going to let Oliver get away with anything.

Chapter Fifty

By the time Sian arrived at the mortuary, it was lunchtime. Lucy and Adele were in the pathologist's office having a sandwich, cup of tea and a chat. Sian walked tentatively through the post-mortem suite. She had attended many autopsies in her career, and although there were never any bodies left on display, she hated her eye wandering and picking up anything she'd rather not see. Gaze fixed firmly on the office in the corner of the room, she headed for it holding her breath and didn't breathe out until she was safely inside with the door closed.

'You didn't have to come down, Sian, I could have emailed you,' Adele said, putting her tuna sandwich back in its box.

'That's OK. I needed to get out of the station. Between there and home I see very little daylight.'

'I know that feeling.'

'How are you doing, Lucy?' Sian asked.

Lucy flicked back her hair. 'I'm OK now, thanks. I think I was slightly overwhelmed.'

'We all were. I don't think any of us is going to forget this case in a while.'

Adele noticed Lucy's face whiten. 'How's Kesinka? No lasting damage?'

'No. She's resting at home. She's back at work on Monday. Not that Ranjeet is too happy about that.'

'I like Ranjeet. He's gorgeous,' Lucy said. She blushed when she realized she'd said it out loud.

'Oh, who doesn't,' Sian agreed. 'He's stunning. Soft skin and that black shiny hair.' She shuddered. 'I shouldn't really. I'm old enough to be his mother.'

'Not to mention the fact you're married,' Adele said with a smile.

'A woman can look as long as she doesn't touch.'

'Would you let your Stuart ogle other women?'

'He doesn't need to. I'm all the woman he needs.' She grinned.

'Right then, Sian,' Adele began, wiping her hands on a piece of kitchen towel and logging on to her computer, 'I've looked up the cases you're interested in and I can tell you there was nothing murderous about their deaths.'

'All accidental then?'

'Well, as you know, there are no such things as accidents, but there was nothing done deliberately that caused the deaths. They were merely unfortunate occurrences.'

'Could they have been avoided?'

'Absolutely,' Adele said without hesitating. 'Although, in the case of Margo Sanders, I'm surprised the surgeon went ahead with the operation. She was incredibly frail. If it hadn't been for a reaction with her medication and the anaesthetic, she might not have survived the surgery anyway. We'll never know.'

'What about the other two?'

'Martin Walken died of a coronary artery atheroma. That's a collection of fat in the blood vessels. The physiological stress of being anaesthetized was too much for his heart to cope with.'

'And the child?'

Adele pulled up the file and let out a deep sigh. 'This is a much trickier case. She had a large tumour on her brain. It is highly likely that it would have killed her within weeks or months. The surgery was a last-ditch attempt to remove some of the tumour to make her as comfortable as possible. However, the ET tube – the tracheal tube – stimulated the vagus nerve which caused her to suffer a massive seizure. Personally, I don't think she should have been operated on. It was a huge risk.'

Sian looked bewildered by the medical terminology. 'OK. So, who's to blame here?'

'Take your pick. Maybe the tumour wasn't spotted early enough; maybe her parents ignored the child's symptoms; maybe the tracheal tube was inserted incorrectly.'

'But none of these three was killed deliberately?'

'Murdered? No.'

'No. I don't mean murder. I mean . . . actually, I don't know what I mean.'

'Do you mean were they killed through negligence that could have been easily avoided if someone was doing their job correctly?' Lucy chimed up.

They both turned to look at her.

'Yes,' Sian said.

Adele thought for a while. 'Possibly. Although, in the case of the little girl, most definitely. They shouldn't have been operating on her. Not with a tumour that aggressive.'

'Would the parents have known this?'

'They would have been informed of the risks. If you're looking for a motive for murder, you're not going to find one here. I'll admit, on paper, it does seem that Clive Mercer was incompetent in the way he was brought before the GMC on three occasions in such a short period of time, but surgeons, anaesthetists, doctors, consultants, all the decision makers, they take enormous risks every day. Sometimes they work out, sometimes they don't. That's the nature of the job.'

'Thanks, Adele,' Sian said, suitably placated.

'How are you getting on with finding the killer?' Lucy asked. She was looking down at the floor. It was obvious she wanted to know about the case without trying to spend too much time thinking of the horror of it all.

'I have absolutely no idea, I'm afraid. This one has us completely in the dark. Anyway, thanks for your help. I'd better be heading back.'

'Sian, how's Scott?' Adele asked, following her out of the office.

'I don't know. I haven't seen him yet today. Why?'

'I just wondered if he'd recovered from last night.'

'Recovered?'

'Yes. He was . . . you don't know?'

'No.'

'I thought Matilda would've told you.'

'Matilda just said he was involved in an incident. What's happened?'

'He was beaten up last night.'

'What? Who by?'

Adele frowned as she thought. 'I can't remember who they said now, hang on. I think his name was Oliver something.'

'Ridgeway?'

'That's it.'

'Oliver Ridgeway beat up Scott? Why?'

'I've no idea. Shit. Should I not have said anything?'

'No. Don't worry about it,' Sian said, a heavy frown on her face. 'I can't believe Matilda would keep something like that from me. Thanks, Adele. I'll see you later.'

Adele watched as Sian slowly made her way out of the autopsy suite. She went back into the office where Lucy was struggling with the easy open tab on a packet of biscuits.

'What's wrong?' Lucy asked when she noticed Adele's worried expression.

'I think I might have just opened up a massive can of worms.'

'How?'

'I'm not sure. But Matilda was very cagey this morning and Chris didn't say anything to me before he left for work. They're keeping me in the dark about something.'

'That's not like Matilda. She tells you everything.'

'Exactly. So what is she hiding from me?'

Chapter Fifty-One

Keith saw his chance of a lift at a row of dilapidated warehouses on the outskirts of Manchester city centre. An overweight man was struggling to load a rusty van, so Keith played the Good Samaritan and gave him a hand out of the goodness of his heart. They started chatting and Keith just happened to mention he was trying to get to Sheffield. The driver said he was heading to the east coast but could drop him as close as he could. An hour later, on the A628, Keith saw the sign for Barnsley. He asked the driver, Richard, to keep going rather than turn off. He didn't know why, but he wanted to see his flat again.

It had been less than a week since Keith had been in his own home, but it felt much longer as he stood across the road from it, hidden behind a bus shelter. He gave a small smile; it was familiar, comforting, but there was a hint of sadness. If Matilda Darke didn't believe him, she'd arrest him on sight and he'd spend the rest of his life in prison for three murders he didn't commit. He would never see this flat again.

He dug in his pocket for the key, checked the coast was clear and nobody was watching, then hurried across the road. He quickly unlocked the door, squeezed in a small gap and slammed it closed behind him, securing it with the key and the bolts at the top and bottom of the door.

Several brown envelopes lay on the doormat. He kicked them to one side and headed up the stairs. He wanted a shower, a change of clothing, something to eat. Ideally, he wanted several days in bed to catch up on sleep.

The living room was cold. There was an opened packet of Bourbon biscuits on the coffee table. He shoved one in his mouth and picked up two more. They were soft but they were food. There was a horrible smell to the flat, a staleness. It wasn't long before Keith realized it was him. He kicked off his battered shoes and stripped off his clothes as he made his way to the bedroom. As he looked at his thin, naked body in the full-length mirror he saw how dirty his skin was.

He stood under the shower and let the hot needles of water cascade down on him. The water ran brown in the bath as the dirt, grime and grease was washed out of his hair and body. He could feel himself becoming cleaner. As he scrubbed his knotted hair, digging his nails into his scalp he thought of the mess he had got himself into. How was it possible he could be accused of triple murder? It wouldn't have happened if he'd stayed at school, concentrated and passed his exams instead of playing the class clown to get a laugh and impress Stephanie Wainwright. Not that it did. She was an optician now. He spotted her in a Specsavers in the centre of Barnsley a few months ago. She still had that trademark crooked smile that had won him over all those years ago. She had made something of herself. She wore a wedding ring, too. Part of him was happy for her. Another part was jealous. She had a good career, probably drove a good car, went home every evening to a man with an equally good career, maybe even a child or two. And there he was, Keith Lumb, nose pressed up against the optician window, living in a one-bedroom flat with rising damp, a tired second-hand sofa, and a temperamental fridge. He was a month behind with the rent, he didn't have a TV licence and the council was threatening him with court proceedings if he didn't pay his council tax by the first of next month. What would Stephanie Wainwright see in him now?

The water ran cold, bringing Keith out of his daydream. He stepped out of the bath, wrapped a thin towel around his waist and went into the bedroom. He flopped down on the single bed with a heavy sigh. Yes, he was only twenty-seven. It wasn't impossible for him to turn his life around and make something of himself. He could go to college and take his GCSEs, maybe a couple of A levels. By the time he was thirty he could have enough qualifications to get a job in an office, a bank maybe. While working, and saving, he could go to night school, learn something else, maybe start up his own business. He and Elizabeth could go into business together. A family firm.

A warm smile spread across his lips. He stole a glance at himself in the mirror and all he saw was a condemned man looking back at him. He was not a killer, but the police thought he was.

*   *   *

'I don't like this, Matilda,' Valerie Masterson said. She leaned back in her chair and folded her arms. Her lips were pursed.

'We don't have any other option. It's the only way I'm going to be able to talk to Keith Lumb.'

'So you're going to go to his sister's house, sit down with the two of them, have a cosy little chat, then walk away at the end of it?'

She shook her head. 'No. It all depends on what I hear. If I'm convinced of his guilt then I'll arrest him.'

'You have bloodstained clothing found at the scene of the crime. You have his fingerprints and a hair under the nail of one of his victims. The forensics say it's him.'

'Yes, but common sense doesn't.'

'You're losing me, Mat.'

'Keith Lumb is a petty criminal. He's a burglar, and not a very good one. You don't go from breaking into someone's home to murdering three people.'

'He broke into the Mercers' home. Maybe it was a burglary gone wrong.'

'No. The violence inflicted on Clive, Serena and Jeremy does not equate to a burglary gone wrong. If that had been the case, they would have been hit on the head or, if they had been stabbed, it would have been once to incapacitate them. These murders were savage. They were personal,' Matilda said, getting herself worked up. 'I mean, for crying out loud, Clive was practically decapitated. Someone wanted to destroy him.'

Valerie remained silent while she thought. 'Fine. Go for your chat. But I want you wired.'

'No,' she said with defiance. 'I need Keith to trust me.'

Valerie took a deep breath. 'Then I want an armed response team on standby.'

'No. Keith does not pose any threat.'

'You seem very sure.'

'I am. It's him that's requested I meet him. It's him that wants to tell me his side of the story. If he was guilty, he wouldn't do that.'

'I am not having you walk into that house without any form of protection. It could be a massacre,' she almost shouted.

Matilda sighed. 'All Keith wants is to explain his innocence. From his point of view he did not commit these murders and he wants to convince me of that.'

'And what if he can't convince you? Do you honestly think he is going to let you arrest him? He was tracked in Maidstone. He was obviously trying to escape the country. He's hardly going to let you put the cuffs on him and walk calmly out of the house. He will try to run again and if you, or his sister, get in the way, he will strike.'

'I don't believe he will.'

'You're willing to risk your life?'

'My life isn't in any danger.'

'I'm guessing Tina Law thought that too.' Matilda looked up at her, mouth agape. 'DI Eckhart had DS Jonson tell me all about her. It's only been a couple of months since we lost DC Faith Easter. I do not want another of my officers killed in the line of duty.'

'I won't be,' she said, sounding less convincing.

'I'll need you to sign something.'

'What?' Matilda frowned.

'I'm in the shit over this, Matilda. I've got the chief constable breathing down my neck and if this all goes tits up, I'm out on my ear. Now, I'm willing for you to interview Keith Lumb, but I want you wired and I want you guarded. If you're going to go against my orders, I want it on paper you're doing this off your own bat. Is that understood?'

Matilda looked aghast. 'You're hanging me out to dry?'

'Yes. I'm sorry, Matilda, but this is how it's going to be. It's my way, or you're on your own.'

'You don't trust me?'

'I don't trust your judgement. Not in this case.'

The silence between them was heavy. Matilda stood up and walked slowly out of the office. She had brought nothing but good results for Valerie over the years. Since a police officer had been unmasked as a killer last year, everything had changed, and the fault seemed to lie with Matilda. Was it her fault Barnsley had allowed Keith Lumb to escape? Was it her fault he had gone on to massacre three people? Was it her fault he hadn't been caught yet? Evidently so.

This changes everything.

Chapter Fifty-Two

'How are you getting on?' Rory asked TDC Finn Cotton. The new member of the team was by the drinks station. The kettle was boiling and the young DC was rubbing at the back of his neck and stifling a yawn.

'Fine thanks,' he said, trying to smile through the pain.

'You sure?'

'Yes. I've just been staring at the computer screen for too long. I think I'm going slowly mad.'

'What are you working on?'

'I'm going through all the photos the wedding guests have sent in to us. I'm trying to identify everyone and work out if there is someone there who shouldn't be.'

'You've been given a very glamorous job,' Rory laughed, patting him on the back.

'I know. Whoever said a specialized team was all car chases and shoot-outs obviously never visits Sheffield. Do you want a drink?'

'No. I'm fine, thanks. Have you spotted someone you can't identify?'

'Yes. A few actually,' Finn said, picking up his coffee and heading back to his desk. 'There are a couple of men who I have no idea who they are but they crop up a few times. They're in the group photos too, so I'm guessing they were meant to be there but haven't come forward yet. I've been speaking to Ranjeet and he said there are still a couple from the guest list outstanding. However, there's one woman who appears only once.'

'Let's have a look.'

Finn placed his mug down on the desk and rifled through the mess of photographs. 'I printed the ones off who I couldn't identify. She's among these somewhere. Yes. Here she is.' He handed Rory the photo. The main shot was of the happy bride and groom dancing. In the background was Serena Mercer having what appeared to be a heavy conversation with a woman in a long black jacket and black trousers.

'The photo was taken fairly early into the evening. Obviously, that's Serena. The woman behind her with the plate of food is a Veronica Miles. I don't know who the woman in black is.'

'I do.'

'Really?'

'Yes. That's Elizabeth Lumb. She told us she didn't go to the wedding. Do you mind if I keep this?' Rory asked, heading for the door.

'No problem. Do I still need to go through all these?'

'Definitely,' he called back. 'Oh, can you make a blown-up version of that picture and send it to my phone?'

'Sure.'

Finn let out a sigh and took a sip of his strong coffee. 'I'm beginning to wish I was marshalling a Sheffield United match.'

'Can I ask a huge favour?' Leah asked Aaron as he led her to her car in the car park.

'Of course.'

'Will you come with me to my parents' house? I've been told

that it's now my responsibility as I'm next of kin. I'm going to have to get one of those specialized cleaning teams in, but I don't want to go inside on my own. Not when it's like it is.'

Aaron looked up at the police station. He had so much work on at the moment. He didn't have time to hold Leah's hand. However, when he looked at her, he saw the pain and horror in her eyes. Her entire life had fallen apart.

'Sure. I'll come with you.'

Her face lit up. 'That's wonderful. Thank you.'

The twenty-minute drive was conducted in silence. Aaron didn't know what to say, and Leah spent the time looking out of the window, watching a freezing cold Sheffield blur by. Aaron pulled up on the driveway and turned off the engine.

'It's a lovely house,' he said.

'Yes. I remember Mum telling me that when she was a child she always dreamed of living in a place like this. She felt lucky, blessed. That's why she did so much charity work to help those less fortunate. She'd had a bad start in life and made something of herself. She wanted to give others a chance too.'

'Shall we?' Aaron asked, making to get out of the car.

Leah swallowed hard and nodded.

They walked slowly to the front door. Leah held her coat firmly to her chest with folded arms. She looked nervous, petrified of what she was going to find once inside.

Aaron put the key in the lock, but Leah reached up to stop him from opening the door.

'Mum always said to me and Jeremy not to take things for granted; to appreciate what we have, look after it. Wise words, don't you think?'

'Absolutely.' Aaron smiled. 'Your mother seemed like a wonderful woman.'

'Oh she was. I wanted to be just like her. I always felt I let her down, though.'

'Why?'

'Because of my illness. I'd have dark days. Sometimes it was an effort to get out of bed. I missed out on a lot of opportunities.'

'Have you always suffered with depression?'

She nodded. 'Since I was a child. Dad used to say I'd grow out of it. I believed him.'

'Were your parents supportive?'

'Mum was.'

'Not your dad?'

'He didn't understand mental health issues.'

A strong wind blew and they both shivered.

'We should go inside,' Aaron said.

Reluctantly, Leah agreed.

Aaron turned the key and pushed the door open. It struggled due to the amount of post blocking the way. They stepped inside and Aaron closed the door behind them. Standing in the hallway, it seemed as if nothing was amiss. The broken hall table had been removed and there was a staleness about the air, but it looked like an ordinary house.

From the hallway, Aaron looked straight into the kitchen. On the central island, the detritus from the wedding reception was laid out. Flies were buzzing around unwrapped food.

Aaron stepped forward first. He hadn't been in the house when it was an active crime scene, but he'd seen the photographs. He knew where Jeremy Mercer had been found: at the bottom of the stairs, slumped against the wall. He approached the stairs, turned, and looked at the aftermath of the massacre. His heart sank.

'How bad is it?' Leah asked from the door.

'Just tell yourself they're at peace now,' Aaron struggled to think of something reassuring to say.

Leah held out her hand. Aaron took it. She squeezed hard and approached the stairs. She turned, saw the blood and immediately collapsed. Aaron caught her.

'It's all right. I've got you.' He held her firmly against him.

'Is that where my brother—?' she couldn't finish through the tears.

'Yes.'

'Oh my God. Poor Jeremy.'

Leah held onto Aaron tightly. She looked up and saw his kind face staring down at her.

'Thank you for being here with me, I couldn't have done this on my own,' she said through her tears.

'That's all right.' He smiled.

Leah stretched up on tip-toes and kissed Aaron on the lips.

Chapter Fifty-Three

Scott was in the canteen. He felt sick and wasn't hungry, but it was going to be a long night so felt he had to eat something. On a plate in front of him was a pile of chips, a slice of cheese and onion quiche and a mound of mixed vegetables. It looked like it had been sitting under a heat lamp for several hours and tasted bland. However, it was fuel, and that was all that mattered. As he stabbed at the soggy chips and struggled to chew, he looked up and saw Rory heading towards him. His heart sank.

Rory pulled out the chair opposite and sat down. He had the steely look of determination in his eyes.

'What's going on?' Rory asked.

'Nothing. Why?'

'You've been avoiding me all day.'

'I've been busy.'

'What happened last night?'

'Nothing.'

'Then why didn't you come home?'

'I stayed out.'

'I guessed that. Matilda said you were involved in an incident. Sian said that Adele told her you'd been beaten up. What's going on?'

'Nothing.' He gave up on the food and pushed his plate away.

'I was on my way to see Chris, for a run, and I was set upon. A chance mugging, probably. As I was closer to Chris's than ours I went straight to his. Matilda was there and I ended up staying over,' he said without making eye contact.

'You're lying,' Rory said firmly.

'Why would I lie?'

'I've no idea. Look, Scott, come on, we're colleagues, we share a flat together, we're mates. You can tell me anything.'

Scott swallowed but it was painful, and it was nothing to do with the food. He took a deep breath. 'You know Paul over there?' He nodded towards a uniformed officer who was shovelling a fry-up into his mouth.

Rory looked over his shoulder. 'Yes. What about him?'

'What would you say if I told you he was gay?'

'Oh. Well, I wouldn't say anything. It's nothing to do with me.' He shrugged.

'What would you say if I told you I was gay?'

'I'd say it's about time you told me.' He smiled.

'What?'

'I think you're probably the last person in the team to know. We've all been waiting for ages for you to tell us.'

'Really?' Scott asked, blushing slightly.

'Yes.'

Scott bit his bottom lip to control the tears that were forming. 'I'm sorry I didn't tell you sooner.'

'Don't be. You've told me now, that's the main thing.' He looked at his friend and squinted. 'You're dating Chris, aren't you?'

'Bloody hell, are you psychic?'

'No. Just observant. I'm an excellent detective, remember.'

'Then why are you leaving?'

'I haven't made my mind up yet, and don't change the subject.'

Scott looked down as his bland meal. 'You won't tell anyone, about Chris I mean? I don't think Adele knows.'

'A secret? Cool. Are you open to blackmail?'

'I'm not cleaning your bedroom.'

'Damn.' He smirked. 'Scott, you're a great bloke, you're a bit of a neat freak and you have a shit taste in films, but you're my mate. As long as you're happy, that's the main thing.'

'Thanks.' He smiled.

'Come on, let's head back. Matilda mentioned something about wanting backup tonight.'

'So, how come you all knew then?' Scott asked as they made their way out of the canteen.

'Well, what confirmed it for me was when Joseph Glass joined us as family liaison officer. You were well smitten.'

Scott smiled at the memory of the young officer who had been attacked while they were chasing a suspect. He later died when his parents agreed to have his life support machine turned off. 'I did like Joseph.'

'I could tell. Did anything happen between you two?'

'He invited me to the pictures, but, we didn't get to go. Maybe something would have done.'

'Maybe in a parallel universe you're married with kids.'

Scott gave an exaggerated shiver. 'Kids? I can't think of anything worse.'

'I've been looking for you everywhere,' Finn said when Scott and Rory entered the suite. He looked flustered.

'What is it?' Rory asked.

'I've had a call from the team in Barnsley who were posted to keep an eye on Keith Lumb's flat. They got there this morning and everything was normal. When they went back this afternoon, the bedroom curtains were closed.'

'What do you mean, when they went back? They left?' Rory asked.

'They must have done. I didn't get the full story. I've been calling Sian and Christian but I can't find them anywhere.'

'That's OK. I'll sort it. What the fuck are they playing at in Barnsley? Matilda's going to go ballistic when she finds out.'

'Shit. I'm so sorry. I don't know why I did that,' Leah said, stepping back from Aaron.

'It's OK. Don't worry about it.'

'I just looked at you and thought . . . Jesus!'

Aaron led Leah into the kitchen, away from the crime scene behind her. He pulled out a stool at the breakfast table and sat her down.

'I don't know what's happening to me. Everything has just fallen apart at once.'

'It's a lot to take in.'

'Less than a week ago, everything was perfect. I was getting married. Everyone was so happy. Now look at me. My husband has been leading a double life. My mum, dad, and brother have been killed and I am completely alone in the world.'

'No you're not. You have Rachel.'

Leah looked up at Aaron. 'Oh my God, poor Rachel. What's going to happen to her?'

'I don't know.'

'Do you think they'd let me have her, become her official guardian?'

'I don't see why not.'

'But, I'm, you know, not exactly normal, am I?' she said, tapping the side of her head, hard.

'I think social services like to do what is best for the child.

In this case, it would be to live with you. You're her only surviving relative. You have a house to live in, and you have the means to support her.'

'Will you put in a good word for me?'

'I'll do whatever I can.'

'So, how do I go about getting this house cleaned?'

'There are specialized companies you can contact. They'll all be online.'

Leah stood up and went over to the marquee at the back of the house. She looked out at the remains of her perfect day. What was left of the wedding cake was crawling with flies, the white tablecloths were stained with dropped food and spilled wine. Chairs were scattered, some overturned. It had to be a metaphor for her life.

She took a deep breath and held her head up high. She turned back to face Aaron and looked completely different. There was a determination about her.

'Right then,' she clapped her hands together, 'as far as I'm concerned, Oliver can go to hell. My main priority is to get this house cleaned so it's a safe and happy environment for Rachel and Pongo. This may be a nightmare at the moment, but I can overcome this. If my mum taught me anything, it's that women are survivors. We're strong, and we're a hundred times better than men. No offence,'

'None taken.' Aaron smiled.

Chapter Fifty-Four

Pat Campbell knocked on the front door and stepped back. She was hot and slightly out of breath from rushing to get here.

Her mobile had rung just as she was stepping out of the shower. She knew who would be calling without even looking at the screen. Sally Meagan had received a fourth phone call from, she assumed, her son. An hour later, and Pat had arrived at the fortress that was Meagan's home.

Philip answered.

'Oh, Philip,' Pat said, taken aback. 'I'm sorry I'm late. You'd think at my age I'd know to put petrol in the car before it ran out.' She gave an embarrassed laugh.

He didn't say anything. He stepped to one side to allow Pat to enter. He looked different in casual clothing. Pat had only really seen him at the restaurant when he was dressed in his best suits. Now, in his home, he was wearing an old pair of jeans, an oversized woollen sweater and carpet slippers. His hair was uncombed, and he was unshaven. He looked smaller, more fragile. Philip Meagan, the restaurant owner was all an act, a show of bravado. When he was at home he could be the father of a missing boy, the husband of a damaged wife.

'Sally's not here,' he said, heading into the kitchen. 'She's had to take Woody to the vet.'

'Oh. Nothing serious I hope.'

'No. He's been scooching around the carpet on his bum. It usually means his anal glands need emptying. Coffee?'

Pat pulled a face. 'Please.'

She sat on one of the high stools at the central island and watched as Philip made the coffee. He went about the ordinary, simple task in what seemed like slow motion.

'Sally said she had another call this morning.'

'That's right,' he said, his back to her.

'Were you here for it?'

'I was in the shower. I turned the water off and I could hear Sally screaming for me. I thought she'd fallen or something,' he said, pushing the plunger down slowly on the cafetière. 'I came charging down the stairs in just a towel, soaking wet, and there she was in the living room, tears streaming down her face.'

'Did she say what the caller said?'

'The usual. He called her mummy. She asked him where he was and he hung up.'

Philip brought a mug of coffee over to Pat. His hand was shaking. Pat looked down at his wrist. It was so thin and bony. It was strained over the weight of the cup.

'What happened then?'

'She held her arms out for me and I just sat and held her while she cried herself out on my shoulder.'

'At least you were here for her this time. That's a comfort for her.'

'Yes.' He let out a deep sigh. 'I don't know if the caller really is Carl, or someone playing a cruel joke, but they've brought us closer together. That's a bonus I suppose.'

Pat offered a weak smile. 'It must be very difficult for you both.'

'It is. All I seem to be doing at the moment is offering support and hugs. It feels empty.'

'You're there for her. That's the main thing.'

'She actually came to bed at a decent time last night rather than passing out on the sofa from exhaustion. I held her until she fell asleep with her head on my chest. When she woke this morning, she said it was the best night's sleep she'd had in months.'

'That's good. Philip, did you get the number of the phone that had called Sally? I know it will probably be another dead number but it's worth tracing.'

'Yes. It's written down on a pad in the office.'

Philip placed his cup down on the marble worktop and left the room. Pat sipped her coffee. A heavy frown appeared on her face as a thought entered her head. Something was worrying at her brain, an idea, but she couldn't quite put her finger on what it was. She nibbled at her bottom lip.

'Here you go,' Philip said, placing the small square of note-paper in front of her. 'Is everything all right?' he asked when he noticed her frown.

'Yes. Thanks for this. I'll send it to Matilda; get her to trace it.' She looked at the number written neatly in pencil. She took her own mobile out and quickly fired off a text, including the number. 'Do you know what time Sally will be back?'

'No. She said she was going to take Woody to the park afterwards. He gets a bit excited going to the vet. It's good to let him run off some of his energy.'

Pat smiled. 'He's a good dog.'

'Yes, he is. He's great company for Sally. When I'm not here.'

Pat was playing with her mobile. She was turning it over in her hands, wondering whether she dare try something she would probably live to regret.

'How are the restaurants doing?' she asked. She wasn't really interested but it was a distraction.

'They're doing very well. In November we had our best ever month.'

'That's good. Have you been out at all this morning?' she asked.

'No. I was going to but Sally asked me to stay on for you.'

'Oh. I hope I'm not keeping you from something.'

'No. It's fine.'

Pat pressed her thumb down on her mobile and closed her eyes tightly shut. The clock in the background seemed to be ticking loudly. She could hear herself breathing shallow, shaking breaths. Somewhere in the house, a phone began to ring. She opened her eyes.

'Is that your phone?' Pat asked.

'It must be. Excuse me,' he said. He placed his cup down with a heavy thud and headed out of the kitchen at a fast pace.

Pat followed.

Philip went into the living room, picked up his jacket from the armchair and pulled an outdated Nokia from the inside pocket. He looked at the number calling and hesitated over whether he should answer it or not. Eventually, he pressed the green button.

'Hello?' he asked hesitantly. His voice was cold and shaking.

'Daddy?'

Philip turned around and saw Pat standing in the doorway. Her own phone pressed to her ear. If it was possible, his face paled even more.

Pat ended the call. 'Philip, how could you?' she asked.

'It's not what you think,' he said as his bottom lip began to wobble. 'I don't know where Carl is. I wish I did, but I don't.'

Tears began to fall. He dropped into the armchair as if his legs had given way. 'It's heartbreaking not knowing where Carl is or what's happened to him. It's even more terrifying seeing what Sally's going through. She's dying. Slowly, each day, she's dying more and more. I've tried to offer her support, love, hugs, she just cringes every time I try to touch her. I thought, if I could get her to need me again, then we'd be OK, and we'd be able to get through all this, together. Since she's been getting the calls, she's talked to me, she's let me hold her. Last night, in bed, I said we should go away for a weekend, have a break. She said yes. That's the first time in three years she's even entertained the notion of leaving the house for longer than an hour.

'I know what I did was wrong, but I need my wife. I need my wife to need me and I couldn't think of any other way to get her back.'

He broke down and sobbed loudly.

Pat didn't know what to do. She remained in the doorway and watched as a desperate man collapsed in front of her. She looked up and saw the framed photograph of a smiling Carl on the mantelpiece. This house was too big for just the two of them. The atmosphere was heavy and depressing. Philip was right; Sally did need to get out and have a break, even if it was only for a weekend. She needed to have a laugh, stretch her legs, do something other than search the Internet looking for her missing son.

Pat went over to Philip and placed her arm around his bony shoulders. 'I can't agree with what you've done, but your heart was in the right place. I know you didn't mean any malice in this.'

'I didn't,' he said, looking up at the retired detective with wet eyes. 'I want my wife back. That's all.'

She pulled him into a tight embrace. 'Promise me no more calls,' she said in a loud whisper.

'I promise.'

She took the phone from him. 'I'll get rid of this.'

'You won't tell Sally?'

'No, I won't. Do me a favour, take her away for that weekend. Tell her that she can still have some kind of life as well as look for her son.'

'I will.' He smiled through his tears.

Pat stood up and headed for the door. She stopped and turned back. 'I won't give up looking, Philip. Neither will Matilda. We will find him. Eventually.'

Philip didn't say anything. He gave her a weak smile and continued to cry.

Pat turned and left the house, closing the door firmly behind her. She had been researching the aftermath of a child going missing or being murdered and the effects it had on those left behind. The majority of parents split up – grieving, not grieving, moving on, not moving on. People deal with these things in their own way; sometimes, it takes over their lives. Pat didn't want Sally and Philip to be another statistic, another couple who fell apart over the loss of their son.

She walked slowly down the gravel driveway with a heavy heart. She had solved one mystery, but there was nothing to celebrate. She wouldn't tell Sally, but she needed to tell Matilda.

Chapter Fifty-Five

Matilda was sitting behind the wheel of her new Range Rover a few doors up from Elizabeth Lumb's house on Trap Lane. She had received a few baffling text messages from Pat which she would need to see her about later. She looked out of the side window. It was getting dark.

The front passenger door opened and Scott lowered himself into the seat next to her. He'd been to the shop at the end of the road and bought them both a few provisions to keep going.

'Is it me or are Mars bars getting smaller?' he asked.

'You should have been a child when I was. KitKats for twenty pence and much bigger fingers than you get now.'

'Smaller bars yet more money and for some reason we just accept this. Shouldn't we be boycotting the chocolate companies?'

'We should but we're a nation of chocoholics so we don't seem to care; except when it comes to Christmas and we see how small the tubs of Roses are. Then, we're outraged.' She smiled.

'But we still buy them.'

'Because it's tradition.'

'We're quite weird, us Brits, when you think about it,' Scott said with a smile as he bit into his Mars.

'How are you feeling now?'

'I'm fine,' he said with a mouthful. 'I ache a bit, but I'll be back to normal in a few days.'

'Has anyone at work said anything?'

He smiled and nodded. 'I've had a few pats on the back. Aaron shook my hand; I'm not sure why. Sian gave me a hug. And, do you remember Ryan, used to be a SOCO but left and is now a personal trainer?'

'No, but go on.'

'He sent me a friend request on Facebook and welcomed me to the family. Who knew!'

Matilda's smile was huge and warm. 'Nothing to worry about at all, was there?'

'No. Nothing's changed. The sun will still rise tomorrow. Chocolate bars will continue getting smaller.'

Matilda studied Scott. He had gone through a monumental upheaval in his life. From this point on, everything had changed. To look at him, you wouldn't think so. He'd faced the potential backlash and, despite a few worries, had emerged unscathed. Was it his age that made him seem unbreakable? It was three years since James had died. Yes, she'd moved to a new house and was getting on with life, but always, at the back of her mind, was the realization she was completely alone.

'Can I ask you a question?' Matilda asked as she looked back at Elizabeth's house.

'Sure.'

'In your drawer, I found a photograph of you with a young man. On the back was the date of ten years ago. Who was that?'

Scott blushed slightly. 'His name was Jake Skeeter. He was my first boyfriend. We went out for about six months. Looking back, it seemed longer. He was the first . . . you know . . . I'd ever done anything with. I don't know why, but a couple of months ago I looked him up on Facebook. He lives in Truro with his husband. They've adopted twin girls and they run a garage together. It made me realize what I was missing out on. Ten years ago we were exactly the same. Now, he's got a family, a business, he's happy. I'm still exactly where I was.'

'No, you're not,' Matilda interrupted.

'I am. I know I've got a good career going on but that's it. There's nothing else. No partner. No family. Nothing on the horizon. It started to get to me.'

'Is that what you want? A life similar to this Jake Skeeter?'

'Yes,' he said quietly with watery eyes. 'It's not too much to ask for, is it?'

'No. There's no reason why you can't settle down. Scott, about last—'

Matilda was interrupted by the back door opening and Rory climbing into the car. He slammed the door closed behind him.

'Bloody hell it's cold. My nipples could cut glass,' he said. 'Right then, there's been a car outside the nursing home Keith and Elizabeth's mother is in all day and he hasn't been there. I've been talking to the matron of the home, can you believe they still have matrons? Anyway, she said the only person who has been to see her recently is Elizabeth. She goes three times a week.'

'How is the mother?' Scott asked.

'The same as she was last week, last month and last year.'

'Is it true what Finn said; that Elizabeth pushed her off a balcony?' Scott asked.

'I guess I'll find out the truth when I go in there,' she replied. 'Anything on Keith's flat?' Matilda asked, turning in her seat.

'Yes. Keith's definitely been back. It looks like he's had a shower, change of clothes and a shave. His dirty clothes were on the floor in the bedroom. We've bagged them up.'

'Anything else?'

'No. Oh, DI Brady spoke to DI Eckhart in Barnsley. He was full of apologies. Christian got a bit annoyed with him. He said you'd be paying him a visit in a day or two.'

'Too bloody right I will.'

'Are you really going to go in there on your own?' Rory asked, looking out of the window at Elizabeth's house.

'Yes.'

'With a suspected triple killer?'

'Personally, Rory, I don't believe Keith Lumb is the killer.'

'But the evidence . . .'

'I'm aware of what the evidence says, but it seemed too obvious to me. Someone wants us to believe Keith is the killer. That's what I'll be finding out when I go in.'

'But what about Elizabeth? She could be all kinds of crazy.'

'And she lied about being at the wedding,' Scott said.

'I'll be asking her about that too.'

'Then should you really go in there alone? You don't know what you're going to face once that door's closed and locked behind you,' Rory said.

'It has to be done this way or Keith won't talk. What he says is likely to be the missing piece. Now, you two should make yourselves scarce. If they see me in the car with others they'll think it's a trap.'

'Are you sure?' Scott asked.

'I'm positive. Just, keep an eye on the house.'

Hesitantly, Scott and Rory exited the car. As they slammed the doors closed, Matilda was plunged into silence. She watched through the wing mirror as the two DCs retreated to a car parked further up the road. However, for now, she was on her own.

She hunkered down in her seat and kept both eyes firmly

fixed on Elizabeth's house up ahead. The curtains were drawn. There was a faint light in the living room but the rest of the house seemed to be in darkness. She wondered what Elizabeth was doing in there. Was Keith already inside?

Matilda was reminded of the last time she sat in a car waiting for an urgent phone call. She was at the entrance to Graves Park. On the front passenger seat was a bag with two hundred and fifty thousand pounds in used notes. When the phone rang, the kidnappers would tell her where to go with the money in exchange for Carl Meagan. Unfortunately, it didn't work out the way she had hoped. Her mind was elsewhere. Earlier that day her husband had died. The brain tumour had won and stolen James from her. She was all alone in the world. She was angry, sad, frustrated, tired, annoyed. She should have gone home straight from the hospital, but there was nobody to go home to so what was the point?

Matilda's mobile rang, bringing her out of the dark, depressing room in her mind she often found herself edging towards. The display told her Elizabeth was calling.

'Hello.'

'DCI Darke? It's Elizabeth Lumb. Keith has arrived. He'd like to speak to you.'

'I'll be a few minutes.'

'I'll put the kettle on.'

Matilda rolled her eyes. To Elizabeth this was a chance to get the teapot out, open a packet of biscuits and sit around the fire having a good chat. Did she not realize the importance of the situation? Was she so blind as to the danger her brother was in? Or was she simply naïve? A lost, lonely woman with nothing and no one in her life; where the prospect of interrogation about three murders was seen as a pleasant way to spend a winter's evening?

Matilda sent a text to Scott telling him she was going in. She turned her phone to silent and placed it in her inside jacket pocket. She took a deep breath and left the car.

Once outside in the chilly January evening, she turned and smiled as Scott flashed the headlights of his car. She turned back and headed for Elizabeth's house.

Matilda was cold. Her breathing was fast and her heart was pounding in her chest. If she didn't believe Keith was guilty of three murders, why was she so nervous? She climbed the three steps to the porch and rang the bell. There was no turning back.

Chapter Fifty-Six

The front door opened, bathing Matilda in a warm yellow glow. Elizabeth Lumb was wearing a floor-length dark red skirt. She had a heavy knitted cardigan wrapped around her. Her dark hair was flowing down her back. She had the expression of a woman with a lot on her mind.

'DCI Darke, welcome. Please, come on in,' she said, stepping to one side.

Matilda took a final glance at the car up ahead with Scott and Rory keeping an eye on the house before entering. She stood in the dimly lit, cluttered hallway and listened as the door was firmly closed behind her. She half expected to hear it bolted, locking her inside, but there was just the sound of the catch being dropped.

'Keith's in the living room. I've made a pot of tea,' Elizabeth said, squeezing past Matilda and leading the way. As she brushed by, Matilda caught a hint of cheap perfume mixed with mothballs.

The living room was dark, lit only by a standard lamp in the corner. Long shadows gave the room an ominous air of mystique. Keith stood by the fireplace. He looked older than the photographs Matilda had seen of him. He had dark circles under his eyes: the effects of sleeping rough the past few days, or the grim shadow from the light.

'Keith, this is DCI Darke. My brother, Keith,' Elizabeth said, as if making introductions at the beginning of a party. 'Take a seat. I'll pour.'

Matilda sat down on the sofa but Keith remained by the fireplace. He looked calm. He wasn't biting his lip or playing with his fingers. He wasn't waffling his innocence or pleading his case. This seemed like a man with not a care in the world. Matilda suddenly felt frightened. Her eyes flitted between the siblings. Keith's gaze was fixed firmly on his sister while Elizabeth set about pouring them all cups of tea.

The teapot, cups and saucers were all matching. There was a large plate in the middle of the table with an assortment of neatly arranged biscuits. She smiled as she passed each of them a cup. She was enjoying the company.

'Before we begin,' Matilda broke the silence, 'I'd like to ask you, Elizabeth, once more, if you attended Leah and Oliver's wedding on Sunday.'

She looked up from the rim of her cup. 'No. I told you. I wasn't invited. I sent a card.'

Matilda placed her cup on the coffee table and brought out a photograph from her pocket. 'This is a photograph taken from one of the guests on their mobile phone. In the background you can clearly see you talking to Serena Mercer.' She placed the picture on the table.

Both Keith and Elizabeth leaned forward for a closer look.

She closed her eyes tight. 'I felt so embarrassed,' Elizabeth eventually said. 'About a week before the wedding, I received an invitation through the post. I was invited to the reception but not the actual wedding. So I went. I got all dressed up. Did my hair and make-up. When I got there, Serena seemed surprised to see me, but not in a good way. She looked shocked. I showed her my invitation and it wasn't anything like all the others.

Someone had sent it to me as a joke.' Her bottom lip wobbled.

'Who would do that?' Matilda asked.

'I don't know.'

'Do you still have the invitation?'

'No. I was so angry when I came home that I threw it on the fire.'

'Did Serena throw you out?' Keith asked. The first time he'd spoken. He sounded tired.

'No. She was very kind. She offered me a drink but I just had a few sips then came home. I couldn't believe it. I felt so ashamed.' She pulled her cardigan tighter around her.

'Elizabeth, can you think of anyone who would want to deceive you in such a way?'

'No. When I got home, I started thinking, why would someone want me out of the house? I hadn't been burgled, nobody had tried to get into the house. It just didn't make sense. I put it down to a cruel joke.'

'Does that sort of thing happen often?'

'No,' she answered quickly. 'Well, the neighbour kids knock on my door and run away, but that's just kid stuff. Whoever did this, had the invitation especially printed. It looked very professional. Quality paper.'

Matilda looked at Keith and Elizabeth in turn. If Keith was being framed for these murders, why? and why was Elizabeth being brought into the trap too?

'Is the only connection your family has with the Mercers the fact that you work at the same charity?' Matilda asked.

'Yes. As far as I know.'

'Keith, you've never been to the Mercers' house?'

'No,' he said, sitting down. 'I don't even know where it is. Well, I do now, but I didn't before.'

'Have you ever met any of the family?'

'I met Serena. A few years ago.'

'In what context?'

He moved from the fireplace and sat on the edge of a chunky armchair. 'I'd been sacked from this decorating job I had. I was behind with my rent and the landlord chucked me out. Elizabeth put me in touch with Serena at the charity. She helped me get my flat in Barnsley.'

'That's all?' Matilda asked.

'Yes. I probably met her three or four times, tops. I moved in and she moved on to her next charity case.'

'Keith, be nice,' Elizabeth chastised.

'We have forensic evidence of you being in that house on the night of the killings.' She dug into her pocket again and pulled out three photographs of the bloodstained clothing found at the scene. She placed them on the table. 'Are these your clothes?'

He leaned over and looked at them each in turn, taking his time. 'Well, yes. I mean, I have clothes like that.'

'There were found in the Mercers' home. As you can see, they're covered in the blood of the victims. Your hair is on these clothes. We've also found one of your hairs under Serena Mercer's fingernails.'

'Keith!' Elizabeth exclaimed.

'But I've never been there,' he said, visibly distressed. 'I don't know any of them. Apart from Serena, I could walk past them in the street and not know who they are.'

'Then how do you account for your clothes and hair being at the scene of the crime?'

'I can't,' he said, running his fingers through his hair. 'All I can assume is that someone is trying to set me up.'

'Who?'

'I don't know,' he said, getting exasperated.

Matilda took a deep breath. 'Keith, to be perfectly honest, I don't believe you're guilty of these murders. You were arrested for burglary and you absconded from the police station because you didn't want to go to prison, right?'

'Right.'

'So, a few months for burglary against a whole life tariff for three brutal murders doesn't make any sense. Can you tell me where you were on Sunday night?'

'I don't know where I was on Sunday night,' he said, shaking his head.

'You must have been somewhere.'

'I was. I was here until early evening.'

Matilda looked at Elizabeth.

'That's right,' she said. 'He came asking for help. I told him, I wouldn't call the police on him but I wasn't hiding him. That would get me in trouble with the police too, and I—' she stopped herself.

'What time did you leave here?'

'About five-ish?' He looked to his sister for confirmation. She nodded.

'And where did you go?'

'I went to the bottom of the road. I caught a bus into town. I got a lift from a guy in a van to Chesterfield. He wasn't going any further. I asked a few drivers to give me a lift but they were all going north. I wanted to go south. I found a quiet spot near the motorway services and managed to get some sleep.'

'Did you speak to anyone?'

'No.'

'Did you go anywhere where you might have been caught on CCTV?'

'I don't think so. The bit of money I had on me I wanted to save for breakfast the next morning.'

Matilda studied Keith. He looked genuinely frightened by the situation he had found himself in. The evidence against him was undeniable. On paper he seemed to be as guilty as if he was found standing over a dead body with a knife in his hand. However, here and now, in this living room, Matilda knew she was sitting opposite an innocent man. If only she could prove it.

'Keith, have you had anyone come to your flat lately? Any friends, or, I don't know, a gas meter reader maybe?'

'No. I don't have many friends. The ones I do have, we tend to meet in pubs.'

'So nobody comes to your flat?'

'No.'

'What about break-ins?'

He sniggered. 'I don't have anything worth nicking.'

'Have you lent any clothes to anyone?'

'No.'

'So how did your clothes end up in the Mercers' house?' Matilda asked, raising her voice.

Keith shrugged his shoulders.

'I'm trying to help you here, Keith, but you need to give me something in return.'

'I don't know what to say. If I knew something, I'd tell you. Look, I know I'm no good. I know I'll probably end up in prison at some point or getting beaten to death by someone I owe a couple of quid to, but I am not a killer. I can look you in the eye, swear on my sister's life, my mother's life, that I did not kill the Mercers.'

The living room fell silent after Keith's outburst. Matilda believed him. She just couldn't prove it.

'What about what happened with Tina Law?'

Keith shook his head. 'Who's she?'

'An ex-girlfriend of yours. You were suspected of beating her up on several occasions.'

Keith looked perplexed. 'I don't know any Tina Law.'

Now it was Matilda's turn to look confused. 'DS Jonson from the station in Barnsley you were taken to said you were suspected of assaulting your girlfriend, Tina Law.'

'I've never had a girlfriend called Tina.'

'I'm sure he said Tina,' Matilda said to herself. 'I'll have to call him.'

'DCI Darke,' Elizabeth said, leaning forward, 'my brother is many things, and I'll be the first to admit that he's made mistakes, but one thing he isn't and that's a woman beater.'

'The truth is, I've never hit anyone before in my life,' Keith said.

Matilda squeezed her eyes closed. She could feel a headache coming on. Nothing seemed to be making any sense. 'Keith, I'm going to have to take you into the station.'

'What?' he said, jumping up. 'No. I can't be done for murder.'

'Look, from an evidence point of view, you're our prime suspect. I need to place you under arrest.'

'But you said yourself you believe he's innocent,' Elizabeth said.

'And I do. But I can't prove it. And neither can Keith.'

'No. I'm not going with you.'

'While you're in custody, I'll still be looking for the real killer.'

'Can't you do that now?' Elizabeth asked. 'Can't you place him under house arrest or something?'

'It doesn't work like that. I'm sorry.'

'I'm not going,' he grabbed a poker from the fireplace and held it aloft.

'Keith, this is not helping. You're only going to dig yourself in deeper.'

'Elizabeth, give me your car keys,' Keith said, holding his shaking hand out.

Elizabeth remained in her seat. Her eyes were locked on her brother. She wanted to help but knew she would be arrested if she did.

'Elizabeth, keys. Now!'

'I'm sorry, Keith.'

'Fuck!' he yelled.

'Keith, put the poker down. We'll go to the station and make a statement. We'll hold you for twenty-four hours. I'll apply for an extension. Your solicitor will apply for bail at magistrates' court.'

'They won't give me bail. I'm a triple killer, apparently. They don't give murderers bail. Fuck!' He kicked the coal bucket at the side of the fireplace.

Elizabeth jumped up. 'DCI Darke, is there nothing you can do? You said you believe him. You don't want to arrest him; I know you don't. I can read it on your face. There's someone out there who wants to frame him for these murders, someone dangerous enough to plant evidence. If you take my brother into the station, that'll be it. Your boss won't let you keep digging because they'll believe you have the real killer. Please. I'm begging you.'

Matilda took a deep breath. She felt hot and sick. Maybe it was the heat coming from the fire and radiators. Maybe it was the oppressive atmosphere from the cluttered living room and the desperation radiating out of Keith and Elizabeth. Either way, she needed to get out of this house and she had to take someone with her.

'Double Deckers,' Rory said. 'I remember they used to be huge when I was a kid. I can fit one into my mouth whole now.'

'Nothing to do with the fact you've got a big gob?' Scott shivered from behind the steering wheel.

'I haven't.'

'Remember that time when you were drunk and you bet me a fiver you could fit your fist into it then you got it stuck?'

'Oh yes,' he said, laughing. 'Did you ever give me that fiver?'

'The door's opened.'

They both leaned forward and looked out of the windscreen at Elizabeth's house. They saw Matilda on the doorstep. She turned back to the house, said something, then walked down the steps alone. The front door closed behind her.

Rory opened his window as Matilda reached their car. He let in a blast of winter air and pulled his coat tighter around him.

'Boss?'

'He didn't turn up,' Matilda said.

'What?'

'He wasn't there.'

'But you've been in about half an hour.'

'I know. I was talking to his sister.'

'Did she explain why she lied about being at the wedding?' Scott asked.

'Yes. I'll bring you all up to speed back at the station.'

'I can't believe he didn't turn up. If that doesn't point to his guilt, I don't know what does,' Rory said.

Matilda didn't say anything. She offered them a weak smile, pulled up the collar on her coat and headed back for her car.

* * *

From behind the steering wheel, Matilda watched as Rory and Scott drove slowly past her and headed for the station. She'd blatantly lied to them. She had hand-picked her team because she knew she could trust each and every one of them. In return, they offered their total support and commitment. If Matilda believed in something, then so did they. So why had she lied to them?

'You're acting like a one-woman police force,' she told herself. 'You can't solve this on your own. Let them in.'

Unfortunately for her, the others believed in hard evidence, and everything they had pointed to Keith slaughtering Clive, Serena and Jeremy Mercer.

All Matilda had to go on was the word of a potential triple murderer.

Chapter Fifty-Seven

Elizabeth Lumb couldn't sleep. As soon as Matilda had left, Keith went straight to bed in the spare bedroom. Elizabeth had sat in silence in the living room. Despite Matilda giving them her word she wouldn't arrest Keith, she half expected to see a fleet of police cars come screaming up the road. They'd break the door down, charge into the house and tear it apart looking for her brother. They'd drag him out of the house kicking and screaming and shouting his innocence. All Elizabeth could think about was the mess they'd create.

She went to bed around midnight and read half a Catherine Cookson before putting the paperback down with a sigh. It was no good. She threw back the duvet and climbed out of bed. As she made her way down the stairs, tying her dressing gown around her waist, she could hear her brother snoring lightly in the spare room. How could he possibly sleep so soundly when their lives were being systematically destroyed? She shook the thought away and headed for the kitchen.

The curtains were wide open and while Elizabeth waited for the kettle to boil, she looked out onto the back garden. The sky was a sheet of black, pierced with an infinite number of stars and a brilliantly bright moon which shone down on the grass, causing the frost to twinkle on each blade. It was beautiful, serene, calming.

The kettle boiled. She made herself a mug of strong tea, took the last piece of angel cake from the pantry and sat at the table. She let out a heavy sigh and tucked in.

'We should have looked after him more,' she began, her voice shattered the silence, echoing around the room. 'He took Dad's death harder than the rest of us. He idolized him. If we'd stepped up and took on a more parental role, Keith could have done something with his life, something respectful. Don't you think?' She looked to the seat next to her. It was empty. 'I should have seen the signs.'

'Who are you talking to?' Keith asked from the doorway.

Elizabeth let out a scream and slapped a hand on her chest. 'You scared me half to death. What do you think you're doing, creeping up on me like that?'

'I wasn't creeping up on you.'

'Well . . . you should have made your presence known.'

Keith, wearing his father's old dressing gown, flicked the switch on the kettle and took a mug from the top cupboard. 'Is there any more of that cake left?'

'No. There's some biscuits in the barrel.'

'Who were you talking to?' he asked, pouring hot water into the mug.

'Nobody,' she said, blushing slightly.

'You were. I heard you.'

'I was talking to myself.'

'You were talking to Ruby, weren't you?'

'No.'

'Lizzie.'

'Don't call me Lizzie,' she snapped.

Keith sat in the chair opposite her. He looked at the empty chair to Elizabeth's right, knowing that's where Ruby would have sat. He reached out and took his sister's hand.

'I'm sorry,' he said. It sounded heartfelt and purposeful.

'What for?'

'Putting you through all this. I've been very selfish. I've never thought about others, what my actions do to other people. I've never once asked how you're doing on your own. I know we're very different, but we're family. I should have been there for you more.'

Elizabeth gave a weak smile. 'Ruby meant the world to me. I know she was your sister too, but when you're identical twins, there's a much stronger bond. It's almost like you're one person but in two bodies. We tried to live a normal life, and it didn't work.'

'Do you think, if you'd found someone, like Ruby did, you'd have been able to be happy?'

Elizabeth swallowed her emotions and shook her head. 'We wanted to be normal, like everybody else, but, we were drawn back to each other. When she married Guy, I felt like I'd lost a limb. The day she moved out of here she said she'd made a mistake, and wanted to come back, but she couldn't. She was married. She was round here more than she was at her new home. Guy, give him his due, he tried to understand, but, eventually, he told her to make a choice, him or me. She didn't hesitate. She chose me.'

'Do you ever hear from Guy?'

'No. He came to see me the day after Ruby's funeral.'

'You never said.'

'He really laid into me. He said some cruel, nasty things; blamed me for Ruby killing herself. Said I was a sick, twisted, lonely woman. Maybe he was right.'

Keith squeezed his sister's hand tighter. 'He's not right. Like you said, the bond between identical twins is too strong.'

A tear fell down Elizabeth's face. She turned to the empty chair. 'All Ruby wanted was a normal life, but she couldn't have one.'

'Elizabeth,' Keith said after a long silence, 'the invitation from the Mercers' wedding . . . there wasn't one, was there?'

She closed her eyes tight. When she opened them, tears streamed down her face. 'I just wanted to be accepted by other people. I never get invited anywhere.'

'What did Serena say to you?'

'She said it was a private party for family and close friends only. She gave me a drink out of politeness, but it was obvious she wanted me to leave.'

Keith went around the table and took his sister in his arms. He held her tight. 'You should have told me you were so lonely.'

'You've got your own life to lead. You don't want me around.'

'Some life,' he scoffed. 'And you're wrong. You're my sister. Of course I want you around.'

'I've made a real mess of everything, haven't I?' she asked, wiping her nose on a battered tissue from her pocket. 'Your DNA is all over the house and I'm photographed there. The police will think we were both in on it. We both have criminal records.'

'What happened with Mum was an accident,' Keith said, squeezing his sister harder.

'It wasn't, though, was it?' She pushed Keith away, wiped away her tears and sniffled. 'Mummy blamed me for Ruby's death like everyone else. She said I should have stayed away from her and Guy, let them live their own lives. I couldn't. She didn't understand. Nobody understood.'

'Are you ready now to tell me what actually happened?' Keith asked.

'We argued. She was cruel. I mean, really horrible to me. She went out onto the balcony to get her cigarettes from the table, and I just saw red. I pushed her. We were only one floor up; I didn't think she'd be seriously hurt,' she sobbed. 'It was the way she landed, apparently. I remember the doctors telling me she was unlucky the way she hit the ground.'

'Oh, Elizabeth.' Keith reached forward and took his sister's hand. 'Nobody blames you for what happened to Mum. I certainly don't.'

'But I do. The police did. That horrible detective hounded me day and night. That's why they don't believe us about this. It's a complete mess, Keith.'

'I think DCI Darke will get to the truth.' He offered a smile that didn't reach his eyes.

'What if she doesn't?'

'Then we're both screwed.'

Chapter Fifty-Eight

Matilda looked at herself in the mirror of the ladies' toilets in the police station. She looked shattered. She felt worse. By the time she had got home last night, she was drained and exhausted by the weight of the investigation and the pressure she had placed upon herself. She hadn't told anyone about Keith turning up at his sister's house, not her team, not Valerie, and not even Adele when she called.

She'd closed the front door behind her, keeping the crazy, insane world locked firmly outside, and headed for the sanctuary of her library. There were piles of books everywhere and empty shelves waiting to be filled. It was a mammoth task that lay ahead of her, but it was one she relished. She'd put on a pot of coffee, opened a packet of biscuits and set to work cataloguing her collection.

The doorbell rang.

She looked at her watch. It was almost eleven o'clock. Who would be calling so late. Fortunately, the library was at the back of the house and there were no lights on in the rooms at the front. It would look like she was out, or in bed. Unfortunately, her car was parked outside as the garage hadn't been made secure enough yet. Shit.

Matilda edged out into the hallway and looked towards the door. There was a looming shadow on the other side. The letterbox was lifted, and Matilda felt her heart sink.

'Matilda, it's Pat. I know it's late but open up. It's freezing out here.'

She smiled with relief and headed for the door.

'Why are you so frightened of answering your own door?' Pat asked as she entered the house.

'I'm not,' she lied.

'Every time I come round it's like I have to pass a test before I'm allowed in. Or are you just trying to tell me something?' She smiled. 'Are we through here?' she asked, heading for the lounge and the warmth of the fire.

'Pat, what are you doing out so late?'

'To cut a long story short, I've been at our Cheryl's babysitting all evening while she ran her oldest up to the Children's.'

'Is he OK?'

'He is now. He's got a nut allergy and he must have eaten one without realizing. He needed an injection, that's all. Anyway, as you're on my way home, I thought I'd pop in seeing as you haven't replied to my messages.'

'I know. I'm sorry. It's been one of those days.'

'You look like you've got the weight of the world on your shoulders.'

'I feel it.'

'Well, if you want to offer me a strong drink and unburden yourself, I don't mind,' she said, making herself comfortable on the sofa.

Matilda smiled. She poured Pat a large glass of Highland Park and a small one for herself.

'Fill me in on the Meagans then,' Matilda said.

'I thought you were going to be doing the talking,' she said, smacking her lips after downing half a glass of whisky.

'After the day I've had, I'd rather not have to relive it.'

'Fair enough.' She made herself more comfortable and filled Matilda in on Philip Meagan's deception; how he had been behind the phone calls to Sally all along.

'Oh my God. I can't believe he would do something like that,' Matilda said, wide-eyed.

'He's a man, isn't he? We all know how depraved they can be.'

'But to put his wife through such torment.'

'To be honest, he looked slightly tormented himself. He's lost his son and he's close to losing his wife. He needed her to need him again. The more I think about it, the more I can see it from his point of view. I'm not denying he went about it completely the wrong way, but they did need pushing back together.'

Matilda slumped back in her seat and blew out her cheeks. 'Even so. It's a rotten thing to do.'

'It seems to have worked though. An hour or so after I'd left I had a call from Sally. She said Philip was taking her away to the Lakes for a long weekend and would it be OK for me to pop round when she got back.'

'She's willing to go away?'

'They must have had a serious talk when she got back from the vet with Woody. I think it will do them all good.'

Pat didn't stay too long after that. Long enough to have a second drink, but not long enough so she was unfit to drive. She had tried to get Matilda to open up, tell her about her disastrous day, but Matilda wouldn't budge. She filled her in on her urbexing exploits then headed for the door.

Matilda returned to her library but her heart was no longer in it. Philip's deception prayed on her mind. What he did was wrong, but he had had good intentions. She couldn't help but think the same about the Mercer case. In her eyes, Keith wasn't the killer, yet someone was obviously willing to plant evidence to frame him so they could get away with it. To them, they had a reason for killing Clive, Serena and Jeremy.

From the ladies' toilets, Matilda headed for the HMET suite. From the doorway she could tell she still hadn't received any extra staff. TDC Finn Cotton looked suitably harassed as if he'd been with the team for years rather than a few days.

As soon as Sian spotted her, she picked up her pad and headed towards her. 'Keith Lumb seems to have disappeared from the face of the earth. Uniformed officers are still outside his flat but it's as quiet as the proverbial. We've had a few phone calls, but nothing we can take seriously. I've sent his photo to all train stations, bus stations, ports and airports.'

'Good work, Sian.' Matilda smiled but gritted her teeth. She knew exactly where Keith was and she was wasting resources she couldn't afford looking for him. 'Kesinka, nice to have you back. How are you feeling?' As soon as Matilda saw the heavily pregnant DC, she headed over to her desk. Anything to change the subject.

'I'm doing OK, thank you.'

'You've been told about restricted duties?'

'Yes. I'm just happy to be back at work. I don't care if I'm making everyone coffee.'

'Two sugars, Kes,' Rory shouted.

'If you need anything, let me know. Or, better still, get Rory to do it for you.'

'Will do. I'm covering the control room for a few shifts. The ACC said I won't be needed here all the time. Is that OK?' she asked nervously.

Matilda wanted to vent some anger, but Kesinka shouldn't be on the receiving end. 'That's fine.' She smiled coldly.

Matilda went into her office and closed the door behind her. She hadn't been sitting down a couple of minutes before there was a knock on the glass and Christian entered.

'I've had the DI from Barnsley on the phone. He's not happy about all the uniformed officers we're using covering Keith Lumb's flat.'

'Well I'm not happy about his officers allowing him to escape in the first place. His officers screwed up, they can pay for it. Sian,' Matilda called out over Christian's shoulder, 'are we closing the door on the GMC angle?'

Sian edged around Christian and entered the office. 'I think so. I've printed off the files. They're on your desk if you fancy glancing through them. I've been trying to trace the invisible man all morning. Do you think we should bring the sister in?'

Matilda quickly looked away. She remained silent.

'You know where he's hiding, don't you?' Christian asked.

Reluctantly, she nodded.

'What?' They both asked at the same time, mouths agape.

'OK, calm down. Keith was at Elizabeth's house last night. I had a good talk to both of them.'

'And you left the house with a killer in there?' Christian shouted in a loud whisper.

'He's not a killer,' Matilda said, flustered.

'You should have brought him in for questioning. We could have interviewed him formally and found out what links him with the Mercers.'

'Nothing links him with the Mercers. Well, nothing concrete.'

'I don't believe this,' Sian said, obviously annoyed. 'Having a chat in a living room is completely different to a formal interview. Under interrogation, who knows what he would have revealed.'

'I'll go and have another word with him.'

'I'm not happy about this,' Sian said. 'I'm sorry, Matilda, I've always trusted your judgement in the past, but what if you're wrong on this? What if Keith is the killer and is just a very clever man? He could be playing you.'

'If I'm wrong, then I'm wrong.'

'It's not that simple. If you're wrong, more people could die. And if it gets out, you could lose your job.'

The silence was palpable. Matilda looked everywhere but at the DI and DS sitting opposite her. She knew Sian was right. Sian always seemed to be right, but she had to go with her gut feeling on this, and that was telling her Keith Lumb was innocent.

'Sian, I believe Keith is innocent. I don't believe more people will die. Someone killed the Mercers for a reason.'

'But we don't know what that reason is.'

'Then we need to find out.'

'How? We've interviewed friends, family, neighbours, colleagues. Apart from digging up abuse from Clive and Oliver hiding his sexuality, there's nothing in their pasts that would lead to them being murdered,' Sian said.

'There has to be.'

'We can keep going over the interviews and statements time and time again, but the solution is not there. I'm sorry, Matilda, but Keith Lumb should be arrested on suspicion of murder and held while we formally interview him. If he's innocent, he'll have an alibi.'

'Yes,' Christian said. 'Did he tell you what his alibi was for Sunday night?'

Matilda looked down as her desk.

'He doesn't have one, does he?'

'No,' she replied quietly.

'I don't believe this,' Sian said. 'In past cases we've waited for forensic evidence to come through. Once we've got a result, we use it to find the killer, arrest him, and that's it, case over. Why is this case so different?'

'Because Keith Lumb is not a killer,' Matilda replied with defiance.

'Despite the evidence saying otherwise?'

'Yes.'

Sian and Christian exchanged glances but neither of them said anything. Sian turned and left the room.

'Shit. I need Sian on my side.'

'Sian's an evidence woman. She always has been. If the evidence tells her to go one way, she will.'

'What about you?'

'I'm anybody's for a cup of tea and a bag of chips,' he said with a smile. 'Personally, I think the killer is someone close to the Mercer family. It's someone who had a grievance against them. It's probably someone we've already interviewed. To have killed them in such a violent way, the killer had to have known them to feel such hatred to inflict such overkill.'

'And who would fit into that category?'

'Somebody close to the family.'

'That only leaves Leah and Rachel.'

'And we know Leah was in France.'

'Maybe she knows more than she's letting on, though.'

'Why wouldn't she tell us who's destroyed her family?'

Christian thought for a while. He scratched the back of his head. 'I can think of two reasons.'

'Are you going to share them with me?'

'She's scared,' he began, counting his theories off on his fingers. 'Or she's protecting the killer because she has strong feelings for him.'

'Oliver Ridgeway? I doubt she has strong feelings for him now. Besides, he was in France with her.'

'Maybe she hired someone.'

'Then why leave Rachel alive?'

'Only she can answer that question.'

'Hang on a minute,' Matilda interrupted. 'Are we really suggesting Leah hired a killer? This is Sheffield for crying out loud, not 1930s Chicago.'

'You said you wanted to go through everyone.'

Matilda slumped on her desk, her head in her hands. 'I'm getting a headache.'

'So am I. I'm also fancying a bag of chips.'

Matilda smirked. 'Christian, I'm really struggling here. I honestly have no idea which way to turn.'

'Do you want to know what I think?'

'Go on.'

'I think you're screwed.'

Matilda rolled her eyes. She couldn't disagree with him. As he left the office, she leaned forward and placed her head on her desk with a bang and closed her eyes.

I am screwed.

Chapter Fifty-Nine

Aaron received a call from the front desk telling him Leah Mercer was here to see him. He bounded down the stairs like a five-year-old on Christmas morning. When he went into reception, he saw a different woman waiting to see him. Leah was all smiles. She was dressed smartly; her hair was neatly styled, and she was wearing make-up. She looked a decade younger than when he last saw her.

'A bit of an improvement, don't you think?' she asked when she noticed Aaron staring at her.

'You look a million times better.'

'Thank you.' She grabbed Aaron's arm and led him over to the seating area, away from the prying eyes and ears of the desk sergeant. 'I have a favour to ask you. I know it's a cheek after what you've done for me, but I was wondering if you'd come with me to see Rachel and Pongo?'

'Of course,' he answered quickly.

She visibly relaxed. 'Thank you. I've been on to social services and they've contacted the family Rachel's staying with, temporarily, and they're expecting me. I have a plan.' She smiled. 'Jeremy and Rachel's house in Liverpool is standing empty. I'm going to move there while my parents' house is cleaned and sorted, then, if Rachel wants to, we'll move here permanently. If she'd rather stay in Liverpool, then I'll sell up here.'

'Wow.' Aaron was taken aback by the sudden transformation. 'What about Oliver?'

'What about him?'

'He's still your husband.'

'Not for much longer. I've been to see a solicitor. I think I may be able to have the marriage annulled.'

'You don't want to try and make it work?'

'What's the point? He doesn't love me. He doesn't even love women. I certainly won't be sad to close the door on that particular chapter. I never liked his parents, anyway. No,' she said, pushing her hair back, 'I've made up my mind. What's happened has been a tragedy for all of us, but it's also been a wake-up call. Life is incredibly fragile. From now on, it's going to be me and Rachel. We're going to have fun, live our lives and try to put the past firmly in its place. We'll survive, just the two of us.' She smiled.

'I'm really pleased for you,' he said. He took her hands in both of his and held them tight.

The visit to see Rachel and Pongo was fraught with emotion. Rachel cried the second the door was opened and Leah entered. They hugged for an age and Rachel only let go when Pongo started barking. While they chatted in the living room with the social worker, Aaron went into the kitchen with the emergency foster parents. An hour later, Leah was ready to leave. Back in the car, she took a deep breath and wiped her eyes.

'Are you all right?' Aaron asked.

'I am. I really am.' She smiled. 'Rachel said she wants to go back home to Liverpool. I said I'd go across this evening, sort the place out, come back for her tomorrow morning and take her home. Social services seem to be happy about that. They're putting me in touch with the people in Liverpool in case we need any help.'

'A new chapter.'

'Absolutely. Aaron, I want to thank you.'

'What for?'

'For what you said at my parents' house yesterday. You were incredibly sweet. I think I would have gone back to the hotel and drowned myself in the bath if you hadn't made me see what was left. I can't thank you enough.'

She leaned forward in her seat and kissed Aaron on the cheek. Her turned to face her. She kissed him on the mouth and he reciprocated. It wasn't a long kiss, but it was full of passion and excitement.

From his inside pocket, he pulled out his card. 'If you need anything at all, call me. My mobile's on there.'

She smiled. 'Maybe you could visit us in Liverpool from time to time.'

'Maybe.'

Chapter Sixty

Matilda decided to go home. It would be the first time in as long as she could remember when she would have an early finish. She hoped that if she took a step back from the case, even for a couple of hours, it may give her a fresh perspective. Fingers firmly crossed. As she was leaving, she stuffed the GMC files in her bag and went for a quick word with the ACC before going out of the station via the back way to the car park.

Fortunately for Matilda, it was Adele's afternoon off. They arranged to meet in the centre of Sheffield and went for a late lunch in the Blue Moon Café next to the cathedral. Matilda ordered a strong black coffee and a piece of homity pie. She had tried to make it herself for her and Adele once, but it never came out the way it did here. She sat in the corner and looked at the four clocks on the wall, all giving the same time. Beneath them were cities from around the world – Bradford, Doncaster, Sheffield and Rotherham. They always made her smile. The atmosphere in the café was relaxed as usual and she found her headache easing slightly.

Adele started talking about work, about the Mercer case, and if there were any leads. Matilda had escaped the office to get away from the Mercers. She was beginning to wish she'd never heard of them. She gave monosyllabic replies to Adele's questions and eventually had to be honest with her best friend.

'Look, can we change the subject?'

'OK,' Adele conceded defeat. 'So,' she began, 'I hear Scott's gay.'

'Oh. Yes he is. How did you find out?'

'Rory told me.'

Matilda smiled. 'I've never known such a big a gossip as Rory.'

'Do you think Scott and my Chris are a couple?' Adele asked, playing with her leftover food with her fork.

Matilda looked up from her pie. She hoped her face wasn't giving her away. She was sure she could feel her face blush. 'What? No. Of course not. What makes you say that?'

'Because Chris is gay.' She shrugged.

'Is he?'

'He hasn't told me, but a mother knows. I like Scott. I think they'd make a great couple.'

'Scott does have feelings for Chris. I think they may be reciprocated,' Matilda said gently.

Adele smiled. 'I hope they're happy.' She looked off into the distance.

'Are you all right with it?' Matilda leaned forward and placed her hand over Adele's.

'Of course I am. All I want is for Chris to be happy. I don't care if it's with another man or a woman.'

'But wouldn't you have liked grandchildren?'

'Can you honestly see me as a grandmother? Besides, it's 2018, two men can have children these days. Now, do you think you could move your hand from mine? We're getting funny looks from the old couple at the next table.'

Matilda looked across to see an elderly man and woman watching them out of the corner of their eyes. She couldn't hear their lowered conversation but the tuts were loud enough.

Matilda was driving along Ringinglow Road. As she turned onto the dirt track and the car disappeared under the cover of trees, a figure jumped out up ahead. She slammed on the brakes. When she opened her eyes she saw Keith Lumb looking straight at her.

'What the bloody hell are you doing here?' she asked as she opened the window.

'I can't stay at Elizabeth's any longer. She's doing my head in.'

'How do you know where I lived?'

'Elizabeth said you'd told her you live close by, that you'd bought a rundown farmhouse. This is the only one I know. I took a shot.'

'I told you to stay at your sister's.'

'There's police camped outside her house. She was getting nervous. She thinks she'll be arrested as aiding and abetting a fugitive. She's not as strong as she likes to make out.'

'You can't stay with me.'

'Where am I supposed to go?'

'I should take you to the station . . .'

'No fucking way,' he said, backing up. 'You even think about it and I'll run. I mean it. Once you get me into a cell, that's it, you'll lock the door and I won't be coming out again.'

'Shit,' Matilda said under her breath. 'OK, you can stay, but only for one night.'

I'm so going to get fired for this.

* * *

'Why do you have so many books?' Keith asked. He stood in the doorway to her library while she set about making him a drink and a snack.

'I enjoy reading,' she said without looking up.

'But they're all crime. Don't you get enough of that at work?'

'What do you like to do in your spare time?' She avoided answering the question.

'My whole life is my spare time.'

'You don't have a job?'

'Bits of cash-in-hand stuff.'

'You should get yourself a legitimate job.'

'Maybe I should join the police.'

Matilda laughed. 'You'd hate it. Here, I've made you a sandwich. Look, I could lose my job over having you here. I should take you into custody, for your own protection at least.'

'My protection?' he said with a mouthful of cheese and pickle.

'I don't believe you killed the Mercer family, but the killer has chosen you for a reason. If he thinks you're going to get away with it, you could be a target. He could come looking for you.'

'And you don't want my blood all over your shiny new kitchen?'

'I don't want your blood anywhere. I'd also like to keep my job.'

She pulled out a chair opposite him and sat down, taking the file of GMC cases out of her bag.

'Do you live here on your own?' he asked once he'd finished his sandwich and was washing it down with a mug of tea.

Matilda looked up from the files. 'Yes.'

'It's a bit big, isn't it?'

'I like my space.'

'How many bedrooms has it got?'

'Why?'

'Just curious.'

Matilda ignored him and went back to reading.

'You're not married then?' he asked.

'I'm a widow.'

'Oh. Sorry,' he said without emotion. 'No kids?'

'No.'

'Why not?

'Why all the questions?'

'Just being friendly,' he said with a smile.

'I'd rather you didn't. Look, why don't you go and have a shower or something?'

'I had one the other day.'

Matilda rolled her eyes and went back to reading the files. She read through the first two cases in which Clive Mercer had had to justify his actions. When she came to the final case, she sat up.

'What's wrong?' Keith asked.

'Nothing,' she said with a heavy frown. She rummaged in her back pocket for her mobile and dialled. 'Scott, it's me. On one of the white boards, there are three names. Can you read them out to me, please?'

'Yes. Hang on,' he said with his mouth full. 'Margo Sanders, Martin Walken and Milly Johnston. Who are they?'

'They're the people who died in surgery, and why Clive Mercer was referred to the GMC. How is Milly Johnston spelled?'

He spelled it for her.

'Oh my God,' she said.

'What?'

'I'll ring you back.' She hung up before he could say anything else.

'What is it?' Keith asked.

'Does the name Ross Jonson mean anything to you?'

He thought for a while. 'He's a DS in Barnsley, isn't he?'

'Yes. Do you know him?'

'Not really. Why?'

'Let me think for a moment,' she said, raising a hand to silence him. She picked up her phone, opened the Google app and typed in the name 'Ross Jonson'. Then pressed on the news heading and there it was. She fell onto the sofa and scanned the story.

How could I have been so blind?

'I don't believe this. I've known exactly who the killer is from day one. In fact, if we'd been doing our jobs properly in the first place, these murders could have been prevented.'

Chapter Sixty-One

S cott was staring at the white board. There was something in Matilda's voice that didn't sound right. Yes, she was stressed, but there was a hint of anger, nerves, fear that belied her confidence. It was connected with the GMC files. Why had she asked how to spell Milly? Surely there was only one way to spell it.

'Sian,' Scott called out, looking over the top of his computer. 'Could you email me across those GMC reports?'

'Sure. Why?'

'I just want to check something.'

'OK.' She hammered on her keyboard. 'Done.'

'Cheers. Do you fancy a coffee?'

'I'd love one.' She smiled and visibly relaxed in her seat.

Scott went over to the drinks station and began making them both a drink. Most of the detectives in HMET were out so the office was relatively quiet.

'Scott, is everything all right?' Sian asked.

'Fine.'

'Nobody's had a go at you, or made any snide comments about . . . you know?'

'Being gay?'

'Well, yes.'

'No. Everyone's acting like it's no big deal. I suppose it isn't, really, but I'd built it up in my head as being this life-changing thing. It shouldn't be, should it? As long as I can do my job, then who I sleep with is my business.'

'Exactly. So,' she said the word 'so' as if it had about a dozen o's in it. 'Are you seeing anyone at the moment?' Her question was innocent, but she was eager for the gossip.

Scott felt himself redden slightly. He stirred the coffees and handed her a mug. 'It's early days.'

'Anyone I know?' She grinned.

'Like I said, it's early days,' he said as he sat at his desk. He could feel Sian's eyes burning into him. He looked up and saw her smiling. 'What?'

'Nothing. You look different.'

'Do I?'

'Yes. You look . . . I don't know . . . happy.'

'Really?' He thought for a moment. 'I feel happy.'

Scott took a sip of his coffee and opened the email Sian had sent him. He wanted to read the Milly Johnston file first, as that was the one Matilda seemed most interested in. His eyes widened. He looked to the white board then back to the computer.

'Who wrote those names on the board?'

'I did,' Sian answered. 'Why?'

'You didn't copy them from these files, did you?'

'No. My email has been down for a few days. The bloke from the GMC sent them over but I couldn't access them. I called him and he gave me the bare bones over the phone. Why?'

'You spelled Milly's name wrong.'

'Did I?'

'Yes. It's M-I-L-L-I-E.'

'Oh. Well, no disrespect meant.'

'No. I don't mean it like that. You've spelled her surname

incorrectly too. The thing is, the correct spelling would have changed our whole approach to our line of questioning.'

'What are you talking about?' Sian went over to Scott's desk and looked at his screen over her shoulder. 'Oh, Jesus Christ! What have I done?'

Chapter Sixty-Two

Matilda was on the A61 heading for Barnsley. She had tried to persuade Keith to stay behind but he was adamant he was coming with her. Her head was full of thoughts she didn't really want to think about. She understood that during exceptional circumstances the most sane and rational of people could do things they would later regret, but the carnage at the Mercer house was something else. It was savage. It was pure evil. What kind of a warped individual could inflict such pain and horror on another person? There was one shred of light among the darkness; her theory about Keith Lumb was correct. He was innocent. He would have to face the consequences of his burglaries but at least he wouldn't go to prison for three murders.

By the time Matilda pulled up in the car park at Barnsley police station it was dark and most of the day shift had gone home. There were very few cars around so Matilda had her pick of spaces. She looked at the building through the windscreen. It looked desolate. No windows were lit up. There was a sense of foreboding about a police station at night. Matilda had never liked being one of the last officers to leave. In her opinion, they should be a hive of activity twenty-four hours a day. She was beginning to wish she'd called Sian or Christian, told them of her theory, but with the way they reacted to her harbouring

Keith Lumb, she'd prefer to confront a fellow colleague by herself. There was always a lingering doubt that she could be wrong.

'I want you to stay in the car,' she said firmly.

'Are you sure you don't want me for backup?'

'No, I don't. You're to keep well out of the way until I know what's going on.'

'But what if he's violent?'

She took a deep breath and looked up at the building. 'He won't be.'

'You could try saying that with more conviction.'

She sighed. 'Look, if I'm not out within half an hour, call 999 and tell them I need help.'

'I'll wait twenty minutes.'

'Fine.'

It was a cold evening. Matilda picked up her jacket from the back seat and headed for the main entrance. She expected it to be locked but was surprised to find it open. There was nobody at the reception desk, which wasn't a surprise, so Matilda let herself through into the main body of the building.

Her heels clacked loudly on the floor as she made her away across the quiet, dimly lit corridors. She looked into rooms as she passed them, but most were in darkness. She headed up the stairs to the first floor and made a cleaner jump who was emptying the bins and wearing headphones.

She reached the CID suite and found who she was looking for standing at the window looking out over the town.

'DS Jonson,' Matilda called out.

Ross jumped and turned around. He looked stunned to see Matilda standing in the doorway. He was a tall man with unkempt salt-and-pepper hair. His face was drawn and thin, his eyes dark and sunken. His suit looked too big for him, as if he'd lost a lot of weight quickly. If Matilda was correct, he'd had more on his mind recently than cooking a decent meal.

'Where is everyone?' she asked, looking around at the empty desks.

He gave the hint of a smile. 'We have a very skeleton staff at night.'

'Why are you here?'

'I'm just finishing up a few bits of paperwork I haven't got around to doing. We've had a spate of arson attacks in the area over the past couple of days.'

'You didn't look like you were working.'

'Just taking a break,' he said, heading back to his desk with heavy limbs. He slumped into his seat with a sigh. 'Did you want to see someone in particular?'

'I came to see you, actually,' Matilda said, moving further into the room.

'Oh?'

Ross couldn't say anything. He was looking in the black mirror of his computer screen. His body slumped.

She pulled up a chair and sat beside him. 'Do you want to tell me how you know the Mercers?'

He flinched at the name but didn't say anything.

'During a murder investigation we look into the victim's background, as you know. We discovered that Clive Mercer had been brought before a board at the GMC on three occasions. We looked into those cases to see if anyone could have had a motive for killing them.'

Ross remained impassive. He looked down at his untidy desk. His face was blank.

'Your name came up. More accurately, your daughter, Millie.'

Ross looked up at Matilda. His eyes were full of tears.

'Do you want to tell me about her?' Matilda asked.

There was a long silence. It was obvious Ross was fighting with his emotions. Eventually, he spoke. 'Me and Hattie spent years trying to have a child. It was all we both ever wanted, but it just never happened. We used all of our savings up for IVF but that didn't work either. Then, suddenly, out of the blue, she fell pregnant. We couldn't believe it. We were so happy. Millie was born on her due date. Our lives were complete.'

Ross picked up a small framed photograph from the side of his desk, hiding behind his laptop. It showed his wife, Hattie, grinning to the camera with a young girl sitting on her knee. The picture of happiness. He looked at the picture and smiled. He gently brushed the faces with the tip of his finger, as if stroking them.

'Millie started with headaches when she was about two. They weren't just normal headaches, they were crippling. She'd burst into tears sometimes. We took her to the doctor but they were useless. They kept saying we were being overly cautious because we were new parents. They told us to take her to an optician, but we'd already done that and she was fine. Eventually, we were referred to the Children's Hospital in Sheffield. Then they sent us to this specialist at the Northern. Specialist. That was a joke. We saw this arrogant doctor who said Millie was attention seeking. Can you believe that? She didn't need to seek attention, we doted on her. Nobody would listen to us. We knew she was ill.

'Finally, we got to see this neurologist. She didn't even look as if she wanted to be there, like we were some kind of an inconvenience for her. She came into the office and started talking about Millie's diet. She was asking us what food we were giving her. Then she's asking us how long we sit her in front of the television for. Bloody useless.' Ross's frustration was growing as he recounted his story. He had obviously relived it many times over the dark months since Millie had died. Matilda felt his pain. She had done exactly the same thing after James had died.

'This neurologist,' Matilda said, 'it was Serena Mercer, wasn't it?'

Ross nodded. 'We saw her again. I kept asking her to rerun the tests. I knew there was something wrong. Millie would be curled up on the sofa, clutching her head, rocking back and forth. She was tired all the time and feeling sick. It's not normal behaviour for a three-year-old. It was obvious for crying out loud. She had an MRI scan and there was a tumour on her brain. I knew it. I fucking knew it,' he spat. 'She had an operation . . .' he couldn't continue as emotion got the better of him. He showed Matilda the photo in his hand. 'Look at her beautiful blonde hair. She loved her hair. She loved having her mum brush it and put it into plaits. It all had to be cut off. She was devastated.' He looked back at the photo and smiled through his tears. He placed it back on the desk.

'I could never pronounce what kind of tumour it was. Hattie could. She did a lot of research into it. I think she knew more about it than the doctors. They said they could operate, but it would be tricky due to where the tumour was. They tried radiotherapy first. She had a course of that lasting four weeks. It didn't do anything to the tumour and it just made Millie sick. In the end, they decided to risk operating. Hattie wasn't convinced. It was me who said she would be better afterwards. I mean, they wouldn't operate on a three-year-old if they didn't have to, would they?' He looked at Matilda with pleading eyes, as if begging her to agree with him.

'No. They wouldn't,' she said, sympathizing with him. She

was on the brink of tears herself, remembering the endless appointments, scans and courses of treatment her husband had had to endure. The chemotherapy had made him vomit, made him listless and constantly tired. He sometimes thought it would be better to let nature take its course and allow the tumour to do its job. It was only Matilda's constant badgering that made him return to the hospital for more treatment.

'The first operation was a success,' Ross continued. 'They were able to remove more of the tumour than they thought. A few months later we were back to square one. It was a fast-growing tumour and it was bigger than before. It was obvious Millie wasn't going to live much longer, but while she was here, they could keep cutting away at the tumour, relieving the pressure and making her more comfortable. Like I said, Hattie didn't want to keep putting her through the torment of more surgery, but I convinced her. It was that second operation that killed her.'

'Ross, I'm so sorry,' Matilda said. Her words sounded baseless but she genuinely meant them.

'There had to be a post-mortem,' he said, swallowing hard. 'They had to cut open my little girl. The results came back that she'd been given too much of the anaesthetic drug. They tried to blame the anaesthetic nurse. She hadn't been in the job long, but I tracked her down. Yes, she was the one who drew the syringe, but the anaesthetist is supposed to check everything before he administers it, and he didn't. He took the syringe from her and injected it straight into Millie without giving it a second thought.'

'The anaesthetist was Clive Mercer, wasn't it?'

'Yes. What a remarkable team husband and wife make,' he said, his comment oozing with venomous sarcasm. 'Between them they killed my daughter and my wife.'

'Hattie?'

'She couldn't cope with losing Millie. We'd tried for so long to have her. She fell apart when she died. It took all her energy to make it through the funeral. Afterwards, she wasn't interested in anything. She hardly got out of bed; she stopped eating. I came home from work one Thursday and found her still in bed. She'd taken everything in the house she could get her hands on – paracetamol, ibuprofen, old antibiotics, some pain relief I had for my dodgy knee. Those two bastards ruined my life.'

'But what you did was horrific.'

'They had to pay.'

'You slaughtered them.'

'They killed my wife and daughter. The hospital released a statement after the inquest and said lessons would be learned in the future. What the fuck does that mean? I've got to live the rest of my life on my own because my daughter died and my wife killed herself. Meanwhile, those responsible are still working, they're walking around like nothing has happened. They probably didn't even remember Millie's name. Three times Clive Mercer went before the GMC. He should have been struck off after the first time. Maybe my Millie would still be alive. If not, I'd still have Hattie.'

'But what about Jeremy Mercer? What had he done?'

'I didn't know he was going to be there.' Ross shucked Matilda off. He stood up and went back over to the window. It was pitch-dark outside and all he could see was his tired reflection in the black mirror. 'I saw in the newspaper the announcement about the big family wedding. They were all smiles, getting on with life as normal. That's when I realized I had to do something. I couldn't have them rubbing my nose in it.'

'So where does Keith Lumb fit into all of this?' Matilda asked.

She folded her arms in defiance. Yes, she felt sorry for what Ross had gone through, but she had been through similar with James. It hadn't turned her into a murderer.

'That wasn't my idea. My plan was to just break in and stab them as they slept. I didn't give a fuck what happened to me afterwards.'

'So, what happened? Whose idea was it to fit Keith Lumb up for murder?'

'Mine.'

The voice came from behind Matilda. She turned around and saw someone standing in the shadow of the doorway. The lights were flicked on. Matilda blinked against the brightness of the strip lighting on the ceiling. She recognized the figure straight away, but she couldn't take her eyes off the baseball bat he was holding.

Chapter Sixty-Three

D C Kesinka Rani was bored. She hated being given lighter duties. She was a detective constable for crying out loud. She should be out there interviewing suspects, knocking on doors, not sitting in a cramped office listening to all the excitement through the radio. She cradled her stomach, as, once again, the baby made its presence felt. Ranjeet popped in to see her when he could and Sian had sent down a few snacks, but she felt like she was missing the gossip and the fun of being in the HMET suite.

A mug of tea was placed in front of her.

'Thanks, Karen,' she said to her new colleague who had the station next to her.

'Uncomfortable?'

'Very.'

'I'll have a word with Sergeant Bowler, see if we can get a more comfortable chair in.'

'That'll be lovely. Help yourself to a Club; Sian sent a couple of packets down for me.'

An alarm sounded that made everyone in the control room freeze. It wasn't heard very often but when it was, everything was dropped. It was the sound made when a police officer was in distress and the emergency button on their personal radio was pressed for urgent assistance.

Sergeant Bowler, a huge barrel of a man, went over to Kesinka's desk and looked at her screen over her shoulder. 'Who is it?'

'Oh my God. It's DCI Darke,' Kesinka replied.

'Get me a GPS location.'

With shaking fingers, Kesinka tapped on her keyboard. 'She's at the Churchfield Sub Divisional HQ in Barnsley.'

'What's she doing there?'

'I've no idea.'

'Is the ACC still here?'

'Yes, sir.'

Minutes later, ACC Valerie Masterson was in the HMET suite with Sian, Scott and Christian. None of them had had any idea Matilda was planning on visiting Barnsley. She'd told them she was going home early. Scott filled the ACC in on Ross Jonson and what he and Sian had found out about him in the past half an hour or so.

'It looks like DCI Darke found out the same information,' Valerie said. 'But are you really suggesting DS Jonson committed such brutal murders?' she asked, looking up at the crime scene photographs on the murder board.

'Until we know all the details, we're not saying anything,' Sian jumped in. 'However, I think we should proceed with caution.'

'Agreed.'

'Do you want me to give DI Eckhart a call? See if he's seen DCI Darke?' Sian suggested.

'Better not. DI Eckhart has a personal interest if this is the case. DS Jonson is his son-in-law.'

Ross Jonson looked on in silence as Nigel Eckhart explained how he'd laid the trap for Keith Lumb to escape from his cell and do a runner. They'd had some of his clothing when they arrested him and had the power to search his flat for stolen items, where samples of the DNA could be lifted. Keith had been in and out of custody many times over the years. His one fear was being sent to prison, yet he never seemed to be able to change his criminal ways. He was perfect to be set up for murder. Who was going to believe his pleas of innocence against his background and the indisputable forensic evidence?

'But why Keith Lumb?' Matilda asked.

'It didn't have to be him. He just happened to be the first loser we had brought into the station.'

She turned to Ross. 'All that stuff about Tina Law . . .'

'I made it up,' he said, ashamedly. 'I wanted you to believe he was violent.'

'And there wasn't anything wrong with the cell door?' she asked Nigel.

'No.'

'So, Bella Slack is in on it all, too?'

'Bella and I have been seeing each other on and off for years. She'd do anything for me,' Nigel said with a smirk. 'The plan was for Ross to kill Clive and Serena, make it look like a robbery gone wrong, plant the evidence, then leave. I'd be his alibi, should he need one. I had no idea he was going to be so frenzied.'

'I couldn't stop myself,' Ross said, looking down at the floor. 'I was just so angry.'

'You wore a forensic suit for the murders, didn't you? Where is it?'

'I burnt them,' Nigel answered. His voice was steady. 'Everything Ross wore that night was burnt. There's no evidence to trace back to him.'

'What about the knives?'

'They're in a secure location until I need to use them again.'

Matilda thought for a moment. 'You're going to plant them in Keith's flat, aren't you?'

'The man is a grade-A loser. He's done fuck all with his life. He'll end up in prison sooner or later. This way, he's off the street and the little old ladies of Barnsley can sleep easy in their beds without the worry of some pointless wanker stealing their jewellery because he can't be bothered to get a job.'

'I can't believe I'm hearing this. Nigel, this isn't you?'

'At the end of the day, Matilda, we're all trying to get through this fucker of a life in the best way we can. However, there are some who think they're above everyone else and their incompetence forces us to act because the law won't. My daughter,' he choked when he mentioned Hattie, 'my daughter killed herself because she couldn't live without Millie. I lost my only child and grandchild and look at that poor bastard over there.'

Matilda glanced at Ross. He was leaning against the window. He looked defeated. His face was ashen. 'Nigel, I know where you're coming from, I really do. I lost my husband to cancer. He had a brain tumour, just like Millie. When he died, I was devastated. I went through so many emotions, but there was nobody to blame. It was just one of those things.'

'A three-year-old child dying is not one of those things,' Nigel barked.

'If she'd been run over or murdered, I'd agree with you. We can't argue with a brain tumour. Nobody is to blame for that. I'm going to need you both to come with me. Bella, too,' Matilda said, stepping forward.

'Don't you think Ross has suffered enough?'

'Yes, I do. I have a great deal of sympathy for him. I felt all the emotions he went through too. But never once did I think about killing the doctor who diagnosed him, or who operated on him.'

'We all react in different ways, DCI Darke.'

'We're police officers. We don't take the law into our own hands.'

'They were getting away with murder,' Nigel shouted.

'Millie had an aggressive brain tumour. There was nothing anyone could have done about it.'

'And what about Hattie? She was my only child and they drove her to suicide.'

Matilda shook her head. She couldn't think of anything to say.

'You heartless bitch.' Nigel swung the baseball bat and hit Matilda on the side of her head. She dropped to the floor. She was hurt, but still conscious.

'Nigel!' Ross called out.

Matilda crawled along the floor, trying to pick herself up. She put a hand in her coat pocket, felt for her personal radio and pressed the emergency button. She didn't see the second swing of the bat coming, but she certainly felt it. She dropped back to the floor and stayed there.

'What the fuck!'

'It's all right, Ross. Calm down. I know what I'm doing.'

'Really?'

'I know all about Matilda. She's a basket case, has been since her husband died. Last year, DI Hales killed himself in her house. She's had to move. She fucked up the Carl Meagan case; his mother wrote a book about the investigation. It didn't show Matilda in a very good light. She's a suicide waiting to happen.'

'But you've just hit her over the head.'

'So. We'll put her in her car and drive it off the Snake Pass or something.'

'What? Nigel, no. You can't do that.'

'Ross, listen to me. There is no other way out of this. Ring my office; Bella's in there. She can come and help.'

'No,' Ross began, backing away. 'I shouldn't have listened to you in the first place. I should have just gone away or did what Hattie did.'

'Jesus Christ! I always knew you were soft. You're in this up to your neck. There's no backing away from it now. I've killed one detective this evening, I can kill another,' he said, pointing the bloodstained bat at his son-in-law.

*　　*　　*

Sitting in the front passenger seat of the Range Rover, Keith's patience was wearing thin. What was taking Matilda so long? He always knew most police officers were corrupt, but to use him to cover up their own crime was beyond belief. He leaned back in the car and closed his eyes. When he opened them, a light was on in a downstairs corridor. He squinted while he tried to make sense of what he thought he'd seen – two men carrying a woman. Carefully, he opened the passenger door, and slipped out of the car, closing the door firmly behind him. He sneaked up to the building and cupped his hands around his eyes so he could see better through the window.

'Fuck me,' he said to himself when he saw it was Matilda Darke who was being carried. She looked dead. As the door to the main entrance opened, Keith edged around the side of the building and remained in the shadows so as not to be seen.

*　　*　　*

Nigel Eckhart held Matilda under her arms, Ross Jonson was holding her legs. Bella Slack was trotting alongside them.

'Which is her car?' Nigel whispered loudly.

'The Range Rover,' Ross replied.

'Brand new, too, judging by the number plate. How did she afford that?' Nigel seethed. 'Bella, check her pockets for the keys.'

'Do I have to?' she whined.

'Just do it, Bella, for fuck's sake.'

Bella plunged her hand into Matilda's coat pocket and picket out the personal radio. The car keys were in the other pocket. Bella opened the boot and they put Matilda inside, slamming it closed.

'Right, me and Ross will go in this. Bella, you follow us in yours.'

'Where are you going?'

'I don't know. The Snake Pass might be a bit dodgy at this time of night. Ross?'

'Ladybower Reservoir or maybe Derwent,' Ross suggested.

'It's a bit far out.'

'It's closer than the Snake Pass.'

'True. OK. We'll head for Ladybower. We could get a few rocks in her pockets, make it look like she jumped in.'

'Nigel, is this the right thing to do?' Bella cried.

He stepped forward and held her by the shoulders. 'There's no other way. It's for Hattie and Millie. Just think about those two.' He kissed her firmly on the lips.

Bella stood back, shivering in her uniform, minus the jacket, and watched as Nigel reversed Matilda's car out of the visitor's space, turned left out of the car park and headed for the Derbyshire countryside.

Bella dug around in her pockets for her car keys and ran over to the Nissan in the corner.

Keith Lumb stepped out from the shadows. With a rock in his hand from the ornamental garden, he grabbed Bella by the shoulder and spun her around. She cried out and cowered when she saw the rock looming over her.

'Give me your keys,' he said.

'Who are you?'

'Keys. Now!' he screamed in her face.

She quickly handed them over.

He snatched the handcuffs from her utility belt and dragged her over to the railings by the main entrance, where he secured her to them. He took her personal radio, and the one that belonged to Matilda, before running back to the Nissan and setting off in the same direction as Nigel and Ross.

* * *

'What the fuck is going on?' ACC Masterson asked as she stormed into the control room.

'Hello? Can anyone hear me?'

Valerie's question wasn't answered, as she was interrupted by the unusual call coming over the radio.

'Who is this? This is a secured police channel,' Kesinka said.

'DCI Matilda Darke has been attacked and kidnapped. They've dumped her in her own car and are heading for Ladybower Reservoir.'

'Who is this?'

'My name is Keith Lumb. I'm wanted for the Mercer murders but I didn't do it. There are two detectives in Barnsley who have attacked DCI Darke.'

Valerie ushered Kesinka to move so she could talk to Keith.

'This is ACC Masterson; how do you know all this?'

'*I was with Matil . . . DCI Darke this evening. She went into the police station at Barnsley. She didn't say why. She was in there for about half an hour. Two detectives carried her out. I don't know if she's dead or just unconscious, but it doesn't look good. There's a woman officer called Bella who I've handcuffed to the railings outside Barnsley station.*'

'Where are you now?'

'*I've no bloody idea,*' Keith said.

'That's OK. We can track you with the radio.' She turned to Sergeant Bowler. 'Trace the radio and get armed response to Ladybower. I want this car followed too. No sirens and keep well back until we know the situation. Keith are you still there?' she said into the radio.

'*Of course I'm still bloody here.*'

'Can you still see DCI Darke's car.'

'*Yes. Just about. I heard one of the detectives tell this Bella woman to follow them. I'm in her car. It's a dark green Nissan. I'm keeping well back. I don't want them to see it's me driving.*'

'This bloke would make a good copper,' Kesinka said.

'Stay well back, Keith, but keep us updated.' She stepped back from the console and ran her fingers through her hair. 'I can't believe this. I've got a DCI kidnapped, two detectives looking for somewhere to dump her body and a petty criminal, who's wanted for murder, in pursuit. You couldn't make this up.'

* * *

Scott, Christian and Sian had been listening to the whole exchanged over the radio in the HMET suite. Scott grabbed his keys and headed for the door.

'Where are you going?' Sian called out.

'We're closer to Derbyshire than they are. We can be at Ladybower before them.'

'Good thinking,' Christian said, grabbing his coat.

'Wait for me,' Sian said, following.

With Scott driving, Christian in the front passenger seat, and Sian in the back, they headed for the outskirts of Sheffield at speed. Sian called the ACC and told her what they were doing.

'Armed Response is on its way. I'm going to phone Elizabeth Lumb. I want to know where Keith suddenly figures in all this.'

'Do we know who's got Matilda?' Christian asked turning around in his seat.

'No. I'm guessing it's Ross Jonson and his father-in-law, but who knows how many people are involved in this if Sergeant Slack is helping them too.'

'There is going to be one hell of a shit storm when all this is sorted,' Christian said.

'Let's just concentrate on finding DCI Darke for now,' Scott said as he sounded the horn to clear the traffic ahead of him.

* * *

'I can see the Nissan,' Nigel said, looking through the rear-view mirror.

'I can't believe we're doing this,' Ross said. 'This is wrong.'

'We don't have any choice.'

'She said she'd been looking into the GMC files. Others will too. They won't let this drop.'

'We can get around that.'

'How?'

'I don't know,' he said, slamming his hands down on the steering wheel. 'Let's concentrate on one thing at a time. Look, we can pass her death off as a suicide, that's not a problem. I'll be your alibi for the night of the murders. Bella will too. They'll believe us over Keith Lumb.'

'I can't tell anymore lies.'

'Do you want to go in the boot with her?'

'Jesus, Nigel, what's happened to you?' Ross asked, looking across at his father-in-law.

'They deserved it. Clive, Serena, Matilda, they all deserved what they got. There are some people in this world who should never be given positions of power because they can't cope, while others have to fight for every little thing.'

Nigel's rage was growing. He was gripping the steering wheel hard; his knuckles were white and his foot was pressing the accelerator further and further to the floor.

* * *

From the direction Nigel turned, it was obvious he was avoiding driving through Sheffield. He was taking the longer route around Penistone, along the A616 and via Glossop. The quicker way was through Sheffield then on the A57 straight through the country-side to Ladybower. Dropping back, Keith turned and headed for Sheffield. He relayed the information back to the control room telling the ACC there was no nobody tailing DCI Darke's car.

* * *

'He's going to end up following us,' Scott said once Sian got off the phone to the ACC.

'He's using his initiative,' Christian said. 'He'd make a good copper.'

'Well it sounds like there'll be at least three vacancies soon, if not more,' Scott said.

They were out of Sheffield now and charging through the Derbyshire countryside. It was dark outside which was a shame as the views really were gorgeous to look at. It was hardly the time for sight-seeing, however.

'I hope she's all right,' Sian said. 'Keith said he didn't know if she was dead or alive.'

'She'll be fine. You know Matilda, tough as old boots,' Christian said.

Neither of them believed him. They were all worried for their boss.

'Matilda's believed in Keith right from the start,' Sian said to break the silence. 'We all went on the forensics, but she knew otherwise.'

'The forensic evidence seemed planted,' Scott said. 'Rory went through it with Matilda at the murder house. She pointed out all the discrepancies at the murder house, but he still thought it was Keith, too.'

'We can beat ourselves up about this when it's all over. Sian, what did Elizabeth say?'

'Elizabeth said that Matilda had it all worked out. She needed to buy herself some extra time to prove Keith's innocence and figure out who the real killer was. Apparently, Keith was hiding at Elizabeth's house but she panicked with the police outside so he went to Matilda's.'

'Bloody hell. She took a hell of a risk having him in her house. What if she'd been wrong?' Christian shook his head in disgust.

'Valerie is going to burst a vessel when she finds out.'

'Let's hope this works out for the best then. A good result is the only possible outcome for this without the shit hitting the fan.'

Scott drove through the village of Ashopton, where he had to slow his speed. He pulled over just before Snake Road which acted as a bridge, crossing over the reservoir.

'Why have you stopped?' Sian asked from the back seat.

'This road runs right alongside the reservoir. If they're going to throw the boss in, this will be the best place to do it from.'

'You can't see a thing,' Sian squinted, leaning forward. 'It's pitch-dark.'

'We need to get a helicopter up here,' Christian said, digging out his phone and dialling.

'We need more coppers too, so we can have posts at various points along the road.'

'For all we know they could have beaten us to it. The car could be sinking below the surface and we might not even know it.'

'Scott, don't.' Sian shivered.

Scott opened the glove compartment and took out a torch. He checked it was working then got out of the car.

'Where are you going?'

'To check she's not already drowning.'

'But if they've not been yet, they'll know something is dodgy.'

'Shit. OK, Sian, walk with me. We can be two lovers having a stroll.'

'Shouldn't you take Christian?'

'I'm not really into balding men,' he said with a smirk.

Sian linked arms with Scott and they set off at a slow pace along the edge of the reservoir, trying not to make it too obvious they were looking for a car sinking in the calm water.

Behind, a Nissan screeched to a halt and Keith Lumb jumped out of the front passenger seat.

'Are you the cops?' he called out.

Scott and Sian turned around and walked back. 'DS Sian Mills. I'm guessing you're the infamous Keith Lumb.'

'Have you found them?'

'Not yet.'

'I don't think they wanted to risk going through Sheffield. They went via Penistone then will have probably gone around Glossop.'

'You know the area pretty well,' Scott said.

'I lived in Bamford for a while, with a girlfriend, years ago.'

Christian got out of Scott's car and joined them. 'A helicopter's on its way.'

'What are we doing then? Just standing around here waiting for them to dump a body in the water?' Keith asked.

Scott stepped forward. He was just about to open his mouth to tell Keith who was in charge here when he was lit up from behind by a pair of headlights.

'That's Matilda's car,' Sian said.

They all turned and looked across Snake Road. At the other end, the Range Rover had stopped, the engine slowly ticking over.

'They've seen us,' Scott said.

'Shit.' Keith turned and got back in the Nissan before anyone could stop him. He turned on the ignition, slammed his foot down on the accelerator and charged, at speed, along Snake Road, the Range Rover in his sights.

'What the fuck is he doing?'

The Nissan would be no match for the Range Rover. If he tried to ram it, he would come off worse.

*   *   *

'What the fuck is she doing?' Nigel Eckhart said as he leaned forward looking out of the windscreen. 'She's driving far too fast.'

'Maybe she's panicking,' Ross said. 'I know how she feels.'

'Shit! That's not Bella driving.'

'What?'

'That's someone else. A bloke. Fuck.'

Nigel put the car into reverse but another car was behind him, waiting to get onto Snake Road. Another car was behind that. He had no option but to drive on and hopefully avoid the Nissan that seemed to be on a suicide mission.

Nigel slammed his foot down and set off at speed. The tyres screeched on the dry tarmac road and echoed through the quiet night.

A loud banging was heard from the boot. Ross turned around in his seat. He turned back to see the Nissan's headlights blinding him. It was almost upon them.

The Nissan showed no sign of slowing down, or of turning. It was up to the Range Rover. Nigel swore, swung the steering wheel to the left and hit the concrete barrier. It smashed through and the car plunged over the side and into the reservoir with a loud splash.

* * *

Keith slammed on the brakes and jumped out of the car. He ran to the hole in the barrier. He looked ahead as the three detectives came running towards him. Scott was already taking off his jacket, preparing to jump into the cold water.

'Shit,' Keith said to himself. He removed his jacket, stood on the edge and jumped in, diving straight under the surface and swimming for the sinking wreckage.

Sian, Christian and Scott arrived at the broken barrier in time to see the Range Rover sink below the water. There was no sign of Keith Lumb.

Scott jumped in, followed closely by Christian.

It was a cold night and there was no wind. The black water looked like a sheet of glass. As Scott and Christian plunged into it and disappeared below the surface, the water soon calmed and it was as if nothing had been there to disturb it. The reservoir had swallowed them whole.

Sian stepped back from the edge and saw people from other cars had gathered.

'Call an ambulance,' Sian shouted.

With wide eyes and fear etched on her face, Sian looked on. Her heart was pounding loudly in her chest as the seconds ticked by. If it wasn't for the broken concrete barrier, she wouldn't have known anything was happening below the surface. There were no air bubbles, no car, no people.

The water suddenly broke with all the noise of glass shattering. It was Keith, and he was dragging someone with him.

Sian lowered herself and guided him to the edge. She tried to see who he had saved but couldn't make out who it was. With help from a couple of the passers-by, they all heaved the unconscious man onto the road. Sian looked down and saw it was DS Ross Jonson.

Keith stood up, swept back his hair and went to jump back into the water. Sian stopped him.

'What do you think you're doing?'

He was breathless. 'The young guy. He's trying to get the boot open. He needs help.' He didn't wait for Sian to stop him before he plunged back into the reservoir.

Sian turned back to the stricken detective. A woman was leaning over him performing mouth to mouth.

'I've called the ambulance again. They're on their way,' someone said.

Sian looked down at Ross. He had caused all this. It didn't look like everyone was going to make it out of the reservoir alive, yet here was Ross getting emergency medical attention when others needed saving.

Sian's reverie was broken by yelling from the water's edge. She turned and saw Keith and Scott trying to haul an unconscious Matilda out of the water. She ran over and helped them, grabbing Matilda by the shoulders and pulling her onto the road. Her face was bruised and bloodied. She was pale and unresponsive.

Scott turned Matilda onto her back and checked her airways to make sure they were clear before he began performing CPR on her. Keith stood up. He looked at Sian and gave her a weak smile before going back into the water. There were still two other people below the surface.

'We need to keep her warm,' Sian said.

'I've got some blankets in my car,' a woman said. She turned and ran.

In the distance, sirens could be heard, growing louder as they approached. A helicopter appeared overhead, search light shining down on the road, lighting them all up like the scene of an alien invasion.

'Come on, Mat,' Sian said under her breath. 'Come on. You can do this.'

Scott breathed three times into Matilda's mouth. He sat back on his haunches while Sian performed chest compressions. It seemed like an age before Matilda began coughing and spluttering. Scott turned her onto her side so she could spit out the water she had swallowed. Sian closed her eyes in relief and started breathing again.

Chapter Sixty-Four

Matilda opened her eyes to see Sian and Adele sitting by her bed. She tried to speak but her throat was sore.

'I should kill you,' Sian said quietly. 'Having Keith in your house, then going off to Barnsley to confront a killer on your own. Why didn't you tell me what you were up to? I'm so angry with you right now.' She sat back and folded her arms.

'And don't look at me for any sympathy,' Adele said.

Matilda tried to speak again. She cleared her throat and sat up in bed. 'I'm really sorry,' she struggled to say. Her voice was hoarse. 'The fewer people who knew about Keith the better. I knew the killer had extensive knowledge of forensic science, so had to be a police officer or SOCO.' She took a drink of water from a chipped plastic beaker. The water was warm but it helped to lubricate her throat. 'I had to make it look like Keith was still on the run. You have to understand that, surely.'

'I do, but I'm not a detective,' Adele said. 'You haven't pissed me off as much as you have your team. I'm just angry with you for putting yourself in that position in the first place.'

'I didn't know others were involved. I just thought it was Ross Jonson. What happened to everyone anyway? Sian?'

Sian and Adele exchanged glances.

'Ross was pulled out of the reservoir before you,' Sian began.

'He's fine. He's recovering in another ward. He's under police guard. He's been arrested for the Mercer killings. Bella Slack has also been arrested for aiding and abetting.'

'What about Nigel?'

'He didn't make it out of the reservoir.'

'Oh. I'm sorry it ended that way,' she said, genuinely meaning it. 'At least we've got an arrest. Keith can clear his name. That's the most important thing.'

'Mat, Keith didn't come back up either.'

'What?'

'He pulled Ross out. Then he went back under for you. He went back a third time to help Christian get Nigel out, but he didn't come back up.'

'Christian?'

'He's fine. He pulled Keith's body out of the water.'

'Keith saved my life.'

'He certainly did.'

'He wasn't all bad.'

'No.'

'His poor sister.'

'I've been to see her,' Sian said. 'I've told her what he did, how many lives he saved. He may not have lived the purest of lives, but he died a hero.'

'How did she take it?'

'She was in floods of tears. Did you know she had an identical twin sister? She killed herself years ago. They couldn't live apart, but this sister, Ruby, she'd got married. That didn't last longer than a few months. She couldn't live without Elizabeth yet was in love with her husband.'

'A tragic family,' Adele said.

'I've put Elizabeth in touch with a grief counsellor. She's going to try and get over what happened with Ruby and Keith. She's still a young woman, not even forty yet. She's strong enough as she wants to live, but her siblings are holding her back. It'll take time, but she'll make it.'

'At least Leah and Rachel can move on too,' Matilda said. 'They'll know who killed their family. What's that word the Americans love?'

'Closure,' Adele said.

'Aaron said she's having the marriage to Oliver annulled,' Sian said.

'I don't blame her. What's happening to Oliver?' Matilda asked.

'Well, there are no charges for him to face. I've spoken to Scott several times and he doesn't want to press charges for his assault. According to his parents, Oliver is looking for a new job, somewhere out of Sheffield. He wants a fresh start.'

Matilda couldn't blame him for that. She'd been thinking about having a fresh start too, a few days ago. Sheffield held far too many dark memories. However, it was her home, and, bizarrely, she liked it in the steel city. A glutton for punishment.

Matilda leaned back in her bed, resting her head on the pillow. A tear fell from her eye. She thought of Keith. She had liked him, despite his lifestyle. She had seen that he was a good man at heart. He had proved that too.

'We'll leave you to get some rest,' Adele said, standing up. 'I'll come back later.'

Sian leaned forward and kissed Matilda on the cheek. She smiled. 'Still mad at you.'

'I'll make it up to you.'

* * *

When she opened her eyes again, the room was slightly darker, and Valerie was sitting next to her bed reading a glossy magazine.

'How long have you been sat there?' Matilda asked, making her boss jump.

'Not long. How are you feeling?'

'Fine. You?'

Valerie nodded. She didn't look fine. The worry lines on her forehead were cavernous. 'The Barnsley station is going to close.'

'Oh,' was all Matilda could say.

'The building is in a mess anyway. It's cheaper to knock it down than repair it.'

'What about all the officers who work there?'

'They'll be reassigned to other sites.'

'I can't believe what happened,' Matilda said. 'I knew about DI Eckhart's daughter killing herself. I didn't think about the why. I'm sure I knew she was married to a detective but it didn't register. If I'd paid more attention, all this could have been avoided.'

Valerie shook her head. 'That's not your responsibility, Matilda, it's mine. I'm ACC for the whole of South Yorkshire. It's me who should have seen the signs. DI Eckhart and his team are under my control. I knew about DS Jonson's daughter. I shouldn't have allowed him back to work so soon. He should have received counselling, been put on lighter duties. I failed him.'

'DI Eckhart failed him. Not you.' Matilda held a hand out and Valerie took it. 'Will I be facing a disciplinary hearing?'

'You should do for acting on your own like a one-woman police force, but I think I should be able to bury it under the clusterfuck that is the Barnsley inquiry.'

'Thank you.' She smiled.

'That doesn't let you off the hook, however. I'm going to be keeping a closer eye on you in the future, and so is your team. Despite what you think, you're not Captain Marvel.'

'I've got my Avengers.'

'So use them. I'm going to go; let you get some rest.' At the door, she turned back. 'I'm sorry I didn't believe in you.' She didn't wait for a response.

Matilda was in hospital for three days before she was discharged. She had been unconscious for a long time but the endless scans had shown there was no permanent damage. A few days rest at home and she would be fit to go back to work.

Now her house was complete, she was looking forward to relaxing for a few days with a good book and junk food. Living in the middle of nowhere, she expected nothing but peace and quiet. Unfortunately, she wasn't able to get through a chapter before another visitor knocked on the door.

Her mother and father visited, and it took all her effort to stop her mother from moving in for a while. Thankfully, her father was on Matilda's side and persuaded his wife to join him back in Bakewell once their visit was over. She promised to buy her dad a large bottle of Highland Park, as a thank you, once she was recovered enough.

Matilda was surprised to find Sally Meagan on her doorstep with a bunch of flowers. She had brought Woody with her, who bounded into the living room with his tail wagging and plonked himself down in front of the roaring fire.

'We're going away for a few days,' Sally said with a warming smile. 'Just to the Lake District. Philip's idea. He thought it would be good for me.'

'It'll be good for both of you.'

'We haven't had anymore phone calls. It was obviously some sick, twisted individual getting his kicks out of other people's misery.'

Matilda didn't reply. She nodded and smiled. 'How are things with you and Philip?'

'Fine. Matilda,' she said, edging forward on the sofa. 'Do you think there's a possibility Carl is still alive?'

Matilda didn't need to give her reply any thought. 'Yes. I really do.'

Sally visibly relaxed. 'I hope so. It's all I'm clinging on to.'

'When I'm better, we'll have a sit down – me, you and Pat, and we'll come up with some kind of strategy.'

'I'd like that.'

* * *

On the third day of Matilda's recovery, she was just about to ascend the stairs to bed when a knock came on the door. It was Rory.

'Hello, boss.'

'What are you doing here at this time?'

'I've come to tell you I'm not resigning.'

'I'm back at work tomorrow, Rory. You could have told me then.'

'I know but I wanted to get out of the flat.'

Matilda stepped to one side to let him enter. 'Why?'

'I think Scott's making up for lost time. He and Chris are at it like rabbits. And they're not quiet.'

'Jealous?'

'A little.'

Matilda smiled, and blushed. 'You can't complain, Rory. The

stories Scott has told us over the months about the noises you make with the women you bring back. I've got a spare bed if you want it.'

'Do you mind?'

Matilda shook her head. It would be nice to have someone else in the house at night, even if it was just for one night. There were times, when she had been lying in her hospital bed, when she wondered if she had made the right decision moving out into the countryside, into a four-bedroom house on her own. She hated the fact she couldn't feel her husband anywhere in the house, but it helped in the process of moving on. Also, she had three spare bedrooms to fill and there was potential for a flat over the double garage. She only needed to be on her own if she chose to be.

As Matilda finished reading the latest Will Carver thriller, she closed the book and placed it on the bedside table next to a framed photograph of James. She looked into his icy blue eyes and smiled. Yes, she still loved him. Yes, she missed him. Yes, it was unfair he had died at a young age, but if she had allowed her grief and anger to consume her, she could have ended up like Ross Jonson.

'I'm not going to forget you, James, but I need to stop thinking about you so much. I need to start living.'

She turned the light out and snuggled down under the duvet and listened to the distant sound of Rory snoring in the next room. It was an annoying sound, but it was comforting. For the first time in as long as she could remember, she fell asleep with a smile on her face.

Epilogue

The bell sounded. The doors opened, and a swarm of young children came running out of the school towards their waiting parents.

One young boy, blond with blue eyes, stood at the bottom of the steps. His cheeks were red from the cold and he had the wide-eyed look of fear etched on his face.

As other children ran out of the building with smiles on their faces, rabbiting about their day to their mums and dads, the little boy remained where he was, frozen in time.

A woman approached him. She wore a long duffel coat, a black woollen bobble hat and mittens. She squatted down in front of him so they were eye to eye.

'Have you had a good day?' she asked in broken English.

He didn't say anything.

'Did you eat all your lunch?'

Again, he didn't say anything.

'You need to start talking and playing with the other children or people will start asking questions. You don't want us to get into trouble, do you?'

The boy's bottom lip began to wobble, and tears formed in his eyes. The woman wiped them away before they had chance to fall.

'We've been thinking, me and your dad, and we thought it would be nice for you to have a pet. Can you see him?'

The woman moved to one side. Through the crowd of kids, the young boy looked for the man he was to call dad from now on. There, by the silver Volvo, was a tall thin man with blond hair. Beside him, on a lead, was a golden Labrador puppy.

The boy's eyes lit up.

'He's yours. Would you like to say hello to him?'

The boy ran towards him. The dog noticed and his tail began to wag. The boy dropped to his knees and began stroking him. The puppy jumped up at him and licked his face.

'Say thank you to your dad.'

The boy said a muted thank you but didn't take his eyes from the puppy.

'What are you going to call him?' his dad asked.

'I'm going to call him Woody,' Carl said.

Read the Matilda Darke series
from the beginning . . .

Book 1

**Two murders. Twenty years.
Now the killer is back for more . . .**

DCI Matilda Darke has returned to work after a nine month
absence. A shadow of her former self, she is tasked with
re-opening a cold case: the terrifyingly brutal murders of
Miranda and Stefan Harkness. The only witness was their
eleven-year-old son, Jonathan, who was too deeply trauma-
tized to speak a word.

Then a dead body is discovered, and the investigation leads
back to Matilda's case. Suddenly the past and present converge,
and it seems a killer may have come back for more . . .

Book 2

**How many lies does it take to kill a marriage?
Only the killer knows.**

When elderly George Rainsford goes to investigate a suspicious noise one night, the last thing he expects to find is a bloodbath. A man has been killed and a woman brutally beaten, left for dead.

The victims are Lois Craven and Kevin Hardaker – both married, but not to each other. Their spouses swear they knew nothing of the affair and, besides, they both have alibis for the attack. With nothing else to link the victims, the investigation hits a dead end.

The pressure is on for investigating officer, DCI Matilda Darke: there's a violent killer on the loose, and it looks like her team members are the new targets. With no leads and no suspects, it's going to take all Matilda's wits to catch him, before he strikes again.

Book 3

**Eight killers. One house.
And the almost perfect murder . . .**

Starling House is home to some of the nation's deadliest
teenagers, still too young for prison.

When the latest arrival is found brutally murdered, DCI
Matilda Darke and her team investigate, and discover a prison
manager falling apart and a sabotaged security system.
Neither the staff nor the inmates can be trusted.

The only person Matilda believes is innocent is facing prison
for the rest of his life. With time running out, she must solve
the unsolvable to save a young man from his fate, and find a
murderer in a house full of killers . . .

Book 4

There's a killer in your house.

The Hangman waits in the darkness.

He knows your darkest secrets.

He'll make you pay for all the crimes you have tried
desperately to forget.

And he is closer than you think.

DCI Matilda Darke is running out of time. Fear is spreading
throughout the city. As the body count rises, Matilda is
targeted and her most trusted colleagues fall under suspicion.
But can she keep those closest to her from harm? Or is it
already too late?

Acknowledgements

The Murder House is a work of fiction. However, those readers who know Sheffield and its history will know the plot is taken from a real-life murder which took place in the city in 1983. This book is not a reworking of the case, but entirely from my own imagination.

In the writing of this book I had help from a number of sources. A huge thank you to Philip Lumb for post-mortem procedure and Claire Green for information regarding digital autopsies. Simon Browes answered my gruesome questions about stab wounds in glorious detail for which I am grateful, and slightly disturbed. For forensic advice, I have fellow crime writer and forensic officer Andy Barrett to thank. As ever, I am indebted to 'Mr Tidd' for his help regarding police procedure. Any technical information within this book that is incorrect is all my fault. Please do not blame the experts mentioned above.

Once a novel is written, the hard work really begins. A huge thank you to my agent, Tom Witcomb, at Blake Friedmann, who offers wonderful advice on tightening up a story and whose knowledge of Latin is incredibly impressive. I also have one of the best editors in the business working on my books – Finn Cotton at HarperCollins. His comments and suggestions are invaluable, and this book wouldn't be in the shape it's in without him. A special thank you to the eagle-eyed Janette Currie and to everyone else at One More Chapter, Killer Reads and HarperCollins who has had an input in the creation of this novel.

I would like to thank my mum for listening to my ramblings when I need to iron out a plot difficulty. She also makes the best cakes ever which is what a writer needs to keep going. Thank you to Chris and Kevin for taking me out of Sheffield when I've needed a break, and Maxwell, for simply being there. A thank you also goes to my good friend Jonas for keeping me on the cusp of sanity with his . . . erm . . . unique texts.

Finally, there is a group of people who have helped me to get five books published and that is the bloggers and readers who've read my books and shared their reviews on social media. Thank you for taking my books, and Matilda, into your hearts and long may our journeys together continue.

Michael Wood. January 2020.